WHEN ARROWS WERE HEATED UP

A TALE OF TRIBAL STRUGGLE AGAINST BRITISH COLONIALISM

HARI RAM MEENA

NIYOGI BOOKS

Published by

NIYOGI BOOKS

D-78, Okhla Industrial Area, Phase-I
New Delhi-110 020, INDIA
Tel: 91-11-26816301, 49327000
Fax: 91-11-26810483, 26813830
email: niyogibooks@gmail.com
website: www.niyogibooksindia.com

Layout Design: Ganga Rai
Cover Design: Misha Oberoi

ISBN: 978-93-85285-22-6

Publication: 2016

This is a work of fiction. The names, characters and incidents portrayed in it are the work of the author's imagination. Any resemblance to actual persons, living or dead, events or localities, is entirely coincidental.

Printed at: Niyogi Offset Pvt. Ltd., New Delhi, India

Dedicated to

Those Adivasi stalwarts
Who put up a brave struggle at Mangarh
Against the colonial and feudal rulers of India
And to those brave women like Sugani,
Pano and Kamali who undeterred by death
Gave up their lives for the sake of their right to
Water, land, forest and animals

PREFACE

Years ago, I read about the struggle and sacrifice of the adivasis at Mangarh in the adivasi magazine, *Aravali Udghosh,* edited by Pathik Baba (B.P. Verma). Subsequently, I travelled to Udaipur on several occasions and tried to meet Pathik Baba. I also utilised these occasions by meeting the local intelligentsia, authors, NGO activists and the tribals who were more politically and socially aware than others in their community. Discussions would often centre round the Mangarh sacrifice by adivasis.

I tried gathering information and details pertaining to the incident. The task was not easy. I had not studied history in a systematic manner, nor had I ever done any scholarly research. But being a police officer I had developed skills for investigation. I started collecting evidence to corroborate the facts of the incident.

Eventually, in 2001, I found time to leave Jaipur for a purposeful visit to Mangarh. By now I had gathered enough material, references and information to put it all down in a book form. Thus, I set out on the course of writing about the Mangarh incident and titled it *Mangarh: Adivasi Balidan ke Tehkhane Tak* (At the Bottom of Mangarh Adivasi Sacrifice), which was readily accepted by the prestigious Hindi journal *Pahal*-71 in 2002. It pleased me immensely. Suddenly, the story of Mangarh sacrifice attracted attention and began to be discussed widely.

Simultaneously, I read the works of B.D. Sharma, Kumar Suresh Singh, Ram Sharan Joshi and Mahashweta Devi.

The hero of Mangarh, Govind Guru, along with Tantya Mama of Jhabua (Madhya Pradesh) and Jorji of Gujarat (both of whom were hanged by the British in 1880s) were in the same league as the hero of *Jangal ke Davedar* (Claimants of Forest), Birsa Munda.

The history of the adivasis is as old as that of humankind. Their natural and peaceful life was first disturbed in the clashes between the Aryans and non-Aryans, which forced them to leave their habitats and seek shelter in the jungles. To their credit, the adivasis learnt to adjust their lives in their new surroundings. Despite a clear concept of the institution of family and home, the notion of private property, as commonly understood, had not developed among them. Their society thrived on a collective culture.

There were many upheavals during those early days and matters reached a head when migrant Rajputs took away the sovereign rights of the adivasis in Rajasthan. The victor has always looked down upon the vanquished and it happened in the relations between the Rajputs and the adivasis as well. More upheavals followed and the native adivasis of Rajputana lost their sovereignty to outsiders, the Rajputs. Loss of freedom and sovereignty is directly proportionate to the degree of oppression of the vanquished. The adivasis were subjected to exploitation, became victims of usurpers and were relegated to second-class citizenship. However, the impact of these upheavals was minimal on their society and culture. They did not have to face eviction from their habitats in the forests.

Then came the East India Company. In 1818, Company's representative Col James Todd set his foot on the soil of the large region of Mewar in southern Rajputana (as much of today's Rajasthan was then called). Under a strategy prepared by him, the prominent princely states in southern Rajputana, the adivasi-dominated Dungarpur, Banswara, Pratapgarh, Kushalgarh and the nearby states of Santrampur and Idar in Gujarat signed a treaty with the Company. Its chief feature was that the Company would have the rights to all forest produce of the adivasis and the freedom to exploit the minerals found in the area. In return, the rulers of these states would be entitled to draw from the military force of the British to suppress any revolt or protest by the adivasis.

In the states of Udaipur, Dungarpur, Banswara and Kushalgarh the dominant adivasi community was that of the *Bhils,* followed by the *Meenas*. The Pratapgarh state was *Meena* dominated, too. Spread around Mangarh, this was the southern extreme of Rajputana flanked by the states of Ratlam, Sailana and Jhabua in the East and the states of Jhalod, Soonth and Idar in the West. It was clearly an adivasi-dominated area. But the rulers of the area, maharaja, *maharana, maharawal, jagirdar, thikanedar* and *bhaumiya* (feudal designations assigned according to status), were Rajputs of different clans, who held their sway with the help of the minions they had appointed.

The final decisions, however, rested in the hands of the British-appointed political agents, commandants of different cantonments, residents and other officers of the Crown working under the Viceroy, and later the Governor General. The native rajas and maharajas were mere puppets in the hands of the British. This situation was the result of a process that started with the treaty signed by the native states and the Company at the time of the arrival of Col Todd and then continued with the direct rule of the British over all of India as a consequence of the 1857 "war of independence" (or the "Sepoy Mutiny"), the first revolt against British rule in India. The worst sufferers of all this were the adivasis, surrounded as they were by uncertainties and apprehensions. They had to bear the brunt of the reign of terror let loose by the native states, the British interference, oppressive policies, widespread poverty and hunger.

The last years of the 19th century were witness to several tragic events. There were changes in the power structure; the British rulers had adopted newer methods of oppression and resorted to manipulative politics. The sufferings of people increased, leading to a situation that was to give birth to the spirit of rebellion among the adivasis. Mangarh was a silent witness to this invisible fire.

And nobody was familiar with it more than a prominent hero of Mangarh, Govind Guru, and his committed associates.

He had first hand knowledge of the trials and tribulations of the adivasis. There were many adivasis who worked for the British and native states. The British recruited them in their army; in the officers' mess and in the cantonments; the adivasis worked as cooks, waiters and orderlies. In the native states they served as *sevadars* (servants). Hordes of adivasis used to be forced to work in palaces, forts, fields, gardens and construction sites. Due to their "unfortunate" position in employment, they were able to get wind of whatever strategies were planned by the British or the native rulers against their fellow adivasis.

While writing the book, the biggest challenge for me was how to make a correct guess about the number of people killed. The Mangarh hills are at the border of the former states of Banswara-Dungarpur and Gujarat's Santrampur. I toured dozens of villages in this area, met people and talked to the elderly. Former legislator and the chairman of Mangarh Dham Vikas Samiti (Development Committee), Mr Nathuram helped me a great deal. I went through the old records of Khairwada cantonment, studied material available at the archives of Rajasthan state and spent a lot of time at the Tribal Research Institute's library at Udaipur, where the librarian, Mr Sharma, was of immense help. I went through books in the personal library of the erstwhile maharana of Mewar. I was able to collect photocopies of very important documents of the British era from the National Archives, New Delhi. I studied books on history and discovered to my surprise that Gauri Shanker Hirachand Ojha, reputed to be a great historian of Rajasthan, had in his book on the state's history dismissed the Mangarh sacrifice with these words: "The Bhils at Mangarh had gathered to create a violent disturbance, forcing the army to open fire. Some Bhils were killed."

On my first visit to Mangarh, I saw at the residence of Mr Nathuram in Anandpuri village a turban that belonged to his grandfather that had blood stains and bullet marks. During my next visit to the Mangarh fair in December 2006 I asked Mr Nathuram about the turban. He said, "Someone important person from Delhi took it away, assuring me that he will publicise the Mangarh sacrifice." That was a false promise and nothing of the sort happened. It is quite possible that in future that person might use the historic turban for some commercial gain. This is how innocent adivasis have always been cheated.

The source of inspiration behind this work, respected Mr Giriraj Kishore, took time out of his busy schedule to go through the manuscript and offered constructive suggestions. It is a matter of satisfaction that, on the occasion of the 150th anniversary of the first war of independence, my desire to see my work published in Hindi has been fulfilled by Sahitya Upkarm. This publishing house deserves my gratitude.

The idea of getting this work translated into English was given to me by a few literary friends. Mr Atul Cowshish was kind enough to translate the main text. It was really difficult to translate the folk songs used in the novel. However, this problem was sorted out by respectable Prof. R.K. Sharma of Navalgarh. I am grateful to all of them.

I am thankful to the publisher for publishing this work well in time.

Hari Ram Meena

ONE

Kuriya Danot had just collected dried branches of trees from the surrounding area. From a pocket in his jacket he took out a tightly folded, dirty piece of cloth. Slowly, he unfolded it. Out of the many layers of the cloth came two small pieces of flint and a thread. He rubbed hard the fragmented pieces of the stone, close to one end of the thread. From the spark that ensued the thread caught fire. Kuriya quickly gathered straw and hay and shoved them into a pile of firewood and, placing the burning thread in the middle, blew hard.

Flames began to leap up. He adjusted some of the firewood on top of the burning straw. Gradually, a bonfire was lit.

Govind was watching it all very carefully.

"What is the matter, Govind?" asked Poonja, who had come from his village, Dungar, to meet some relatives.

"Yes, Poonja. Now I have got it."

"But I don't get it. Unravel the secret."

"Can you see how the flint hides the fire within? Rub a little and sparks fly out. The sparks with fire..."

"Don't tell me, you are seeing it for the first time. What is so new in it?" Kuriya asked as he placed some corn over the burning fire.

"You are an intelligent man. Turn the corn over so that it is roasted properly. Don't let the intensity of fire go waste. Poonja is thick headed. I will explain to him. Now listen carefully."

"Are you a holy man that I should listen to you carefully?"

"Kuriya, listen to what Govind says. When you were producing sparks from the flint Govind was watching it intently. Maybe, this has created some idea in his mind," Poonja intervened as he made an unsuccessful attempt to read Govind's smile.

"Should I roast corn or listen to Govind?"

"It is simple, brother. You have to use your hands to roast corn while you use your ears to listen to Govind. Every part of the body is for a different function, isn't it?"

This explanation from Poonja silenced Kuriya and he nodded in agreement.

"Kuriya produced a spark from the flint. The spark turned into a fire. It means there is fire in stones. If there is fire in stones then the hills have fire in them. And if the hills have fire in them, then the adivasis who live in those hills must have fire inside them, too. I want to light that fire. The priest in my village says that there is fire inside every human being. The one who recognises that fire sees God. This requires devotion to God. If people worship without any malice, it becomes easier. A fire is a spark on which is deposited the malice in the form of ash. If you dust off the ash, the sparkle of the fire becomes visible, just as a spark rises from a flint and turns into fire. This is the fire that gives people the power to fight evil."

Govind's words took Kuriya and Poonja by surprise. They only partially understood his words.

Govind was born in his family home at Basia, a village in Dungarpur state. His father Besar and mother Lataki were from an ordinary Banjara family with Govaria lineage. In his childhood, Govind had received informal education from Rajgiri Gosai, the village temple priest. Govind used to sit with him whenever he was free. He would listen to Rajgiri's words with great interest and curiosity. Rajgiri liked this innocent youth. Whatever religious books Rajgiri read, he enjoyed conveying their essence to Govind in simple layman's language. Soon, Govind learnt the alphabets. Rajgiri influenced and captivated Govind's mind so much that he liked being called Govind Giri.

The tribe to which Govind belonged used to follow the barter system and traded in merchandise that was ferried far and wide on bullocks. Govind travelled a lot with his father in his childhood. He saw parts of Gujarat, Vagad and Malwa regions. He used to be an avid participant in religious discourses and discussions as well.

Once, when Govind was about 11 years old, sitting on the Bhilad Dev platform under a neem tree, he was addressing five–seven village youths.

The mukhiya (head) of the Bhils scolded him. "Don't you have anything else to do? You do not let our children work."

"Kaka (uncle), that is not true. I am only telling them that education makes a person wise. It helps distinguish between right and wrong. It is necessary to entertain good thoughts to improve one's life," Govind replied.

"Since when have you become a learned man? Off you go. Come on kids; go to your work."

"Kaka, please don't think that I'm trying to mislead them. I'm talking of their betterment. You sit with me and listen; after that I'll do whatever you say."

The innocence on Govind's face and his respectful tone impressed the mukhiya. He sat with Govind. The children stood by the side, a little apprehensive. One or two of them took shelter behind the neem tree.

"Kaka, why do you people treat me as a stranger? Yes, by birth I am a Banjara, but I was born and have lived in the midst of all of you. I consider myself a Bhil and Meena and when I see their poverty and misery, my heart goes out to them. Rajgiri priest used to say: 'There is nothing as sacred as to wish for another's well being; there is nothing as sinful as to wish for another's sufferings'. I will tell you what it means. There is no greater dharma than helping others and there is no sin graver than giving pain to others."

The mukhiya found himself drawn to Govind's words. He talked to him for a long time. In the end, he told Govind: "You are acquiring the qualities of a priest. But we don't get any free time after attending to our household chores and offering forced labour to the ruler. When do we get to listen to such sound discourse? In any case, what do we do after listening to these wise words? We have to lead the same life that our ancestors did."

"No, Kaka! Don't think like that. It is good to learn to live within one's means. But these rulers commit various atrocities on us and the jagirdar asks us to offer him free labour. Instead of thinking about these things, our people get drunk and abuse their mind and body. They also harass their women and children everyday. This is a bad habit. Shouldn't we oppose it? If such things don't happen, wouldn't our lives be better?"

"What! Oppose the Raj?"

"I'm not talking about opposing the Raj. But we can create awareness about bad habits."

Hearing such wise words from a young man left the mukhiya stunned. He had heard a lot about God and dharma when listening to bhajans of Sant Mavji, Surmalji and Narsiji. Govind had impressed the mukhiya. He had no doubt that Govind was a bright and promising boy.

Govind was walking amidst prickly bushes with his friends Hinsallya, Missra, Kuriya and Ruksya, about two miles away from Basiya village along a rocky path on the foothills. A little above, on the hills, was located the site of Hirkuliya Baba, an adivasi deity. The boys moved towards that direction, with Govind in the lead.

Suddenly, he stopped as he sighted a black scorpion near his feet. Right behind him was Kuriya, who also saw the scorpion. Without thinking twice, he removed a *jooti* (footwear) and struck the scorpion hard. The insect became lifeless. Its sting had no poison left in it. Before the other boys could react to the sudden appearance of the scorpion, Kuriya had killed it.

"What've you done, you foolish Kuriya?" Govind asked in an irritated tone. "Don't you know that killing a scorpion is a sin?"

"I don't have brains. I don't know what is moral and immoral. But I do know that had I not killed the scorpion it would have stung you. Don't you realise this?" he defended himself with a thoughtful query for Govind.

"Look, Kuriya, I don't say that you don't have brains. But to kill a living creature for no reason is a sin. Don't believe me, but our elders tell us that a living creature killed by a human being is reborn in human form and takes revenge for his death in the fashion he was killed," Govind told Kuriya.

"I agree. But our elders never said this about scorpions. If we don't kill a scorpion it will sting us. Likewise, if we do not kill other poisonous creatures like snake, *gauhara* (a venomous reptile) and *kaankhajura* (a venomous centipede) don't we face threat to our lives?"

"Yes, perhaps there is no harm in killing a dangerous creature if it enters our house. But this scorpion was going its way. What danger did you encounter from it in this jungle?" It was Missra who after a thoughtful pause rather half-heartedly supported Govind. By now Kuriya had cleaned the sole of his jooti by rubbing it on the grass and had slipped it back on to his foot.

"Now move, Govind. What great feat has Kuriya performed if he has killed the scorpion? Is there a dearth of scorpions and snakes in this world? Each one of them multiply many times over," Ruksya said to end the debate.

Govind moved on and the others followed him.

The site of Hirkuliya god was a stone platform about two or two-and-a-half-feet high and eight to ten-feet-long. In the name of the statue of Hirkuliya was a stone that was half-buried under a triangular platform. Right behind it was a semal (silk-cotton tree) tree. Just five–seven steps ahead a rabbit was pounced upon by a jungle cat, which disappeared into the bushes in a jiffy with its helpless prey secure in its jaws.

"Now, Govind tell me, will this cat not be accountable for the sin of catching and killing that innocent rabbit for its meal? Will these creatures be reborn and exchange their bodies to complete the act of revenge?" Kuriya asked Govind. Hinsallya, Missra and Ruksya were eagerly awaiting Govind's reply.

"I am no learned Pandit who can read and tell about God's mysterious designs. I can only talk about what I have heard and learned from Pujari Baba. As for the rabbit and wildcat, where will the cat get to drink milk in this jungle? Will he not hunt rabbit and mouse to fill his stomach? If you talk about carnivores, will they live on grass? Each living being will live his life the way God has made him. Pujari Baba used to say that man is the only creature who has intelligence, which helps him distinguish between right and wrong. When Kuriya killed the scorpion I had opposed his action only for this reason. If Kuriya had used his intelligence he would not have killed the scorpion."

Hearing this, Kuriya became angry and moved away from the group. Missra tried to reason with him, but he did not listen and left, saying, "Okay Govind, you keep all the snakes and scorpions as pets."

Unpleasantness had crept in an otherwise interesting discourse among this small group of boys. Following Kuriya, others also returned to the village. All this upset Govind. Instead of coming home, he went to a lake near the hillock. A variety of birds were frolicking in the waters. A fascinated Govind watched the scene for some time.

The sun was setting. Clouds had appeared on the western horizon and were playing hide and seek with the sun. Reflections from the setting sun on the clouds were forming many patterns on the sky. One such shape appeared to be that a woman, her hair dishevelled, and appearing to breast-feed her little one. Govind's eyes were fixed on this image. Soon that image was dissolved in the clouds. Govind began to trek back home, wondering all the while what had hurt Kuriya. He became restless. He headed straight towards the thatched hut of Kuriya's family.

In the courtyard was sitting Kuriya's father, Sanwanta, drinking a bowlful of *mahoodi*, a country-made liquor. He appeared slightly intoxicated. In the darkness he could not recognise Govind. Assuming that it was Kuriya, he said rather incoherently: "Hey, lad! Where were you? Crying the whole day? You are returning now when it has got dark. All right! Now fill tobacco in my hookah."

Govind wondered if it would be worthwhile talking to a man who appeared to be drunk. He wanted to return, but was keen to talk to Kuriya. Keeping this resolve in mind, he gathered courage and asked Sanwanta, "Is Kuriya not at home? Kaka, I am Govind, son of Besar Banjara."

"Oh, where have you dropped from? It is you who is leading my Kuriya astray. Now that you have come, do me a favour. Some tobacco and the hookah are kept in an alcove on top of the window of the hut. Light the tobacco and hand it to me."

"Kaka, you know that I am a disciple of Pujari Baba. Till he breathed his last, he used to say that tobacco and liquor destroy both man's body and mind. I also consider these habits to be bad."

"So, the Pujari has also taught you that elders should not be listened to. Son, not obeying elders is a sin."

"Yes. But it is also not right to accept anything wrong that the elders might say. You ask me to do something good and I'd do it right now."

"Your father used to smoke tobacco, too. Why did you not stop him? And you want to teach me. Buzz off. Find out where is Kuriya and bring him here. If you don't, I shall call the panchayat tomorrow and complain that you are leading the youth of the village astray."

Sanwanta was a tuberculosis patient. His body was weak. He did not have the strength to get up in the dark and fill his hookah with tobacco. He also suffered from night-blindness. He thought that by threatening to go to the panchayat he would be able to frighten Govind, making him fill his hookah with tobacco, or he would quickly find out where Kuriya was and make sure he hurried home.

Govind was pained by what he heard from Sanwanta. He left quietly. But all the time he was worried that Kuriya had not returned home even though it was very late. He went searching for Kuriya in the village. At last he found him at Hinsalya's house. The two of them were talking in front of the hut. As soon as he spotted Kuriya, Govind said, "Oh, Kuriya, you did not like my words. Look, I have still not gone home. I am sorry if you did not like something that I said. I seek you pardon. Come, buddy. Let's embrace. If something wrong had slipped out of my mouth, will you keep chewing it?"

Kuriya immediately melted. He leapt to his feet from his sitting posture and held Govind in a tight embrace. The scene had an emotional impact on Hinsalya. Now everything was back to normal.

"Kuriya, your father is not well, still he does not give up smoking and drinking. I was at your house before coming here. This way he will die soon. Why don't you make him understand?" Govind told Kuriya.

"Govind, you talk of his drinking and smoking habits. Only I know what hell is raised in the house when my old man creates a ruckus after getting drunk. I can't make any sense out of it. You are a wise man. Why don't you try?" Kuriya was getting emotional. His eyes were downcast out of a sense of shame.

"Kuriya, don't worry. God will do whatever is right. Go home now. Whatever your father may be, he still worries for you. He is waiting for you."

Kuriya headed home. Govind, too, returned to his hut.

The whole night Govind kept thinking why the father of a bright young man like Kuriya, who was not a bad man, had become useless because of his addiction. Govind was getting convinced that intoxication in any form damaged the body of a human being and affected his behaviour. By the time he stepped into adulthood, Govind had seen many instances of adivasi men ruining themselves and their families due to their drinking habit. They always found an excuse to drink, be it a happy occasion, a tragedy born out of poverty that they wanted to forget, or anger building up due to an unpleasant secret. That night Govind decided that he would dedicate his life to spreading awareness among adivasis about the ills of intoxication and the ignorance prevalent in their society.

Govind was very fond of Kuriya. To Govind it appeared that his friends Missra, Hinsallya and Ruksya were deadly dull. Poonja, though from the village Dungra, had become a good friend of Govind's, and always looked for an opportunity to meet him. He would find excuses to meet him. From the time Govind had first observed Kuriya roast the corn by lighting a flint he had thought of becoming something like "Kuriya's flint". That night Govind had a dream reflecting those thoughts.

In front of a religious place called Mala Bavji was the open square of Bhukiya village. It could accommodate 100–125 people. Surrounded by a rocky terrain were the huts of villagers. On the foot of the surrounding hillock outside the village were the huts of about a dozen families. In all, about 50–60 houses and 80–90 adivasi families constituted the entire village. The total population of the village could not have exceeded 450.

"Hey look, Rama is headed this way with Thamma (branch of tree used during Holi)," said Bhaniya Manat. His words turned the attention of a group of 10–15 people towards Rama Katara and his four–five young companions. These men had brought a tall branch of semal tree to the village. Placing that bundle of tree branches on a platform, Rama took out a brown coarse towel with blue lines to mop the sweat on his forehead.

"Oh Dungar Kaka! Today I was nearly devoured by a female bear. By the grace of Bholanath I was able to save myself." Saying this, Rama and his companion Gomana turned towards the middle-aged Dungar Parmar and looked at the sky above with folded hands. The other youth who had accompanied Rama readily agreed with him.

"Oh! These lads got scared unnecessarily. Dungar Kaka, there is nothing."

Before Dungar Kaka could react, Rama intervened. He said, "What happened was that we spotted a female bear with her children as soon as we had chopped the branches of the semal tree and were about to leave. The beast was startled. Before she could attack us we climbed up the tree. The female bear was disturbed when a small branch, heavily laden with leaves, slipped out of Gomana's hands and hit her. Gomana was not aware that a female bear was sitting behind the bushes. The sight of a furious bear saw us climbing fast on to the tree. The bear snarled for a while and, sniffing at the semal tree branches that were scattered on the ground, disappeared towards the nearby nullah with her two cubs. Gomana is still a kid. He doesn't know that wild animals don't attack unless provoked."

"All of you learn this lesson: Never pass by a new mother bear. She is always extra alert to protect her cubs. On such occasions she can also attack you without any provocation. You all know that two days before last Diwali a female bear had killed the wife of Manji Damor." Dungar Parmar shared his experience.

"Forget this. Now get busy with work and plant the recently brought green branch of the semal tree." To give a break in the story about the female bear Bhaniya Manat called a youth sitting nearby and asked him to light the hookah after filling it with tobacco. The youth took out his flint-stone, rubbing it hard to produce a spark with which he lit one end of a thread. He then inserted the burning end of the thread into the tobacco bowl of the hookah. Bhaniya inhaled deeply and that was enough to light the tobacco in the bowl of the hookah. As soon as he exhaled the tobacco smoke its aroma filled the surroundings. He passed the hookah to Dungar Parmar.

The ceremony of planting the semal sapling began. The priest of Mala Bavji brought a new pitcher, which was filled with water, and placed it in a pit dug where the sapling was to be planted. By its side was planted the lower portion of the sapling by Roopaji, Rama, Bhaniya, Dungar and Manji. They then filled the pit with earth and made it firm by trampling hard upon the filled space. The top of the sapling, which was planted straight, was tied to a red-and-white cloth and covered with some dried grass. Roopaji applied turmeric paste on the forehead of all those present on the occasion. A small lamp filled with ghee was lit near the sapling. Curiosity had brought small children around the place. Women in the nearby huts were watching the proceedings intently.

The abode of folk god Mala Bavji was close by. The Bhookiya village population was scattered around a small courtyard. A little beyond was another hamlet. Amidst the hills, jungle and a stream, in the small patches of agricultural land, shrubs and rocks, crops of barley, peas, linseed, and aniseed were ripe and ready for harvesting. They were irrigated with water drawn from the stream with the help of makeshift wooden pails and those who had wells in their land drew water from the Persian wheel.

The sun was about to set in half an hour. It had been a bright, sunlit winter day. Late in the afternoon, chilly winds had swept the place and it had turned cooler during the sapling ceremony. The winds had gathered speed during the last few hours. The warm sunshine that had given relief during the day from the chilly winds was becoming weak. From the north-western horizon rushed some dark clouds. The sun was hiding behind the western hills. Some scattered clouds could also be seen gathering in that direction.

The day of planting the sapling, a ritual to celebrate Holi, was almost over. It was evening now. But before the village could be engulfed by the darkness of night, the full moon appeared over the hills on the east. The eastern sky was absolutely clear. The children in the village had gone to bed after their meal. The goats, cows and bulls had been tethered in their pens. The cold had forced the hens and chicken to hide in various corners of their coop.

Roopaji had gone after lighting the incense stick at Mala Bavji. But he returned after taking his meals. Some of the devout had left after lighting fire in a pit built in the middle of the platform, using the dry tree branches that were scattered around. Dungar Parmar, Manji Damor, Bhaniya Manat and two-three middle aged men were sitting there, warming their hands. Like everyday, about half a dozen people had assembled at the place.

Two children, Hira and Bhajanya, were struggling to get some sleep in their hut. During last monsoon they had lost their father due to a gauhara bite. Hira used to be the leading participant in the ceremony of planting the Holi sapling. When this ceremony was on during the day, these two youngsters had missed their father. They had come to watch this year's ceremony as a way to overcome their grief. They had come along with their uncle Deena, who was around 32 years old. Besides these three, all others who had gathered at the ceremony were past their middle age. Roopaji had crossed 60, but he looked older.

From Hira, Bhajanya to Roopaji, all of them were short in height but their survival instinct in a harsh world had made them good at fighting and working like the devil. They had inherited from their ancestors the habit of changing the pattern of their lives according to the seasons. Their faces looked shrivelled, their noses were flat, and they were strong enough to make the highest sacrifices for the sake of their pride. Their skins were dark but their hearts and minds were pure white. Despite the abject conditions in which they lived, they were very good people.

On the border of Banswara and Dungarpur states was the village Bhukiya, a small part in the middle of Aravali hills. Thick forests and irregular black hills surrounded the village. These puny, dark complexioned adivasis lived in this range of low black hills. They had strong emotional ties with one other and also with every nook and cranny of the forest and hills. There was perfect harmony between nature and all living creatures in their surroundings. There was no sense of envy, jealousy, inequality or oppression in the minds of these adivasis. They were virtually cut off from the rest of the world. That was perhaps why their rich tradition of respect for living creatures had survived so long. They had held on to their core values. Their inherited asset was an old value system of simple and honest life that had survived for centuries. Too much of worldly knowledge and experiences sometimes make life too complicated and make people tense. It cannot be said whether it will hold true and remain relevant in future, but it appeared that the values followed by these simple adivasis would sustain whatever remained of fellow feeling among human beings.

Roopaji had a limited knowledge of his area, but it was invaluable. He knew enough about the land, forests and hills around him. He knew about the flora and fauna of the area, the herbs and medicinal plants, which were useful in curing snakebites and similar hazards arising out of attacks by wild animals and poisonous insects. Unfortunately, the day Hiralya had died after he was bitten by a gauhara, Roopaji was visiting a relative elsewhere. Hiralya had died by the time Roopaji could answer the summons to attend to him. He repeated this story before the sons of Hira.

"Had I been present that day, Mahadev Baba (God) would have extended his blessings and perhaps Hiralya would have been saved."

"Whatever had to happen has happened. It was the wish of the One with the Blue Umbrella (colloquial expression for God). What is the point of crying over it everyday? Roopaji Baba, why don't you narrate a good story?" Thus spoke Deena as he looked at the audience.

Roopaji understood. Changing the topic, he recalled a Shiv–Parvati episode from the scriptures. It was a tradition that all the fables and stories popular in the area were narrated in the form of songs. So Roopaji began in the same style:

> Hey! Once Shiva and Parvati were at loggerheads
> whereupon Shiva renounced her,
> and lived as an ascetic in the woods
> for years twelve.

The story in the song was this: Lord Shiv carries out ascetic practices in the jungles for 12 years. His wife Parvati is alone at home. She is unable to bathe and feels unclean. How could she go for a bath, leaving the house unattended? She mulls over this problem and gathers the dirt on her person to mould it into a human form and bring a son to life to look after the house; she then leaves for a dip in the sea. In the meanwhile, Lord Shiv returns home and knocks on the door. The child who answers does not recognise him and quarrels with Lord Shiv. When Lord Shiv asks the child to name his parents, he mentions Shiv and Parvati. An angry Shiv chops off the boy's head, which falls into the sea while the body remains where it was. When Parvati returns home, she is overcome by grief at what she sees and demands that Lord Shiv bring the child back to life. At first, he refuses but on Parvati's persistence he relents, strikes at the neck of a passing elephant and plants the upper portion of the elephant on the body of the child.

The moment the story ended all assembled shouted "*Mahadev Baba ki Jai* (Hail thee, Great Lord Mahadev!)"

The assembly at Mala Bavji's site thus came to an end.

The clouds, which had appeared on the west-northern horizon at dusk, now covered the entire western sky. Not a single star was visible. On the other hand, the full moon of the Magh (January–February) month climbed to about 60–65 degree. The stars disappeared over the western horizon. The horizon on the East was clear but clouds were gathering from the West—an indication of some unusual happening?

The air had become still as the second part of the evening was coming to an end. The cold was becoming intense. Next morning the month of Phagun was to begin. This year's winter was a bit more severe. The month of Magh had turned out to be one of bitter cold.

In the forests around the village, trees like the Kalpataru, useful in times of distress and sickness, were standing motionless. Were they sleeping? Or, were they weeping? There is a saying that the mahua tree weeps on quiet and lonely nights. It is, of course, true that water drops trickle like tears from the leaves of mahua, both in winter and summer nights. Who knows what pangs of separation trouble these trees? This much is certain that in this area the trees—be they of mango, black plum, neem, wild fig, teak or wild sandalwood—had all gone to sleep. Suddenly came a roar from the forest…"Hukki…Hukki…Hukki…"

By now the moon had been surrounded by clouds. Only a few stars were twinkling on the eastern horizon. Right above the village there was a thundering streak of lightening. It reverberated loudly through the entire area. A few drops fell at some places in the beginning but soon there was an onslaught of hailstones. Lightning, thunder and hailstorm, all at once, oh! The stillness in this area of Vagad region was disturbed. The jungle came out of its reverie. Everyone in the village, including the children, was awake. Women threw out black pitchers from their houses. The elder among them turned the stone grinder anti-clockwise.

"Oh, You treacherous One of Blue Umbrella, what have You done? Oh, Lord Mahadev! Oh, Mother Parvati! Oh, Mala Bavji! What havoc you have wreaked?" Roopaji cursed the gods. He pleaded with Bholanath, revered by tribals for thousands of years. He called Mother Parvati for help. He hailed Mala Bavji, the folk god.

Despite the cries for mercy and entreaties, the merciless clouds did whatever damage they had to do, all in a jiffy. Then the clouds drifted towards the eastern direction. By midnight darkness was shifting eastwards. On the west, bright rays from the moon were trying to penetrate the cloudy sky. At last, that cursed night was over. The month of Phagun was heralded next morning with a clear sky. A few remainders of the previous night's clouds did appear to be drifting here and there. A bright crimson sun was emerging on top of the Bhairon Dungari situated at the village's eastern corner. None from the village was up to see that sight!

What they saw was the linseed crop flattened in the fields amidst the rough valleys and by the side of the bushes around village streams. The tiny and tender pods in the linseed crop had been brutally crushed by the hailstone. The withered crop had ceased to be of any use to the owners of the different patches. The barley crops looked healthy, displaying thick clusters of grain with bristling spikes. The barley grain appeared to be full of milk. But the crop required another 20 or 30 days to ripen. Now it was sure that the barley crop would not mature. The fields were covered with the flattened crops. The destroyed cumin and aniseed crops in the fields looked like a growth of uneven grass. Their raw seeds were barely visible. At some places one could see the damaged mustard crop. Just the other day, yellow flowers had started to sprout in the mustard crop. The crop was green, ripening well and it was apparent that it would be ready for harvesting in no time. Now all that was lost. The creepers of green pea pods were sprawled dead on the fields.

The villagers were greeted with a horrible sight of their crops devastated and their fields covered with a carpet of hailstone. Instead of looking at the rising sun, their gaze was fixed on their misery. Anyone endowed with the ability to read the minds of the villagers would have seen that for these tribals it was not a simple hailstorm that hit their fields but an attack by all the meteors in the solar system. The adivasis were showing their disgust and disappointment by repeatedly striking their forehead with their hands. For them the destruction of their crops was a tragedy bigger than the death of a dear one.

Excessive rain had destroyed that year's Kharif crop. Hope then rested on the Rabi crop. That, too, was destroyed by the hailstorm.

The pace of life, however, is not impeded by such incidents. Life has to move on constantly. Crying does not help when man is helpless.

Roopaji was a pious man. He kept himself away from worldly matters. Dungar Parmar was a serious and determined person, who believed in hard work and preaching its virtue. The villagers who had assembled at Mala Bavji's place after their crops had been destroyed looked morose. They had passed through a great internal turmoil; they had cursed the skies and complained to God.

Govind was headed towards Garhi with Kuriya and two-three other companions. Seeing the crowd that had assembled at the open courtyard of Bhukiya village, they stopped. After the exchange of pleasantries, they learnt from the villagers about the loss of their crops. Govind and his companions had already seen the damaged crops on the way. The hailstorm had destroyed crops in many other villages as well. Trying to restore their confidence, Govind said:

"It's no use being crestfallen. If God gives us a lot, he also has the right to take something from us. Learn to fill the places rendered empty. You got nothing from this crop. Never mind. Have patience. The jungle is full of grass and there is no dearth of leaves on the trees. There will be no shortage of fodder for the bullocks, cows and goats. As for your stomachs, go far out into the jungles and collect gum, catechu, honey, dry twigs and any other thing useful. Instead of selling these to the village *bania* (trader), if you sell them at the haat (weekly market), you will get a better price. Besides, the mahua tree can always be banked upon to give you something. Have trust in God. Stop crying. Work hard to feed your children. In Lord Rama's tale, Sant Tulsidas has said, 'The world is built by one's sweat'. It means that noble act is the basis of life."

The Bhukiya adivasis were taken aback to hear such words of wisdom from Govind. They whispered among themselves: "He appears to be a holy and learned man."

"Where are you from, oh *bhagat* (follower of God)," Roopaji asked Govind. Roopaji himself was a devotee. He too was impressed by Govind's talk.

"From Basiya village which is towards Dungarpur, Bhai Baba," replied Govind, who was mobbed by the assembled villagers as he tried to resume his journey with his companions. "Some other time! Now I must leave," said Govind as he proceeded towards Garhi with his friends. From Govind he had become Govind Bhagat and, deep inside him, was pleased to hear that name.

Around noon, Govind reached Garhi with his group. Garhi was the main inhabited centre of the *jagir* and a prominent part of the Banswara state. On one side of the village lived Rajput and Pathan families. The Bhil adivasis lived on the small hills around the town. In one corner of the village was the religious site of Bhilardev. Govind Bhagat decided to stay there.

"Jai Bhole Nath," shouted Govind Bhagat as he greeted two or three elders sitting there. "Jai Ramjiki. Son, where are you coming from?" asked one of the elders as he courteously asked Govind Bhagat to sit.

Kuriya introduced the visiting party. "This is Govind Bhagat. We travel with him from village to village with the intention of serving adivasi brothers."

"In appearance and talk you look like decent folks. Anyone who wanders to share the joys and sorrows of us adivasis does a pious work. But what can you do? Even Lord Ram has turned against us. See, all was well till a hailstorm hit us last night. Everything has been lost. This is how the One Up Above has treated us. In addition, the Raj is also after us," the elder man said as he leaned towards Govind and Kuriya. He was Ghasita Katara of Garhi village. He had acquired the name after an ailment in his younger days deprived him of his ability to walk normally and for months he had to trudge dragging his feet. He lived a life of a handicap.

The air still had a chill in it. The day was rising and the warmth of the sun provided comfort to the body.

From behind the Bhilardev assembly ground by the side of a nullah emerged a middle aged man walking unsteadily, apparently drunk. He was heard saying, "I'll see those sons of bitches…I'll jump to my death and become a ghost…yes, a ghost, a ghost. Then I'll kill each one of them by twisting their necks. I'll not spare even their relatives. Three Saturdays have passed…working day and night…shouting day and night… tossing some crumbs like throwing them at a dog…so what, the empty stomach is still craving for food."

This man was Sodana Damor who lived above the nullah. Kuriya took the man's hand and tried to make him sit.

"I'll not sit at Baba's place. Today…for the first time I've drunk liquor. Liquor is liquor…I've committed a sin. Yes, I have...committed a sin. Now I shall commit a bigger sin. I'll become a ghost. Ramji (God) has given a life for incurring debts and forced labour. From the moment I became conscious of my existence, God pushed me to the feet of the Raj. This Devbaba also did not care for me. What can I say of him? He is our ancestor. Even he...yes, even he must have led a similar life. Must have died of hunger...even he. What good can he do? But he is still...our ancestor. Isn't he? I'll not sit in his place. I've heard from my parents and grandparents that he used to consider liquor as a sprinkling of oil."

Speaking thus, Sodana slipped out of Kuriya's grip and tumbled over as he tried to sit on the floor. He was frothing at the mouth. His eyes were fiery. His anger was aggravated by the burning sensation from the liquor in his stomach.

"Throw some buttermilk on his head. I'm seeing him drunk for the first time."

Seeing the state of Sodana, a couple of youth gathered around him. They were from Garhi too. One of them quickly fetched a bowl of buttermilk. The two young men propped up Sodana and slowly began to pour buttermilk over his head. The buttermilk found its way to the ground via his ears and cheeks. As a drop slid near his mouth from his left cheek, Sodana tried to lick it with his tongue. The duo of the youth poured the remainder of the buttermilk in his mouth.

From Sodana's action it appeared that he was feeling better with the treatment of a shower of cold buttermilk and enjoyed drinking some of it. Now he was stretching his eyelids with his fingers to try and recognise the assembled crowd. He had stopped fumbling and seemed to regret his behaviour.

"You worthless creature! Where did you pick up that stuff? Got drunk so early in the day? You left the house saying you would be grazing the goats and you returned taking this demonic shape in the hailstorm," said Sodana's wife as she arrived there after searching for him.

"Your husband is fine now. Very soon he'll be sober. Take him home carefully," Ghasita advised Sodana's wife.

"What will I do by taking this father-eating man home? When I protested at his drinking he started beating me. I pushed him and he, threatening to kill me, rushed out of our courtyard."

"Never mind. After all, he's your husband. Who else will take care of him? Something must have disturbed him emotionally. He was at fault. We have never seen him in this condition. Now take him away. Don't invite ridicule before the world," the second elder said, echoing Ghasita advice.

"Yes, it is me who is inviting ridicule and this man is Bholanath's simple follower who has strayed the first time in his life! What more can I speak in front of you elders?" Saying so, the woman took Sodana's hand and tried to make him stand up.

Kuriya stepped down from where he was sitting and lent a helping hand. Sodana was now steady, standing on his own. He needed no support. He was trying to evade the eyes of the elders. He looked at his wife as though seeking a silent pardon. He was clearly ashamed of his conduct. Lending her shoulders to him, the woman turned towards the nullah and headed for her hut with Sodana.

Govind Bhagat watched the entire scene seriously. He thought of Kuriya's father. Sodana had appeared to be more aggressive than Kuriya's father. Govind turned towards Kuriya and appeared to be muttering to himself, "Oh Kuriya, take care of your father."

Govind Bhagat learned in Garhi that for the last 15 days, Sodana was being forced to offer free labour to the jagirdar. Sodana was childless. He had a small patch of land. Mustard crop was ripening in this field when the hailstorm destroyed it. There was not a grain at home to eat. This morning he had to again go to jagirdar for forced labour. After securing the goat in its corner, he had arrived at his field in the midst of the hailstorm. He kept watching the destruction of his crop. Then he went to the hut of Rama, who also had to offer free labour to the jagirdar.

"I'm feeling cold. Brother Rama, give me some liquor or else I'll fall ill due to cold and will not be able to go to the jagirdar. If that happens then I'll be whipped or will have to serve another two days of forced labour."

Rama felt helpless and offered him a full measure of mahudi (a country liquor)-filled jhavli (earthen pot), hoping that he would take only a few sips. Rama knew that Sodana did not drink. He got busy with household chores. He had no idea of what Sodana would be doing behind his back. When he returned he found that Sodana had finished the jhavli and was drunk. It wasn't easy for Rama to send Sodana home.

Govind Bhagat had watched from close quarters how destruction from the hailstorm and forced labour had affected Sodana. Govind was getting restless.

Ghasita had lived through many, many days of sorrow and pain. In his childhood he might have walked by dragging his feet, but by the time he reached the ripe age he had learned a lot. He had seen how the adivasis had to suffer a double attack from Ram (Lord) and Raj. It had also become part of his life. He could not comprehend the ways of the Lord, but he knew about many misdeeds of the Raj.

On request from Govind and Kuriya, Ghasita called an adivasi chief, Mangalya Damor. He respected Ghasita who was the most intelligent elder of the village. Mangalya used to seek his help and guidance to sort out complicated matters. He immediately arrived on receiving message from Ghasita and asked him: "What's the matter, Kaka?"

In the morning both had shared their grief over the loss of crops. Mangalya had thought that Ghasita was being called in to approach the jagirdar for helping the poor hit by the crop damage. But that was not the case. Govind Bhagat had insisted that the adivasi panchayat, a council of the adivasis, be summoned to discuss the issue of forced labour and other matters. Ghasita had very respectfully introduced Govind Bhagat and his companions to the mukhiya (chief). The mukhiya was able to gather a crowd by using the traditional method of loud drumbeat. By afternoon around 150 people had assembled there.

"By the grace of Mahadev Baba this wanderer has landed in our village," said Mangalya by way of introduction of Govind as he called the panchayat proceedings to order.

"Govind is still very young but he has become a bhagat. He is a Banjara by caste. His ancestors led the life of adivasis, as we do. He is familiar with our travails. Endowed with a spirit to serve humankind, he wanders afar for our good. I had a lengthy conversation with him. He is honest and knowledgeable. All you brothers, please listen to him attentively," Ghasita picked up the thread from Mangalya.

The faces of the people who had assembled at the panchayat wore withered look, the shock due to loss of their crops weighing heavily upon them. They appeared deeply worried. They doubted if any bhagat would be able to help them in providing relief in this hour of extreme misery. But they sat quietly, obeying the command of the mukhiya. Some of them were still looking at the sky. The gaze of some others was fixed on the mukhiya and Ghasita. Now most of them turned their attention towards Govind.

The sky was clear. Not a speck of cloud anywhere. After commanding a force comprising lightening, rain and hailstone to attack the earth all night, as if to settle an old score, and then sending back his warriors with a pat on the back for the successful attack, the all-conquering sky now appeared to be resting peacefully on the swing of a gentle breeze. The sun was weak. There was dense greenery by the side of the nullah with trees of mahua, semal, mango, jamun, sares and neem. Right behind the cluster at Bhilardev was a banyan tree with its heavy branches hanging on all sides. Yellow, lifeless leaves lay scattered underneath it. The trees were shedding leaves on their own. It was the first day of Phagun. But for the down and out, badly bruised and demoralised locality of the adivasis it was an ominous day.

On a cue from mukhiya, Govind cleared his throat, started speaking: "Elders, friends and fellow youth, we have just seen a middle aged man, Sodana, who lives in the cluster above the nullah. His wife took him away a little while ago. It has been said that the man never touched liquor. But deeply grieved at the destruction caused by the hailstorm and the free forced labour that he had to do last fortnight at the jagirdar's, he had consumed mahudi. Seeing his condition, I was shaken thoroughly. If drinking of mahudi ends all troubles then let all of us decide in this panchayat that we shall adopt this habit. But such a decision will be a path to the destruction of homes and families. Intoxication of any kind damages the body and the mind."

"So, what should we do to get over fatigue and our problems?" interrupted someone.

"First, listen to all that Govind Bhagat has to say. It's an insult to the guest to interrupt him like this," the mukhiya said sternly.

"Mukhiya, let me answer that man. The priest in my village had told me that doubts should be resolved then and there. As a medicine, a little of liquor does provide relief to breathing problems. This I accept. But to become an addict is wrong in all circumstances. Let the fruit of mahua fill an empty stomach instead."

Govind gave a detailed account of the damage that consumption of liquor did.

He added: "Another important thing I want to say is that it isn't if an employee or the jagirdar of a princely state forces a hungry man to do free labour. God makes arrangements for filling the stomach of even those who have only a beak. When will a man, who has to do forced labour, have the time to earn a living for his family?"

"We do not have to do forced labour everyday. We do it only on a project started by the Raj or when it is our turn to do so," an adult in the crowd explained.

The mukhiya was not clear about the issue. He kept quiet. The old eyes of Ghāsita were fixed on Govind. The mukhiya was trying to gauge the reaction of the people. He wanted to intervene. As he tried to stand up, Govind put his hands on his shoulders to stop him.

"There's no harm in helping and sharing each other's work. Doing that sort of labour is not bad. This we have to do. But being forced to put in hard labour for free is slavery. This sort of work is degrading for human beings. For the sake of mitigating our hunger—to earn roti, rice and vegetable—we may be forced to work. There is no harm in working for the construction of a well, pond or tank for our area. This is, after all, work for our own good. But to work for someone else without wages is wrong. We should oppose it."

"What! Oppose the Raj?" someone shouted.

"Let Raj do its work. Why does the Raj interfere in our lives? Why should I do anything against my wishes? Tell me one thing: are you happy and cheerful in your heart to be working gratis?"

"Brother Bhagat! It is not a question of our wish. This has been a tradition for generations. Besides, the Raj does render some help in times of famine and epidemic. Look at it like this: we do forced labour as it helps us face trouble that may come in future. What's wrong in it?" asked another.

"A lot of things have been happening down generations. For centuries adivasi mukhiyas have been taking money to protect and guide non-adivasis, especially traders, through adivasi territories so that they face no harm. Most of the money thus earned has been spent for the good of the village. Why did the Raj stop this income? These days, men from the Raj are measuring our fields. I've learnt that the idea is to increase the rent on our land. That's why our fields are being measured. We've owned land for generations and we've cleared patches to make them cultivable. The foremost thing is that the land is ours, so why do we have to pay rent? Okay, let the Raj take rent from us for the sake of attending to our woes in times of distress. But what's the meaning of increasing the rent?"

There was much substance in what Govind was saying. He was right about the intention behind the measurement of land. The audience was startled to hear about the likelihood of increase in land rent.

"Listen! More woes are in store. What grows in the jungles has been ours for generations. What grows there is for our use, but why does the Raj let contractors take that produce? People of my caste have been selling salt for generations. Now the Raj has put restrictions on salt trade. One has to pay for trading in salt. Check-posts have been erected at many places so that no one can trade the way we did earlier. We have to take loan from the rich to buy grain. What kind of accounting is this that the loan refuses to expire even after full payment has been made many times over? We do not understand the dishonest ways of the bania. We've to understand all this to sort out matters. The adivasis from many other places have also opposed these things. Wherever there were protests, the Raj had to withdraw the new rules and laws. We would continue to be exploited by the Raj, jagirdar, moneylender, clerks and minions of the Raj unless we have the awareness to fight the evil within ourselves."

By now most people were listening to Govind attentively. They felt that a really wise bhagat was addressing them. Kuriya and others with him were feeling very pleased too.

The panchayat ended after Govind had spoken. Mangalya had a mixed reaction to this discourse. The mukhiya feared that Govind had spoken against the Raj and this news will duly reach the Raj and from there right to the darbar. This could spell trouble for the village.

When Govind expressed a desire to leave Garhi, Ghasita asked him to stay for the night. However, the mukhiya did not show any interest in pursuing that request.

There was still time for sunset. Govind left for Garhi with his companions. Next day, the jagirdar learnt whatever had transpired at the panchayat. He was at Banswara Darbar for three days. The Thakur quietly sent his men in different directions to find out more about Govind, but they could not get any information. The jagirdar summoned Mangalya to his palace. Mangalya was evasive and avoided further ordeal by promising that in future he would not call a panchayat to discuss controversial issues. The jagirdar was unaware of Govind's future plan for agitations. The mukhiya had not admitted that he supported all that Govind had said, and that, among the adivasis of the village, the message from Govind had taken roots.

TWO

Udaipur Darbar

Maharaja Sajjan Singh was sitting on the throne. Kotwal Rehmat Ali Bakhs, the police officer of Udaipur city, bent in salutations as he entered the darbar. He was wearing the narrow churidar pyjama, buttoned-up achkan and big folded turredar turban. A sword in its scabbard was slung across his waist.

"Everything is fine in the Raj of the darbar. Three locks were broken open in the goldsmith market last night. But not much of the valuables were stolen. Clues obtained from the spot indicate that one of the adivasis from Hiranmagri had committed the crime or someone from the criminal tribe could also be responsible for the crime. I've summoned my informers. The thieves will be caught in a day or two. Apart from this, there was an attempted robbery at the *math* (seminary) of Mahant Sukhdas Maharaj, but the devotees woke up in time to foil it. The principal devotee at the seminary has been asked to be more vigilant. There is no other news that needs to be brought to the notice of the Lord Darbar."

Kotwal Rehmat Ali Bakhs had presented the morning report from the Kotwali with great courtesy before Maharana Sajjan Singh.

"Do pay special attention to the bazaar," said the king as he asked the Kotwal to leave.

It was a practice that the city Kotwal would present a report about the crime situation in the city everyday before the king as soon as he entered the darbar in the morning. Other routines at the darbar followed after that.

Just after the Kotwal left, the personal secretary of the king, Shyamaldas entered the Darbar Khas with some selected courtiers.

"Hukum (my lord), Khamagani," he said in the traditional style of veneration.

"Please sit, Shyamaldasji."

"Hail the darbar. If Hukum be pleased, may I read this telegram? It has just been received from Delhi, sent by the foreign secretary to the Government of India."

Hearing this, Maharaja Sajjan Singh looked a little worried. From the time of the previous king, Shambhu Singh, the British had formed the "Council of Regency" to increase interference in the affairs of the Mewar state. It was still active. Hearing about the telegram made him think that perhaps the British had sent him another instruction.

"Yes, Shyamaldasji. Is there anything important in the telegram?"

"Huzoor (my lord), it says that in view of a likely revolt by the adivasis strict punishment should be awarded to the miscreants," Shyamaldas said as he read out the telegram.

"There has been no news so far to suggest that an adivasi revolt is brewing in our kingdom. How can the Bhil, Meena or any other subject of the state oppose the Darbar?"

"Huzoor, it is not about mere opposition. What is in the telegram mirrors the feeling among the Barapal and Padona adivasis that the British interference is reducing the patronage and protection they enjoyed at the time of Maharana Pratap. The adivasis are growing restless over the question of excise and jungle laws. Huzoor was acquainted about these matters a couple of times earlier too. Since yesterday some adivasis have been here to present their case. If you permit, I shall call them in."

"All right! You go and talk to them first. Is there anything else?"

"No, Maharaj, may I beg your leave?"

After Shyamaldas left, Sajjan Singh got busy talking to some selected Rajput nobles.

The British were introducing new laws to strengthen their policy of interference in the affairs of native princely states to increase their hold over them. Their main target was the income that came from tapping various sources for the expansion of trade and the armed forces. Restrictions on grain production, tax on agriculture and land settlement, excise policy, trade routes through Vagad region, restrictions on trade and production of salt were some of the matters the adivasis were opposing.

All this had affected their lives. It was also an attack on their autonomy, which they could not tolerate. The British policy was that any worsening of situation arising out of repressive economic measures would be blamed on the native rulers and in the event of their failure to control the consequent rebellion these rulers would be held incompetent. This will facilitate further political interference by the British through the Council.

When Shyamaldas met some adivasis they spoke to him in one voice.

"The clerks and other employees of the state are conducting the census exercise. It is widely believed in the area that this is being done to levy new taxes. It has also been said that adivasi youth will be sent to fight war in Afghanistan. Their young women will be left in the care of others. The young daughters of the adivasis will be handed over to the male bachelor adivasis so that their elders can leave for the front without much worry. People are being weighed during the census. This has led to all kinds of speculations in the area. We had never seen such an atmosphere of uncertainty. It must stop. We request the darbar with folded hands to stop all this."

"All these are rumours. You must not believe them. The purpose of the census is to prepare new plans for your prosperity and development, and arrange for timely relief in times of natural disaster. You should go to your areas and tell this."

"But sir, the steps taken by the Raj so far have not been in our interest. In such circumstances it is natural to see any new step taken by the Raj with suspicion. No adivasi is going to believe what you are telling us. That is why we have come to meet the Maharaj and we shall not return till we have conveyed our misgivings to him."

Since there was no other alternative, Shyamaldas was forced to take the adivasi delegation to Maharaja Sajjan Singh. After meeting the king, the advivasis were satisfied only to the extent that they had an opportunity to convey their misapprehensions to him.

"Annadata (bread provider), one thing more," one of the adivasis mustered courage to say.

"Yes, tell me, mukhiya. What else remains to be said?"

"Sir, lengthy roads using stones and iron are being constructed through the jungles. We have heard that on these iron paths bullocks of iron will haul big iron carts. It is said that this bullock will spit fire, which will burn all trees, vegetation and grass in the jungles."

Maharaja Sajjan Singh laughed heartily on hearing this. He was nearly chocked by laughter. One of the servants promptly brought water in a silver tumbler. Gulping a quick draught of water made him regain his composure. The courtiers present in the darbar joined him in the laughter. But only a smile was visible on Shyamaldas's face. The adivasis were clueless about the cause of the mirth. The king spoke after a pause.

"You fools! Have you seen the world outside the jungles? Have you heard about trains?"

"No, Maharaj!" said most of the assembly.

"I'll tell you. What you call an iron path is actually the iron track on which will run trains with many carriages. They will run as fast as the horse. It will make travelling of passengers and ferrying of goods between two points faster and comfortable. Latsahib (Viceroy) will travel on such trains and so shall we. Your life will remain confined to the jungles. There is no need for you to know more. The train will serve its purpose. You have nothing to fear from it. I am your king. Trust my words always."

"Yes, sir." The questioner could manage only this response but a lot of things were going in his mind.

A little later the mukhiya spoke again. "The Raj is bent upon doing it, it will build an iron path and a train will run on it. Whatever is done, sir, you have to ensure that we are not disturbed without any rhyme and reason. But still there is something that is not clear."

"What is that, mukhiya?" The Maharaja was wondering what else remains to be sorted out. He was getting restless because he thought the adivasis were wasting his time. He wanted to see them leave at once.

"The thing is, sir, that while the road is being constructed through the jungle, the jagirdar's men come to us with barbers who chop off the hair of the elders and on inquiry tell us that it is for the road that the Raj is building. Now that a real road is being built then what is the need to cut our hair in a style that makes a two-inch channel on the head? It will be a road on which no one can walk," said another adivasi mukhiya in all seriousness.

Some courtiers burst out laughing again. Maharaja Sajjan Singh, however, turned a little serious on hearing this. The darbaris who were laughing were embarrassed. Shyamaldas joined neither the laughter nor did he change his expression.

"The king is like God on earth. He protects the subjects. As long as the ruler extends his hand of protection over the subjects they are safe and in return the subjects have to repose their faith and trust in him. This is an old tradition. Don't waste your time over it. It is getting late. You may leave," said the Maharaja.

The delegation of *gametis* (adivasi chiefs) returned after talking to Maharaja Sajjan Singh, but none of them was completely satisfied, especially over the matter relating to the laws on jungle produce and excise. They had not been able to decipher the meaning of building "a road for the Raj".

Like a thorn that refuses to come out, the talk about the road for the Raj had stuck in the minds of these adivasis. They associated this analogy with oppression, something that the adivasi society had begun to understand. The revulsion created by increasing interference in their lives by the Raj was increasing and was sowing seeds of rebellion among the adivasis. They now understood better the unwanted obstructions in their natural life, which was based on their customs and traditions that they had followed since centuries.

An initiative may be a boon for the initiator, not for those who suffer on account of it. The adivasis had begun to understand this fact.

Their king had been opaque in his talks with the delegation. How could he make the adivasis of the region understand? With changing circumstances resentment among the adivasis was brewing and that too, rapidly.

A few days later, the head of Barapal police station killed an adivasi from Padona. He was beaten severely for refusing to give false evidence in a case and he died due to this thrashing. A dynamite of anger already building up among the adivasis was waiting to explode.

The next morning on 25 March 1881, hundreds of adivasis left for Barapal. They were carrying bows and arrows, lathis, spears, scythes, axe and other weapons. On the way the Bhils of Tidi joined them. The news about the death of a tribal youth had spread like jungle fire and the adivasis from surrounding areas rushed to be part of the army that was moving towards Barapal. At Barapal, local adivasis also joined them. By afternoon between 1,000 and 1,200 adivasis assembled outside the police station.

The inspector at the police station managed to convey the news to Udaipur. But before that could result in the dispatch of army, the adivasis had surrounded the police station and attacked it. The police inspector, a liquor contractor and a few others were killed. Many buildings belonging to the Barapal and Padona states were destroyed.

After receiving the news of the attack on the police station, the Maharaja of Mewar dispatched 150 cavalry and 500 men of the infantry, all well armed, to the troubled area. They were led by the jagirdar of Lonar village and Raja Amar Singh. The army was instructed to severely punish the Bhils and Meenas of Padona and Barapal and fully crush the rebellion. When the army reached Barapal, it saw vast destruction.

The scene at Padona was almost similar. The army set afire the village, assuming that terror would force the adivasis to surrender. But it only fuelled the spirit of rebellion and more number of people joined the rebels. The adivasis killed the kamdar of Asirgarh. Many police posts were set on fire. They also captured a petty ruler of the area, Akshay Singh.

As soon as the Maharaja learnt about it, he dispatched two more detachments of the army, one of which was put under the joint command of Thakur Pratap Singh of Bhainsrogarh, Thakur Raj Singh of Shivpura and Maulvi Abdul Rehman Khan. One detachment was sent to Kotda. The second detachment was placed under Jagirdar Rawal Rattan Singh of Kurabda, Takhat Singh Mehta and Thakur Madan Singh of Baldhara. Maharaja Sajjan Singh also sent his personal secretary, Shyamaldas, with the second detachment. The army headed towards the Kewra valley. It clashed with the adivasis near Parsad where the army murdered a Bhil.

Shyamaldas later issued a clarification about the incident. According to him, the Bhil youth was moving in a suspicious manner. When a cavalry soldier asked the Bhil to stop, he shot arrows at him. The solider opened fire in self defence and the Bhil was killed. In all, this battle took a toll of 74 adivasis and many others were injured. The dead and injured adivasis were taken away by their comrades into the jungles. The adivasis put up obstructions on the road to stop the army from advancing further. They also damaged the communication lines between Khairwada and Udaipur. At Rishabdev, about 6,000 to 7,000 adivasis gathered and attacked an army unit there. The army opened fire. The adivasis retraced their steps but continued to fight a guerrilla war. This battle had drawn adivasis from Bhikal, Pipli, Sairon and other villages. They unsuccessfully tried to attack the Khairwada cantonment. They were repulsed by the soldiers who were well equipped with rifles and machine guns. This battle took a toll of 20 adivasi lives and many more were injured.

The British officers had kept an eye over the adivasi rebellion right from the beginning. They had instructed Major Temple at Kotda to proceed to Khairwada. Col Blair, who was on leave, was asked to rejoin duties and move from Mount Abu to Udaipur. From his Udaipur camp he kept himself in touch with Khairwada and Rishabdev.

In the hope that it will quell the rebellion, a message was sent to the adivasis that the king will take a sympathetic view of their problems. The rising tension brought the Rajputana AGG., Col Walters, to Udaipur.

After receiving the message from Maharaja Sajjan Singh, the adivasi chiefs decided to open the Udaipur-Khairwada route on the condition that no extra forces will be sent in that direction. British officer Straton, who was to replace Col Blair when the latter was on leave, reached Udaipur. Meanwhile, the representatives of the king and tribal chiefs reached an agreement to start a dialogue at the Rishabdev temple. On behalf of Maharaja Sajjan Singh (also referred to as the Maharana), Shyamaldas was to be the sole interlocutor. The British officers did not want the dialogue to be held without their interference. Therefore, to 'advise' Shyamaldas, Col Blair and Wingate also reached Khairawada.

Col Walters was blunt with Maharaja Sajjan Singh. "It is Col Blair's wish that during the talks at Rishabdev, Shyamaldas should respect his decisions."

The Maharana had no choice. Accordingly, he conveyed the 'advice' to Shyamaldas.

However, before Shyamaldas could receive the message from the Maharana, the disputed issues had nearly been settled with the mediation by Khemraj Bhandari, the priest of Rishabdev temple. Col Walters had sent a report to the Government of India that the Maharana meets him everyday and takes no decision without first informing him or seeking his advice. Around 7,000 adivasis had assembled at the Rishabdev temple when the priest was sorting out their problems.

Col Blair and Wingate reached Rishabhdev before the talks began at the temple. They pitched their tents a mile away from the town. Shyamaldas met them before joining the talks. The two British representatives were not happy with what they had heard from Shyamaldas. They thought that Shyamaldas was exaggerating dissensions within the adivasis to serve his interests. Blair tried to talk directly to some influential adivasi leaders. Shyamaldas' fear was that by talking directly to some adivasis, the British officers would be able to incite them and then bring the area under British control. In their talks with some of the adivasis, the British officers explained to them the importance of the census exercise.

The adivasi leaders were keen that the Maharana should press for the pardon of their fellow adivasis who had taken part in the rebellion. On this, Col Blair said: "Talk about it directly to the Maharana."

While the talks were on, Shyamaldas motioned to the adivasis standing outside to go behind the temple. This signal was misunderstood. One adivasi fired a shot from his rifle. During the pandemonium that followed the adivasis took positions on the nearby hillocks.

Fearing that Khairwada cantonment might come under attack Blair immediately headed there, taking a few men along with him. The adivasis in the meanwhile had looted his tent. Col Blair sent a message to Erinpura cantonment that a force be rushed to Kotda. Simultaneously, a request went out to the big army centre at Ahmedabad that a force of at least regiment strength be rushed for the protection of Khairwada. Similar requests were received at Dungarpur and Mahikantha.

The Government of India ordered the Bombay Presidency to immediately send army for the protection of Mewar region. Col Blair sent some trusted adivasis to the village to restore peace. It was also publicised that armed forces in large numbers were arriving at Erinpura and other places. Before leaving for Rishabdev, Col Blair had expressed a desire that to bring the situation under control, he would take charge of the entire operation. The Maharana was not sure about his intentions. Therefore, he warned Shyamaldas in advance that he must see to it that the British did not dominate during the dialogue to push their point forward in order to serve their own interests. The unspoken word from the Maharana was that he did not want anything to facilitate British takeover of Mewar in the manner Ajmer and Khairwada were lost to them due to a British conspiracy.

Shyamaldas toured the adivasi area without any security and pressed for a resolution through dialogue. The adivasi mukhiyas talked to Shyamaldas at a hillock located at some distance from Rishabdev and came to an agreement on important issues. The agreement was put down in writing and inscribed on a cemented slab, which was fixed to the right of the Rishabdev temple.

As soon as Col Blair got to know about the Rishabdev agreement, he consulted AGG Col Walters, who had arrived at Khairwada cantonment two days earlier. During this conversation held at the Officers' Mess, Col Blair said: "The Maharana has crossed all limits. He has placed too much trust on his advisers. From the text of the agreement it appears that the adivasis were able to get all their fair and unfair demands accepted under duress. This amounts to total surrender of the Maharana before the adivasis."

"I believe it will be a temporary agreement and the Maharana will have to reconsider it after some time," Col Walters observed as his eyes scanned the open space outside the western verandah of the mess.

The sun was setting. Its fast descent below the horizon could be seen minute by minute. Those were the last days of the month of April. There were many palash (flaming trees) in Khairwada cantonment. The soft yellow rays from the retreating sun were turning the crimson flowers of palash into ochre-reddish. The sky was by and large clear with some haze here and there. The strong sun had rendered the day rather uncomfortable. By evening the weather had become pleasant because of a gentle breeze. The cantonment was echoing with the songs of various birds.

Blair was lost deep in his thoughts. He was indifferent to the captivating scene outside. The words spoken by Col Walters kept coming back to him. He then resumed: "I'm not worried about what agreement took place or should have taken place between the Maharana and the adivasis. My worry is that all the taxes levied on the adivasis will be withdrawn or their recovery will be relaxed, in which case how will the Maharana pay for the expenses of our army? His treasury is in poor condition." Blair filled his pipe with tobacco and pressed it into its bowl with his thumb.

"Yes, Colonel, that's right. But it'll be good for us if somehow an agreement is reached and the rebellion is called off. Our main concern is to see that commercial activities between Surat and Bombay in northern part of India pick up. This is possible only when there is peace in the area," Walters remarked as he stared at the western horizon. Blair lit his pipe and taking a deep puff blew a ring of smoke towards the east.

"You're right, Col Walters. Do you agree that Maharana's secretary Shyamaldas did not like my and Wingate's presence at Rishabdev and did not respect the advice that we had given him?" He asked as he took another deep puff and the smoke drifted into the open space making a 45 degree angle.

"There's no harm if sometimes in our own interest we overlook our petty pride or what we consider an insult," Col Walters was staring into the growing darkness advancing from the western horizon as he spoke.

"Colonel, I know you don't smoke. Is this why you are talking to me with your face turned westward?"

"No, that's not true, Colonel. The smoke from your pipe is wafting upwards. You know that smoke always floats upwards. This is an open verandah, so there is no chance of suffocation. The truth is that both of us are sitting in the East. My mind is on the agreement that the Maharana has struck with the adivasis and how London, the headquarters of the Crown in the West, will look at it."

"Oh, you are digressing, Col Walters," Col Blair was laughing heartily.

"No. I'm riveted to our concerns," Col Walters turned even more serious.

The sound of a bugle came from the quarter guard. For a moment it drew the attention of the two British officers. It was time for the evening roll call of the soldiers. The quarter guard bell struck eight times to signal the time. Subedar Major Bhanwata Ram took the roll call and went to the Commander of the Bhil corps and political superintendent, Captain Ansley, who was waiting for a report at his office, which was by the side of the administrative block.

"Sir, the roll call is over. Sepoy Sheru Pargi number 936 and Sepoy Nathuram Meena number 804 were found absent. The duty chart for night patrolling has been read to the guards. The roster for tomorrow morning's duty has also been prepared."

"All right, the absence of the two sepoys be registered."

"Yes sir," the Subedar Major saluted, turned smartly and retreated in army style. Captain Ansley headed for the Officers' Mess, where the two colonels were waiting for him.

"Come, Captain. Hope everything is fine?" Col Walters said as he returned the Captain's salute. The two colonels stood up as they shook hands with the Captain.

"Sit down, Captain," said Col Blair, as he beaconed him towards an empty chair.

The three British officers occupied the chairs laid out in the verandah. Hasmat Khan, the head waiter on duty at the officers' mess, presented himself before them and asked: "Sirs, what will you like to have?"

"Col Walters, tell me what would you like to drink," said Col Blair.

"A gin for me, please. The summer is upon us. And you?"

"I'll prefer to stick to Scotch. Captain Ansley, what will you like?"

"Sir, a Scotch for me, too," Captain Ansley said as he looked at Hasmat Khan, who then went to the Bar Room. He returned a little while later, accompanied by two boys. One of them was carrying gin and Scotch pegs in three glasses neatly kept on a tray. The other carried a jug of water. They kept these on the table and disappeared. Hasmat Khan remained in attendance. The three attendants wore khaki half-pants, white half-sleeved undershirt and white PT shoes. One of the jawans returned to place a plate of salad on the table. "Cheers," said the trio in unison.

"You may go now," Captain Ansley told Hasmat Khan as he took his first sip.

"Sir, anything to eat?" Hasmat Khan asked Commandant Ansley in almost hushed tone.

"What is the menu, Hasmat Khan? Are you fully prepared to serve the Sahibs?"

"There is no question of a 'no' from me, Sir. There is rabbit meat and partridge for dinner."

"Well done! Sir, what shall we order," the Captain asked the two colonels.

"Col Walters?" Blair asked.

"I'll prefer partridge for dinner."

"And so shall I."

"Me too."

Captain turned his face towards Hasmat Khan as though he had placed the order. Hasmat returned soon with a plate of roasted partridge with one large and three small plates, carefully laying them on the table before returning to the kitchen.

"Tell me, Captain. Is the agreement between the Maharana and the adivasis in the interest of the British Raj?" Col Blair quizzed. Col Walters was staring hard at Col Blair. He was perhaps trying to tell him that the talk the two colonels had a little while ago should not be transmitted verbatim to the Captain. Col Blair understood the message from the facial expression of Col Walters.

"Sir, the news received is that after the agreement the old cordiality will return in the relations between the Maharana and the adivasis and there will be no trouble in the area, or at least the area will see very little of it."

"Right! Anything else?" Col Blair sounded curious.

"Well, what else? If you want to know something more specific from me, I shall be glad to share it with you," the

Captain said as he lifted a portion of the partridge from the plate and put it in his mouth.

"I'm not sure that the trade route will still be safe after the agreement," Col Blair said.

"Can't be said with certainty, but there is room for hope."

"Will this agreement not send a message to Mewar, Dungarpur, Pratapgarh, Kushalgarh, Banswara, Gujarat and Malwa states that the influence of the British Agent and officers over the native princely states has waned?" Col Walters broke his silence as he took a large sip of gin.

"It is possible that such a message does go out," the Captain was guarded. The reply pleased Col Blair who thought it was an endorsement of his assessment.

During that session of drinking and informal conversation the three officers were quite frank in exchanging views. Col Blair had termed as "absurd" a certain proposition that the Muslims had made at Rishabdev. He also disclosed that "the treasurer of the temple had instigated the adivasis to make a demand indirectly on his behalf and see that it gets accepted". Blair was also opposed to the pardon granted to officers at Barapal and Padona who were responsible for incidents there. He termed as "foolish" the decision to withdraw the cavalry sent to guard the Udaipur–Khairawad road. He held it "insulting" that the grass and wood cutting contracts were cancelled and prisoners who had served term for more than three years had been released. He did not take the rebate given in the three-yearly tax seriously. He felt that the adivasis had created pressure on the Maharana, but the decision could have been put off. He expressed a similar opinion on the issue of census.

Col Walters chose to remain quiet. The reason was that he had already sent his report to the Governor General in Council, stating clearly that "such a big revolt had been quelled through a peaceful dialogue. The British officers were able to remain neutral. This way the possibility of their direct clash with the adivasis had been put off".

Col Blair appeared somewhat restless. He took out from his bag the book *Annals and Antiquities of Rajasthan*, written by

British Political Agent for Mewar, Col Todd. He began to read a portion of it.

> With regard, however, to the rude tribes who still inhabit the mountains and vastnesses of India, and who may be regarded as the aborigines of that country, the converse of this doctrine is more probable. Not their language only, but their superstitions differ from those of the Rajputs: though, from a desire to rise above their natural condition, they have engrafted upon their own the most popular mythologies of their civilised conquerors, who from the north gradually spread themselves over the continent and peninsula even to the remote isles of the Indian Ocean. Of the primitive inhabitants we may enumerate the Minas, the Meras, the Gonds, the Bhils, the Sahariyas, the Savaras, the Abhiras, the Gujars, and those who inhabit the forests of the Nerbudda, the Son, the Mahanadi, the mountains of Sarguja and the lesser Nagpur; many of whom are still but little removed from savage life, and whose dialects are as various as their manners. These are content to be called the 'sons of the earth' or 'children of the forest', while their conquerors, the Rajputs, arrogate celestial descent. How soon after the flood the suryas, or sun worshippers, entered India Proper, must ever remain uncertain.
>
> If a straight line is drawn from the capital of Mewar, Udaipur to Mount Abu via Ogana, Panarva and Merpur and further down the southern slopes near Sirohi, the distance covered will be 60 miles through the 'hills upon hills' and 'peaks upon peaks' from the height of Udaipur to the slopes of Mewar. In the area till the boundary of Sirohi, the tribals and others living there are found to be living with their tribal culture. Enjoying some kind of freedom in the jungles, they belong to different clans and owe allegiance to their own lineage. Thus, an order from an autonomous *Rawat* can collect five thousand men with bows and arrows. But these men accept no one's sovereignty over them; nor do they pay make presents anyone. They are

the complete masters of their republics. Their habitats of scattered huts are near grazing grounds and secure places near the valleys.

The land of these tribal communities was spread over a wide area. The land management in the Mewar state was surprisingly well planned because surrounding the area on three sides, South, West and East, were the habitations of criminal tribes of Bhil, Mer and Meenas. The fertile land belonging to the state, the source of revenue was fully protected as it was in the middle of the tribal land.

Bappa was the offender, who receiving from his faithful scouts intimation of his danger, sought refuge in one of the retreats which abound in these mountains, and which in after-times proved the preservation of his race. The companions of his flight were two Bhils: one of Undri, in the valley of the present capital; the other of Solanki decent from Oghna Panwara, in the western wilds. Their names, Baleo and Dewa, have been handed down with Bappa's; and the former had the honour of drawing the tika of sovereignty with his own blood on the forehead of the prince, on the occasion of his taking the crown from the Mori. It is pleasing to trace, through a series of ages, the knowledge of a custom still 'honoured in the observance'. The descendants of Baleo of Oghna and the Undri Bhil still claim the privilege of performing the tika on the inauguration of the descendants of Bappa.

Oghna-Panwara is the sole area in the country which enjoys a state of natural freedom.

Attached to no state, having no foreign communications, living under its own patriarchal head, its chief, with the title of Rana, whom one thousand hamlets scattered over the forest-crowned valleys obey, can, if requisite, appear at "the head of five thousand bows". He is a Bhumia Bhil of mixed blood, from the Solanki Rajput, on the old stock of pure (*ujla*) Bhils, of Mewar. Besides making the tika of blood from an incision in the thumb, the Oghna chief takes the prince by the arm and seats him on the throne, while the

> Undri Bhil holds the salver of spices and sacred grains of rice used in making the tika.
>
> On the boundary of Choti Sadari are hilly areas with dense forests, inhabited by half-civilised Bhils and Meenas. There are some subordinate jagirdars here who were appointed to control the criminal acts of the Bhils and Meenas. But their greed for a share in the loot induced them to encourage the Bhils and Meenas to take to criminal activities.

After this assessment of the region by Col Todd, Col Blair began to mull over future strategy.

The fire of rebellion that started in Barapal and Padona spread to other areas. The adivasis in other areas also started making similar demands after news of Rishabdev agreement between the Maharana and Magra adivasis reached them. The adivasis of Bhainsrodgarh and Alsigarh raised their demands rather violently. Those at Kevada ki Naal attacked a police station. The adivasis at Som put up obstructions on the road to Kotda and Khairwada. The jagirdar of Gulora village in the Khairwada was driven away following an attack by the adivasis of Bartol and Khairwada. Also in the Khairwada area, the adivasis surrounded the mansion of the jagirdar of Pol, who was made to sign an agreement. All the 38 clauses in that agreement were in favour of the adivasis. A series of rebellions continued for months. Its impact reached Gujarat. In October 1881, the tent of the political agent of Mahikantha was looted during his absence and the guards were forced to flee.

The infectious adivasi rebellion after the Rishabdev agreement became a serious matter for the AGG and political agents posted in southern Rajputana states, the commandants in cantonments of Khairawada, Kotda, Erinpura etc. and other British officers. All of them put pressure on Maharaja Sajjan Singh through the AGG, Col Walters, for revising the agreement.

A clear message, rather almost a threat, was sent out that the native rulers must be firm in their dealings with the adivasis.

Under pressure, Maharaja Sajjan Singh summoned the *gametis* of different clusters of villages and got a text prepared for another agreement. Its highlight was a provision that in future compensation for any damage caused to a particular area by acts of arson, loot or similar activity will have to be paid by the people of the affected areas through their adivasi chiefs. If the people concerned fail to do so, the army will be sent to catch the culprits, who will be given severe punishment. In such army operations the local adivasis will have to cooperate. In the Udaipur and Girva regions police posts will be established.

Agreements with the adivasis of Barapal and Kharpana were also revised. It was agreed that after the withdrawal of mounted guards from the roads, it will be the duty of the residents to provide security. These locals will be fined if there were reports of any damage. If security was not assured, police posts would be re-established.

Also, many administrative changes and improvements were introduced on suggestions from the British by the Maharana of Mewar and the rulers of Banswara, Dungarpur, Kushalgarh, Pratapgarh, Malwa and Gujarat. The new measures included transfers of officers appointed by native states in the hill areas, changes in the areas under the state-appointed officers, redefining duties of junior revenue and other officials, giving more powers to judicial officials, enhanced punishment for various crimes, opening of new police posts, and in some place new police stations.

The administrative officials received special instructions from the Maharana and the Maharawals, asking them to be generally sympathetic to the adivasis and take them into confidence. They should impress upon the adivasis the need to concentrate on farming. Their dependence on the forest produce should be reduced. The adivasis should be able to buy bullocks, plough and seeds on down payment or on low interest loans from the lagan (land-revenue). Proposals for digging new wells and ponds should be sent to the appropriate authorities at headquarters of the states. The scope of the *begar* (free labour) by tribals should remain true to the ancient tradition. Disputes related to the assessment of probable agro produce should be settled with the intervention of *gametis*. Salt be made available at special depots to be opened at selected places.

However, the special instruction for the officials was that despite these measures if there was even a hint of trouble anywhere, it should be crushed with a heavy hand so that it does not spread elsewhere.

In the first two or three months of 1882, the AGG, Col Walters, toured all the five native states of southern Rajputana to get first hand knowledge of the situation there. He held dozens of meetings with the *gametis*. In the end, he realised that the British officers, Col Blair and Wingate, who were sent to Rishabdev, were not able to play an effective role. He sent a report to the Governor General as a result of which Col Blair was recalled to England and in his place Straton was appointed the new political agent of Mewar.

THREE

The Fawata jungle was dense and extensive. It was a forest of dark hills, hillocks, slopes, valleys and streams with plenty of teak, palash, jamun, and mango trees. It had rich wildlife. At times tigers and leopards could be spotted there. The stormwater flowing from the hills used to find its way through the streams and nullahs into a big tank common to the nearby villages of Kangarva, Virvada and Decha.

The Dungarpur Maharawal Udai Singh was very fond of hunting. But he did not find hunting safe because the dense forests were full of wild animals. During their tours of princely states, the British officers were invariably asked to join hunting expeditions. For this reason, the Maharawal wanted that for safer hunting of tigers and leopard special platforms and fortifications be constructed in the jungles of Fawata. He entrusted this task to one of his wellwishers, Thakur Dalpat Singh. The material needed for constructing platforms included stone, gravel and lime. Gravel was available in the Kangarva nullah. There was no dearth of stone in the hilly areas. Lime was to be transported from Dungarpur. Labourers were needed to collect all this, which meant getting the adivasis to do *begar*.

Accompanied by some of his men and riding his horse, Dalpat Singh arrived in Kangarva village. He asked the gameti to collect villagers. For the villagers being thus summoned for *begar* was nothing unusual.

The festival of Holi was approaching and small patches of adivasi land were ripe with crops of barley, peas and linseed. They were waiting to reap the crop. They also had to prepare themselves for the coming hot months of summer by repairing their huts and strengthen their roofs with thick cover of dry grass and wood obtained from the jungle. Considering this situation, the gameti, while obeying the order to collect the adivasi villagers, requested the Thakur: "Mai-Baap, the crop awaits reaping. Let the adivasis first complete that job which will not take more than 15 days. It will be convenient for them if the *begar* follows afterwards; otherwise, of course, the order from the Raj has to be obeyed."

"Look, mukhiya, I have to carry out the instructions from the darbar. The Maharawal wants the hunting platforms ready by the month of Chaitra so that hunting is possible in the month of Baisakh. It will be too hot in the month of Jyeth." Thakur Dalpat Singh was keen that the work be completed quickly so that he could prove his loyalty to the Maharawal. Not being bothered about any inconvenience to the adivasis, he was blunt with them.

"Just give us 15 days..." said an elderly man.

"No, this is an order from the darbar. No bargaining for time."

The stern voice of the Thakur made the elderly man despondent. He picked up a straw from the ground and snapped it in his hands. The high hope among the adivasis of being able to reap their harvest in time had evaporated in a jiffy.

A distant relative of Kuriya, Bhanwata Katara, was also present there. He knew that Kuriya and some others in association with a bhagat called Govind propagated reforms and opposed the *begar* system. He did not think it proper to say anything about it at the meeting that Thakur Dalpat Singh was addressing. Instead, he quietly slipped out and headed for his village, Basiya.

In commanding tones, Thakur Dalpat Singh told the adivasis: "One healthy male from each family who can toil hard will work at the project. On the request of the gameti this is the only concession I can offer you. Else, I would have asked all the men and women to work on the project."

The words from Thakur did offer some relief to the people who had assembled there. The gameti thought to himself, "He has not agreed to put off the date for beginning the work but now, except for one member of each family, others will be able to work on their fields."

"My Lord, may I offer a suggestion?" the gameti asked.

"Yes, what is it?"

"Kangarva village has only 20–25 houses and the project on which we've to work is big. So, my request is that men from the neighbouring Virvada village also be engaged so that the work can be finished fast as per your wish."

"This is a good suggestion. Your men will begin the work tomorrow morning. I shall return to Dungarpur via Virvada. But I'll come to see that the work begins tomorrow morning." So saying Thakur Dalpat Singh left Kangarva with his men.

The very next day, one man from each family in the villages of Kangarva and Virvada started the work. But the path from the nullahs from where the gravel had to be lifted to the site where it had to be stored was not fit for the movement of bullock cart. This job had become tedious as it could be completed only if the material was hauled manually with the help of wicker baskets and the limited quantity of shallow metal dishes available. Early in the morning Thakur Dalpat Singh, accompanied by his men and six–seven masonry workers, reached the Fawata jungle. The main site for the hunting platform had already been decided by Thakur Dalpat Singh and so were the places for fortification. With shovels and other tools in their hands, the adivasis had started digging the earth, breaking the stone pieces and then transporting it all to appropriate place. The work continued throughout the day. Anyone who was seen relaxing was pulled up by the Thakur's men. For their lunch, the adivasis had brought with them dry rotis with some pieces of onion and chilli. For the Thakur and his men there was a kitchen to cook their meals. They hunted rabbit and partridge for their meals. More than the tiredness from the hard labour they were forced to do, the sight of the lavish spread for the Thakur and his company infuriated the adivasis. A rage was burning within them.

Bhanwata Katara returned to his village the following day. But he did not find Kuriya or Govind Bhagat at Basiya. He had informed his family about the *begar* being forced on the adivasis. Govind and Kuriya were touring villages as part of their mission to improve the lot of the adivasis. When they returned to Basiya, they were told by their family: "Bhanwata of Kangarva had come and left after telling us about the *begar* ordered by the Thakur for constructing hunting platforms. He said that the crops were ripe, ready for harvest and it was at such a time that the Raj was enforcing *begar*. He also said that if Govind Bhagat and Kuriya could provide any relief to the adivasis then they must reach Kangarva. The two can be assured that the adivasis have full confidence in them."

When the message of Bhanwata was conveyed to him, Govind Bhagat took Kuriya, Missarya and Hinsalaya and left for Kangarva. Missarya and Hinsalaya were initially hesitant but found it impossible to say no to Govind, the village boy who had by now been elevated to the status of Bhagat.

On the day Govind Bhagat and his friends reached Kangarva, the adivasis of Kangarva and Virvada had completed five days of *begar*. Bhanwata was one of them. He was dejected. If he had refused *begar*, then his old father would have been forced to take his place.

Govind Bhagat and his companions came to the *begar* site and saw the adivasis toiling hard, crushing stones, loading gravel and assisting in masonry work. Thakur Dalpat Singh was not present there on that day, but two or three of his lieutenants were.

Bhanwata leapt with joy when he saw Govind Bhagat. He immediately roared: "Govind Bhagat has come. This Bhagat is working for our good." It filled him with pride that a relative, Kuriya, was with Govind Bhagat. He rushed towards him.

"Jai Bhole Nath," he greeted Govind Bhagat and warmly embraced Kuriya. Meeting Bhanwata after many years, Kuriya became emotional.

Hearing the call from Bhanwata, the adivasis from the two villages who were working at the site surrounded Govind Bhagat. It took the lieutenants of Thakur Dalpat Singh by surprise. Intuitively, a sense of fear gripped them. They stared at Bhanwata. But Bhanwata's gaze was fixed on Govind Bhagat and Kuriya.

"Who are they? Where have they come from?" one of Thakur's lieutenants asked Bhanwata softly.

"Don't you know? This is Govind Bhagat, the man who takes care of our sorrows and travails."

"But why have you stopped your work? Tell these labourers to go back to work. It is you who had collected them here," said the second lieutenant. At this juncture, Kuriya, who had overheard him, said, "Listen, we have walked a long distance. Can't we even talk to our brothers?"

"There is no harm in meeting and talking. These men are working out of their own free will on the hunting platform. We don't want the pace of the work to slow down. The Thakur has said that the work must be quickly completed. That's what we have in mind." The first of the two lieutenants of the Thakur spoke in support of his colleague. But a sense of fear reflected in his eyes.

"Brothers! What are you constructing in this desolate jungle? The Raj has vast lands. Why construct a stone-gravel building in a jungle like this?" asked Govind Bhagat.

Before one of Thakur's men could reply, an elderly adivasi said agitatedly: "The *begar* has been forced upon us for constructing a hunting platform. The Darbar and his guests will come here hunting. We are being asked to work at a time when our crops are ready to be harvested. We have been forced to abandon harvesting to work here."

The Thakur's men stared at the man angrily.

Kuriya read the language behind those stern looks as he spoke: "The Darbar's orders are supreme. But how can these men work without being paid? Have you paid these men anything for their labour?" Kuriya looked at the Thakur's men as he spoke. The men were nonplussed. They said nothing.

Govind Bhagat took over. Addressing the adivasis he said: "What does the Raj give you? All of you fill your stomach by working hard. If anyone forces you to work, he should pay you, no matter whether he is the Darbar or some rich trader or businessman."

"Yes, Govind Bhagat. You've spoken truly. But who listens to us? The Darbar sent Thakur Dalpat Singhji here and we were pushed into *begar*. You are a wise man. Tell us what should we do?" Bhanwata Katara asked. His confidence was apparent in his tone. Others were silent.

Walking briskly, a gameti from Kangarva arrived there. He looked a little worried. He had learned that a bhagat who opposed the *begar* system had reached the Fawta jungle and was talking to the men. "What is the matter that all of you have stopped the work?" the gameti asked a little hesitatingly.

"Talk to Govind Bhagat, Kaka," Bhanwata said.

"Who is Govind Bhagat?" gameti asked in surprise.

"You are the village gameti. You are intelligent and must know a lot about this area. And yet you haven't heard of Govind Bhagat who wanders day and night to eliminate our troubles and social ills! I am surprised. Since you are older to me what more can I say? You are asking your own men to do *begar*," Kuriya rattled off a little excitedly.

"Kuriya, stop. Yes, now you are the mukhiya of the village. You must be thinking about the problems of villagers. Then, why are you forcing them to work free? Don't you have the courage to tell the Thakur the right thing?" Govind Bhagat told the gameti even as he asked Kuriya to be quiet.

"*Begar* is an ancient tradition. What can I do about it? What wrong have I done?"

"It's a wrong tradition that we have to eliminate. Let's forget about *begar*. Talk about this work being carried out here. Isn't it because hunting platforms and fortifications will be constructed in this green jungle so that the Darbar and his guests, who will be the white-skinned Britishers, kill animals? For them it is a sport, a pastime. But will it not be a sin to kill animals? All of you will be partners in this sin. Is this good or bad in the eyes of God?"

The gameti was left speechless. After a brief pause, he asked: "What shall we do, Govind Bhagat?"

"There is no harm if you do *begar* for the good of man, animal or the jungle. But you'll waste your life if you do something that is sin."

Govind Bhagat's words touched the hearts of the men present there. The Thakur's men were astonished. As they stood mute the others shouted: "Govind Bhagat ki Jai! Govind Bhagat ki Jai!"

Bhanwata was pleased with himself. He thought it was his effort that brought Govind Bhagat to this jungle.

All the adivasis doing *begar* were unanimous in deciding that they would not do any labour without wages. The Thakur's lieutenants lost no time in leaving the Fawata jungles for Dungarpur.

The Thakur was astounded when he heard the story. But he understood the situation and explained it to the Maharawal. "The work was proceeding well. But hunting in that fearsome forest might be a difficult proposition. Forget about horse and carriage, the special guests of the Darbar will have to walk on foot for shikar. The jungles of Fawata are not fit for hunting."

The Thakur gave a twist to the Govind Bhagat-inspired message opposing *begar*. He did not want to give the impression that an order from the Raj had been defied. The Thakur did not want the honour of the ruling class to be compromised. He repeated: "Fawata is a treacherous jungle. There are plenty of tigers and leopards in the jungle, but hunting will still be risky even after the construction of platforms and fortifications."

Maharawal Udai Singh agreed with Thakur Dalpat Singh. The Thakur was his relative and hence, the king trusted him.

Govind Bhagat was receiving all the news of events after the Rishabdev agreement and the follow-up to all the other agitations by adivasis. The Fawata incident encouraged Govind Bhagat so much that taking a select band of colleagues he embarked upon a long tour of the Vagad area. He would collect adivasis and work whole-heartedly among them to help them get rid of their social ills and also expressed opposition to the oppressive acts of the princely states. Govind Bhagat's influence among the adivasis was spreading fast. He began to be addressed more respectably, as Govind Guru.

The adivasis started to gather at the foothills near Suranta village from early morning. Many had come from distant places. The Holi festival was round the corner. They had assembled in a rugged terrain surrounded by dense and tall trees of mahua, teak, flower-laden palash, cluster of bamboos, and thick groves of cactus. There were men, women and children among the crowd. Govind Guru began his address with the intention of creating awareness among the adivasis.

"It is difficult to truly describe all the pain in your lives. Instead of thinking about ways to lessen your sorrows, you have tried to drown them in alcohol. Mahua is your life-saving tree. Do not extract liquor out of its fruit. Use the fruit as vegetable or extract oil from it. Meat is the food of the depraved. You are gentle people. The jungle has plenty of fruits and other eatable vegetation that can provide you food. You are considered as belonging to criminal tribes. Whether you indulge in looting because of hunger or rob the royal treasury as a mark of protest, a bad deed is a bad deed. You get a bad name due to such deeds. After being caught you are sent to prison where you are brutally beaten and then sentenced. Many die in custody. So, give up all bad habits. Hard work is the best worship. Do farming and earn an honest living for your families. Learn to live a life of honesty. Only thus will the adivasi society improve," he said.

He added, "Know the importance of reading and writing. I could not go to school, but I managed to learn a little with some help here and there. You should also educate yourself.

Send children to school, only then will they become intelligent. It is the sacred duty of all those in the village who are even semi-literate to teach others. The right atmosphere at home encourages education. Therefore, adults should also start learning. Don't do *begar* for the raja, jagirdar or hakim. Don't suffer injustice. Face injustice bravely."

Govind Guru continued: "Use things made locally. Imported goods promote alien culture. Slavery is not imposed by the Raj alone; efforts are being made to enslave us mentally. We must understand this well."

"Keep your courtyards clean. Don't eat leftover food. Take bath every day. Keep the clothes that you wear clean. Dirtiness leads to diseases," he said.

"There is only one God. Different communities see Him in different forms. The name and shape may be different, but there is only One who has created life and universe. Great men have understood this. You should also try to understand it. Worship God in your homes by lighting a holy fire and offering drops of ghee and coconut. This will cleanse the mind of the devout of vicious thoughts and wash away the sins that he may have committed. A holy fire keeps the atmosphere in the house pure. Sow good habits and qualities in your children. In every village you should learn to sing prayers and cultivate good habits, learn from those who tell you about proper conduct and traditions. Don't take your quarrels to the police or the courts. Try and settle them by sitting together at panchayats. Don't trust the Darbari courts where judgements are arbitrary. Besides, you unnecessarily waste time and money. It only increases conflicts. It does not end antagonism. The wise panchas are like God. Always respect their decision. Learn to respect panchayats. Also respect the understanding gameti."

Poonja Dhira was three years older than Govind Guru. His father, Dhira Paragi, was a resident of Doongar village in Santrampur state. He was the gameti of Doongar, Bhabri and

Gadra. Officers from the state and the police used to visit him. They would force *begar* on men and insult adivasi women. Poonja and his friends did not like all this. They would react angrily but only after the officials had left. Dhira used to advise them: "You should not be talking ill of representatives of the Raj. We can come to harm if a spy carries the tale." Dhira was afraid that in case the disrespect shown towards the representatives of the Raj by his son and others is made public in the darbar, his own position in society and relation with darbar would suffer.

Poonja did not know what was in his father's mind. Even if he did, he would not have agreed with the views of his father because a fire was burning within him against the atrocities committed against the adivasis. Taking some friends along, in 1878, Poonja formed an organisation called Sampsabha, but it could not become very active due to the political and social influence of his father.

Now five years later, and against this background, he was speaking in support of Govind Guru. "It is necessary for us to pay attention to what Guruji has said; it is in our own interest. If we just sit idle, nobody will descend from heaven to take care of our problems. We must unite to oppose all ills. There are two kinds of ills; one, our own bad habits, and, two, the atrocities of the Raj."

Poonja talked to Govind Guru about the experiences he had with the Sampsabha. Govind Guru liked what he heard from Poonja and endorsed Poonja's idea on the need for intra-community friendliness and threw more light on it. "In the name of 'Samp' all of us, brothers and sisters, will be guided by the spirit of cordiality and cement our ties. It is this kind of harmony that will unite us and enable us to defend ourselves. We shall oppose all ills."

Govind Guru announced the formation of Sampsabha at the meeting. It gave an organised shape to the movement for creating awareness among the tribals. The traditional adivasi panchayats had many flaws. Their influence was localised. There were quarrels relating to clans and ancestries, problems inherited due to the gameti tradition, the practice where the family of the accused in criminal cases like murder and quarrel over women were forced to pay financial compensation. These shortcomings led to groupism and other complications while disputes got bigger. The aims of Sampsabha came to be identified with the well being of the adivasi community. The adivasis understood well the philosophy behind Sampsabha, which attracted two dedicated bhagats, Poonja Dhirji and Kuriya Danot, at an initial stage.

FOUR

On 1 January 1884, the Mewar Bhil Corps was awarded the "Rifle" (a military ceremony) and was merged in the regular army. This armed force became a battalion of the British-controlled Indian Army with Lt Col A. Connolly as its commandant. Earlier in 1862, the Mewar Bhil Corps had been awarded its Colour—its own independent flag. For any military unit the occasion of receiving its Rifle or Colour is a special day. And so it was at the headquarters of the Mewar Bhil Corps on 1 January 1884. Preparations for the day began months in advance. A big operation it was of massive cleaning, painting of buildings, decoration of parade ground, attention to uniform and gear for the special day, including anklets, half-pants, shirt, turban, belt, badge, sash and rifle. All of these items had to shine and sparkle at their best. The quarter guard was specially decorated. Pots with various flowers were arranged neatly at appropriate places. Flower pots in abundance were also kept at some important places like the quarter guard area, officers' mess and saluting base at the parade ground. The two pillars at the entrance of the cantonment were white-washed. A rifle-carrying guard was painted on them. Emblazoned across the pillars, in English and Hindi, were the words "Mewar Bhil Corps Headquarters, Khairwada". It could not have escaped anyone's notice. The path leading from the entrance to the main parade ground was covered with red gravel with white line marks on either side. The turnings in this path were decorated with colourful buntings strung on 2-foot-high bamboo poles. At either end of the wall of the headquarters were fixed big flags; tiny flags and buntings adorned the parade ground and the area in front of the quarter guard. It was a cantonment bedecked like a new bride, full of sparkle and colour.

The chief guest on the occasion was Col Walters, the Agent in charge of southern Rajputana, appointed by the Governor General and Viceroy of British India. The Mewar Maharana, Sajjan Singh, and the Dungarpur Maharawal, Udai Singh, were invited as special guests. All the VIPs and other guests arrived at Khairwada by the afternoon of 31 December 1883. About two dozen important jagirdars and officials of Mewar and Dungarpur states joined them in the New Year festivities, celebrated at the officers' mess in Khairwada cantonment. Liquor was flowing freely till midnight. The Commandant, Connolly, AGG Col Walters, Maharaja Sujjan Singh and Maharawal Udai Singh were a little restrained in consuming the freely flowing spirits. The British and other guests consumed liquor in different quantities, depending on their conception of how much is appropriate. Some worried about their reputation which could be marred if they got drunk. On the other hand, some guests were swayed by their feudal pride. Their friends and well wishers tried to hold them in check, though not always with success.

The New Year party reached its climax by midnight. There were exchanges of New Year greetings, followed by dance and a lavish dinner with a tasty spread of vegetarian and non-vegetarian dishes. The party had to be wound up by 1 am because everyone had to attend the "Rifle" and special parade ceremonies early next morning, the New Year day.

The weather on the first day of January 1884 was not in tune with the joyous spirit of the occasion. Strong winds were blowing across. The curse of a cold wave loomed large. There was fog, though light. The sky was cloudless; the warmth from the sun was coming out reluctantly.

It was part of his daily routine that the AGG would leave the cantonment guesthouse on his horse exactly at 6 am. The corps adjutant was at the portico of the guesthouse by 5:45 am to greet him. A soldier with a horse was waiting outside. Wearing a woollen shirt, breeches and turban, the soldier was clearly uncomfortable in the cold. As soon as the quarter guard bell struck 6, the AGG came out of his room, impressive in his tunic, breeches, boots and hat. He returned the salute given to him by the adjutant and soldier. But he felt a little uncomfortable when he saw a fog developing.

"Can't ride the horse," he declared. An icy draft had pierced his body. He was shivering as he went back to his room. The adjutant knew why he had gone back, but the soldier did not. He came out a little while later, this time in a tracksuit and a woollen cap on his head.

"Let me go jogging," he announced as he came out of the officers' mess gate where two army guards were already posted. The adjutant appeared to be signalling to them. Immediately, the two soldiers started to trot a little ahead of the AGG, who reached the playground-cum-racing track. The adjutant had already signalled the two horsemen who walked with the horse to return to the stable.

Exactly an hour and a half later, the AGG was back at the guesthouse and after another hour he came out all properly attired and looking fresh after a bath. But the fog had not faded. He sat on the sofa kept in the verandah and lit his pipe. He blew a smoke that became undistinguishable from the fog.

"Won't it be better to put off the time for the parade salute by an hour?" he wanted to know from the adjutant.

"Yes, Sir. Nothing is visible because of the fog," he agreed without hesitation.

"All right," the AGG seemed to say as an order.

A subedar was standing at the gate of the officers' mess, close to the decorated horse-carriage of the AGG. The coachman was standing by its side holding the bridle in his hands.

"Subedar!" shouted the adjutant.

"Yes, Sir. Good morning."

"Good morning," acknowledged the adjutant as he informed him, "the salute time has been postponed to 9 am."

"Right, Sir," he replied as he gestured towards the coachman, saluted the adjutant and left. The revised programme was conveyed to the quarter guard, armoury, all officers and men at the parade ground.

The original time for the salute was 8 am. The jawans who were to take part in the parade had taken out rifles from the armoury. The buglers were on duty. The commanders of the three platoons who were detailed for the parade were ready for their task. The parade commander, the commandant of the Mewar Bhil Corps, Lt Col A. Connolly, had inspected the preparations at the parade ground at 7:45 am.

As soon as it was announced that the parade time had been shifted to 9 am the officers and jawans looked a little relaxed in their movements. They stopped scurrying around. It was necessary for them to be alert and look smart for the parade. But an hour's rest before the parade was not a comfortable thought. The jawans were keen to get over the parade. The main reason was that the brisk exercise they would have gone through during the parade would have warmed their bodies and given them some relief from the biting cold.

The Mewar Maharana and Dungarpur Maharawal, being special guests, were put up at the officers' mess. They knew about the change in the parade schedule. The other jagirdar and thikanedar guests had their own havelis (mansions) in Khairwada and that is where they had spent the night. The news about the change in the parade schedule could not be conveyed to them in time. It was possible that because of the confusion over the parade schedule nobody remembered to inform them about the revised plan. Of course, every part of the entire day's ceremony had a separate person in charge and things were proceeding meticulously. The change in the saluting ceremony had come unexpectedly. That is why the invited jagirdars, thikanedars, selected businessmen and traders and some personal friends of the Mewar Maharana and Dungarpur Maharawal had reached the parade ground a little before eight in the morning and taken their seats at the places designated for them under the *shamiana* (big tent) behind the saluting base. Most of them were guests at the previous night's party. Some of them had bleary eyes and their faces looked puffed, apparently the result of the previous night's binge. Some others were trying to duck the glances of their superiors. There were some who could be seen staggering as they moved to their seats; their unsteady gait visible to all. The guests were anxious for the ceremonies to begin. They whiled away their time gossiping and talking about the magnificent way the cantonment had been decorated for the occasion.

By now the fog had begun to lift. The sun now looked like the real blazing sun. The bite of the morning cold was also becoming less severe. The three platoons consisting of selected jawans from the entire Bhil corps had taken up positions at the ground.

Just half a minute before 9 am, the four buglers standing at the terrace of the quarter guard sounded the fanfare. It was a signal that the chief guest was about to arrive at the parade ground.

The chief guest inspected the parade and returned to the saluting base. The officers and jawans in the parade went round the ground. The parade went past the chief guest. The whole ground was filled with lilting tunes being played by the band.

The ceremonies for the salute at the parade ground were over in an hour and half. The band then struck some new tunes. The jawans displayed feats of physical exercises, the mounted men showed their skills on the horse, the wrestlers grappled with each other, and also on display was the skill of self defence by the unarmed. All this was to let the guests see for themselves the capabilities of the corps. This part of the programme lasted for another half an hour.

Afterwards, the second in command of the Mewar Bhil Corps, Capt C. Brightland, read out a prepared written report that gave details of the role played by the corps in maintaining peace in the area in the last 50 years:

"In 1844, a fight erupted between the adivasis of Magrapal and Salumber over a theft. The fight between the two sides had reached such a scale that the situation threatened to get out of control. A company of the Mewar Bhil Corps brought the situation under control by a unique show of bravery and understanding. The same year, a platoon of the corps was sent to help the Dungarpur Maharawal where the former ruler was trying to establish his second son on the throne. Thanks to the help from the corps a revolt was avoided. In 1848, there was trouble and an increase in the incidence of theft under the Sayana Mukhiya in Juda area.

On the request of the Maharana, two companies of the Bhil corps were sent there, which were able to overpower the criminals. In 1853, a company of the corps was sent after receiving information that the Rao of Panarva had given shelter to many adivasi rebels. About a dozen fugitive criminals surrendered to the corps near Khairwada and the Rao of Panarva had no choice but to seek the Maharana's pardon. In 1856, when the Rao of Salumber tried to incite people to revolt against the Maharana, the Mewar Bhil Corps was able to quell it."

Capt Brightland did not confine himself to giving an account of how the Mewar Bhil Corps had done a commendable work in putting down rebellions and catching criminals involved in theft, robbery and murder. He also recalled the important role of the Bhil corps in fighting some of the social ills and superstition, such as witch-hunting, child sacrifice, exorcism and other hocus-pocus practised in the name of curing ailments.

He illustrated all this with some examples.

"In 1852, Sampla, a Mewar Bhil Corps sepoy, killed an old woman mistaking her to be a witch. He was given a sentence of seven years in prison. A similar incident that had taken place in 1851 came to light in 1853. Many adivasis were given severe punishment on the charge of murdering that woman. On advice from the British resident Brooks, the Mewar Maharana issued an order in 1854 to ban the killing or torture of witches. It was decided that criminals involved in these acts would be sent to prison for six months, or awarded death sentence if they were guilty of murder. The Bhopas (village men who spread superstition) who are accomplices in such offences would receive similar punishment. Those who shelter such criminals would also be punished and fined ₹200. Similar orders were issued in the states of Dungarpur, Banswara and Salumber. Yet such incidents did occur. Another sepoy of the Mewar Bhil Corps was absconding after he killed his aunt in 1861, suspecting her to be a witch.

On the advice of the Corps commandant, the Maharana sent his police force, which also received help from the Corps in tracing the sepoy. Despite protests by the villagers, the sepoy was arrested. Later, during inquiry it was found that the sepoy was innocent. Some employees of the state had tried to protect the real culprit, who was arrested with the help of the Mewar Bhil Corps."

Capt Brightland recalled incidents that had taken place in 1862 in Dhor, Dhandor and Jhajol villages, in Punoorva and Pipli in 1863, and Jhanjur in 1870, even as he appreciated the role played by the Mewar Bhil Corps.

Capt Brightland spoke a lot about the Bhil Corps but did not tell why the adivasis of the area were getting rebellious. And why the Mewar Bhil Corps had to come forward to help the rulers of native states, sometimes on its own initiatives. He did not disclose that behind the rebellion of the tribals was the termination of *Bolai* and *Rakhvali* (guiding and ensuring safety) taxes at the instance of the rulers. Under that tax system, the adivasis used to provide safe passage by guiding non-adivasis through their territories, especially traders, by taking *Bolai* tax, and when they stayed in the adivasi areas, the tribals protected them in lieu of *Rakhvali* tax.

He did not mention that the jagirdars and thikanedars used to collect extra taxes from the adivasis in the name of *Hal Barar* and *Tirsala* (per plough and tri-annual tax). He said nothing about the increase in the lagan. He had kept mum about the fact that in 1880 a separate department for forests was opened as a result of which the adivasis lost their right to forest produce. The adivasis had stood up in opposition to the system of settlement and measurement of land. He made no reference to the fact that the adivasi opposition was led by Neema, the gameti of Belak, and Khema, the gameti of Pipli. Their rebellion in support of their lost rights spread to Barapal, Tidi, Padona, Rishabdev, Parsad, Nathara, Pipli ki Pal, Alsigarh, Pai, Kotda, Kewara ki Nal, Bhorai ki Pal in Magra Mewar. The adivasis declared that if the Maharana of Mewar and the Maharawals of Dungarpur and Banswara extended their support to them they could overthrow British rule. But the Maharana did not support them and the adivasi rebellion was suppressed with the help of the Bhil Corps.

Capt Brightland's report omitted reference to the fact that the adivasis being opposed to land settlement and measurement scheme had not sown in their fields. Many adivasis were arrested and the state forced them to sow crops. He blanked the fact that this protest campaign of the adivasis had led to a revolt in 1881 and again in 1882. At the Javadmata temple about 4,000 adivasis took a pledge to fight for their rights. As they intensified their struggle they set afire Barapal police station and a police post.

Capt Brightland did not give this important information that the British had allowed liquor shops to open in adivasi areas in order to boost revenues and that during their agitation, the adivasis had attacked liquor traders and vendors. In order to crush the rebellion, the Maharana's army took the help of the Bhil Corps. The houses of the tribals were burnt. Hundreds of adivasis lost their lives. But they did not bend; instead they became more determined to carry on their fight. The adivasis united and came together to fight for their rights, oppose oppression, and break the unholy nexus between the British and native rulers. The role of the Bhil Corps in crushing the adivasis was completely censored by Capt Brightland.

The occasion of receiving the "Rifle" was an honour for the Mewar Bhil Corps. It was also an occasion to convey to the adivasis that the Mewar Bhil Corps was now much stronger and better equipped than before. It had become a part of the (British) Indian Army, a force that could be reckoned to deal with any rebellion.

Finally, the AGG, Col Walters, presented the "Rifle" to the Mewar Bhil Corps. The parade gave him a Royal Salute. Guns were fired. The Mewar Bhil Corps enclave reverberated with joyous shouts and slogans. At one corner of the quarter guard area guests were served refreshments under a *shamiana.* Everyone was showering praises on the Mewar Bhil Corps. The Commandant, Lt A. Connolly, was receiving congratulations from the guests for the display of high standards at the parade. Refreshments over, the AGG left in his horse carriage. He was followed by the Maharana Mewar, Maharawal Dungarpur, the jagirdars, thikanedars, British guest officers and other invitees.

FIVE

"Guru, an idea has come to my mind but I hesitate to express it," Kuriya announced.

"Look, Kuriya, even if a bad idea comes to mind it should be blurted out or else a man remains confused. You can speak without any fear. It is good that hundreds of adivasi brothers and sisters are assembled here, listening to me attentively, taking me to be their guru and considering me enlightened. They may be illiterate but questions arise in their minds too. They can hesitate in my presence because they think I am superior. But you and Poonja are my two strong arms. You should not hesitate and ask me anything that is in your mind." Govind Guru said this a bit loudly as though addressing the assembly, though Kuriya, sitting close to him, had expressed his hesitation in somewhat suppressed tones.

"The thing is, Guru Maharaj, that a whispering campaign has started against you in these parts, suggesting that you have become a disciple of a Sanyasi Baba who is actually living in luxury in the palace of Udaipur Darbar. He is supposed to have come from outside. We, including the Bhils, Meenas, Garasiyas and other non-adivasi, all of us have been suffering under the Raj. In such a situation it will not be in our interest to have someone in our midst who can be influenced by a guest of the Maharana." Many in the audience agreed with what Kuriya had said.

"Kuriya, be more frank. What are the rumourmongers saying? I should know to what extent these loose talks can influence your mind. There should be no ambiguity about these matters. I shall tell you the truth and try to clear the air." It required some courage for Kuriya to speak. His biggest fear was that the Guru would stop believing him. He had left his home to be with the Guru. It was almost impossible for Kuriya to speak any further. Govind Guru read his thoughts. The rumours that the others had heard were perhaps less reliable and beyond their belief. That is why no other person spoke. Govind Guru answered the questions that had arisen in the mind of simple and innocent Kuriya. He addressed the assembly with full confidence.

"All adivasi brothers, sisters and children present here, listen to me carefully. It is nothing new to hear criticism of those who come forward in support of the oppressed, either by their own people or by the Raj. It is possible that one of your *panch-patels* (headmen) or *gametis* felt that I wanted to become the sole mukhiya (head) of the adivasis. It is also likely that such a rumour has been spread by one of the officers of the Raj or one of the smaller fries, assuming that Govind Guru holds panchayat sittings among the adivasis with this end in mind. Their fear must be that the adivasis are being united to rise in revolt. There could be some other reasons which I cannot guess."

The words of Govind Guru impressed the audience, which appeared eager to listen to him further. All eyes were now fixed on the Guru. But some eyes turned to Kuriya, as though they wanted to put him in the dock to ask "Oh, you Kuriya, why did you disturb the Guru's discourse?"

Govind Guru continued: "The saint's name is Dayanand. Many years ago he was with the Udaipur Darbar. It is said that the Maharaj had sent for him after hearing about his fame. He accepted the invitation. At that time I was about 20–22 years old. It is not a very mature age but I had travelled a lot by then. I had travelled with goods loaded on bullocks to Mewar, Sirohi, Dungarpur, Banswara and Abu in Rajputana and Idar, Palanpur, Revakantha, Soonth (Santrampur), Jhalode, Dahod in Gujarat. In all these places I met villagers, the poor and oppressed sections, especially the Bhils, Meenas, Girasiyas and other adivasis of these areas. I held lengthy discussions with them. Their pains and sorrows became my pains and sorrows. Let me also tell you. The Guru of my childhood days, Rajgiri Gosai, had taught me that one should always walk on the right path, help people in distress, as far as possible oppose ills and have hopes for better days. My village, Basia, is about 11 km from Dungarpur. This entire Vagad land is my motherland. Its children are my brothers and sisters. Can I ever distance myself from them? This area had produced a saint, Mavji Maharaj. All of you are familiar with his name. Many saints were born before him too. There are many famous names like Kabir, Nanak, Raidas, Dadu, Narsi. Mavji was in the same tradition. He had established a *Nishkalank Samuday* (Clean Society), he also taught lessons of dharma and devotion and opposed social ills. The lot of the adivasis in his time was no better. That was the time of Maharawal Ram Singh (1702–1730). We had to suffer only at the hands of our rulers. Now these *phirangis* (foreigners) have also arrived. It is said that all the maharanas, maharawals and jagirdars are scared of these *bhuratiyons* (white-skinned foreigners). The outsiders are encroaching upon our jungles only because of these foreigners. Earlier we used to be unhappy about the *begar* and tax on our agriculture produce (lagan). Now we have to pay lagan even if we have nothing to cultivate. Earlier, we were free to use the forest produce. Now everyday more and more restrictions are being imposed on that. Do I support all this? Don't I oppose all this? Sant Dayanand preaches swadeshi (indigenous products). What's wrong in it, brothers? We also talk about swadeshi. We have been feeding ourselves on whatever was being produced in our jungles and hills. We have ancestral rights over them. That right should not be taken away; this is what swadeshi preaches; to remove the ills in the society. Is it wrong to talk about piety? Our sacrifice is unique. I am not talking about calling a priest from outside. Whatever goes against our interest and the outsiders who are causing us harm, I am talking about these things. Am I wrong?"

Govind Guru continued: "There were three famous sects at Mavji's time—Chisti, Suhrawardy and Kavri. During his time there were jogis (saintly figures) who wore strange clothes and ate excessively. Mavji would say, 'They are outsiders. We should not be influenced by them'. Sant Dayanand talks about swadeshi and if I learned something from him, am I going to harm you?"

The audience appeared glued to his words. But also written on their faces were queries on what he was saying. These queries were related to the anger that had been building inside them. This anger had also entered the minds of Govind Guru, Poonja Dhira and Kuriya. Govind Guru understood the turmoil going inside their minds. He did not want anything to disturb the gathering of the good and honest adivasis who had collected in the midst of rich natural surroundings and flat lands of Bhukiya village.

Govind Guru remained quiet for a while and concluded his talk with these words: "None of us should mind what Kuriya has said. There may be some others who think the way he does but could not express their views. Kuriya said what he had been bothering him. This is good. I spoke something to remove the doubts. What I would like to add is that it is quite natural for such doubts arise. We should keep our eyes and ears open. Instead of magnifying rumours we should try to understand the truth. Intelligent people should not start believing in rumours."

"It is quite late now. We were to talk about the bad habit of drinking. We shall talk about it later. I request everyone to go home and attend to your chores."

Loud cries of "Jai Gurudev, Jai Gurudev" pierced the air and its echoes travelled to the nearby hills.

Govind Guru, Poonja, Kuriya and three–four adivasis left Bhukiya for Mangarh hills where they were camping. They watched the sight of the setting sun and after that Govind Guru got busy in prayers. In the meanwhile, his companions gathered some firewood, lit a fire and baked maize rotis and cooked a vegetable, *lahalra*.

Kuriya looked distraught while eating, as if he was going through an internal turmoil. It did not take long for others to notice it.

"What is the matter, Kuriya? Why do you look so unhappy?" asked Surtya Meena, slightly older than him.

"Nothing."

"Small things snowball into big and important issues. You tell us what the matter is," the experienced Poonja Dhira supplemented Surtya's query.

"Yes, brother Kuriya, and you Poonja, Surtya! It is people like you who give me strength. All of us should be one in heart and mind. There should be no differences in our understanding and thinking. Even if some differences arise, we must remove them by discussing it. We have a long way to travel and the path is full of obstructions. It will not do to become despondent," Govind Guru explained as he put a morsel in his mouth.

All this while Nanji Gameti was looking at Kuriya with some suspicion and the latter was aware of it.

"Guru, it is nothing important. Even then let me tell you. When your discourse got over and we left Bhukiya some people were staring at me. My mind was full of all sorts of misgivings," Kuriya spoke these words directly facing Govind Guru, but he also threw a glance towards Nanji.

"Look, Kuriya. You were right. The problem was sorted out during the discourse. No one else had raised the issue. If anyone nurses any ill will towards you, tell us about it without any fear. There is nobody here. We are in a close-knit group."

"Guru, you and these brothers know that I believe in taking everyone along. I have no enemies in the village and among relatives. I am a bachelor, so there is no other problem."

"Then, what is the fear?" Surtya cut him short.

"Don't interrupt, Surtya. Let him complete," Govind Guru said sternly.

Kuriya had by now finished half roti, but remained disturbed. He got up and placed the remaining rotis on a stone slab nearby. Much of the gravy from the vegetable on top of the rotis trickled to the ground. He tilted the pitcher containing water with his left elbow to let water drop on his cupped right palm. Cleaning his hands and face with water, he perched himself on a platform under a mahua tree, some hundred steps away. Nobody thought it proper to disturb him when he was in that state of mind.

The night in the middle of that Ashad (June–July, the initial month of the rainy season) was getting darker. The chirping of the birds had stopped long ago. A rustling sound came from behind the hills. Perhaps, a wildcat had grabbed a prey. Somewhere further away could be heard the "Huki, Huki" call of the jackal.

"The jungle has its own rules. Oh You Big Blue Umbrella (God), please protect us all," said Govind Guru as he went to his hut made of dried grass spread over sturdy twigs of acacia. Spreading his thin towel on the cot he went to sleep. Poonja Dhira and others spread themselves on the stone platforms nearby. How and when they actually managed to sleep was not known.

Kuriya folded his coarse towel, which he had tied on his head, to use it as a pillow. Joining his knees he sprawled himself on the platform. The branches of the old mahua trees spread over a wide area. Despite dense green trees around him Kuriya could see stars twinkling in the sky. He was immersed deeply in his thoughts. The gentle cool breeze was gathering speed but inside Kuriya's head a fire was raging at the same speed. He was confused with all kinds of thoughts. He feared that Govind Guru might weaken the adivasi unity.

Maybe, under the spell of Dayanand he might have supported the state. Far from helping them in their moment of trouble, he might have betrayed them and gotten them killed or arrested. Govind Guru was a nice man, talked of dharma and also about the adivasis getting rid of their bad habits. But why did he talk about the dharma of the dhooni (something like the yajna practised by the brahmins) instead of their tradition of worship?

It is said that those who own horses can sleep well only after selling them. The adivasis had nothing. Hope had brought sleep to some of them but most of them did not have even that and looked half-awake permanently. A troubled man does not get sleep easily, if he does get some sleep, it is the result of sheer tiredness.

Kuriya could not get any sleep. He quietly left the place. Where to? Even he had no idea.

SIX

The diamond jubilee of Queen Victoria was being celebrated in Udaipur with great enthusiasm and pomp. The entire city was decorated like a new bride. Welcome arches decorated with velvety clothes were put up at several places. Festoons of jamun and mango leaves hung at every gate. The main roads and crossings looked colourful with rangoli patterns in white, saffron and red lines of lime and ochre dye.

Spring was in the air. Even in ordinary course it was the season when Udaipur brightened up with colourful flowers. This year was special and preparations for the Queen's diamond jubilee had started much in advance. At every crossing, empty space was left for laying flowers beds in rectangular and circular shapes. All of Sajjan Niwas Palace looked specially bedecked. The grass lawns in the extensive palace gardens were well manicured. The trees in the palace gardens, chandni (crape jasmine), nagchampa (cobra saffron), raat ki rani (cestrum noturnum), gudhal (china rose), din ka raja, gulmohar, amaltas were all in full bloom.

The tiny branches of mayurpankhi trees were trimmed and given the shapes of elephant, horse and peacock. All around the palace gardens were trees of mango, jamun, neem, sheeshum and gular. The Victoria Hall in the garden was given a special attention. Directly in front of the hall stood a majestic marble statue of Queen Victoria, a reminder of her exalted status. It was the statue of the famous Queen of an empire where the sun never sets. It was inaugurated in 1890 by Prince Albert.

In 1887, Maharana Fateh Singh had been lavish in spending money from the state exchequer to celebrate the golden jubilee of Queen Victoria. The entire state was illuminated, prisoners were given amnesty and released and the hungry were fed liberally. The Maharana had donated ₹10,000 to the Imperial Institute, London, and another ₹5,000 was contributed to a charity run by the wife of Viceroy Duffrin.

On the joyous occasion of the golden jubilee of the Queen and in view of the generosity displayed by him, the British government had decorated Maharana Fateh Singh with the Grand Commander of the Star of India (GCSI). Prior to that, in 1885, the Maharana had the new building of Walter Female Hospital inaugurated by Madam Duffrin, while her husband was on a visit to Udaipur. A year before the diamond jubilee of the Queen, in 1896, the Viceroy, Lord Elgin had visited Udaipur. He was presented a golden bracelet at the Jagdish temple.

The diamond jubilee of the Queen was celebrated in style against the background of close ties between the British government and the Mewar state.

All the thikanedars, jagirdars, bhaumiyas of the state came to the bedecked Sajjan Niwas Palace, wearing the round Mewari turbans made of colourful striped cotton. They also wore dhoti and darbari angrakhi, the traditional long coat, with swords tied to their waist. Their swirling smart moustaches and facial expressions showed how deeply they were steeped in feudal pride and customs. The prominent rich traders of the state were also invited to the ceremonies. There were hundreds of them. All of them had their heads covered with small round turbans, which were tied in the peculiar Mewari style. A few selected adivasi heads came in their traditional dresses to participate in the festivities. Prominent charans (bards) were also present.

Among the invitees was a man believed to be nursing anti-imperialist views—Kesari Singh Barhat of Shahpura, stood apart from all of them. The Maharana liked and respected him a great deal. That is why he had been invited to join the celebrations. His heart though was not in the festivities.

In his splendid royal attire the Maharana himself looked imposing as he sat on his throne. In front of him on either side seated in their designated places were the ministers of the darbar, special advisers, other officers and special invitees. Next to the Maharana's throne was the VIP guest, AGG Trevor and the political agent of the Bharatpur state, Mortelli. Col Miles, the British Resident in Mewar (formerly political agent), had been forced to go on long leave following differences between him and the Maharana over transporting train passengers between Udaipur and Chittorgarh by mail cart. Mortelli was deputising for him.

After the formalities of welcoming of the distinguished guests, the Divan of Mewar began his speech in praise of the glory of the Mewar state and the British Empire. He began with a historical reference: "Maharana Pratap of this Mewar state had challenged the powerful Indian emperor of the time, Akbar..." These words made AGG Trevor squirm with unease.

The Divan continued: "Our Fateh Singhji is a descendant of the same Pratap dynasty. The Mewar state is prosperous and powerful. The Thakur of the Bhomat area and the adivasi mukhiya had gone astray for a while. But the present bhaumiyas and mukhiyas are loyal to the throne." The Maharana looked askance at the Divan when he heard this. He thought the reference to what had happened in the Bhomat area in the past was inappropriate to the occasion. But AGG Trevor paid special attention to that reference, twice whispering to the interpreter to clarify that portion of the speech.

The Divan was effusive in his praise for the British government and the Empire and also Empress Victoria while he recalled the history of the traditional good relations between the British and Mewar state that has continued right till the present day. He made a special mention of the statue of Queen Victoria in the Sajjan Niwas gardens, the background in which it was installed, and the Udaipur visits of previous Viceroys including Lord Rippon and Lord Duffrin.

Now it was the turn of AGG Trevor to speak. "I would like to remind Maharana Saheb and all his subordinate sardars that in the background of the 1857 revolt relations between the Company and the native princely states had come under some strain, leading to many misunderstandings. This was the reason why the British government abolished the Company's rule, and in the interest of this country, took over all the rights and duties. The British minister for India, in a letter that he wrote in 1862 to the Governor General Lord Canning, had stated clearly that 'only by providing security to the native princely rulers can we can establish our power permanently in India'. The British stuck to this stand and granted the adoption right to all the rulers. Lest it led to any doubts, this right was backed by a legal document." He then repeated the assurances given by Lord Caning.

"Her Majesty Queen Victoria wishes to see that the rights and powers that the rulers in India and their sardars have over their states and the prestige and honour they enjoy should be preserved forever. In fulfilment of this wish, the British Crown wishes to assure you that in the absence of a natural heir if you or the future rulers of your state adopt a son in accordance with your traditions and the Hindu religion, that adoption will be recognised legally."

Maharana Fateh Singh was relieved to hear this from the AGG. There was a special reason behind it. The former Maharana, Sajjan Singh, did not have a son and Fateh Singh, who belonged to the Shivrati family, was declared his heir with the consent of the political agent.

"Let you be assured that as long as your kingdom remains a well-wisher of the British and continues to honour all the contracts, deeds and agreements, which detail your duties towards the British government, there will be no breach of this promise." AGG Trevor then went on to dwell on the glory of the Empire that was spread over most parts of the world, the illustrious dynasty represented by Queen Victoria, her qualities as a great ruler and the power of the British government and the British army, before expressing his gratitude to Maharana Fateh Singh.

When AGG Trevor was delivering his speech, Kesari Singh Barhat, who was sitting in the darbar, was seen frequently raising his eyebrows. Once or twice he shook his left hand. In the AGG's speech he detected a clear hint of British arrogance and threat to the Mewar state. He remembered Maharana Pratap repeatedly. The expressionless face of Fateh Singh, who occupied the throne of the Maharana of Mewar, was creating revulsion in his mind and anger was writ large on his face. He thought of going out into the open air but somehow decided against doing so. Inside himself he remained restless, almost shaking in rage, feeling uncomfortable as though scores of thorns had pierced his veins. His eyes frequently rested on the portrait of Maharana Pratap on the wall opposite to him.

Drawing attention of the audience, AGG Trevor made an important announcement.

"On this great occasion of the diamond jubilee of Queen Victoria, the British government has decided that henceforth the Maharana of Mewar who was entitled to a 15-gun salute will receive a 21-gun salute."

The announcement lit the faces of everyone in the audience. It was greeted by a round of loud clapping. Cries of "Maharani Victoria ki Jai! Maharani ki Jai! Maharani ki Jai! (Long live Queen Victoria) echoed in the air."

AGG Trevor then drew the attention of the audience again to make another announcement.

"Maharana Fateh Singh Bahadur has displayed allegiance to the British Crown and the British government. For this the British government congratulates him and has decided that in lieu of this show of faith by him, he is decorated with the title of 'Order of the Crown of India'. I take this opportunity to congratulate the Maharana Saheb Bahadur for receiving this honour."

More clapping followed. The spirited atmosphere reverberated with more cries of "Maharani Victoria ki Jai! Maharana Mewar ki Jai!"

Maharana Fateh Singh expressed his gratitude in a brief speech. The AGG formally handed over the decoration to him.

Kesari Singh Barhat had in the meanwhile quietly slipped out. Nobody had noticed his exit in the tumult of the happy occasion.

AGG Trevor was staying at Sajjan Niwas. The grand ceremonies had overwhelmed him. He was resting after lunch when he received a telegram announcing the death of Col Showers. The colonel had played an important role in crushing the 1857 revolution on behalf of the British. He had said goodbye to the world at the ripe age of 86. He was an elderly but distant relative of AGG Trevor, who was overcome by grief on receiving the news of his death. He took out the book *The Missing Chapter of the Indian Mutiny* written by Col Showers and began to read the eyewitness account about the 1857 development from that book:

The Indian units of the British Army posted in Meerut cantonment sounded the bugle of revolt on 10 May 1857. The news spread to other parts of the country. On May 18, the soldiers at Neemuch cantonment joined the ranks of the rebel. They set fire to the cantonment, killing a British woman and two children. The rest of the British there escaped. Among them was the commandant of the cantonment, Capt Lloyd. Along with some colleagues of his, he sought shelter with the Maharawal of the Pratapgarh state in southern Rajputana. The Maharawal sent his forces to Neemuch for his help. But his soldiers beat a retreat after the rebels repulsed their attack.

'The adivasis are joining the mutinous soldiers. Your army will not be enough. Your own jagirdars don't trust me. It is possible some of them may be supporting the rebels,' Lloyd had said wiping his sweat. Those were the hot days of the month of May.

'Captain Saheb, tell me, what can I do? There is no need to worry too much if one or two jagirdars side with the rebels. What I fear are the adivasis.'

'Please send four or five mounted men immediately to Udaipur. Showers, the political agent in Mewar, has to be

informed at once,' Capt Lloyd sounded alarmed. He was shivering with fear, his voice quivering. He was desperate to send the message across. As he walked towards a conference room of the palace, the Maharawal asked him to sit by his side on a divan, placing his hands over his shoulders, a gesture that was supposed to convey to him a silent assurance from the Maharawal. Pride was writ large on the Maharawal's face. He began to see visions of an opportunity to get closer to the British government. Capt Lloyd was not comfortable with the Maharawal's gesture of placing his hands on his shoulders. But he kept quiet. He was busy writing the message. The Maharawal decided to summon a confidante, Thakur Abhaya Singh, and dispatched him with three other mounted men and Capt Lloyd's letter to Udaipur.

When Thakur Abhaya Singh reached Udaipur I was talking to Maharana Swarup Singh about the revolt some time earlier by the Rao of Salumber, Kesari Singh. After a brief wait, Abhaya Singh handed me Lloyd's letter in the presence of the Maharana. The letter took me by surprise. The Maharana too was stunned for a while.

'What is the matter, Agent Saheb Bahadur?' Maharana Swarup Singh asked him.

'There is revolt in the Neemuch cantonment. Please alert your forces immediately. I shall personally go there. It will be difficult to send the army from Khairwada. It is already deployed in Salumber. You know it.'

Maharana Swarup Singh instructed his army chief to ready the army. I got up from the chair and paced up and down. I was restless. I had received the information from Meerut well in time. After the Meerut revolt, Governor General Lord Caning had informed all his political agents that 'possibilities for revolt exist everywhere'. The mutineers should be dealt with strictly with the cooperation of the native rulers and theirs as well as the British army.

Maharana Swarup Singh sent his army with me. The command of this armed, mounted force was entrusted by the Maharana to his trusted counsel Arjun Singh. The Maharana talked separately to Thakur Abhaya Singh of Pratapgarh. After consulting me, it was decided that if any action needs to be taken on the way from Udaipur to Neemuch, I will direct Thakur Abhaya Singh who will act in cooperation with Arjun Singh. En route we met the Bhil mukhiya, Devji, who was known to Abhaya Singh. He said that 'about forty British men, women and children who ran away from Neemuch, have taken shelter in the fort of the jagirdar of Dungla village.' This information was conveyed to me by Abhaya Singh. I left for Dungla with the army. Thanking the jagirdar, I sent the British refugees with a British platoon to Udaipur. The Maharana lodged them in the Jug Niwas Palace.

The rebels from Neemuch were going round villages in the areas of Chittorgarh, Nimbahera and Choti Sadri, asking villagers to fortify themselves against the British. Under my command, the Mewar army clashed at many place with the rebels and the villagers. The rebels were much smaller in numbers compared to the trained Mewar army, so it did not halt my onward march. Near Neemuch, the revolt had taken a more violent turn. The Neemuch cantonment was destroyed and the armoury had been robbed of all its arms and ammunition. Led by the rebel soldiers, the adivasis had attacked the Pratapgarh fort. They suspected that the Pratapgarh Maharawal had hidden the Neemuch commandant, Capt Lloyd. It was true, but Lloyd had safely gone back to Neemuch before the attack on the Pratapgarh fort. Some jagirdars tried to convince their trusted adivasi heads that neither Capt Lloyd nor any of his men were hiding in the fort. After they were convinced, the rebels and the adivasis retreated from there.

I arrived at Neemuch on 14 June with the Mewar army. Thakur Abhaya Singh left Neemuch for Pratapgarh. He had gone up to Neemuch on my request. But at Neemuch a false story had been circulated among the Mewar army personnel that in order to disrespect their religion the British had mixed crushed bone powder in the flour. The soldiers were enraged by this rumour and they united in opposition to the British. The Mewar counsel, Arjun Singh who had come along with me, commanded a good influence over the army. He was himself a religious person. He tasted the flour for its dubious contents, found nothing but it was with some difficulty that he was able to pacify the soldiers.

To subdue the revolt, two companies of the army arrived from Devli cantonment also. A little before Neemuch, some of the rebels were able to contact these soldiers. A rumour spread: 'The East India Company has decided to send the Indian soldiers at Neemuch to fight a war abroad. That is why they have revolted. Now they are being called back so the soldiers from Devli can be sent abroad.' Because of this rumour, the soldiers from Devli refused to tame the rebels. Instead, they joined the ranks of the rebels. The Mewar army and the Devli soldiers fought near Neemuch. A platoon commander and two Havildars of the Devli army were gunned down in this fight. All three of them were adivasis. The platoon commander was Parihar Meena and the two Havildars were Bhils. Most of the men in the Devli army were adivasis. Now all the adivasi soldiers from Devli were in a rebellious mood and had escaped to the forests. Joining the rebels from Neemuch, they fortified positions against the British at various places. The Mewar army remained loyal to the British. With the help of the British army under my command we were able to overcome the revolt in Neemuch.'

Nimbahera formed part of the Mewar state. The Rao there had revolted and met the Nawab of Tonk. The Nawab agreed to help the Rao. But after some time he managed to depose him and handed over the control of Nimbahera to a trusted Pathan of his.

'Now is the time; you should get Nimbahera freed from the control of Nawab of Tonk and have it returned into the fold of Mewar. This will be an appropriate reward for the help given by the Mewar army,' counsel Arjun Singh told me. Maharana Swarup Singh had obviously well instructed Arjun Singh on this matter.

'The Maharana had not presented such a demand before me,' I replied, surprised by the unexpected suggestion.

'Sir, our Maharana is a very far-sighted man. He never talks lightly. Besides, he never tells his mind before the appropriate occasion.'

'Has he sent you with these instructions?'

'Yes, you may think so.'

'Shall I then consider it a pre-condition?'

'No, it is not. What I say will strengthen the ties between Mewar and the Company.'

'Yes, I agree,' I nodded with a smile.

'You are sagacious and loyal to the Maharana. That is why you were sent with me. I shall remain convinced about one thing. The Mewar army would not have helped us if it did not have faith in you. I shall never forget for the rest of my life how you cleared the air and scotched the rumours about bone powder in the flour.'

'You are very kind. Also, a living proof of the friendship between the Mewar Darbar and the Company.' Counsel Arjun Singh's words made me laugh heartily.

'I shall have to take permission from the Company headquarters, which will be possible only after the revolt has been crushed. For the time being the transfer of Nimbahera to the Mewar state shall remain temporary. I accept your proposition on this condition.'

'I played a trick. I told the Nawab of Tonk in a letter sent to him secretly: The jagirdar of Nimbahera is helping the rebels against the British. I think he is not under your command either. Until the rebellion is quelled, the East India Company rule over Nimbahera has become necessary. We assure and promise solemnly that just after the restoration of peace Nimbahera will be returned to your control. Other than this we have no interest in Nimbahera.'

The letter also clarified that 'the Mewar army helped the British army in quashing the rebellion in the Neemuch area. That is why Nimbahera will be under temporary control of Mewar. You should not have any misunderstanding over this temporary measure.'

The Nawab of Tonk, Vazir Khan, received this letter at a trying time for him. During the soldiers' revolt the Nawab had sided with the British but a large part of his army, under his maternal uncle, Mir Alam Khan, had revolted. Alam Khan was killed by men loyal to the Nawab. But about 600 'Mujahids' (fighters) of Tonk were able to reach Delhi to help the Moghul emperor, Bahadur Shah Zafar. Some of the rebels from the Tonk army had taken the Divan of Tonk, Faizullah Khan, as hostage and had the prisoners freed. They declared Tonk to be under their rule. The Nawab of Tonk sought the help of the British army, which he received a little later. Major Eden arrived in Tonk with a large contingent of the army and was able to restore peace there.

The Nawab of Tonk had received my letter when the state was in turmoil. That is why he had no reason to reject the offer I had made.

I led an attack on Nimbahera with the Mewar army on 18th September. The Mewar army easily ran over the opposition. The jagirdar of Nimbahera ran away and joined the rebels at Mandsore. I restored Nimbahera temporarily to Mewar.

Peace had returned to Neemuch. Some of the rebel soldiers had been arrested, some others had been slain. At important places, platoons of the army had been posted. There was strict vigilance over the whole area.

I was sitting in the rest house at Neemuch cantonment. Capt Lloyd and three or four British officers were with me. It was evening time. The sun was not about to set but was barely visible. There were clouds in the sky and flashes of lightening. Rain fell with the thunder of clouds. The showers had started to hit the vicinity of the verandah where I was sitting in the company of some others. We were sitting in chairs, holding our glasses with pegs of scotch. We stood up and looked for a dry place. Just then a drenched Indian astride a horse came rushing in. He had come from Khairwada cantonment. Leaving the horse under a tree and tying it to a branch, he entered the rest house.

'Come to the verandah. Is it an important message?' Capt Lloyd asked the man. He had realised from the uniform the man was wearing that he was from the Mewar Bhil Corps.

'Yes, Sir, a special and secret message! This is for Showers Sir,' said the man as he pulled out a secure envelope from a leather pouch and stood at attention before saluting the officers. He was looking at Capt Lloyd who had first noticed his entry

and spoken to him. The man hardly knew me. He had the letter in his hand and looked at me with curiosity.

'Showers, Sir, it is for you.' As soon as Lloyd looked at me the visitor understood who I was and saluting me handed me the envelop. I put my whisky glass on the table, opened the letter and read it. My brows arched as I read the letter and tension began to show on my face. I was tense as I stood up muttering 'Ah, Ah'.

'The contents of the letter need not have been kept secret from the British officers who were sitting with me."

'You may leave now,' I told the man. 'Oh, listen. Come back after half an hour. Go and rest somewhere,' I instructed him.

'The stable is over there, go there,' Capt Lloyd gestured to the man who had come on a horse to deliver the message. The man saluted him and left. Capt Lloyd also asked an orderly at the rest house to help the visitor.

The rain was becoming intense. The trees outside the rest house were thoroughly drenched. The birds on the trees sat huddled because of the incessant rain. At the other end of the rest house four or five langoors (the black-faced monkeys) sat looking a little scared. They were flashing their glances all around. At that moment, an orderly came from the direction of the kitchen which was by the side of the rest house. He was carrying a tray with tumblers containing drinks. He came straight to us.

'All right! Leave them on the table. Don't bring anything else,' Capt Lloyd told the orderly. He had understood what was in my mind and so had the other officers. I wanted to discuss something important with them.

'Mister Showers! Is there something to worry about,' asked Robert Linley.

'Yes, Robert and all of you listen to this carefully,' I said as I took a sip of whisky and ran my fingers over my drooping moustaches to stretch them to reach my French cut beard and then lifted my fingers. I rubbed my eyes and spoke.

'Two weeks ago, the adivasi head of Khairwada had tried to instigate the soldiers of the Mewar Bhil Corps against us. Luckily, Commandant William Hunter got to know of it well in

time. The mukhiya did not succeed but he had revolted with the help of 3,000 Bhils and Makraniyons (migrants from Makrana) he had gathered at his mansion.'

Many relatives of these Bhils and Meenas are in the Mewar Bhil Corps. Fourteen soldiers are absent. It is feared they may have joined the rebels. It will influence other soldiers. Elsewhere, near Banswara Ganga Rawal (Bhil) has attacked the Morikheda post with hundreds of his accomplices. Three soldiers have been killed, rest have escaped. Of course, the jagirdar of Morikheda faced the attackers with his men and Ganga's brother, Jeeva, was killed in the fight. Ganga Rawal has created trouble in many other places. He is active. Hundreds of adivasis are joining him. There is this information that a group of adivasis has attacked the Pipalkhoont post and one solider has been killed. Three or four others have been taken hostage by the attackers. There have been violent incidents near Saagwara. In the hilly track near Salumber, the Khoomji Meena gang has looted 30 traders. It is a very dangerous gang which is inciting the adivasis against us and helping them with money and in other ways. Another worrisome news is that Tantya Tonpe has crossed the jungles of Narmada and is heading towards southern Rajputana. He has some good guerrilla fighters with him. The problem is that unrest has spread to all the five states in southern Rajputana. If Tantya Tonpe enters in such a situation extra forces will have to be deployed to meet his challenge. That will affect the task of crushing the local rebellion with depleted forces. Apart from the Maharana of Mewar, the rulers of Pratapgarh, Banswara, Kushalgarh and Dungarpur and their army are with us. But the local population, the mukhiyas and many of the jagirdars and thikanedars are opposed to us and the native rulers.

The officers present listened to me with attention. I went on. 'I shall have to rush to Khairwada to take control. Capt Lloyd, I suggest you ask that messenger with the horse to stay here for the night. I shall leave for Khairawad in the morning. Send a message to counsel Arjun Singh that a platoon of the Mewar cavalry will accompany me. And Major Roberts, order one company of the force that you have brought from Nasirabad cantonment to accompany me to Khairwada. We shall also have a company of the cavalry. Send this information on my behalf to the office of the Ajmer Residency.'

We had finished our dinner by 8:30 in the evening. It was earlier than usual. We had also cut our liquor intake that evening. By the time we finished our dinner, instructions for keeping the Khairwada-bound army had been issued. Counsel Arjun Singh was a little reluctant to send the Mewar army to Khairwada without the permission of the Maharana, but he had the Nimbahera agreement and so he was certain that the Maharana would agree to send an army unit to Khairwada. Arjun Singh was, after all, a trusted lieutenant of the Maharana.

The month of September in 1857 was closing. I reached Khairwada in the afternoon amidst an atmosphere of suspicion. Apart from the missing 14 soldiers of the Bhil Corps, all other soldiers were discharging their duty responsibly. They had performed the brave task of crushing the rebellion of previous days. But Hunter, the commandant, feared that deep inside the Bhil Corps soldiers were restless, which he had guessed by looking at their faces.

I was tired. But I preferred to hear about the situation from the commandant of the Bhil Corps. As soon as I entered the officers' mess I asked him: 'Capt Hunter, I have read your letter and I felt I must reach Khairwada with the army. Please, update me on the situation.

'Sir, I am grateful to you. I was sure you will not lose even a moment to help me. That is why I had sent a message, both to you and the AGG.'

He continued: 'The rebellion in the Salumber area is not under control. At other places…'

'First tell me, has there been any message from the AGG,' I said as I cut him short.

'No, not so far.'

'I'll tell you what. I have a strength of two companies with me. All are mounted soldiers. You may, if you wish, send the company from the Mewar army to Salumber.'

'Yes, that will be better, Sir.'

'A message for me from the AGG Lawrence had reached the Neemuch commandant, Lloyd.'

On the cover of the letter was written: 'This message should also be seen by the Neemuch Commandant.' The commandant handed me the 'urgent' letter as soon as I reached Neemuch. The information in it was brief. What transpired was that when the AGG was spending his summer vacation at Mount Abu, 90 soldiers from an army contingent of the Jodhpur state, the Jodhpur Legion, had been sent to the British cantonment, Erinpura for army exercise. After reaching there, these soldiers had mutinied when they heard about the anti-British rebellion that had spread to various parts of the country. They fired at British soldiers at Mount Abu. About 15 soldiers lost their lives in this incident. One Captain was seriously wounded. The British soldiers repulsed the attack by the Jodhpur Legion. They returned from there to their headquarters in Erinpura. A dispute had arisen between the native and British soldiers over a trivial matter, which soon led to violence. Four Legion men were also killed in the violence. This information set off a rebellion by the Jodhpur Legion against the British. The British cantonment was in Shivganj, about two kos *from Erinpura, beyond the Sukri River. That was the place for recruiting the Meena adivasis. It was an area dominated by the Meena and Garasiya adivasis. When the news of revolt by the Jodhpur Legion reached Shivganj the soldiers in the cantonment also joined the rebellion.*

They also received support from the non-adivasi men and junior officers. The rebellion at Jodhpur Legion and Shivganj cantonment was led by Thekedar *(contractor) Moti Khan and Subedar Sheetal Prasad. With the slogan* Chalo Dilli, Maro Firangi *(Onward to Delhi and kill the British) the rebels from Shivganj and Erinpura marched to Sumerpur. From there they left for Delhi. On the way, Thakur Kushal Singh of Aaua with his army joined the rebel soldiers.*

The AGG wrote to Maharaja Takht Singh of Jodhpur to crush the rebels and he himself arrived at Udaipur from Mount Abu, from where he kept an eye on all of Rajputana. Under the leadership of his 'Kiledars' who had worked in the army, Aunar Singh Panwar and Faujdar Rajmal Lodha, the Maharaja sent 10,000 soldiers and horsemen and 12 guns to Aaua.

The letter had specifically asked that the rebellion at Aaua and its nearby areas be crushed most decisively.

After lunch I decided to rest for a while. A company of the Mewar army was dispatched to Salumber in the afternoon. A platoon of the reserve company of the Mewar Bhil Corps was also sent with it.

After all the arrangements had been made, Capt Hunter came to see me at the officers' mess at about 5 pm. I had rested enough by then and I was planning a strategy to rout the rebellion. On the table in front of me was a map of southern Rajputana on white cloth with black ink markings. Important points on the map were marked in red ink. I was also making cross marks in red ink over sensitive points, which were strategically important. From the window I could see Capt Hunter entering the steps to the verandah. Anxious that I was, I shouted from my room: 'Come Captain. I was waiting for you.'

Capt Hunter was a little startled. He realised that I had seen him coming. An Indian orderly was in the verandah. Before he could convey to me the news of his arrival, Capt Hunter had passed by the orderly and came directly into the room. I stood up and answered his salute by shaking his hand and told him: 'Look Captain, except for some small incidents in Kushalgarh state, the situation on the whole is under control. But rebellion has spread in much of the southern Rajputana area, Jodhpur state, Khandesh, Malwa, and other nearby areas. We are in direct touch with the rulers of these states. Some of their jagirdars are with the rebels. Your corps is safe till now?'

'Yes, Sir.'

'I am worried about your 14 missing soldiers. I'm afraid they may have joined the rebels.'

'No, Sir, except for two, others have returned to duty. I had warned them of severe punishment while serving them the recall notice. They started to return as soon as they received the recall notice. About the two missing ones, it is learnt that they are not

in a position to return because of illness. I am sure they will do no such thing.'

'But?'

'Yes, they are also under observation. The two come from Khanpur and Sanjaria villages which are not very far from Khairwada.'

'I hope they are not depending on black magic for their treatment; I could not control my laughter.'

'Get them here. The corps doctor will treat them and there will be no need to keep an eye on them.'

'Yes, that is right, Sir. They will be here by tomorrow.'

I got busy preparing a foolproof strategy to crush the rebellion in consultation with other officers and representatives of the five states in southern Rajputana.

I received information on September 30 that ahead of Aaua, near Chelavas, the political agent at Jodhpur, Col Mason, died while fighting. It left me shocked. We were good friends and both of us had joined the same regiment in England at the same time. I remained disturbed for many days.

The details of that incident were something like this. A fierce battle ensued when a unit of the Jodhpur army under Kiledar Aunar Singh Panwar and Faujdar Rajmal Lodha arrived at Vothoda, near Aaua, to confront the rebels. Panwar was killed in this fight. The rebels had taken guns the army had used against them, as also other fighting equipment and rupees one lakh.

AGG Lawrence on being informed about it arrived at Ajmer from Udaipur and from there left for Aaua with the army and political agent Mason. The rebellion, which had begun in Erinpura and Shivganj, had gathered strength. Led by Thakur Kushal Singh thousands of rebels had reached Chelavas. AGG Lawrence and political agent Mason surrounded the rebels there and launched an attack on them. The British army lost this battle and Mason was killed. The more brutal among the rebels went round Aaua with his severed head and hung it at the Sadar (main) gate of the fort. There was pandemonium in the army that had come with Lawrence, who had taken shelter in Ajmer.

When Governor General Lord Caning learnt about the incident, he dispatched large units of army from Palanpur and Nasirabad to Aaua under the command of Col Holmes. He surrounded the fort at Aaua and brought the situation under control. The rebels were thrown out. Most of them had managed to escape, but 124 were arrested. Twenty-four of them were hanged. The small town of Aaua was destroyed, burnt and looted.

The strategy that I had prepared at Khairwada proved to be successful. By October–November the rebellion was brought under control. Though some odd incidents continued here and there, the Vagad region remained calm for one year. But under the surface of this calm was the dormant fire of a volcano. All it needed to explode was a slight spark and my fear was that it could come any moment.

On a November afternoon I was enjoying the sun sitting in the verandah at the Khairwada officers' mess. Maj Gen Roberts had arrived there. He was sitting there with the Mewar Bhil Corps Commandant, Capt Hunter.

Maj Gen Roberts had planned to celebrate Christmas at Khairwada. He had remained very active during the 1857 revolt also. He had defeated Tantya Tonpe army on August 9 near the Kothari River in Bhilwara. Tantya Tonpe was forced to flee to Chittor with his men.

Capt Hunter was in blue tracksuit. We, the other officers, were in casuals. Conversation tended to be about our deeds of bravery in quelling the rebellion. But the black shadows of the death of Col Mason hung over all the tales of bravery, courage and strategy and left us despondent. During that particular moment of leisure, we three officers were trying to forget that sad episode.

There was a strong feel of cold in the air. Simla had a snowfall in the previous week. But the sky was clear. In the neatly laid out beds in the lawn at the officers' mess marigold, chrySoonthemum, Gudel and other flowers of various hues were in bloom. The Nagchampa was overflowing with white-yellow flowers. The lawn had been freshly mowed and its lustrous soft grass looked lovely under the sun. There were abundant plants of the local rose. Surrounded by this beauty of nature, we three officers were enjoying a drink of gin. In usual course, gin was to have been an evening summer drink, but if he wanted to drink any liquor, it had to be gin for Maj Gen Roberts. Capt Hunter and I normally used to avoid drinking during the day, except for an occasional beer. That afternoon we had decided to have gin in deference to Maj Gen Roberts. He was a decent and easy-going man. He did not like to treat everything too seriously and took many things lightly. When asked for his preference for the drink, he said without hesitation 'gin.' In order to show our respect for him, we said: 'Sir, we shall go with you.'

'No, it is not necessary, nor is it a formality. Here in the officers' mess we are friends. It is not in the culture or tradition of the mess to look at someone as senior or junior, especially during the leisure hours of taking refreshments when all the officers are equal. The idea is that we should talk freely.'

We kept our thoughts to ourselves while responding to Maj Gen Roberts with a yes. This was, after all, our first meeting with him. We thought it necessary to be a little formal with him.

Maj Gen Roberts had a distinct identity in the British army. He had fought the Russians in the Crimean war, where he proved his bravery. He was a colonel at that time. Later, he was knighted by the Crown. Major General Sir William Roberts 'Eagle', to give his full name, told us that afternoon the complete story behind the suffix 'Eagle' in his name. It was nothing but the story of how he had bravely fought against the Russian army in the war.

We were deep into light chatter. Suddenly came the roar of a tiger from over the southern hills of Khairwada cantonment. At that very moment, John Black Smith, adjutant of the Mewar Bhil Corps, entered the mess with a snappy salute. Commandant Hunter went up to him and asked: 'What's the matter, adjutant?'

'There is an urgent mail for Col Showers,' he told Col Hunter as he handed him an envelope. Hunter passed that envelope on to me. I opened it and read it. The news is that 'on November 11, Tantya Tonpe attacked Banswara and occupied the fort. The jagirdars of the state have given their support to him and the

Maharawal of Banswara had left the capital and gone into the jungle. You should rush there with army. A larger detachment of the army will be reaching there from Nasirabad under the command of Brig Park.'

This was the message from the AGG and I conveyed it to Maj Gen Roberts.

'Oh! He has come again! I had driven him out on August 9 from the banks of river Kothari near Bhilwara. He had escaped towards Nathwara after I chased him. He managed to dodge and reach Jhalawar via Chittor where he received help from the state army. He arrested the ruler of Jhalawar, Prithvi Singh and took the treasury of the state, elephants, horses and the armoury. We had all of these released by him as we drove him out. I was recalled and the responsibility of dealing with him was handed over to Brig Park. I was impressed by the instant recall of the story by Maj Gen Roberts.'

'He is a very dangerous man. A specialist in guerrilla attack. But Brig Park is a great fighter, no less than me. So don't worry. He can be easily chased away. My best wishes to you. Yes, you may have to leave soon,' Roberts said as he leaned towards me.'

Next day, I left for Banswara.

On the last cover page of Col Showers' book was a sketch of his. Below it in his handwriting was a special note: 'This story of Sepoy Mutiny in India is based on my own experience and later on discussions with British officers who controlled the mutiny in the area where I was posted.'

After reading the book, AGG Trevor took a deep breath. It remained a matter of guess whether it was to express his sorrow over the death of Col Showers or an expression of his satisfaction over the bravery shown by Col Showers in controlling that revolt. The AGG was then lost in his thoughts.

SEVEN

"I, Sengaji Sadh, profusely thank God for creating this planet dotted with wonderful hills, rivers, streams, oceans, and producing strange creatures like man, animals, birds, etc. No one can ever know the secret of His great craftsmanship. In this unique world the other mysterious thing is black magic. Once it traps a person he cannot wiggle out of it. Therefore, I want to tell all the Hindus, Muslims, fakirs, saints, maharajas, rajas and all the seven–eight monarchs in Europe with folded hands that all that we call magic, witchcraft, sorcery etc. is a big evil. Raja Indra had started it to take control of the riches of the people. He began to lead an ostentatious and lavish life. He became carefree after building a castle in the sky and handed over all the material riches he had to Kuber, who turned himself into a black cobra and sat over all the wealth of the world. Later, Bajrabu, the Black Brahmin, Raja Kans and Haroon the King all used sorcery to trouble people. After them, came the Betal Raja. Then these men began to distance themselves from this black art but now these foreigners who have come from across seven seas have mastered this black magic. They have deluded the rajas, maharajas and mahajans of this land and led them astray. Just as the Shani God had discovered the truth about black magic and warned people to stay away from it, I want to tell you all that I have understood the trap that the foreigners (British) are laying and appeal to you not to fall into it. You will lose everything if you fall in their trap. People do not even realise why they are suffering and what can be done to find a remedy. The world built by the Creator has many good people, but these magicians have captivated them with their magic. These magicians are wicked; they are rajas and maharajas, money lenders and the British."

This is how Sengaji Maharaj began his morning discourse in Rohida, a small town. He was 60–62 years of age. It was the monsoon month of Sawan (July–August, early rainy season). But not a drop had fallen during the entire season. A congregation of about 200–250 was listening attentively to Sengaji Sadhu. Sometimes their eyes strayed from the face of the sadhu and looked up in the sky. Gradually, the number of followers of Sengaji increased many-fold. His spell spread over thousands of Hindus, Muslims, followers of Kabir, farmers, adivasis and others living in and around Rohida, Pindwara and Mount Abu. His message was spreading like wild fire.

It is said that some days ago a cow near Bhoola-Viloliya village had died due to snakebite. When Sengaji was passing by that area, the adivasis told him about the incident. He patted the cow on its shoulders and it sprang to life and walked away. After this miracle, Sengaji became known far and wide as the miracle baba.

Sadhu Sengaji continued his discourse.

"The bad practice of magic has been used under different names. It was first used by Raja Indra. It was called Indrajal after him. Lord Shani exposed it before the world. Raja Kuber continued with the aforesaid mischief and called it *Mahamaya*, which was unmasked by Lord Shankar and the evil started by Raja Kans was called *Jaaduchala* (magic) and uncovered by Lord Krishna. The evil started by King Haroon was called Infidel's Knowledge, which was laid bare by Guru Nanak. As you can see the wickedness was the same but different names were used because its perpetrators feared that they would not be able to practise their evil craft long if it continued under one name. If the name is changed frequently then our designs will not be revealed all of a sudden, they thought. What the

Hindus, Muslims and others call Kalukaal or Kalyug is an extension of the sins the magicians had spread. The British are now resorting to the evil black magic that was started by Raja Indra and others. These British plunderers are bringing back the same evil to the world. The oppressive rulers, wicked money lenders, shallow scholars and preachers have used this evil power by writing the so-called holy books, which are being widely circulated. This is an illusion, being watched by all Hindus, Muslims and the entire world. How clever are these men that they have mentioned the names of the future satis (saints) and have also written that the future will be so hard that anyone who has one *seer* (around one kg) of bronze will be considered rich. These sorcerers have circulated all these books of dark forebodings written with the help of their evil knowledge."

"The talk about *seer*, bronze and famine was first started by the baniyas and later they attributed it to this or that sadhu or sant (saints). If these so-called saints knew about it in advance, they would have also written that these wicked men would use this evil craft to harm the world. Those poor sadhus and sants were simple devotees of God and lived by His name to improve their lives. I request all of you with folded hands, the subjects and rulers, to come together and rid the world of the evil these plunderers are spreading. If your children do not survive, these evil people will reduce this creation of God to dust and take control of all the wealth of the world."

"These clever people have manipulated many. But it is not the fault of these people because you can do anything under a spell."

"I am only trying to caution you to save your children and warning you that fake brahmins are going round houses narrating dark stories. Reading these stories from books does not tell about good or bad future or what misfortune awaits us. But these people, intent on causing harm, spread these false tales six months in advance, quoting their books. To prove that their books are correct these people use witchcraft to perpetrate an evil. When a disease enters the body, they attribute it to the forecast in their books. By such misleading methods they prove that their books are right. Oh, you brahmins, Senga Sadh humbly tells you that these books are fabricated by these magicians and should be returned to them. To the Raj-Darbar my entreaty is: beware of these people."

"The loan sharks prepare false documents in the names of Hindu and Muslim clients, deceive them in the name of recovery of loan and deprive these poor people of their meagre worldly possessions—cows, bullocks, buffaloes, goats and whatever they can lay their hands on. They prepare fake documents by getting signatures of three-four of their employees as witnesses and present these documents in courts for facilitating auction of the poor people's possessions. The courts accept them as genuine documents and the bania makes them look more so when he presents them before the courts. The poor man is made to look like a liar when confronted by the bania in the court. This is court justice because these banias have in their possession bonds in black and white. But these are false bonds and notes that mention the names of the ancestors of the poor people. After the death of their ancestors the banias tell these poor people to return the loan that their grandfathers had taken from the bania's grandfather, as mentioned in the fake documents. 'We have the fingerprints of your grandfather on the documents as proof of the loan taken. Return the loan or we recover it by filing a lawsuit against you.' The poor man pays out of fear. But if he doesn't, the lawsuit will go against him because of the false note that carries his ancestor's thumb impression on it. On court orders the bania takes away all that the poor man possesses. The bania who lied thoroughly is proved right and the honest but poor man becomes a liar. The Raj dispenses this kind of justice because of the magic performed by the clever moneylenders who claim to be the repository of all the intelligence in the world. In any case, the voice of the poor is not heard in the courts. That is why the poor are not believed when they speak the truth. It is something to ponder over that those who toil day and night die of hunger and those who are experts in deceit and sit idle the whole day accumulate huge wealth through trickery and fraudulent means. Similarly, the foreign magicians have denuded the Indians of their wisdom and after taking over all the treasures of India they want to control the wealth of the entire world. That is why I want to forewarn all Hindus, Muslims and followers of other faiths about the dangerous conspiracy of the foreigners and ask you to rid the world of their evil designs."

"Just think what goes through my mind when you call me crazy at the instigation of these people when actually all that I speak is for the sake of a better future for you and your children. I feel like smashing my head. But I stop myself from doing that when I think that if I do not tell you about the magic spell these magicians try to cast over you then who else will? They have used their jugglery to harm me. I wish to expose their craftiness. With folded hands I beseech you to recognise the illusions they create and do something quickly to come out of their spell. The important thing I wish to tell you is that we have to suffer pain because of the sins committed by British and the Indian rulers. It was part of the tricks they play that this year we had no rain..."

"Sadh ki Jai Ho! Sadh ki Jai Ho! Let the jugglers die a black death! Let them die a black death!" an excited Mema Bhil started shouting suddenly. Sitting in the back rows, he was listening to Senga Sadhu very attentively.

The disturbance he caused first took the audience by surprise; then the atmosphere echoed to the slogans he had raised, as most of them joined him. Some of the special devotees of Senga Sadhu restored order and pleaded with Mema Bhil to listen quietly. But Mema Bhil appeared to have been overtaken by a spirit. He left the place shouting alone.

Mema was a resident of Bisoriya, a village near Sarda. Hit by the failure of monsoon rain, he had gone to Kotda in search of work. Things were equally bad there. But somehow he was able to find some odd work that partially met his hunger during the last 10–15 days. Today he had attended the congregation of Senga Sadhu by accident.

Nobody knew anything about the birthplace of Sengaji. Many believed he had come from Malwa region. He had been around for five–six months. He never stayed in one area for long duration. When people asked him about himself, he merely said that he was the son of this earth and he had a part of the spirit of Bhartari Baba in him. He did disclose that for 12 years he had done penance in Bhartari's capital, Ujjain. His Guru was a Baba who had both his ears pierced.

He used to preach in villages and at night used to rest in a cave in a hill near Kotda. What he did in the cave was not known to anyone. Around a month ago he had revealed the secret in a village that about 10 years ago his Guru had told him in his dream that he had become a sadhu with supernatural powers. Now his job was to create awareness among the people and expose the oppressive ways of the rulers, the wicked ways of the loan sharks and how the British were enslaving Indians. "Then alone will your life be a success."

Following that dream he had traversed long distances over Malwa, Khandesh, Vagad and Mewar before his present halt.

By the time he left, Mema had been deeply impressed by what he had heard from Senga Sadh.

Mema was unwilling to return to his village Bisoriya as he asked himself: Who was waiting for me there?

His mother had died when he was a child. She was grazing goats in the jungle. A flock of wolves arrived and attacked the goats. She gathered courage and tried to save the goats. She yelled for help. Before anyone could arrive, she had been badly mauled. She died on the way to her home. Her dying words were: "Oh, Mema's father, I am leaving with you our only child. Do take care of him. He will be your support in old age." But Mema's destiny was written with black ink. A few days later he lost his father too, killed by a dreaded disease.

Mema was brought up by his kaka (uncle), Haridiya. But when he became an adult, the uncle did not arrange for his marriage. The uncle was dishonest. He thought if Mema got married, a stranger would come to the house as his wife. It is likely that Mema may set up a separate household and there may be no one to look after him and his wife when they would be old. The childless Haridiya made Mema slog a lot. Mema too worked for him frantically, in and out of the house. The village was hit by famine. How could Mema provide for three people?

Haridiya would do nothing but get drunk and curse a lot. "You bastard! I brought you up and you refuse to attend to me." He would abuse Mema 10 times a day. What could kaki Bhajani do? She suffered from tuberculosis. What chore could she perform when Mema had to help her even to lie on bed?

Mema was more than 40 years old. Who would give him his daughter? But he was strong. He looked like a sprightly youth of 25–30. He would sprint through on any errand. Short in height, flat nosed, round faced, black hair, athletic body and a complexion as dark as the clouds of Asadh, but his face was always lit. He had an unspoilt look on his face and his eyes were bright. Those who knew him used to say that after the death of his father he cried a lot more than he did over the loss of his mother. But afterwards nobody ever saw him cry.

Burning with a desire to live Mema, who stood like a solid bamboo, arrived in Pindwara from Kotda. There was a dharmshala, an inn, at the entrance of Pindwara, called Patniyon (one clan of banias) ki dharamshala, which was built by a trader of Patni sub-caste. Later, that family had settled in Sirohi. A group of Banjara grain dealers was staying in the inn. When he passed by them he greeted them with "Jai Bhole Nath ki!"

"Jai Ramji ki! Who are you? Come here," one of them returned his greetings.

He went up to him and introduced himself. The traders were 10–12 in number, adults and youth and one or two elderly, who belonged to Banaskantha. They travelled in groups from Gujarat to Rajputana and then central India. Pindwara fell on what was known as the traders' route. There were two prominent routes for travel between Gujarat and central India. One, from Ahmedabad-Mehsana to Banswara via Abu Road-Udaipur and then central India. The second route led from Himmatnagar to Sirohi and then Pindwara–Kotda–Udaipur.

These Banjara traders mainly dealt in salt, selling the famous salt of the Rann of Kutch, carrying it on bullocks and donkeys via Rajputana to central India. Their more traditional occupation was trading in animals, especially bullocks and cows. But here we had the salt trading Banjaras.

On an oven made out of stone blocks was placed a broken pitcher that served as a round plate to bake millet chapattis. The aroma of an onion-based gravy cooked on a cauldron was wafting through the air.

In the company of friendly Banjaras, Mema had a delicious meal after a long time. More than the food, it was the feeling of companionship that thrilled him.

It was a tradition among these Banjaras and the Rebaris of Rajputana to leave their homes after Diwali to carry out their trade. Because of the poor monsoon that year, the Banjaras had to leave earlier than usual to sell salt. They were also called *lamana*. This name was familiar in central India also. The term was derived from *lavan*, the vernacular name for salt. The thrifty Banjara community, which would not allow even a drop of water to go waste, was known to be rich. Barter was the special feature of their trade.

"The rest of your family, I mean your wives and children etc. are left behind in the village?" Mema asked Sohna Banjara as he handed him a chillum stuffed with tobacco.

"Brother Mema! If there are a few drops of rain in the next 15–30 days, it may be possible to sow moong (green pulse), millet or barley. That is why the family members have been left behind. They will also leave after Diwali and join us in Neemuch town in Malwa region. This is the understanding we had before we left. We would have left with the full family after Diwali. But there was nothing for us to do at home because of poor rains. We thought it better to leave early and do some business," Sohana puffed deeply at the chillum as he replied to

Mema's query. As he drew another puff, he was nearly choked by a sudden bout of coughing. He kept coughing for a while. Then he spitted at one side and covered the saliva with some earth that he had shoved with his heel.

"Any hope for sowing another crop?"

"No, brother! There has been no rain for sowing millet and barley. If the rain is good around Dussehra then there are chances of raising a good crop of barley, gram etc. for which we leave the task of sowing to Gujars on crop-sharing basis. Whatever they give us on our return is ours, the rest is theirs, or God knows. But if we wait till the time has come for sowing that crop, we shall lose our business," Sohana informed him as he passed the chillum on to Sundar Baba.

"When do you return home?"

"Around Asadh," replied Sohana. Sunder was enjoying his chillum as he recalled the story of Lakha Banjara.

Lakha Banjara was travelling through a dense forest. On the way he met goddess Badatri Mata and asked her, "Where are you going?"

She told him that she was going to write the fate of a Rajput's son.

"What will you write?" Lakha Banjara was curious.

"One day he will own the property of Lakha Banjara," she replied.

She immediately vanished after saying this and arrived at the house of the Rajput. Lakha Banjara followed her, disguised as a sadhu.

The Rajput did not know what she had written about the fate of his baby. But the Banjara knew. He hatched a plan and told the Rajput:

"Your son will create dissension in the family when he grows up and give you a lot of trouble when you become old. So you better give me that cursed child. I shall give him good education and when he grows up, I will send him back to you. He will then serve you and the baleful period of his life would have passed. Your child was a king in his previous birth. I shall remind him about his previous birth and make him a gentle but brave human being. He will make you proud."

The Rajput took the bait thrown at him by Lakha Banjara. Lakha Banjara left with the baby after the Rajput had given him silver coins equal to the weight of his son. When he reached a forest, he wanted to kill the baby, but he could not gather courage to commit that sin. He merely wrapped the child in a cloth and left him in a bush, hoping that he will die either of hunger or some wild animal will eat him. This way, he thought, could prevent the possibility of his fortune falling into the hands of the child and also save himself from committing the sin of infanticide.

A cowherd from a nearby village happened to be passing by when he heard the cry of the baby and took him home. On inquiry he learnt that it was the newborn baby of a Rajput of the village. He handed over the baby to the Rajput, who was overcome by a sense of remorse that a thug disguised as a sadhu had taken away his child. A wave of happiness swept through his family on getting the child back, alive and kicking.

The child grew up. One day his parents told him the story about the fake sadhu. He left the house with the pledge that he will trace that fake sadhu. At last he managed to find him and took employment with him as a cowherd. To know what was in the mind of Lakha Banjara, one day the young boy, who had not disclosed his identity, told him the story of the fake sadhu. Lakha Banjara was worldly wise. As a trader he was used to read faces of people. He grew suspicious about his employee and on inquiry his doubts proved to be correct.

Lakha then planned to kill the young Rajput. He handed him a letter and said, "Go and deliver this letter to my brother in my village."

He had written in the letter that his brother should kill the bearer of the letter. The job should be finished by the time he returned from his business tour. The young Rajput mounted a horse to deliver the letter. It was summer time. The young man reached Lakha's village and rested under the cool shade of the banyan tree near the trader's mansion. At that moment, Lakha's daughter was passing by. She was young, beautiful, a little literate, and unmarried. When she saw the mare that was owned by her father, she went near it and found a young man sleeping under the tree while the mare had been tethered to a tree in one corner. The young man was well-built and handsome. She was bowled over by him.

The letter given to the youth by her father was jutting out of his pocket. She pulled it out and read it. She was shaken by its contents. She tore that letter and quickly wrote another one, addressed to Lakha Banjara's brother: "My dear brother! This man is reaching our house. Get him married to my daughter at once. Do not wait for me otherwise we will lose a fine groom. I have tested him. He is accomplished in all manners." Putting the letter in the pocket of the youth, she returned to the mansion.

The young man handed over that letter to Lakha's brother. Following the instructions in the letter, the young man was promptly married to Lakha's daughter. Lakha learnt about it on his return and was left shell-shocked. He was not at all prepared to accept the young man as his son-in-law. He hatched another conspiracy to kill him. He lured a shoemaker from a neighbouring village and asking him to keep it a secret, told him, "I'll send this young man to you. Kill him and bury him somewhere."

Lakha Banjara then told the young man: "Son-in-law, please go to the shoemaker's house and get yourself a new pair of shoes."

The young man left. On the way he met his brother-in-law, the only son of Lakha Banjara, who was about his age. The latter asked his newly married brother-in-law not to bother about going to the shoemaker, as he would visit the shoemaker himself to get him the new pair of shoes. The shoemaker had never seen the young man who had come to him, nor was he very familiar with Lakha's son. He assumed he was the young man Lakha had written about. He threw him into a pit full of leather, which he covered with more leather and then smothered the young man to death by pressing a heavy stone slab on him. Lakha's only son died.

When Lakha saw his son-in-law return to his mansion, he asked him: "You haven't still gone to get your pair of new shoes?"

The son-in-law replied: "I met brother-in-law on the way. He said that I need not take the trouble of going to the shoemaker and he would go to him and return with the pair of right size shoes."

Lakha immediately ran to the house of the shoemaker. But he was too late. By then his son had already been killed.

Lakha did not give up and prepared another plot to kill his son-in-law. He bribed four men with one hundred rupees each and instructed them to dump the man who had fraudulently become his son-in-law in a river along with his cot when he was fast asleep.

Somehow, Lakha's daughter came to know about this plan. She told her husband: "Lie quietly in the bed, pretending to be asleep when the men come, or else they will tie you up. They'd not throw you into the river before daybreak. You should escape at night. They would not know whether you have swum your way to safety or floated down the river as a dead body." She also instructed him about a rendezvous point and told him, "I'll come with lots of money. We shall then move elsewhere." The young man did as instructed and escaped at night.

Early in the morning, Lakha arrived near the riverbank. He found the four men he had hired in deep slumber, sprawled on the ground. He also saw that his son-in-law's cot was empty. He assumed the quartet was resting after accomplishing the mission he had entrusted them. He then retired on the empty cot. Overtaken by anxiety and tension, he had not been able to sleep the previous night, so he fell asleep within minutes. The four men got up as the dawn was breaking. But it was still a bit dark. They lifted the cot on which Lakha was sleeping and threw it into the river. The swift currents took Lakha to his doom and thus the Rajput youth became the owner of all his property.

"It is rather late in the night. Go to sleep. We have to leave early in the morning. Better to cover as much distance as possible during the day," Sunder said to Mema, as he handed him a tobacco-filled chillum. Except these three, all others had already retired for the night. The three were so engrossed in talks that they did not realise how late it was. At last these three also went to sleep.

For some reason and force of circumstances, the communities of Kanjar, Sansi, Bawri, Kalbeliya, Pardhi, Sikligar, Gadiya Lohar used to live the life of vagabonds in tents. The Banjaras did have a permanent abode but when out for trade, they were like nomads and used to move with their dogs. This had become necessary for guarding their tents. Two handali (dangerous and big) dogs were guarding the Banjara tents one night. It was considered impossible that any of their possessions, bullocks and merchandise, would be even touched by any outsider at night.

It was the night of *teras* (13th day) or *chaudas* (14th day), close to the full moon. In a couple of days, the month of Bhadon (August–September) was to end. There was very little hope for rain in the month of Kanwaar, more so when that particular year was a bad one. If the months of Aashadh (June–July), Sawan (July–August) and Bhadon (August–September) did not bring any rains then what could be expected in the month of Kanwaar? Clear sky—not even a speck of cloud anywhere. The westerly had not changed its direction and there was not even a whiff of easterly. The innumerable stars in the sky were watching the earth through their twinkling eyes. The moon over the head had sailed towards the west. Moonlight was generously sprayed all around. From a distance came the noise of all-night prayers at a holy site. Various musical instruments like drums, cymbals, conchs and bells were being played with synchronised rhythms. Some of the prayers went like this:

Hey: On Saturday wert thou canonised, Lord,
And in a jiffy, did thou create the earth.
Hey: Wrath incarnate, O Lord Saturn!
Worshipped thou wert
Before came the universe into its being.
Hey: Entertained thou art, Lord,
With chalices, full to the brim.
Hey: Mounted on thy horse thou roam through the streets
And make the mortals look pale and panicky.
Lord, thou hit hard
At the bronze and brass and iron
And they all turn dull and dark.
Hey: Thou fall on kings and queens and commoners
And the stars on them turn heavy and harsh.
Hey: So hard, did thou hit King Harishchandra,
He had to lose his home and honour
And Tara, the Queen, had to serve the low and ill-bred.
Hey: Thou struck the Royal Prince, Lord,
And sent his body straight to the graveyard.
Hey: The poor Harishchandra cried to God
For His shelter and prayed to Him
To save his integrity and honour.

The Banjaras were up at the crack of dawn. Before leaving Pindwara for Udaipur, they finished their morning chores by collecting water with the help of a *lota* (a small metal vessel), tied to a string and lowering it into a well. Overruling many objections, Mema Bhil accompanied the *dera* (the group of Banjaras). Covering a distance of about 10 *kos* (one *kos* = two miles) a day, the *dera* took about 10–12 days to reach Udaipur. They had to spend some time in Udaipur for business reasons. Mema Bhil took leave of them.

Mema did not know where to go. He had nowhere to go; no one was waiting for him at home. Like a floating dried leaf of a tree, he was drifting with the wind of the time. He took the route to Banswara. The wandering, illiterate Mema had taken many knocks in life but that did not break him because he had gathered a lot of experience as well. Dark and short in height, barely 5 ft 3 inches, his eyes were yellow like the light from the setting sun on a clear day. But despite poverty and hardships, these eyes did not show despondency. Though uprooted early in life, he was not willing to concede defeat. The discourses of Sadhu Sengaji and the company of nomadic Banjaras had taught him a lot. When his father died, the village Bhopa had given him an amulet in lieu of five *sers* (unit of weight around one kg) of maize. He wore it round his neck. At that time the Bhopa had predicted, "You will marry a girl from a rich family and your indigence will not stand in the way". The forecast had proved false. He had crossed 40. Mema immediately thought of the 'magicians' Sengaji had spoken about. He smashed the amulet. Mema stopped over at Sura Bawadi, 14–16 miles from Udaipur.

A man was addressing a crowd of 50–100 adivasis at a hamlet, 200–300 yards away from Sura Bawadi.

"The famine has been terrible. Not a grain for people to eat. There is no fodder for the cattle. Our right to fruits, vegetables and other vegetations in the forests has been taken away by the Raj. Now we have to take permission from the representatives of the Raj to collect these things and, worse, we will have to pay for them. For centuries we have been collecting money from wayfarers. It was not extortion; it was our inherited right to seek payment for ensuring safe passage to those who traversed our territory. The Raj has imposed a ban on this custom. The state had never done so; it is all because of these white men. The system of *begar* continues like before. We have been tolerating it. But now all limits have been crossed. There is famine and we still have to do daily *begar*. Should we do free labour with empty stomachs or earn a living somewhere?

"I am conveying the message of Govind Guru. He talks of dharma, not about ways to attack the enemy. The Raj will not listen to our complaints if we do not attack. Hundreds of adivasis like me toiled day and night to establish Sampsabhas. When

Guru framed the rules of Sampsabhas, it dealt with matters relating to dharma and social reforms. I am not opposed to them. All this is necessary. The bad social practices must end. We must rid ourselves of wrong habits. But I must raise my concerns about the lagan on our lands, restrictions and levies on forest produce, *begar* and other atrocities. State officials, jagirdars do not hesitate to dishonour our sisters and daughters.

"All adivasis living in Vagad-Mewar, Gujarat, Khandesh and Malwa are equal. People in the Raj mislead us. They say 'you're a Bhil, you're a Damore, you're a Meena, you're a gameti, you belong to this community, this is your local territory, you belong to that clan, that is your sub-caste.' They spread lies that our ancestors were not at peace with each other. These talks are designed to divide us. Our ancestors had united to fight for their rights and they won. You don't know that in ancient times we had our own rulers, our rajas and maharajas. No outsider could rule over us. A sadhu had announced at a fair in Benesar Dham that Dungarpur was founded by Dungar Bhil. Banswara was named after Bansya Bhil. Similarly, Bundi was named after Bundi Meena and Kota took its name from Kotya Bhil. These Rajput outsiders took away our states and now they rule over us. It is these Rajput rulers who have called the foreigners. Together they are now sucking our blood. The loan sharks and traders are their friends. They do not allow us to be free of debts. Our troubles will not go away if we do not stand united to fight them."

The audience of adivasis listened to all this with great attention. A lot of what was being said made sense to them. Mema was listening with the same attention with which he had listened to Sengaji Maharaj.

The speaker of these good words was Kuriya Danot, an associate of Govind Guru. Mema got introduced to Kuriya. They were very pleased to meet each other. Kuriya was impressed by Mema's intelligence and his reference to Sengaji Sadhu. Kuriya particularly liked what Mema had recalled about Sengaji Sadhu. "Sengaji Sadhu says that you cannot achieve anything unless you have a Guru."

"Yes, brother Mema! You're right. Nothing can be achieved unless you've a Guru. Govind Guru also says so. He also learnt his wisdom from his Guru," Kuriya said thoughtfully.

They decided to go back to Govind Guru at Mangarh. For the last month or month and a half, Kuriya had made Sura Bawadi his headquarter. He would visit neighbouring villages to promote the Sampsabha ideology and explain his views. He also met two–three willing followers who left their homes to be part of his group. Sura Bawadi was left behind. Accompanied by Mema, these four–five adivasis left for Mangarh.

It was said of Sura Bawadi that it was an ancient place and was built by Lord Bhole Nath with his own hands. Lord Shiv with his consort Parvati had lived there for a long time. Apart from their folk gods, it was only lord Shiva whom the adivasis had worshiped from ancient times. Many small Shiv temples dotted this area. It is said that before they went on any battle, the adivasis would drink water from Sura Bawadi. It was a belief that such was the effect of the water of Sura Bawadi that after drinking it, the adivasis never lost any battle.

Also, there was a hearsay that about a generation ago a Jain saint had done penance there. He breathed his last while still in the state of worshipping. The Jains wanted to construct a temple in his memory. But the superstitious adivasis opposed it saying, "If a Jain temple is constructed then Jain sadhus will control the rain gods, and wherever that happens they do not allow it to rain. They tie up the clouds with incantation". The adivasis announced that a Shiv temple would be constructed there. It is said that for days tension prevailed between the two communities. A little distance away was a small village inhabited by Oswal Jains. They left it to settle in Udaipur during those days. After the Maharana's intervention, no temple was built at the site.

Beneshwar at the tri-junction of Mahi, Jakham and Som rivers was a place known far and wide. It came to be called the *kumbh* of adivasis. Sabla was a village next to it. Kuriya and his companions learnt there that Govind Guru was at Kahvada village. Fifteen years ago, there they had established dhooni, a place of holy fire. Kuriya himself had been a keen participant in that event.

It was afternoon. The adivasis had returned to their villages after listening to Govind Guru's morning discourse. On a platform under the neem tree sat Govind Guru with his 20–30 disciples.

Kuriya's heart was shaking like a peepal leaf. He was angry with himself as he realised that Govind Guru knew everything though he had not told him anything. two–three young men who had just left Govind Guru's dhooni were singing this bhajan (prayer) as they walked.

> Do keep in thy heart the words of the Master
> And never ever flout the moral laws of life.
> Never renounce the faith in finer feelings
> And live together in harmony as a unit
> O brethren mine!

A little hesitant, Kuriya went up to Govind Guru and touched his feet.

"Where were you Kuriya Bhagat?" he said, patting his shoulders. Govind Guru was not at all surprised on seeing Kuriya after so many days. He looked calm with a friendly expression on his face. Poonja Dhira and other bhagats present there did look surprised though, wondering where Kuriya had been all these days. They had looked for him here and there on the Guru's orders. Kuriya held on to Guru's feet as he cried. The Guru hugged him.

"Good that you have come back, Kuriya! We are all very happy. Now tell us where all have you been?" Govind Guru asked him as he looked at those who had come with Kuriya and had touched his feet. Kuriya narrated his story. What Govind Guru and other heard from him about Sengaji Sadhu impressed them a lot. After about a week, Govind Guru and his followers left for Balwani village.

EIGHT

The Dungarpur Darbar

Maharawal Vijay Singh was sitting on the throne, attired in a white *achkan* (long coat), a dress of gold and silver lace, a Hydrabadi pearl necklace, a neatly folded round Mewari turban on head with a white *turra* tucked in its fold just above the forehead and a sword fixed to his waist. His face was taut. Even as he glanced around, his eyes had framed the short stature of Govind Guru.

"So, now you have started inciting the adivasis?" he demanded to know, as his eyes turned dark red.

"No, Maharaj! What are you saying? I'm like a sadhu. I'm trying to rid the adivasis of their bad habits and I also talk to them about piety."

"We know about this talk of piety. You talk of ending *begar*, abuse the British and, we are told, also raise fingers at us." His left hand was on the armrest of the throne. As he spoke that hand started to twist the armrest and the right hand moved towards the sword's hilt.

"Maharaj, I don't talk ill of you. But the jagirdar, thikanedar and officers of the state harass adivasis almost daily. Such news must be reaching your ears also. And…?"

"You worry about what news reaches the darbar and what people under us do! It does not worry you that these Bhils and Meenas loot wayfarers, commit thefts and robbery and create nuisance? I had heard that you're a decent man and had come to the darbar a couple of times previously. Why have you started working against the Raj?" Maharawal Vijay Singh interrupted Govind Guru. He was beginning to mellow a little, but his tone was still tough.

"Maharaj, if you really want to wish your subjects well then please do something about the unrest that has spread in this area. People are migrating to Malwa and Khandesh. There has been no crop last year and this year. All wells, step-wells, rivers, nullahs and ponds have gone dry. There is no water to drink. Most of the cattle are dead. The rotting filth is spreading diseases. There is no arrangement for medicine and healthcare. Hunger, thirst and epidemic have spread everywhere," said Govind Guru with courage.

"Drought is God's curse. It has always led to hunger, thirst and disease. Because of this scourge, the treasury of the Raj has gone empty. In the adivasi areas the sale of liquor has drastically gone down. The income from ganja (hemp), bhang (cannabis), opium and tobacco has been affected. For this you alone are responsible. I don't say that the use of these intoxicants is good for health. But the world knows that it helps those who toil day and night to relax."

"Pardon me Sir. I don't accept that any intoxicant really helps a person relax. Intoxication of any kind makes both the body and mind sick. After the adivasis started giving up intoxication, thousands of families have been saved from ruination. Disputes and fights have decreased. Conditions in families have improved..."

"All right! I don't want to argue on this subject. You were talking about famine. So listen, we had arranged for grain and fodder. Didn't you know about it?" The Maharawal changed the topic after he had become defensive on the issue of intoxication.

"Maharaj, you have certainly arranged for grain and fodder for the famine victims. But the fact is that the middlemen are stealing this relief material. Only a small quantity reaches your subjects. The adivasis living in distant areas have not received any relief material."

Maharawal looked somewhat surprised. Govind Guru was not entirely wrong. The Maharawal feared that if the Raj did not come to the rescue of the adivasis at this hour of their travail, they might rise in revolt. He was also aware of Govind Guru's popularity among the adivasis and his leadership qualities. After considering all this, the Maharawal said: "Look, Govind. I've heard only sketchy accounts about you. It is possible that there is an exaggeration in what has been conveyed to me. It is not wrong to work for the eradication of bad habits among the adivasis. It is commendable that you are working for famine relief. But you will concede this much that these Bhils and Meenas can be incited easily. They are not very sagacious and can be easily provoked. You also know about their revolt against the Raj. Extorting money from wayfarers and refusing to do *begar* or refusing to pay lagan, you know all this is wrong. The situation will deteriorate if these activities continue. We want to end such wrong activities and also that the relief work for the adivasis should progress satisfactorily. Why don't you help the Raj in this work? I shall assign you five villages. You shall get the powers of a Thakur. You'll not be short of funds."

"Pardon me, Maharaj. I am a sadhu. These villages and jagirs are God's gift to you. You take care of them. My job is to work among the adivasis. Please let me continue to serve them."

"This power of a Thakur will not be granted to you for any ostentatious purpose. It'll be a sort of title to help you work for the relief of the adivasis. With this power no one will oppose you and you'll find it easier to work."

"No honour need be bestowed to help mankind. I'm doing my work according to the traditions of saints. Please allow me to continue doing that." As he spoke, Govind Guru was troubled with the thought that the young Maharawal was insulting a bhagat like him. He may be a ruler but he was not mature enough. He laughed within himself over the Maharawal's childishness, though he did not let it reflect on his face.

The Maharawal was hurt by Govind Guru's words even though he was impressed by the greatness of his personality. The handful of trusted lieutenants of the Maharawal who were present there raised their eyebrows in disapproval. Presently, the Maharawal's face also became taut. The quilt-like fan attached to the ceiling of the darbar appeared to move slower.

On the wall behind the throne were large paintings of the previous Maharawal Uday Singh and Maharana Pratap. Looking at them, Govind Guru continued: "Rajaji, please remember Maharana Pratap. He fought the emperor of India for the sake of independence. He did not accept slavery. The adivasis supported him with their body and soul. The world knows that the adivasi fighters were the real power of Maharana Pratap, who had blind faith in them. Why have things changed today? Why had the adivasis been angry with the Raj even before I started my efforts to create awareness among them? Wasn't the power of the state working against them? Groaning under the twin attack of the Raj and the British can these adivasis be expected to be loyal to the Raj? Are you not aware of the atrocities committed on the adivasis by the officers of the Raj? Have you seen how these adivasis suffer from hunger, poverty and disease? Have you ever thought how hard an adivasi works and what does he get in the end?" Govind Guru was emotional.

The Maharawal was taken aback. He consulted Diwan Ganesh Ram, who was also listening to Govind Guru, in whispering tones.

"Govind! I wanted to respect you. But you are becoming too defiant. What you are saying is treason. I give you the last warning. Will you listen to me or keep inciting the crude and quarrelsome adivasis?"

"I'll fight against injustice," Govind Guru said after a pause, expressing his opinion firmly, as tension permeated the darbar.

"Shut up! Take him away from me! Arrest him!"

Divan Ganesh Ram did not agree with the Maharawal's one-sided decision to arrest Govind Guru. The Maharawal had taken that decision in a fit of rage. There was only one way to reverse that decision, and that was that Govind Guru sought his pardon. But that was impossible. In fact, after the death of Maharawal Uday Singh, Vijay Singh succeeded him in 1898, but being barely 16 years of age he did not get the powers of the ruler. These powers were with the Regent Council, headed by the Assistant Resident. Divan Ganesh Ram was a member of that council and he was of the view that an important decision like the arrest of Govind Guru should have been left to the council.

Govind Guru was sent to prison.

The news of his arrest spread like wildfire in the entire adivasi belt. They did not have communication facilities, but they had traditional medium of communication.

About a dozen of his closest associates arrived in certain important points in the adivasi belt. At their level they hurriedly gathered some volunteers. Messages were conveyed to villages verbally. In the hilly hamlets people were gathered by the loud beats of drums. The news of Govind Guru's arrest was relayed through shouting from treetops. The prominent panch, patels and *gametis* who thought that their importance had declined because of the expanding influence of Govind Guru and his associates, also stood up against his arrest. Protestors began to assemble at different places.

After the formation of Sampsabha, Govind Guru had become a popular mass leader in the adivasi area of the Vagad region. For the elderly, adult, youth, women and children, "Jai Guru Maharaj" was not just a friendly greeting but a slogan for uniting adivasis. The Sampsabha had been formed for a clear purpose. It was for ending the widespread habit of drinking among adivasis, resolving mutual disputes, a clean daily life, staying away from criminal tendencies, and on cultural-religious front to discard the family traditions of worshipping ancestors and identifying families on the basis of their sub-castes and to replace them with the belief in one God. The organisation extended all support to its disciples, especially those who had become bhagats who wore rudraksha necklace and cleansed their minds and ideas by performing havans. In brief, the Sampsabha movement was confined to social reforms and that remained its main purpose till the end.

Meanwhile, political fronts were being opened against atrocities that were being committed by the nexus of princely states and the British. Govind Guru had acquired the halo of a great man of deliverance. People touched his feet and treated his words as a command. His fame spread not only in the adivasi-Rajputana areas of Dungarpur, Banswara, Udaipur and Sirohi but also in adjacent areas, in Gujarat. The number of adivasis attending his discourses went up to thousands from hundreds. Havans were being performed in every village. Wearing rudraksha necklaces, bhagats and their adivasi followers were uniting people against oppressive practices of the rajas, jagirdars and their minions. They toured extensively to proclaim the end of *begar* system and it had a positive impact. The few literate among these adivasis bore the additional duty of informally teaching adivasi children how to read and write. The news of adivasi anti-slavery movement became known over a very wide area.

Under the leadership of Govind Guru, the first big conference of the adivasis had taken place in Suranta village, where the formation of Sampsabha was announced formally. In subsequent years, Govind Guru intensified his efforts to unite adivasis. He became the supreme leader fighting for adivasis.

Since the last few years, people in Vagad were suffering due to poor monsoon and a severe drought hit the area in 1898. Corresponded to the Vikram Samvat year 1956, it had come to be known as the *chchappanya* (fifty–six). There was shortage of food and fodder. There was unrest and tumult all around and many diseases like cholera were spreading like epidemic. The sole goal before Govind Guru was to ensure that relief reached all affected adivasis. He had called a second big conference of adivasis in Basiya, which was also known as Chhani Magari.

As conditions worsened, he consulted his close associates, the bhagats, to make sure that they showed more zeal and courage in working for the affected people. By this time, the initial circle of Govind Guru's associates had enlarged from Poonja Dhirji, Kuriya Danot, Surtya Meena and Nanji Garasiya to include Kalji, Thano Lala, Jorji Lakhji Lembar, Nagji and many others who had become popular as second-rung heroes.

The work that Govind Guru had taken up at the beginning of chappanya was very important for the welfare of the adivasis. Guided by his associates, the adivasis were fighting natural calamity at their own levels. This was the time the adivasis heard the shocking news of Govind Guru's arrest. Another news spread in the area with lightening speed: The British had hanged Joriya Bhagat.

In Revakantha and Panchmahal jungles of neighbouring Gujarat lived the adivasis of Nayakdas Khanp (sect). Amongst them was born Joriya Nayakdas in Badek village near Jambugoda. Wherever he travelled he used to raise this query: "Why do we, the adivasis, who do not like to be dependent on anyone, agree to do *begar* for the Indian rulers who are subject to the British authority? Why is our traditional right to the produce of the jungle being taken away?" He had only one reply, that the adivasis were not united in opposing the erosion of their rights.

He succeeded in organising the adivasis of the area. The people endorsed the purpose and methods of Joriya. They began to see him as a liberator. He had a religious touch in his message. "The achievements of our ancestors made them a part of the divine and such people are the true bhagats. A result of this message was that adivasis began to regard Joriya as a bhagat devoted to God and called him, Joriya Bhagat. One of his associates was Roopa Nayakdas."

As a result of the treaties between the native states and the British during 1818–1848, the princely states of Gujarat came under indirect British rule. Resident commissioners were appointed to keep an eye on the states. They kept the East India Company headquarters in Calcutta (Kolkata) informed of developments. After the 1857 mutiny, everything came under direct British rule. Joriya Bhagat's agitation became a challenge for the British because by then their supremacy had been established over the entire area.

Roopa had a burning desire to free his motherland. Joriya and Roopa joined hands to oppose tax on agriculture. It was known to all that the lagan was recovered by employees of the state. A large part of it went to the British, who used to help the states with their army to suppress the anti-lagan agitation. When the government stepped up its campaign against the anti-lagan agitation, adivasis responded by rallying behind the leadership of Joriya and Roopa.

The Rajgarh police station was the centre of activities aimed at curbing the adivasi revolt led by Joriya. Under his leadership the adivasis decided to attack the police station. Thousands of adivasis gathered outside the police station. A uniformed policeman at the gate of the police station asked the adivasi leaders in the front row: "What is it in Joriya that makes all of you follow him?"

Joriya was among those standing in the front. But the policeman did not recognise him. As Joriya kept quiet, an agitated adivasi, Nayak Galaliya, took out his sword and acting on an impulse severed the policeman's neck. The other men and officers at the police station ran helter-skelter and escaped. The adivasis took over Rajgarh police station. An adivasi delegation left for Jambugoda. On the way it clashed with the police and chased them away.

The British reacted with rage to this news and dispatched soldiers carrying arms to suppress the revolt. In the jungles near Jambugoda, the adivasis armed with traditional bow and arrow, swords, spears and pikes bravely confronted the armed forces.

But how long could they stand against the rain of bullets from rifles and machine guns? Joriya Bhagat thought it wiser to end the confrontation. Many adivasis had already become martyrs. He ordered his followers to retreat to Badek village. The British army chased them. The retreating adivasis kept fighting the British forces as they looked for safety in the hilly and forest areas. Instead, they found themselves trapped in an unsafe place with water all around. They were surrounded by the British, who showered a hail of bullets on them. Hundreds of adivasis were killed. Some of them managed to escape into the jungle. The British forces were, however, unable to capture Joriya Bhagat, Roopa and Galaliya.

The British knew this for sure that unless these three, especially Joriya, were arrested, it will be impossible to quell the revolt. Keeping this in mind, the chase of the adivasi leaders was not given up. On the pretext of searching all possible places of hiding of their leaders, many atrocities were committed on the adivasis. They were arrested, tortured in prison, and some were offered allurements to spill the beans on their leaders.

The three were not willing to leave their areas. How could they quit their activities after giving a clarion call for freedom? The inevitable arrest of the three followed and they were charged with treason. That was used as an excuse to hang them.

The harassment of the adivasis was widely prevalent at the time. They would be arrested under any pretext and killed in fake encounters. Whenever a revolt was smelt, the potential leaders would be slapped with false charges and awarded stiff sentences or the death sentence. This kind of naked oppression had become common.

Joriya Bhagat was not an ordinary adivasi. He was an extremely devoted person and the adivasis looked up to him as a god. The leaderless adivasis may have become quiet for a while, some of them may have shifted to other places, and many may have died in the battle, but the fire of revolt was burning in them. The flame raging inside them was to explode later.

The followers of Govind Guru, especially in Dungarpur state, were familiar with the name of Joriya Bhagat, who along with his associates was sent to the gallows a little before the arrest of Govind Guru. All this information trickled across the length and breadth of Dungarpur state. It was confirmed by adivasis from Revkantha, Rajgarh, and Jambugoda who had escaped arrest. For adivasis, already angry over Govind Guru's arrest, the news added fuel to fire.

The sepoys at Khairwada cantonment were in a jovial mood after finishing their evening meals. It was autumn, a time of gentle breeze. At 30 degrees to the east was shining the moon, spreading its pleasing light everywhere. From behind the fence on the western boundary of the cantonment came a singing voice.

The black cuckoo'd love to be in the forest
And in the forest she'd stay long, feeding on the fruits.
On the fruits she'd feed and drink from the pond
And roost on the mango or mahua tree.
Who did she wait for?
Lo! over there above the valley twinkles
The colourful crest of the groom's turban.
Here comes the groom at last.

Sepoy Rajia, number 423, was sitting alone on a stone slab under an old wild fig tree behind the mess. He had been sitting there much before the musical notes reached his ears. He was low in spirits because he had learnt in the morning that his childhood friend, Kubera, was going to be married soon. He had applied for leave, but Subedar Major Roopji had turned it down, much to his disappointment.

The song made him nostalgic about his village. It also brought memories of his beloved, Sangi. When Rajia joined the Bhil Corpse, Sangi had tried to dissuade him. The families of Rajia and Sangi had agreed to their marriage. She belonged to a neighbouring village. The two had fallen in love while grazing goats and it was to culminate happily into matrimony. As a sepoy, Rajia would be spending a lot of his time living in a distant place and it would not be possible for him to live with his wife. That is why despite an earlier agreement, Sangi's father decided against marrying his daughter to him. Rajia came to know later that Sangi had been married off to someone else. The day he learnt it, he had cried a lot. Today he again remembered Sangi. He had even toyed with the idea of running away to village and kidnap Sangi. But that was not possible.

One of the merry-making sepoys at the mess, Dhanna, number 329, went towards the rear of the building to relieve himself. He saw Rajia.

"Brother Rajia, what is the matter that you are sitting all by yourself?"

"Dhanna, my pal, I don't know what to tell you."

"Look, we are employees of the Raj, and in the army. Are we in need of anything? We have plenty to eat and clothes to wear, we learn good skills and at the end of the training we'll get a good pay packet every month, which will help our parents fight poverty, and they'll be pleased."

"What you say is right. But my engagement has been called off and you know it. Now, a close friend of mine is getting married and I have been refused even a short leave. This is how we are shackled." As he completed his sentence there appeared a brown rabbit from behind a bush and it hopped towards a mango tree a little away.

"Look, Dhanna. This rabbit lives within the boundary of the cantonment, still he roams freely the way he likes. We can't do everything that we like."

"Can we keep our hearths burning by following our wishes? Here, at least we get enough to fill our stomachs. This bonded life is better than living a life of hunger and want. Understand this and be happy. Now, get up and join the fun with the friends. We have to be up early tomorrow. Come with me. You'll feel light."

Rajia dragged Dhanna to the company of the rest of the friends. On a request from sepoy Teja, Dhanna recalled a story that he had heard in the village:

"Two brothers lived in a village. Once there was a severe famine. There was nothing to eat or drink. One night the two brothers went out to steal. On the way a ghost in the form of a man met them. The ghost asked them, 'Where are you going?' They replied, 'To steal.' The ghost took them home and gave them roti and fish to eat. The brothers asked for his leave after they had finished their meals. But the ghost decided to accompany them. The three entered the house of a bard with the intention of committing theft. The ghost liked the drum that he found in the house and expressed a desire to play it. The brothers advised him against it. 'Return the rotis and fish that I gave you for eating or else I'll play the drum.' But the food was in their stomach and they could not have returned it. The ghost played the drum loudly, waking up people in the village. They chased away the thieves who hid in the forest. They saw a wild buffalo on the way. The ghost said, 'I'll call the buffalo.' The brothers said, 'No, you'll not.' The ghost hit back: 'Return my roti and fish or I call the buffalo.' The ghost called the buffalo. With the buffalo in hot pursuit, the two brothers hid themselves in a lion's den. The lion was sleeping soundly. The buffalo waited for the brothers at the entrance of the den. The two brothers were sandwiched between the lion and the buffalo. The ghost said, 'I'll wake up the lion.' When the brothers pleaded with him against it, he demanded his rotis and fish. Impossible! The ghost woke up the lion. An enraged lion came out of his den and in the ensuing melee killed the buffalo. Devouring half the buffalo, the lion went to the river to drink water. The two brothers hiding in a corner in the den came out and taking a portion of the buffalo rushed to hide on a tree in the jungle.

"It was summer time. The wedding party of a Mahajan trader was resting under the tree. The ghost said, 'I'm throwing the buffalo meat down.' He repeated his condition when the brothers asked him not to do so. Again, it was going to be impossible to meet his condition. The ghost threw the meat piece down the tree. It scared the Mahajan party and they ran away, leaving their valuables including jewellery on the spot. The three of them collected the valuables and left. They stopped at a place and divided the booty into three parts. The ghost said, 'I am a ghost. What will I do with the jewellery and coins? You two brothers divide it between you.' The two brothers merrily brought all the wealth home and began to live a lavish life."

"Your story is fascinating. But it's hard to swallow the part about the ghost," Teja said with a puzzled expression on his face.

"Yes, Teja is right. Hakim (jail officer) had said that all this talk about ghosts, witches and sorcery is nothing but superstition. Isn't it so?" Rajia said in support of Teja, but with some reservations because the influence of traditions and old beliefs still existed in his mind.

Subedar Major Roopaji in the meanwhile, came that way while going round the cantonment. As soon as they sighted him, one by one all the sepoys went back to their barracks.

NINE

Thavara, the son of Gopi Gameti of Jharkara village, was returning to his village after about 15 years. He had suddenly disappeared one night. Govind Guru had formed the Sampsabha by then. There were about 100 or 125 houses in Jharkara and the nearby villages of Movai and Tamta. In these and some other villages close by lived mainly the adivasis of Pargi sub-caste. Gopi Gameti was the chief of these adivasis. A whisper had spread that Gopi's son wanted to work as jagarti, a motivator for awareness campaigns of the Sampsabha. Gopi Gameti was opposed to it. After all, Thavara was his only child.

Gopi had stopped his son from attending Sampsabha meetings, telling him: "A king's son becomes a king, a mukhiya's son becomes a mukhiya and a gameti's son becomes a gameti." He did not like the idea that a gameti's son should spend his life with a babaji and lead the life of an ascetic. It was just not acceptable to him.

Gopi was overcome by repentance after his son left home. He spared no effort to trace him, but all in vain. Gopi was a stubborn and somewhat unpleasant sort of a fellow. He was not used to allowing anyone his say, though he was famous as a *panch* who delivered the right judgement in the panchayat. But he found it impossible to overcome his guilt after his son's disappearance. After a while, the doubts in his mind about Govind Guru disappeared. He enrolled himself as an active member of the Sampsabha.

He hugged his son on his return; his joy was evident from the tears of joy that flowed from his eyes. He felt as though he had got back a lost treasure.

The news of Govind Guru's arrest deeply shocked Gopi. But the joy at his son's return made him forget all that. He questioned his son in detail about his life and acquainted him with adivasis' organisation, the Sampsabha. For Thavra, it was a matter of satisfaction that he would now be able to work for the Sampsabha without any hindrance.

Gopi had taken a decision all by himself and announced it by loud beating of drums. In no time, the news spread like fire and drew adivasis in droves to the low hilly area, called Magra, at Jharkara village. By afternoon around 1,200 adivasis gathered at the place.

In normal course, wheat and mustard crops should have been in full bloom at the time. There should have been a big green cover all over the jungle and hills. Most important, people should have looked contended and their cattle should have been grazing there. All this had become a mirage.

The harsh fact of a famine! Never before such a bad time had been seen or heard. It was the same *chchappanya* famine that had previously hit many parts of the country. Half-fed, half-naked people, starving cattle with many skeletons and rotting corpses strewn all over, parched land and thirsty life! But despite all that life must go on, the will to live defied defeat, fatigue.

The adivasis assembled at the Magra in response to the drum beats. The crowd was talking in soft whispers. Most of them had heard about Govind Guru's arrest. They also knew that Gopi's son, Thavara, had returned home after many years. Everyone assumed that they would be told to protest against the arrest of Govind Guru.

After hearing about the arrest of Govind Guru, Poonja Dhirji, Kuriya Bhagat and other functionaries of the Sampsabha mounted on camels to tour the area. They were propagating a simple line wherever they went: "Govind Guru left his home for our good and the Maharawal arrested him, which is unjust. Guru has committed no crime. We must oppose his arrest."

At another level, the other members of Sampsabha were preparing a strategy to get Govind Guru released. They rushed to Jharkara. They had assumed that the adivasis were being summoned there to protest against the arrest of Govind Guru. But it turned out to be something else that completely stumped Poonja, Kuriya and their associates.

"Gopi Gameti's son has returned. There is Diwali at Gopi's house. He wants to host a community feast for the people of the area. Preparations for the feast have been on throughout the day. There can be no bigger joyous occasion for him," someone commented.

"It's good that the Gameti's son is back. For him it is a matter of immense happiness. For us too! But it is incomprehensible that as a Sampsabha member Gopi would host a feast. Govind Guru has been arrested. It is our foremost duty to get him released. Should we forget him and rejoice with Gopi?" Kuriya asked at the top of his voice, standing on a high platform.

Most people were thinking about what they had heard from Thavara. They turned their attention to Kuriya when they heard his angry loud voice. People started crowding around him. Poonja Dhiraj was standing next to Kuriya, lending his silent support to him.

"What's wrong in it? Gopi Gameti is a popular figure of the area. He has some money too. If a well-to-do family spends money to celebrate an occasion like this and orders a feast for the community what's so bad about it," someone in the crowd shouted.

Nobody paid attention to his words. The attention of the people was riveted to Kuriya Bhagat. Even children were familiar with the names of Kuriya and Poonja.

Kuriya was a tough man who believed in blunt talk. He was short, his complexion dark, his eyes bronze, his nose flat and his round pock marked face had an untidy beard but a curly moustache. This man, who had never had enough clothes, no proper roof over his head, was addressing the crowd. The assembly had lent its ears to him, reading the impressive expression on his face. Kuriya was turning into a noble personality, an honest darling of the hills; he was the epitome of confidence.

The sun was about to set. Irrespective of the time of the year, the setting sun always looks bigger than the rising sun. Is it because the rising sun has to serve the universe the whole day while the setting sun goes to rest for the night? In the haziness over the western horizon, the sun went down with its tired rays.

"Gopi Kaka, is the happiness of your son's return bigger than the blow we have received from the arrest of Govind Guru? Is it an occasion that demands that we overlook his arrest?" Kuriya asked Gopi as he pushed his way through the crowd.

"Perhaps for me, but not for all of us," Gopi replied.

"In that case, are all these preparations for the feast justified?"

"Kuriya, you are a bachelor. What do you know of affection for family? Do you recall how I wandered like a mad man around the valley for months after the death of my wife? The roar of the lion and my wife's last shrieks when he devoured her still echo in my ears, and when Thavara disappeared how lonely did I find myself? I was completely broken from inside. The restrictions I had placed on my son against visiting the Sampsabha used to trouble me. Now that he has come back after 15 years I am naturally extremely happy and I want to share this happiness with my brethrens. That's why the drum calls had gone out. What wrong have I committed? You tell me."

Kuriya looked at Thavara's face who was sitting by the side of Gopi. He remained silent.

"And think about this too, Kuriya, that the people who have assembled here have been hungry since morning. In this time of famine when do they get two square meals a day? I've saved some grain, rice and vegetable. All this has to be used for the good of the needy. I'll support whatever all of you decide to get Govind Guru released."

After listening to an emotional speech of Gopi, Poonja, Kuriya and other members of the Sampsabha and all those who had assembled agreed to join the feast. They helped in preparing a meal of rice, maize rotis and a dish of mahua vegetable. After a late night dinner, all of them decided to leave for Dungarpur at the crack of dawn and put pressure on the Maharawal for the release of Govind Guru.

The tales brought by Thavara were the subject of night-long conversations among the assembled people. They were tired and needed rest, but only some of them were able to get a proper sleep.

What Thavara had told them was something like this: Thavara could not sleep the entire night when he was not allowed to join the Sampsabha. He leapt out of the string cot on which he was sleeping two–three times at night and wandered aimlessly. Over the western horizon, three stars of Hirni (a form of constellation in southern sky called Canis Major) had descended to 45 degrees, that is to say it was the beginning of the third phase of the night. Except for the clothes that he was wearing and a bamboo staff (lathi), he carried nothing else.

By sunrise he reached the Anas River. He bathed in the river. By afternoon he reached Bansala village, where he had food at an adivasi's house and rested for a while. He did not disclose his identity to his host. By late evening he was in Banswara town. He spent the night there and early in the morning he again moved on. He had no idea where the path in the hills and jungles would take him. After two days he was in the central province. By night he found himself trapped in the middle of a forest. There was no sign of any inhabitation for miles. He decided to pitch his tent on a plateau near a jamun tree. He had no choice but to spend the night empty stomach. Had it been daytime he might have tried to look for some fruit or vegetable in the jungle. But waking up trees and plants at night is a sin—that is what his traditions had taught him.

Collecting some dried branches, he lit a fire with a flint. He used to carry in the pocket of his *bandi* (a waistcoat) two small pieces of a stone and piece of string. He did not fear the jungles, except the wild animals and poisonous snakes and scorpions. Fire was an easy and safe way to ward off this danger. Thavara was at peace with himself and prepared to sleep for the night. It was the best course for someone who had remained hungry the whole day and was tired too. He did manage to sleep.

Suddenly he was shaken by a stranger's hands. He got up by start. The fire had weakened long ago. The ambers were still smouldering. The gentle breeze was lighting up few splinters in the ashes. It was from the light from these splinters that Thavara saw the man who had shaken him. He could not recognise his face. The man had placed his right hand on Thavara's lathi. About 10–12 feet away was a group of men, all carrying arms.

"Who are you and why have you come here?" asked the man, looking suspiciously at Thavara. Taking the men to be dacoits, Thavara shook in fear and said nothing.

"Are you someone fleeing from the police or a police informer?" asked the same man.

"I…I…" was all that he could manage to mutter.

"Don't be afraid. I am Tantya Bhil. I am fighting for the rights of adivasis. Calm down and tell me who are you?"

"I'm Thavara, a Bhil of Pargi sub-caste. I've come from Dungarpur." The fear in Thavara dissolved into thin air after listening to Tantya Bhil. He was totally composed. He narrated his story to Tantya and also told him about Govind Guru and Sampsabha's activities. The group with Tantya had some youth from the Korku Banjara tribe and some from the Bhil community. A couple of the Banjaras had heard Govind's name because they were distantly related to him. Govind's name was not exactly unknown to Tantya either. But all that he knew was that under the influence of a saintly figure, Govind, a Banjara, had become a sadhu (saint), preaching the adivasis of the Vagad area to give up their bad habits. The Tantya gang knew nothing about what Govind Guru was doing to protect the rights of the adivasis and his fight against oppression.

Tantya and his associates were happy to learn about the activities of Govind Guru. Tantya was tall and stocky with a bulging chest, strong arms, sharp eyes, taut face, a uniquely shiny broad forehead and curly long hair. His moustache looked like an extension of his beard. A dirty cloth was wrapped across his legs as dhoti and he wore a half-sleeved blouse of dotted brick-red colour. On his left shoulder slung a rifle tied to a leather strap and live cartridges in a casement that spread across from his right shoulder to the left. His shoulders also carried a bow and by its side a brown quiver of pointed arrows, while a dagger was tied to his waist.

Because of the generous financial help he would offer for the marriage of poor adivasi girls in the area, Tantya was famous as Mama (maternal uncle). Tantya led a gang of 15–20 men who also looked strong and fierce like him. He had by then thousands of followers who looked up to him as a hero or a superman. People had started advising patients of serious ailments and victims of epidemics to wear amulets and talisman bearing Tantya's name.

The dialogue between Tantya Mama and Thavara continued till dawn. For Tantya it was a safe forest and he and his companions knew each and every corner of it.

It was 25 March 1884. On March 24, Tantya's gang had attacked a zamindar of Melghat for revenge. A joint police team of the British and the Holkar state had fanned out to arrest him. Tantya was in the habit of issuing advance warning about his impending revenge attack. Despite the police being aware of this practice of Tantya, he was able to attack the zamindar. But the police managed to surround him. There was a fierce exchange. Lachman, a member of Tantya's gang, was injured after a bullet hit him. The police whisked away the injured man to the police station. As soon as they learnt it, the Tantya gang intensified the attack. The senior officer in the police party was killed, which immediately caused a panic in the leaderless police contingent. The Tantya gang escaped into the forest where they ran into Thavara Pargi.

Tantya read the thoughts that came to the mind of Thavara and invited him to join his gang, which he did gladly. He was now an active member of Tantya Mama's gang.

After the encounter at Melghat, the campaign for the arrest of Tantya intensified. Only a little earlier, the British and Holkar police had formed a special "Tantya Police" group to trace and arrest him. But it had no success. The incident at Melghat was a challenge for the Raj. It had seen a senior police officer killed and this had demoralised the police force. In view of this, the Holkar Maharaj had specially selected Captain Mehmood Khan to nab Tantya. In another encounter a few months later, a policeman died of bullet injury.

A few days later, an associate of Tantya, Dauliya, was arrested. Tantya retaliated by attacking more fiercely. His victims were zamindars and lagan recovery agents who were despotic, and other oppressive officers of the Raj. Tantya was relentless in launching his attacks and took revenge for each of the oppressive acts against the adivasis.

Meanwhile, the police arrested two more members of his gang, Bhauliya and Auliya. The cleverness shown by a sepoy, Bapumang, posted at the police post in Sugan Banjari village, played a key role in this arrest. Tantya was not going to spare such a person, whether he was a police informer or an employee of the Raj. He led his gang to Sugan Banjari village, caught sepoy Bapumang, cut his nose with his sword and let him go. Naturally the news spread like wildfire.

Upset over this incident, Holkar Maharaj made many changes in the police administration. Many officers were sacked and replaced by men called from outside. He also sought help from the British government. It was decided that the Agent for Central India, Sir Lapel Griffin should lead a team for arresting Tantya. Major Ishwari Prasad was made his assistant.

Tantya's popularity was spreading like a hurricane. Nobody was willing to spy on him and become police informer. On the other hand, people took pride in giving him shelter, saying, "we have served our brave and magical superman, Tantya Mama."

At last a joint action was launched by 'Tantya Police', Malwa Bhil Corps and a platoon from Bhopal. Shivaji Rao was the ruler of the Holkar state. He exhorted the police to launch a vigorous campaign for Tantya's arrest. Various allurements were announced for informers. Tantya had crossed 47 years by then. Age does have a way of showing itself. Near Banet village, the Rajputs betrayed him and got him arrested. This happened on 11 August 1889.

Those who were victims of his terror hurriedly started proceedings to prosecute Tantya Mama on true but more often on trumped up charges. On 19 October 1889, the Sessions Court in Jabalpur awarded him death sentence. On 4 December 1889, he was hanged in the Jabalpur central jail. After his death his gang was bound to scatter. Some were arrested; others were awarded life imprisonment or death sentence. Tantya Mama fought with courage for the rights of the adivasis and became immortal.

The British had already given him a name in his lifetime—"The Indian Robin Hood." Tantya Mama was born in 1842 to Bhauji Bhil in Barda (Ghatikheri) village of Pandhana tehsil of Khandwa district in Central India.

After spending five years with him, Thavara changed track along with some other members of Tantya's gang. They gave up arms and transformed themselves into sadhus of sorts. They had to do so because they were vulnerable and under pressure. They were likely to be arrested. As sadhus they could wander in the adivasi villages, speak to audiences about the atrocities they had suffered and before moving on tell the villagers about the harms that can come to them from their bad habits. They followed this routine for nine years. But Thavara was not able to fulfil his heart's desire which was to do his work on a large scale.

At last he remembered his place of birth, his parents, the near and dear ones, his activities as a Sampsabha member and follower of Govind Guru. He recalled the pains and sorrows of the adivasis, the oppressive policies against them, daily atrocities on them, all of which he had witnessed from close quarters. He mulled over the question of what could be the best way to rid them of these problems.

The adivasis who had gathered at Jharkara village got to know about Tantya Mama from Thavara. Both Thavara and Tantya Mama remained the focus of their conversation right through the night.

Each one of them drew their own conclusions after they had learnt something from his narrative. Listening to the tales of Tantya Mama's bravery, Kuriya became stronger in his convictions.

TEN

The police had not used any forceful method to arrest Govind Guru. A messenger of Maharawal Vijay Singh of Dungarpur had come and announced: "The Maharawal sends his remembrance to Govind Guru and wishes to discuss something with him."

"Look, Kuriya, I've met Maharawal Udai Singh, father of the present Maharawal. His son, Maharawal Vijay Singh, has sent for me. I must go. I'll talk to him about the problems of the adivasis, especially in this trying time of a famine. I'm confident that he'll do something for us. That's why I've agreed to go. You take charge of the situation in my absence. See that rumours are not spread to ignite unrest," Govind Guru left clear instructions to Kuriya and six–seven other associates before he leaving for Dungarpur.

Many were under the impression that he would return soon after the meeting. But a rumour also spread that Guru had been arrested. It provoked some people. At some places, adivasis called panchayat meetings. But Kuriya, Poonja and others did not allow the situation to take a serious turn. Just three or four days after Govind Guru had left, there came the unsettling news of death sentence given to Joriya Bhagat and Tantya Mama. All kinds of doubts arose in the minds of the people.

A furious Kuriya made an announcement: "Brothers, all of you must proceed towards Dungarpur. Take along everyone that you meet on the way. We must return only after getting Govind Guru released." The message had a stirring effect on the listeners. The news of the adivasis' march to Dungarpur reached the darbar before they set out.

A small group of adivasis from Jharkara drew hundreds of others after travelling a distance of barely four–five *kos*. Eventually, 1,500 to 2,000 adivasis, carrying lathis, choppers, spears, axes, rocks, bows and arrows were on the march to get their beloved Govind Guru released.

These people were hungry, lean and thin, but high in spirits and determined to free Govind Guru. Their eyes glowed in the hope of a better future. It was a group of adivasis who were ready to sacrifice everything for the Guru who had taught them: "To an extent we are ourselves responsible for our miseries. If we unite against atrocities and oppressive policies, things will start moving in our favour." This kind of talk by the Guru had left a deep impression on their mind.

In the mythical battles between gods and demons and historical ones between Aryan and non-Aryan clans, people had taken shelter in the jungles and hills, but the communities uprooted from their native soil had not give up hope.

Within the natural bounds of a desire to live, the adivasis fought for independence. But they had also allowed themselves to be trapped by joint conspiracies of feudal rulers and the British government, accepting it as their fate. Thanks to Govind Guru, this belief in the fatalities of destiny had begun to disappear. There was awareness of conspiracies against them. Voices were uniting to oppose them. How could such people tolerate the arrest of their Guru? Hence, they marched towards Dungarpur.

Govind Guru was quietly sitting cross-legged in a prison cell of the Dungarpur state. The sun had just gone down. The ebbing yellow rays were giving way to darkness. Govind Guru's cell was becoming darker. He could hear noise of marching feet of the guards outside his cell. A lizard on the wall had just been rewarded for its long vigil for a prey.

"Brother Guard! Can I please have some water to drink?"

The well-built guard of wheat complexion heard the voice of Govind Guru. He came up to the cell door. A white dhoti was fastened to the Rajput guard's waist in dulangi style. He wore a thick orange-coloured vest and a turban covered his head. He had a sword with its scabbard fixed to his waist and carried a spear in his hand. He stared at Govind Guru for a while. He thought for a moment and then returned with a pot full of water taken from a utensil placed in the verandah. He extended the pot towards Govind Guru, who knew that the pot would be stuck between the narrow iron bars at the entrance to his cell. He extended his cupped hands through the iron bars. The guard poured water in them. He washed his hands and sprinkled some water over his face. He took another cup-full of water to drink and looked at the guard with gratitude. The guard smiled a little and left.

Govind Guru sprayed the drops of water in the cell as though he was purifying it. He then sat down on the floor for prayers. Closing his eyes for concentration he went into an unknown deep territory. It was pitch dark all around. He felt as though he was trapped in an ocean of darkness. He saw in all the 10 directions nothing but turbulent waves of darkness. Was it darkness that was flooding the ocean of darkness or was it the catastrophic storm of darkness which was swallowing the universe?

Slowly, all murky movements in the already darkened environment came to a halt and in its place was an all-pervasive vacuum. Govind Guru was immersed in his prayer to the spiritual supreme power. Suddenly at a distance appeared a jot of light. Govind Guru's attention was concentrated on it. Slowly it began to move towards him, becoming brighter and brighter. In no time all the surrounding darkness vanished, paving the way for a pleasing spell of brightness. The speck of illumination magnified to present the sight of a light brown flat field in front of him.

Within seconds, the field was filled with green grass. From the tiny leaves of the grass emerged multi-coloured flowers, adding sparkle to the field with myriad colours. Adding to the richness of the ambience was the music of chirping birds. The closed eyes of Govind Guru suggested that he was still concentrating on his prayer. His smiling face was lit up with an aura of spiritual greatness and high intellect. Suddenly, out of nowhere herds of elephants invaded the field, trampling upon the tender green grass and multi-coloured flowers. Just when the elephants were coming, the sky was covered with flocks of shrieking vultures. Within minutes the cacophony of wailing vultures and rampaging elephants created a mayhem. The beautiful creation was destroyed and soon it looked like a crematorium.

The shine on the face of Govind Guru turned into a tensed expression. The field was still there, but from light brown it had turned into blood red. The grass was there, but crushed; the birds were there, but in the shape of scattered wings. The soothing fragrance of flowers was replaced by an intolerably rotten smell.

Having finished their job of wreaking havoc, the elephants and vultures disappeared. The earth began to shrink in a deathlike solitude. It was a site of dark hills, black plateaus and deep foreboding valleys. No sign of any tree, plant, creeper, bush or grass. A desolate, uneven place! Echoing through the hills from a distant valley were the refrains of a song.

> Well known is Kanheng in the hamlet of *thoor*, brother.
> It was for *thoor* that Kanheng laid down his life.
> Brother, *thoor* suffers today from a severe drought.
> Out of reach are going things needed to survive.
> The cows are dying, brother
> And the stores have grains little.
> The folk are dying, brother,
> And we are frightened with more and more deaths.
> Beat the drum, brother, and blow the siren.
> Go and find out if thou can
> And money or wealth anywhere.
> Brother, there's a mount in our region
> Famed for its gold and silver
> And in Hitol lies an ascetic's treasure.
> O my brother, they killed Kanheng.
> 'Take care of my kids' were the last words of Kanheng.
> Well known is Kanheng in the hamlet of *thoor*, brother.
> It was for *thoor* that Kanheng laid down his life.

Even as he paid attention to the prayer, Govind Guru's mind was weighed down by the tragedy brought in by famine. No matter how much he kept his mind focussed on the shapeless God he could see only the sight of famine.

"Here, take your meal," shouted Deena Damor, a cook in the jail kitchen. He stood by the iron bar outside Govind Guru's cell with a meal of thin watery lentils in a bowl of dry leaf and some small chapattis. Govind Guru's spell was broken. He gestured that he did not want to eat. Deena said again, "Eat or you will die." That had no impact on Govind Guru. Deena went away as he had other things to do.

Govind Guru did not have a wink of sleep that night. In the morning he was handcuffed and brought out of his cell. The prison compound was large. There was an open space near the main jail, full of wild growth of grass. All round the compound were walls, high and solid. A guard asked Govind Guru to ease himself behind the bushes. Guru had eaten nothing the previous evening. He did not feel like moving his bowels. He was allowed to take his bath under a tap with his handcuffs on. He was brought back to his cell and locked. He said his morning prayers. Folding his hands before God and finishing his prayer, he sat downcast in his cell.

At about nine Deena again came back with a meal. He had by then learnt something about Govind Guru from his colleagues. He had developed a sense of respect for him. This time Govind Guru ate after insistence from Deena, who also got talking to him.

"Guru, I heard a little while ago that thousands of people are coming to protest against your arrest. I have also heard that Raja Saheb has ordered his army to stop them and told them that they should not hesitate to shoot any adivasi if it became necessary to stop them."

Govind Guru was taken completely by surprise by this news. Before leaving for Dungarpur, he had specifically instructed Kuriya to see that nothing troublesome took place in his absence. Then how did this happen? Govind Guru was not able to understand anything. Another sepoy at the prison got a whiff of what Deena had told Govind Guru. He informed the jamadar. The matter reached the jail in-charge. Deena was held responsible for committing the crime of passing information to Govind Guru and was severely beaten as a punishment. His shoulders turned red with whiplashes. It took two days for him to recover.

Behind the jail barracks on a rocky piece of land a dead banyan tree had been lying for many years. Its branches had gone into the jail kitchen. The thick and ugly trunk was still lying on the ground. Deena and Sopat Meena were sitting on it, exchanging their stories of joys and sorrows.

Starting his work early in the morning and after serving the evening meals to prisoners and jail staff and cleaning the utensils, Deena normally used to hit the sack by nine. He used to snore heavily, as though waiting to sleep since morning. He was much disturbed and dejected that morning. Sopat belonged to his village. Both of them had taken up the prison job on the same day. Sopat was tall and athletic. He became a sepoy. Deena was short so he could be employed only in the kitchen. Deena used to share all his thoughts with Sopat.

"Brother Sopat, what sin did I commit that I was whiplashed in front of all? What I told Govind Guru was common knowledge. Not only inside the prison compound but all over Dungarpur state it is known that the adivasis are marching towards Dungarpur in protest against the arrest of Govind Guru. What secret did I convey to Govind Guru that I was punished for acting as his spy? I'd have accepted the punishment if I had committed a wrong, if I was guilty. But what I cannot accept is that I was innocent and yet punished." Deena was sobbing. Tears trickled down his cheeks and chin to his vest. He removed the towel of thin cloth from his shoulders to wipe his tears.

"No, Deena! Don't think like that. Look, we are all employees of the Raj and an employee is like a slave. We get paid for our labours; we have to obey our officers. At the time of our recruitment, the officers had told us that we'd earn much more than what we could by working elsewhere. And that is true. The conditions they put on us were that we had to complete the tasks given to us, we could not go out without permission, and we could not talk to prisoners on our own free will. You remember how our friend, Kisna, who was on duty as the prison guard, was fooled by the dacoit Dhanna, who told him 'Guard Sir! I suffer from a strange disease. I can't rest unless I've sucked at an iron piece for two-three hours.' The naïve Kisna brought a piece of pickaxe and handed it to Dhanna. Kisna did not realise that he could have very well asked Dhanna to suck at the window bar in the prison. He made a foolish mistake.

That night Dhanna used the pickaxe piece to remove stones from the wall in his cell and escaped. Nobody had a clue about his escape till the time he reached the safety of forests. Till today he remains untraceable. Dhanna is out and Kisna is in prison. For the Raj, all prisoners are alike, whether he is Dhanna, the dacoit, or Govind Guru. So, were you then not foolish enough to make that mistake of talking to Govind Guru?"

"Sopat, you are right. But Govind Guru is a saintly person. He is not a criminal. If I allow a bhagat to go to sleep hungry, will it not be a sin? That bhagat had not eaten in the evening. It was I who had taken food to him. When again he refused to eat next morning my sin was mounting. What could I have done? I begged him to eat and he relented. All this took a while and during that time I told him what everyone knew."

"Don't think of other matters. You'll agree at least that it is wrong to talk to a prisoner?"

"Yes, that is correct."

"You also know that for us this prison job is important."

"Yes."

"What could you have done if the officer had sacked you?"

"To hell with my job! Are we animals that we should accept this kind of beating over small matters?"

Deena's dormant self respect surfaced, and he clinched his fist. His eyes turned red. His forehead narrowed. His face was burning.

Sopat realised the gravity of the situation. He had known Deena since childhood. He also knew that in a fit of rage Deena could go out of control. He put his hands on his shoulders. He tried his best to ensure that he became calm.

After some hard persuasion he escorted him to the jail kitchen and helped him sleep.

Sopat returned to his barrack. Deena could not sleep that night. He recalled the days of his childhood. The hilly area, green forests, flowing river, ponds full of water, his heady life, fairs and the festivals—every memory re-surfaced. His mind went back to the carefree dances of young boys and girls. He remembered Gurlya Bhopa who spent his days treating the sick with exorcism, chasing away witches, throwing grain of urad to drive away evil spirits. Deena remembered him as Gurlya Baba who would retire to his hut after the day's work, sit under a mahua tree and stare at the innumerable stars in the sky as if searching for Jamani, his wife, who had died in the fullness of her youth without bearing him a child after being bitten by a black scorpion. Nobody knew what were her dying words, because she had died before anyone knew about the accident.

He recalled the words of Gurlya that a shooting star symbolises the death of a person on this earth. He also used to say that the spirit of the dead person shines when it takes the place of a shooting star. The shooting star takes birth on our planet in the form of a human and the human spirit turns into a shiny star in the sky. It was the man of such extraordinary thinking that Deena remembered. Deena also remembered a song that Gurlya used to sing when he failed to find his wife among the stars.

A scorpion has crept and settled in
The bodice that thou bought for me
From the Ranapur fair.
Ah, my love, I won't survive.
Who, then, will grind the wheat
Lying in the store, my love?
Ah, my love, I won't survive.
A scorpion has crept and settled in
The bodice that thou bought for me
From the Ranapur fair.
Ah, my love, I won't survive.
She, my rival and your another love

Will grind the wheat
And enjoy swinging with thee.
A scorpion has crept and settled in
The bodice that thou bought for me
From the Ranapur fair.
Ah, my love, I won't survive.
Who, then, will fetch from the well
The pitchers of water, my love?
Ah, my love, I won't survive
She, my rival and your another love
Will grind the wheat
And enjoy swinging with thee.
A scorpion has crept and settled in
The bodice that thou bought for me
From the Ranapur fair.
Ah, my love, I won't survive.
Who, then, will remove
The waste of the cattle, my love?
A scorpion has crept and settled in
The bodice that thou bought for me
From the Ranapur fair.
Ah, my love, I won't survive.
She, my rival and your another love
Will grind the wheat
And enjoy swinging with thee.
Ah, my love, I won't survive.
A scorpion has crept and settled in
The bodice that thou bought for me
From the Ranapur fair.
Ah, my love, I won't survive.
Ah, my love, I won't survive.

This was a song that Gurlya's wife had sung for him once.

Gurlya never married again. He kept himself immersed in his family avocation of Bhopayas. He shared the pains and sorrows of the people and was satisfied helping people with exorcism, the craft that he had inherited.

Deena remembered his wife, Manbhari, also his only son, four-year-old Heera. His mind was flooded with memories of his village, its surroundings, Gurlya, the bodice bought from the Ranapur fair and the scorpion hidden in it, death of a young woman, hooting star and innumerable bright stars...It was all inscribed in his mind as a mixture of memories and ideas.

In the end, Deena recalled the words of his wife when he was leaving to take up his job: "Women have to suffer on two occasions when they are separated from their homes. One, at the time of famine, and two, when their men take up employment with the Raj. It does not really pain much to leave our village during the famine because we move with our families. But for a job in the Raj, the husband has to go alone and has to leave his wife behind who cannot bear the pain of seperation. Don't take up the job. We shall toil here and fill our stomachs with whatever little we get here. At least, we'll live together."

Just after their marriage, she had told him: "You sit under the mahua tree on the slope of the magari (hillock) and play the flute while I'll collect mahua flowers. You'll hear the music of my anklets. When that music reaches the skies then there will be thunder, lightening and it'll rain. You hide the flute in your waist so that it is not damaged by rainwater and make a necklace of wild mogar flowers and tie it on my bun. Also put a yellow naag champa flower in my bun. I shall make a peacock shape crown of date leaves for your turban."

At five in the morning Deena left the kitchen and came out after informing the guard on duty and jail superintendent, "I shall return soon after visiting a relative of mine who is admitted in a hospital in Dungarpur." His pay for the month was due in another three-four days. He had left without collecting his salary. He headed for his village.

The crowd at Balota swelled to 5,000–6,000. One of the main reasons for this was that Govind Guru had addressed his first meeting in the nearby Suranta village. He was very popular, apart from Balota and Suranta, in Huti, Aantri, Mobai and Tamta.

News about this large gathering reached Dungarpur darbar. The Maharawal consulted his trusted lieutenants. On the advice of Divan Ganesh Ram it was decided that it is best to release Govind Guru at this juncture. The problem was what excuse should be found to release him?

It would be too much to coax him into changing his views after he had so resolutely presented them. He was not a person who could be cowed down by threats. He had helped people suffering due to famine. This had made him more respectable than before. As a saint his image had acquired more lustre. The famine was spreading with a destructive fury. At such a time people needed helpful souls like Govind Guru. If he was not released the adivasis' anger would take a fearsome turn. The Maharawal was in a fix to find a way out of his dilemma. He had to choose between his feudal pride and the need to nip adivasis' revolt in the bud.

Govind Guru too was getting restless, as he was very keen to help the famine-hit adivasis. He wanted to be released from prison. The Maharawal's false pride did not allow him to talk under any pressure. Govind Guru was a bhagat and had a large heart. He had no ego. But he was a self respecting person.

Dalpatrai Mehta was a well-known and rich businessman of Dungarpur. He was a philanthropist and a liberal person. Often, he would help the poor. At the time of natural calamities he always provided help to the needy. Maharawal Vijay Singh sent for him at once. He gladly came to see him.

"Sethji, we've remembered you in the hope that you'll help us in fighting the famine," began the Maharawal.

"Annadata, I am doing whatever I can. Please let me know what more should I do."

"Mehtaji, you must have heard of Govind Guru."

Seth Dalpatrai nodded. The Maharawal continued.

"He has served the people during the famine. At its own level, the Raj is distributing food, fodder, clothes among victims at different places. We want that you, we and Govind Guru and all other voluntary organisations should join hands in providing relief to the people. This will make the relief job better organised."

"Maharaj! This is an excellent idea. What are your orders for me?"

"We've heard that in some villages families are receiving relief material in excess of their demand and thus many needy are deprived of help and relief. Lack of coordination is the primary cause for this. That's why it will be better to complete this task cooperatively."

"Yes, Maharaj! You are right about it."

"But there is a problem."

"What is that, Annadata?"

"When he does good work like helping the adivasis at the time of famine and telling the tribals to give up their bad habits, he also incites them against the Raj. That is why violence has broken out in many places."

"This is wrong, Maharaj."

"Yes. That's why we called him and talked to him about it. But he speaks a different language. He has started to think that he has become too big just because a couple of hundred adivasis are behind him. We've arrested him for showing arrogance. But you know, we are kind and generous. We can't sleep when our subjects are in trouble."

The deliberately chosen respectful references to Govind Guru by the Maharawal in order to impress Mehta appeared to be acquiring a different colour.

"Maharaj, it's also rumoured that some adivasis are coming to meet the darbar to take up the matter of his release."

"Yes, it is not a rumour. It's a fact. But it is not important. We shall explain things to them. If they still create problems, we shall deal with it. In no way can treason be tolerated."

"Please tell me what I can do to help you?"

"You should talk to Govind Guru. But do not refer to this conversation we had."

"Annadata! Can I dare betray any secret of the Raj?" the businessman said promptly.

"Fine, then listen carefully. Try to make Govind Guru understand that the most urgent thing at this time is to render help to the victims of famine. This is our collective responsibility. Tell him to discard this obsession with rebellion and join hands in helping the needy. We are sure you will be able to influence him. If he accepts that, we shall set him free."

The Maharawal used very calculated words tutored by Divan Ganesh Ram.

"All right, Maharaj, I shall talk to him and do my best to persuade him."

Seth Mehta had a lot of respect for Govind Guru. Respecting sadhus was his family tradition. He looked at Govind Guru in that light. He used a clever ploy by not telling the Maharawal about his feelings regarding Govind Guru.

Mehta had a one-to-one talk with Govind Guru. Mehta was careful that during this conversation there should be nothing that went against the dignity of the Maharawal or the self respect of Govind Guru. Mehta was, after all, familiar with the ways of the world. His life was full of varied experiences. He was good at reading a person's mind. Mehta was able to bring Govind Guru round to his point of view.

"All right, call Kuriya Bhagat," Govind Guru told him.

"You are a sadhu. It is a matter of great satisfaction for me that you've understood and agreed with what I said."

Mehta told the Maharawal about his conversation with Govind Guru. It was agreed that Seth Dalpatrai Mehta and the priest of the Durga Temple, Rasbihari Goswami, will bring Kuriya Bhagat. The two went to fetch Kuriya in a horse carriage. By that time the adivasi march had crossed Balota.

Many of the adivasis knew Seth Dalpatrai Mehta. Kuriya had also heard his name. They had a good impression about the Seth. Mehta and the priest talked to Kuriya and some other leaders of the adivasis, who had doubts in their minds about the reasons behind the talks. Later, after receiving some firm assurances from the duo, they felt confident. The duo brought Kuriya to the darbar. That is where the Maharawal talked to Govind Guru after he was released on a surety from Kuriya. Hoping to generate goodwill among the adivasis, the Maharawal had Govind Guru and Kuriya return home with Mehta and the priest. Mehta was keen that he should escort Govind Guru back to the adivasis to convey the message that they could trust Mehta anytime. But Goswami, the priest, was not interested in all this.

The adivasis were pleased to see Govind Guru back with them. They felt obliged to the Seth and priest. The Seth was enamoured with the idea that he was instrumental in solving a difficult problem. He had, after all, managed to win the trust of not only the Maharawal but also of Govind Guru and adivasi leaders. The adivasis saw it as a great victory for them. The air was echoing to the shouts of "Govind Guru ki Jai! Guru Maharaj ki Jai!"

ELEVEN

The severe chchapanya famine.

People longed for even a miserly quantity of food and water. There was no fodder for the cattle. The hungry and thirsty people wandered around helplessly, some died. The cattle at home and wild animals in jungles were reduced to carcasses. The macabre dance of death could be seen everywhere. Corpses, rotten smell and epidemic! No one knew how many people had already left home to escape this hell.

Food and water was not reaching the far flung areas of Banswara, Dungarpur, Kushalgarh and Pratapgarh in Vagad region and Idar and Santrampur states in neighbouring Gujarat, all because of the mismanagement and irresponsible conduct of the feudal rulers.

The Rajputana AGG wrote a letter about the famine to the Government of India. "This is the worst affected area in the whole of India. The outbreak of cholera epidemic has taken a heavy toll of the adivasis, 20 per cent of whom are from the states of Dungarpur and Banswara and 15 per cent are from Pratapgarh..."

In one place, four adivasis sold some of their silver ornaments to buy wheat flour, which was sufficient for making just a single roti. They divided it into four parts and ate it. At another place, two adivasis walking past a mahua tree saw a fruit on it. They plucked it and divided it between them.

During the 1898–1900 famine, a large number of adivasis died in all the five states of southern Rajputana—Mewar, Dungarpur, Banswara, Kushalgarh and Pratapgarh. The adivasi population in the area was 612,459 in 1891; in 1901 it came down to 272,708. About 55 per cent of the adivasi population fell to the famine. The situation arose due to insufficient food, epidemic and migration of people. If there are no human beings on earth where will you rule? Perhaps this thought worried the British as they appointed Captain Pinhay to monitor famine relief works, which were started under his supervision in these states.

The famine started in 1898, but the relief work did not begin in Mewar till 1900. The situation in Dungarpur was equally bad. The relief that reached there was inadequate. In Banswara, too, relief work began only in 1900.

The proverb "a hungry man can commit any sin" proved to be true, considering the dreadful conditions of the adivasis who were desperate for food. In September 1899, the Bhils looted a group of wayfarers in Aantari near Dungarpur. During 1899–1900, there were 108 incidents of robbery in Mewar in which 4,989 people were found to be involved. Of these 261 were arrested. The looting of a dak chowki (a small post office) on the Rishabdev-Salumber road by a group of 30 was considered a serious incident. The Garasiyas of Kotda attacked the house of a trader in Banswara, resulting in the death of eight. The house was set on fire after it was looted. Discontentment was widest among the adivasis of Dungarpur and Banswara because of the perceived danger to their very existence. That was the prime motive behind these criminal acts.

The adivasis worried about filling their stomachs; the rulers worried about crime. Army units from Mewar Bhil Corps were sent to these two states to bring the situation under control. Incidents of theft increased in all the adivasi-dominated areas. Special police forces were raised to stop those activities.

In his report on famine that Capt A. F. Pinhay sent to the Government of India, he wrote that 30 per cent of the deaths in Mewar state had taken place in its hilly areas. In Dungarpur, Pratapgarh and Banswara states, 12, 8 and 15 per cent respectively of the total human population had perished. This report was sent by him at the end of 1900. In April 1901, the AGG of Rajputana sent a report to the Government of India, which said that the situation in the hilly areas of Mewar was "extremely pitiable and there was widespread dissatisfaction among the adivasis. Riots, violence and looting incidents are spreading everywhere. In Pratapgarh, Dungarpur, Kushalgarh and Banswara the situation has gone out of control".

In many places, the jagirdars incited the adivasis to commit acts of robbery and looting. The adivasis were assured protection if they parted with a portion of the loot after committing the crime in the border areas. This is illustrated by what happened to the Thakur of Nandli and his son in Dungarpur state. They were arrested and punished after their role in a criminal conspiracy was exposed.

To curb the growth of robbery and theft by adivasis, the Regent Council notified the Bhil, Meena and Garasiya communities of the Dungarpur state under the Criminal Tribes Act. Similar steps were taken in the affected areas of Idar, Banswara, Kushalgarh, Pratapgarh and Mewar states. This Act was first introduced in the Bombay Presidency in 1871. Under its provisions, every adivasi child of over 12 years had to report at the police station. He had to report to the police station concerned when he went to another village on any account.

This Act became a handy tool for committing acts of oppression against adivasis. They would be summoned to the police stations or posts and residence of jagirdars under any pretext and tortured. They would be whipped, beaten with shoes and hung upside down on the trees. There were also instances when their feet were cut off so that they could not walk. The Council ruled in Dungarpur and Banswara. The Council started recruiting Pathans from outside the state in the state police. These Pathans used to look down upon the adivasis and called them *bandra*. This became another major reason for the migration of adivasis.

To deal with the famine, the British government encouraged Christian missionaries to join the relief work. The Presbyterian Church of Udaipur opened a shelter for the famine-affected people in Khairwada. The missionaries took many orphans with them. They arranged medicines for the treatment of cholera and plague. They also converted many adivasis to Christianity.

In a 1902 report, a British officer observed that compared to others the adivasis of Dungarpur lacked the capacity to work. The famine had lowered their morale. The British Resident in Mewar wrote in 1901 that "hunger and diseases, as a result of famine, have considerably reduced the population of the adivasis. In such a situation, conditions for a rebellion by them in future should be considered non-existent".

Undoubtedly, some famine relief works were taken up. Many roads were constructed—Jooda to Kotda, Manpur to Jeliwara, Oguna to Genjur, Madari to Pipalwara, Jaisamand to Kewara, Mandwa to Bikarni and Loharia-Umaria-Valoch road. Roads were also constructed connecting Pipalkhant in Banswara to Kushalgarh and from Banswara to Ratlam. But all these efforts were like "cumin in a camel's mouth"; they were too little. The reason was that the British had other priorities and the native rulers had to work under pressure from the British while the Christian missionaries had their own future plans.

Govind Guru had lost his wife and both the sons in the *chchapanya* famine. This had broken his heart. He decided to move to some other place.

"Guru Maharaj, please don't leave us," people pleaded with him, trying to persuade him not to go.

"The adivasis of Idar and Santrampur are in equally bad situation. I have to work for awareness there too. I'll return after spending some time in the states of Idar and Santrampur. I shall not be very far from you. I'm a Banjara by caste, a nomad. What other work can I do other than fighting against the atrocities of the rulers? As long as I live I am with you," Govind Guru's voice was choking with emotion.

"Guru Maharaj is leaving us"—this news spread like wildfire in Dungarpur-Banswara-Kushalgarh areas. The realisation that people had such deep faith in him gave some solace to his disturbed mind. But how could he bear the setback of the loss of his wife and sons due to the epidemic. He was a broken man inside. He did not know what he should do, surrounded as he was by a crowd of adivasis at Chhani Magari in his own village, Basiya.

'My mind repeatedly goes back to my wife and sons. I spend days and nights in sorrow, in their memory. Sometimes I can't sleep. If I go and spend some days elsewhere, everything will be all right. In your midst are men like Poonja and Kuriya who will keep running the affairs of the Sampsabha with courage and responsibility. Don't stop me now." His words showed his abounding love for the adivasis.

He cast a sweeping glance at Chhani Magari. Resting his eyes somewhere at a distant hillock, he appeared to be staring at a vacuum. The moist eyes of hundreds of adivasis were riveted at the face of Govind Guru.

"All right, Guru Maharaj! We shall convey the news to you if something important occurs," Kuriya told him as he awaited the response of the crowd of adivasis.

"Don't stop Guru Maharaj now," Poonja said supporting Kuriya. The adivasi men, women and children were standing with their heads down. That was their consent, though an unhappy one.

Govind Guru travelled far beyond Dungarpur. He started staying in Natwa village in Santrampur state of Gujarat. He married again, a widow by the name of Gani. He cleared a piece of fallow land, making it cultivable, to start a new life. He had two sons from his second wife, Aru and Amru.

One day when his wife had gone to pick up firewood and he was sitting alone on his cot in the verandah of his thatched hut, a middle-aged sadhu came up to him. Govind Guru welcomed him.

Blessing Govind Guru, the sadhu said: "First of all through samadhi, that is extreme concentration, master the art of controlling the five senses that tie mankind to the world. Then concentrate on remembering God, the Almighty. The adivasis in Vagad and nearby areas are living a dark life. They are forgetting God and becoming superstitious. They are being exploited and oppressed at every step. It is your duty to save them from their plight by initiating them into the acts of devotion to God and kindling their spirits to fight against oppression." Govind Guru was already dedicated to serving the adivasis. The sadhu's words cemented his resolve. The unknown sadhu did not stay long. He neither ate anything nor did he accept any alms. After he left, Govind Guru thought he must have been some extraordinary sadhu. Maybe, a divine messenger! Perhaps, he came to warn me that I should not get stuck here after marrying again and raising a family.

That unnamed sadhu left a deep impression on Govind Guru.

Natwa village of those days was a cluster of scattered settlements, each of five to 12 houses. Most of the settlements were on the slopes of low hills and valleys. In the adivasi areas, villages of this type are called *pals*.

Normally, one *pal* has people of the same clan, which reflects the family's distinct identity. The clan and its distinct identity have a lot of commonality. It could be called the mark of an adivasi community. Culturally, there were a lot of similarities between the Banjara community and the adivasis. Govind Guru's *gotra* (sub-caste) Govaria, was derived from the identity of Gau clan. Gau (cow) was the sole symbol of economics of the Gau clan.

Govind Guru's hut was at the eastern end in the middle part of this settlement. Its walls were of stone slabs put one top of another and the roof consisted of dried branches of teak wood covered with a layer of grass and leaves. Outside the hut, there was a row of nagphani in the open compound. In the middle of the compound was a mahua tree. Above the tree was the open sky. Anyone who climbed the hills on the east could see not only the sky but also the wide horizon beyond.

Govind Guru remained restless throughout the day recalling the words of the unknown mahatma. By evening, he went over to the platform at the old Shiv temple. He looked carefully at the setting sun. The sun hid behind a hill on the western horizon. The birds were returning home from west to east. It has been observed that the flock of birds flies from east to west in the morning and reverses the direction in the evening.

Govind Guru, who was watching the flight of the birds till the sunset, was lost in his thoughts. He returned home late, by then his wife and sons were fast asleep. His wife was familiar with his odd routines.

In the courtyard of his hut, Govind Guru was lying on his string cot. It was past midnight. The Canis Major in the sky was hanging close to the western horizon. He was looking at the night sky but his sight was also fixed at the smaller stars by its side in the sky and the hunting star behind them.

"Who is this hunter? And the frightened stars?" asked Govind Guru while still lying.

Govind Guru alone knew who he had addressed his query to. It could be guessed that it must have been addressed to his wife, or his children, the bushes, the mahua tree or self.

The jute rope is thinner than the cotton twine, thinner is the rope of Indian hemp and still thinner is the rope of long reed. That was the rope used in Govind Guru's cot. The mystery of universe and the three little stars in the night sky was stuck in a corner of Govind Guru's mind. The third phase of the night was coming to an end. Sleep has to eventually overcome a tired body to give it some relief. His eyes were flickering with less frequency. Guru Govind did not realise when he lapsed into sound sleep.

The light and invisible body of Govind Guru was transported beyond the dense forests to the foothills, and then into a tunnel through the big rocky caves. His body entered the tunnel which was intensely dark. But it was not a frightening darkness. Like a boat sailing gently in a calm lake, Govind Guru kept going ahead through the layers of darkness in the tunnel. His feet did not seem to be touching the ground. He felt weightless when he stood in one position and when he moved in the pitch-dark tunnel his hands hit the rocky walls frequently. He was finding it difficult to observe the caution required in walking through a dark and unknown tunnel.

"How long do I have to walk in this tunnel? What'll come at the end of it? Is there an end to this tunnel? Or is it a never-ending tunnel, which I'll have to traverse all my life before I die anonymously? Is it that dark tunnel from where it is impossible to come out?" Govind Guru was assailed by many doubts.

"Is it an endless cave? A tunnel has to end no matter how long it is and how zigzag is its path. Just as a night that may be frightening, dark and long, must come to an end to make way for morning. At least you are not encountering thorny bushes, the inconvenience of boulders hitting you at every step on an uneven path. All that is needed is some patience to negotiate through the rocks on either sides of the path. Now that you are in the tunnel, it will lead you somewhere in the end. That will be your destiny, your future. What you have to do at that precise moment, you have to think when that moment comes." His inner consciousness was trying to solve the puzzles he faced.

Like the ripples that come to a halt after a piece of stone has hit the pond, Govind Guru's agitated mind became calm after listening to the voice of his inner self. Govind Guru, the traveller in a dark tunnel, was now at peace with himself, sure of the future.

After covering a great distance he saw a dot of light that came though a hairline fracture in a piece of rock on the upper side of the tunnel. It was a very narrow ray of light, though somewhat bright. However, the light was still not sufficiently bright to make it possible to illuminate the entire tunnel. But the beacon of light from the rock began to walk ahead of Govind Guru. He was pleasantly surprised by this miracle. He was now sure that he was not going to be lost. In fact, he realised that he was on the right path.

Govind Guru reached the end of the tunnel after he had travelled the same distance that he had covered so far. It was very hot inside the tunnel. He did not realise that he was drenched in his perspiration. He was greeted by the pleasing sight of morning sun rays. The darkness had lifted, whether swallowed by the tunnel he had left behind or dispelled by the morning light, he did not know.

Emerging from the rocky tunnel he saw that the forests and hills too had disappeared and in their place was an expanse of sandy flat land. It felt like winter to him. The soft sunlight was giving him some comfort from the cold that he felt. He did not feel tired after his long journey through the tunnel. An extraordinary day was coming to an end. Out of the blue, without any lightening and thunder or clouds from the clear skies came showers. Falling against the sunlight, the raindrops looked like silver particles. The sun was in the middle of the third phase of the day. An eye-catching rainbow was formed just above the right horizon.

Govind Guru's spirits soared. But it remained a surprise how did it start to rain. The rain stopped after a while. The brown earth had been soaked over a wide distance. In no time at all, flower buds were sprouting, emitting a musical noise of "chat-chat-chat til-tadkan".

In the next few moments the entire land was filled with tiny green plants and then in the next few moments they had grown to knee length as multi-coloured blossomed flowers. The sunlight was pleasing, the breeze was gentle and cool, and the plants were swaying with many flowers.

Govind Guru smiled within himself at this sight, as if saying something to himself. It was the smile of a man who did not have words to describe the happiness of his great spiritual experience in words. But he could not contain his happiness as he burst out laughing loudly, a hearty joyful laugh.

It was such a loud laughter that it reached the ears of his wife over the rough scratching noise of the millstone she was using to grind wheat flour. Surprised, she came rushing out where she saw her husband laughing loudly in his sleep. She woke him up with a tug at his chest.

"Where is my sun, where has the gentle breeze eloped, where has the rainbow disappeared, where are the raindrops hiding, what has happened to my flat brown land and where have all the multi-coloured flowers gone?" Govind Guru muttered, half asleep.

"There is nothing here. Why are you blabbering? Don't you know that laughing in one's sleep is considered a bad omen?" said his wife as she lent her hands to make him sit up on the cot.

Govind Guru was now fully awake. The dawn was breaking. Across the eastern horizon was spreading the red glow of the morning. From the trees and plants of Natwa village came the musical chirping of birds. The morning star was shining alone in the sky at 45 degree. Sunrise was seconds away. That morning Govind Guru left Natwa.

TWELVE

"I've been speaking these simple words for years. What many regard as god Indra is a deceitful human being who has spread a wide net of illusions to control the wealth of the universe. He built a magnificent palace for himself in the sky with beautiful gardens and a boundary around it to stop any intruder while the magician occupying it leads a life of pleasure. Indra has ruled on the strength of his magic. After him, that magic was used and taken all over the world by the rich Kuber, King Kans and Badshah Haroon. Today, the British are using the same tricks. It has not been raining for three or four seasons and famine has hit the world.

"They say that god Indra is the lord of clouds. He has plenty of showers for his gardens and orchards while famine hits the earth. It is because of his tricks that poor farmers and adivasis who depend on forests are dying of hunger while Indra as god lives comfortably in his city. The British have mastered his tricks to weave a magic that has brought famine. They have taken a grip over the clouds with their magic so that it does not rain and the hungry and thirsty people live under their control. They want to see that times become so harsh that they, the rajas and maharajas who depend on them, and the unscrupulous mahajans and fake pandits dictate the lives of the distressed people. The people should lose their senses and blame their miseries on their fate and do not realise that the real culprit behind their troubles are the British tricksters.

"I am talking to you having understood the truth behind those tricks. In this age, you should stay away from the tricks of the British and your children should not die of hunger. In the days of Indra's rule your life was equally miserable and you continued to be poor and helpless during the reigns of King Kuber, then King Kans and finally, Haroon Rashid. Those were the days of gold, silver and bronze. The magicians possessed those precious metals. In this Kalukal (Bad Era), it is iron that is precious and so the British control it. That is why they run trains, which are made of iron, as are the tracks on which they run. Iron is black. That is why this age of iron is Kalukal, the black age. Because of the trick the British have played on you, you are not able to see that for them iron represents power and for you it represents Kalukal. You should understand the secret that Kalukal represents darkness for you. I have taken birth on earth to instil some sense in you and save you from the darkness that has been spread by the sorcerers. I have no other intention. If you do not follow what I, Sadhu Sengji, tell you then you shall be destroyed."

Sengji Sadh was addressing the adivasis at Kewara ki Nal. He liked to live alone. His speech had immense power. He cast a spell over anyone who came in contact with him and listened to his words of wisdom. While wandering, he would stop anywhere he liked and start talking casually before a small audience. Slowly he attracted a crowd. Because of his virtually nomadic life, Sengji got to know a lot about many places and the people in those places. Wherever he went he would talk to people about their life and origin. People listened to him with interest.

Kewara ki Nal had a population of Bhils and Meenas. During a discourse on the origin of the universe he narrated a story about a pair created by God: There was a childless couple, Birma and Bhaimata. Keen to start the human race, they collected bits of soil from different places and kneaded them into different shapes the way a potter does with earth. This way they made as many shapes of human beings as were the colour of the soil they had collected from earth.

First of all, Bhaimata made a male and female couple. Birma infused life into the couple who were handed over a bow and arrow. Birma and Bhaimata blessed the couple and told them they would live in the forest. If anyone intruded into their territory to harass them, they should use the bow and arrow to drive the stranger away. This is how Birma and Bhaimata produced the first human couple on earth and called them Bhil.

After this, Bhaimata made another couple and Birma again put life into the duo. They were also given a bow and arrow and blessed like the previous Bhil couple were. The second couple was called Meena. The Bhil couple was made out of purely black soil and the Meenas from black soil mixed with a little of brown. Then Birma asked Bhaimata to build people of different hues for whom soils of brown, yellow and red colours were used.

The man using the red soil was built the last. The last couple made of red soil prayed to Birma as soon as life was infused into them; the man said, "Please, teach me the art of magic". Upon this Birma and Bhaimata told him: "We have not taught this art to anyone else, so why should we teach it to you?" The couple made from the red soil was wordless.

After creating them, Birma and Bhaimata created more species of human beings. Then they created Indra and adopted him as their *dharma poot* (son). He was taught the art of magic, which made him stronger than all the other human beings. When Birma was teaching the intricacies of the magic, the man made from the red soil had hid himself to listen to the mantra secretly. As soon as Birma learnt about it, he cursed that red couple: "You have learnt the mantra for magic but you will be able to use it only in the Kalukal."

"So, all you brothers and sisters understand what I am saying and realise that the British are the same ones built from the red soil and know the magic for this age. It is because of the power of this magic that they have control over all the rajas and maharajas of the world, mahajans and brahmins and now they use it to overpower you all. That is why you should guard against their tricks and stay away from the net they have spread or else you shall be destroyed. They are all traders who earn without any effort but they will capture with the help of their magic all your earnings that you have made out of your hard toil. They are single-mindedly pursuing a policy to acquire the wealth of this world and destroy it. They have created an illusion to help them rule over the world and mislead Indians so much that even the rajas and maharajas are unable to see their evil intentions. With the help of the mantra received from my Guru, I have discovered the secret of their magic and I am asking you to beware of it so that your land stays in your care. The brothers and sisters who have gathered here to listen to me, especially the Bhils and Meenas, do listen to this that Birma god and Bhaimata created you to protect the forests, hills, rivers and streams. You should think about that and act accordingly."

As soon as he got up after finishing his discourse, the air was rent with the cries of "Sadhu ki Jai! Sadhu ki Jai."

A couple of elderly people urged Sengji not to go, as it was getting dark. He could stay in the village. All others supported the idea. He said in response: "I'm a wandering minstrel. I don't like to stay long in one place. The reason for this is that if the British magicians learn about it, they will try to trap me and what I have learnt from my Guru will be wasted."

Sadhu Sengji went towards the hills on the east. That was the last time he was seen by anyone.

THIRTEEN

Govind Guru returned to his place of birth, Basiya after five years. His second wife, Gani, and their two sons were with him. The news of his return spread in the nearby areas. He went to his ancestral hut which would have been without any roof of thatch had not the neighbours taken care of it. After looking deep into the hut, Govind Guru and his family went to dhooni, the sacred place, at Chhani Magri in the village. It looked intact.

The villagers had lit an eternal light there. Every full moon day a fair used to be held there, as instructed by the Guru. Adivasis from the neighbourhood used to assemble there and offer coconut, pour ghee into the sacred fire and sing Sampsabha songs. A crowd of adivasis had collected around Govind Guru; most were from Basiya and nearby areas. Govind Guru was pleased to learn that the dhooni was intact and people flocked to the full moon fair. He was satisfied that his initiative for creating awareness had picked up. The local leaders of Sampsabha had taken its activities forward in his absence.

During his stay at Natwa village, Govind Guru was not very active. He was completely broken after the shocking death of his first wife and their two children in the *chchapanya* famine. His routine used to be mostly confined to prayers in solitude or light talks with the villagers. His second wife used to be somewhat troubled because of his introverted nature. His young sons used to long for proximity to their father. It was a happy coincidence that Govind Guru had met that unknown sadhu who revived his spirits.

Govind Guru's joy knew no bounds on regaining the love and affection of the people of Basiya. The memories of his first wife and children did not overwhelm him the way they used to. He was determined to carry forward his mission with Sampsabha with renewed enthusiasm. Not that he was ever away from that mission but he did face a temporary obstruction.

Guru Govind, his wife and sons, who had arrived in Basiya a little before sunset, were tired after their long journey. Just after sunset and after polite conversation with some villagers he headed towards the dhooni where he immersed himself in his evening prayers. The villagers, not wanting to disturb him in the prayers, started returning home.

But a childhood friend of his, Bhartya, who belonged to the neighbouring village of Bedsa, stayed back. Occasionally, he looked at Govind Guru's new wife. He was trying to guess how much did she share Govind Guru's first wife's passion for prayers. Gani, the second wife of Govind Guru, was straightening his second pair of waistcoat and dhoti from the sack of clothes she had brought with her. She put the clothes on a wide stone slab. Close by was another larger stone slab where she spread out a cotton mattress for her two sons to sleep on. She then pulled out a brass lota and walked towards a stream to fill the rounded pot with water.

"Sister-in-law, stop! Let me fetch water. There may be a poisonous insect near the stream," Bhartya warned her about the snake prowling around.

"It is all right. I'll bring water myself," she replied softly though Bhartya's words had initially startled her.

Prayers over, Govind Guru ended his padmasana. He had listened to the dialogue between Bhartya and his wife. He asked Bhartya; "Oh! You haven't not left? Listen, this sister-in-law of yours is familiar with the ways of the forest. You need not worry on that account. She can do all the chores. And, tell me. Is everything is fine at home? You've a son and a daughter, no?"

"Yes, brother Govind! You are now a Guru. I can't talk to you as equal. I know you can't forget the past. But you have been a 'gyani', a knowledgeable person, right from childhood."

"Don't talk about big and small people. For you, I am still the Govind of yore—the inseparable childhood pal of yours.

First, tell me how is your wife and the children?" Govind Guru said. For Bhartya to talk about his wife and children would have meant reviving old wounds. The *chchapanya* famine had forced evacuation of his village. His daughter was with her in-laws and the news from her suggested all was well. During the famine Bhartya and his wife with some friends had left the village for Malwa in search of work and food, from where he had returned without suffering much. His son, Gabru, had gone to Ratlam with some young men where the British were constructing a railway line. He had heard that wages for working at the railway project were good but his young son did not return. According to the prediction of Bhaimata, Gabru had only a short life and Bhartya did not know when the messengers of Yam (death) had taken him away. He had heard that Gabru was "red with fever and his whole body looked a fiery red". No medicine could save him and within two days, while still muttering something to himself, he had closed his eyes forever.

Bhartya was not even able to see his body. His friends had cremated him. Bhartya had learnt of the tragic end of his son when the other youth from the village who were also working on the railway project returned home. Though Bhartya had cried a lot when he heard about the death of his son, he was able to compose himself somehow.

But the news had left Nanka, mother of Gabru, virtually paralysed. Her eyes remained wide open as though staring in disbelief at the body of her son. She became insane with grief. The village sorcerer tried his best with all his tricks, including treating her eyes with burning chillies, and repeatedly threw her on the floor at the place of Baba Hirkuliya. All of it was in vain. She is still mentally ill. She sits silently in the courtyard in front of the hut. Whenever she sees a young man pass by she runs towards him. People unfamiliar with her story think she is a witch or a ghost. Children are scared of her. But adults know that the shock of the untimely death of her son was responsible for her condition and there is no cure for it.

Amidst sobs, Bhartya told this story to his friend Govind who was meeting him after a long time. Govind Guru knew about many other similar sad tales. He had himself experienced the pain of the loss of his wife and children. He understood well the feelings of Bhartya. He consoled Bhartya as much as he could while sharing his sorrow.

In the meanwhile, Ramota Meena came to the dhooni with two boys. He had brought meals for Govind Guru and his family. He was a good worker of the Sampsabha, having been among the first adivasis to join it. Ramota was an active participant when Govind Guru organised the second big meeting of the Sampsabha in Chhani Magari.

He had gone visiting a relative during the day. When he came back home in the evening he learnt about the return of Govind Guru. He wanted to go to see Govind Guru straightaway. But his elderly father told him, "Guru Maharaj has returned to the village after a long time. You, Ramota, are a devotee of his. So, son, you should go to him with some homemade rotis. It may be a simple fare, but feed him with respect."

Hearing her father-in-law, Ramota's wife immediately cooked eight or ten maize rotis with kachri vegetable. She wanted the rotis greased with ghee, but there was no fresh ghee in the house. There was some ghee made out of goat milk in a pot which had begun to smell because it was becoming stale. She did not think it proper to use that kind of ghee on the rotis. Ramota was, of course, a known devotee of Govind Guru, but his wife revered him equally. She had closely watched the proceedings of the Sampsabha at Basiya. Ramota saw the humble meal he was carrying as a grand treat for his Guru and his family.

After an exchange of pleasantries with him, Govind Guru told him, "Ramota, you've just come back after visiting your relatives. You must be very tired. Go home, take your meals and rest." He turned towards Bhartya and advised him, "Bhartya, you too go and attend to your wife. She must be hungry and thirsty. Who else but you will look after her?"

Bhartya had enjoyed the moments he had spent with Govind Guru. He had forgotten about his mentally ill wife. But memories kept flooding back to disturb his peace of mind.

He saw the image of the silent, "insane" woman sitting in the courtyard. He felt sorry for her but he also felt irritated. Anger was building within himself. What was in his mind came out of the mouth. "Oh, Mahadev Baba! Oh, Hirkuliya Dev! Oh Guru Maharaj! My son has gone. He had only this much life to live. He did not allow me to even treat him with medicines. But what do I do with this liability! Neither she recovers nor does she die. Her insanity is a life-long disease. I shall feel relieved if she dies. I shall be able to earn enough for myself anywhere. But I can't leave her in her present condition."

Bhartya took a deep breath as he spoke this. For the first time he was opening up before Govind Guru to share his secret thoughts with him.

Bhartya's tragedy reflected more clearly on his face than in his words. Guru Govind had read his face in the dim light that came from the eternal lamp lit at the dhooni. All manners of doubts came to his mind. He began to feel the unbearable pain suffered by Bhartya more intensely than his own pain on account of the untimely death of his first wife and their two sons. Guru thought that sharing even the biggest of personal pain with others brings some relief. Bhartya may be able to share his pain by talking to people. He has come out with his secret thoughts too. But this kind of mental state could have unpredictable consequences. Is Bhartya thinking of doing something unexpected? So much for Bhartya! But what about his wife? Who knows what storms may be brewing in her mind? Her mind is not working and she is in deep shock. How can one lighten her mind?

After thinking over this, Govind Guru realised that he understood the world of insanity. But the matter with Bhartya was more serious. Govind Guru knew of many cases when hunger, adversity and incurable diseases had led to some unfortunate tragedy, self-inflicted or otherwise. Will Bhartya do some such thing? Govind Guru was troubled by this thought. He took Ramota aside and told him, "Ramota, please take care of Bhartya. It is necessary that whatever time he has after attending to his wife should be spent in doing the Sampsabha work. Come to me tomorrow with Bhartya. Now take him away."

As Bhartya and Ramota and the two boys who had come with the latter began to leave, Govind Guru called Ramota and said: "What shall we do with so many rotis. Here, take some back." Govind Guru's wife had already looked at the pile of the rotis that had been brought wrapped in a piece of cloth and quietly told Govind Guru that they were more than what they could eat. Govind Guru returned the extra rotis to Ramota.

After finishing his meals, Govind Guru lay on a stone slab near the dhooni in Chhani Magari. By his side on another slab were lying his wife and their two sons. For a while he and his wife talked about the tragedy in Bhartya's life. She was too tired and turning sideways she was fast asleep in no time at all. The children had already gone to sleep.

Govind Guru was worried about a hundred things—the sorrows of hundreds of people like Bhartya. How to hasten the pace of Sampsabha activities where it is slack? How to win over the adivasi brethrens who are becoming an obstruction in Sampsabha activities? How to find out what intrigues are being plotted against the adivasis in the states of Dungarpur, Banswara, Kushalgarh, Udaipur, Pratapgarh, Soonth and Idar? How to confront the conspiracies that are being hatched against adivasis by the British with the Rajas and the Maharawals?

Govind Guru was lying straight on the stone slab. It was the month of Baisakh. The blue sky above was studded with innumerable stars. From their positions, these shining stars were transmitting some unknown message to the earth. Thinking about that message, Govind Guru went to sleep. He too was tired. Late at night, at the other end of the dhooni an elderly person and three-four youths were also quietly sleeping on the stone slab. They were members of the Sampsabha and faithful guards of their Guru.

The stillness of the night had engulfed the entire area. If the silence of the night, it was because of the noises made by wild animals, who may be half asleep but were agile enough to look for their preys, waiting patiently at one place or hiding behind the bushes.

"Intelligence sharpens a person's awakening." This is what Govind Guru had said in the form of a proverb at the house of Poonja Paragi (Poonja Dhirji) in Doongar village. Poonja was engaged in working for Sampsabha in his village for some days. His influence had spread in the village. But his son took no interest in anything except farming and his household duties.

Poonja did not waste his time thinking about other matters. He was going to attend a meeting along with Paragi, Kuriya, Kalji, Mema, Jorji, Lemba and Nagji. It was a secret meeting which was to be attended by the Soma family also. He was informed about it but had not showed up. Why did he not come? Govind Guru and his followers could do nothing but wait for him to find out.

The message about awakening had not fully registered with the followers. They merely looked at each other when Govind Guru had spoken of that proverb.

"Guru, please talk simply and straight. Time and efforts are wasted in explaining things which are complicated," Kuriya Bhagat was attempting to find a way for easier understanding of the message in the proverb.

"Oh! It is easy to understand things if you have intelligence. And awakening comes with understanding. You can move ahead if you are aware, conscious. Wisdom comes with education and experience. If we have the experience and have had some education, then only can we become intelligent and wise and then only can we spread awareness among the simple, illiterate and ignorant. When an entire community is awakened then the whole area is transformed and its bad days are over." Govind Guru explained at some length and received understanding nods from the audience.

He further said: "All you Bhagats are dear to me and are special workers. You have done well to advance the cause of Sampsabha. The meetings in Suranta and Basiya were highly successful. The Sampsabha message was taken to different corners by putting up dhoonis. Women and children also attend our meetings. This is all very good. But I think all this is done in the name of God as part of religious rituals. People are still victims of superstition and bad customs. It pains me a lot when I hear from here and there that a woman in a village has been killed because she was thought to be a witch, or if I hear of the sacrifice of a goat or a hen. People are enticed by tricksters like Ojhas and Bhopas. People seem to have more faith in treatment by hocus-pocus than by herbs and medicines. It surprises me a great deal that many people see me as a Miracle Baba.

Mema Bhagat, you had once told me that a child in a village was bitten by a snake and chanting my name, his parents smeared him with 'holy ash', and the child was all right within a short time. It must have been a coincidence. Can 'holy ash' remove poison from a body? Surely, either the snake was not poisonous or the effect of the poison was not going to last long.

"The problem is that we are not trying to make them understand certain facts, which bhagats like us do, but not our adivasi brothers. We can understand easily by trying to find answers to certain questions like how does the Bania (trader) become rich without doing any farming or by selling anything that is procured from the forests? How do employees of the Raj acquire property disproportionate to their income? The laws that Rajas, Jagirdars and big contractors make, who do they favour? It says in our scriptures and is also said by our ancestors that 'sweet is the fruit of patience'. If it is so, then why don't the adivasis get any fruit for the *begar* that they do? Why are we made to pay lagan' even when there is no crop? It is said that the subjects are like the children of the ruler. Then why do the officials of the Raja and the Thikanedars and their lieutenants play with the honour of our daughters and daughters-in-law? We have to understand all this."

"We do try to make them understand all this, Guru. What new action shall we plan?" asked Kalji Bhagat.

"You've asked the right question, Kalji. The thing is that it is difficult to change certain ideas and traditions that are enshrined in our minds for centuries. It is not impossible, but we must keep trying. If we educate the new generation, the youth and especially the children, properly then our message will travel far and awakening will spread to distant corners. There is only one way to achieve that, and that is to open schools everywhere to spread education."

"That's very true," was the unanimous verdict of the people.

The meeting decided that along with the members of the Sampsabha, the youth who have gone in search of jobs to Dungarpur, Banswara, Khairwada, Udaipur and other towns and who have had some education at certain level should be associated with the job of spreading awakening. Another important decision taken at the meeting was that the Mangarh hills should be the headquarters of all activities of the Sampsabha. The reason for this decision was that the hills of Mangarh were at the centre of the states of Dungarpur, Banswara and Santrampur. The object for imparting education was that apart from teaching the letters, it should touch upon many other issues that lead to awakening, and these were more or less the same as the principles of the Sampsabha. The main aim was to get rid of the bad habits, avoid litigation, adopt swadeshi (indigenous products) and say no to *begar*. The most important decision was not to pay any agriculture-related tax because of acute *chchapanya* famine for the last three consecutive years.

This meeting at the house of Poonja Paragi in Doongar village lasted till late at night. The bhagats who attended it rested for a while there and early in the morning left for their homes. They suddenly saw Deena Damore when they were going past Kadana village. He recognised Govind Guru and touched his feet as he burst out crying.

"Hey, what is the matter?" asked Govind Guru as he propped him up, placing his hands on his shoulders. Govind Guru had at first failed to recognise him. When he looked at his face carefully, it dawned on him that it was the same Deena, the cook, who used to bring his meals in the prison.

"How are you here?"

"When you were in prison I had informed you that a large number of adivasis were heading towards Dungarpur to get you released. Somebody told the officer in-charge in the prison about it. Upon this I was punished for spying for you. I could not tolerate it and I quit the prison service. Since then I've been roaming a lot, looking for you, Sant Maharaj. Now that I've met you, my mission is complete."

"What mission are you talking about? Tell me."

"I want to join the Sampsabha. I shall be safe in it. The thing is that there is arrest warrant against me because I left the prison service without any notice. Now you've to save me."

"Right. You be assured. You have not committed any crime. From today onwards you will be with Kuriya Bhagat and observing the rules of the Sampsabha, you will work for awakening."

Deena expressed his gratitude. He again touched the feet of the Guru, took his blessings and joined his group.

Talking among themselves, this small group with Govind Guru went beyond Kadana. Deena Damore sprang a surprise by asking: "Guru Maharaj, do you know that someone has killed Gul Mohammed Pathan, the police inspector at Gadra village? The suspicion is on the adivasis, but a name that has surfaced is that of Soma Parmar. This information was given to me by the gameti of Kholar village. This gameti was quite friendly with the police inspector at Ghatola where the police have been informed about the absconding Soma."

"Soma is a bhagat. He can't commit such a heinous act." Govind Guru was taken aback by the news but he recovered as he responded.

"Guru Maharaj, I know, the inspector at Gadra...he...yes he, that Gul Mohammed Pathan. What a base man...! Tota Bhil of Thurpura. Guru Maharaj, you know about him, don't you? Once when we were leaving Thurpura somebody told us that an Ojha had looked at the skin of Tota's corpse said that there was the shadow of a bad spirit on him. But people told me that the bastard Pathan inspector had raped Anati, the daughter of Tota, and then threw her into the well after strangling her to death. This is the story that everyone has heard in the villages around Thurpura. Tota also learnt about it and pleaded with the Thakur of Bawangarh. It is said that one evening the Pathan inspector reached the Thakur's Haveli. He handed over the contraband goods that he had brought in a bullock cart. It is believed that the Thakur helped save the sinful inspector and Tota was killed the same evening. It was said that someone drove poisonous needles into him when he was roaming like a mad man."

"Kuriya! Whatever the truth about this story, not only a bhagat of the Sampsabha but even an ordinary worker of the Sabha cannot commit the sin of murder."

"Guru Maharaj, I myself would have killed such a base man. If Somabhai did it, he discharged my responsibility," Kuriya said interupting Govind Guru.

"No, Kuriya! You are a hot headed person. It'll not do to commit such sins. If Soma has done this, the police will arrest him and you know very well the punishment for murder. Do you, or do you not know? Death sentence! It will affect us. We want that the Sampsabha work should proceed through peaceful means. Nothing should happen that tarnishes our image or brings a bad name to the Sampsabha. What Soma has done is a sin."

"No! Please pardon me, Guru Maharaj. Senga Sadhu says that the sinner should be finished. It will reduce the burden of sin on the earth. What bad had Joriya Bhil and Tantya Mama done? Tantya Mama had sliced the nose of the police inspector and killed an oppressive jagirdar. Was it a sin?"

Govind Bhagat was very fond of Kuriya Bhagat. He did not respond directly to Kuriya, but he said: "Kuriya, you'll understand these things later on. Right now your blood is boiling with the poison of anger. I don't believe in killing poison with poison." He had spoken these words with great seriousness. The other followers stared at Kuriya, who, though not appreciative, decided to be silent as he understood the situation.

The dhooni at the Mangarh hills used to have a popular adivasi fair on the full-moon day. All day long men, women and children in hundreds used to attend it. People from other villages and the adivasis also used to flock the fair. The flame would be kept lit the whole day. People would pour ghee into the dhooni according to their capacity and degree of respect. Some left corncobs as their offering. Offering ghee, corn and making a resolve to give up at least one bad habit came to be regarded as an act of great virtue.

This is what the Sampsabha workers had told the people. Men had covered their loin with a small piece of dhoti, the young and the middle-aged had covered their head with a cloth and the old wore a turban. They were all modestly clothed. The young women wore the traditional ghagra, choli and odhani. Their feet were covered with toe rings of gilt and their wrists and arms with other rings, bracelets and bangles. Their foreheads were decorated with Faini and Boralas. Some had Mogra and Champa flowers in their buns. Most of the elderly women were dressed in simple ghagra and blouse with an ordinary-looking Odhani to cover their head and practically no ornaments on their body. Almost all the children were naked. They were not conscious of the need to cover any part of the body. But all, the elderly, the middle-aged, the young, all were immersed in a spirit of devotion towards the dhooni. For the children, the hustle and bustle of the fair was more exciting than devotion to the dhooni.

The groups that had gathered at the fair had great faith in Govind Guru and respect for prominent workers like Kuriya and Poonja. Everybody knew them. The visitors touched the feet of Govind Guru who was sitting on a flat stone slab near the dhooni as they threw respectful glances towards him. There was no idol or statue anywhere at the dhooni. The adivasis believed in no other gods except the gods of their own folklore. But they did regard Lord Mahadev as their ancient God and his consort, Parvati, as their mother. In his heart Govind Guru respected a formless God, which was apparent during his long morning and evening prayers with closed eyes.

In the afternoon when the fair was at its peak, Govind Guru began his discourse.

"Without awakening in him, every human being is like an animal. Only awakening separates man from an animal. There is ability to comprehend in every human being. I call it awakening. Apply the mind to judge what is right and what is wrong. Understanding comes from mind. A man who uses his mind is never defeated. This is what intelligence is about. When someone says that such and such person has lost his mind then it simply means that he does not apply his mind and such a person cannot distinguish between right and wrong. You cannot take the right path in life if you do not know the difference between right and wrong. You can live your life without knowing the right path but it will be a wasted life. It is better that such a person is not born on this earth as he will be a burden on this earth. So when I talk of awakening, I talk of ability to understand and when I talk of understanding, I talk of mind and intelligence.

"I feel very sad when I hear someone say in a Sampsabha meeting that we are animals of the hills living in the forest, how can we grasp the intricacies of the worldly affairs? If you use a bit of your brain such a doubt will never arise in your mind. Does anyone learn to talk while in his mother's womb? The child learns to talk in the company of others in the family. In this world it does not help to be mute, or remain silent and not being able to give form to your voice. The child learns it all slowly. We do not have schools in our areas. If we had, we could proceed beyond the form of learning to speak to learning to read and write. That is why I say that those who have had a little education should share it with others. Whatever I have learnt from my Guru I share with you. The Sampsabha workers understand this and they are relaying this knowledge further. This is what awakening is. We do not learn before our birth how to till our land, collect useful things from the forest like herbs, medicines, honey, gum, catechu, and remain alert about poisonous insects, recognise deadly diseases. So how do you say that we are like animals?"

Everyone was listening to Govind Guru with great attention. Most of them understood what he was saying but were still quite unable to fully grasp his message. But it was not an impossible situation. Inside themselves they there stirred by a desire to make the impossible possible. It looked they had started to search for something within themselves. They felt a new sense of satisfaction. Kuriya, Poonja, Deena, Mema etc. were active among the crowd.

"Whatever you learn comes from the company you have after your birth. This task of learning has to be taken forward. It will move only if you sit and discuss things in good company. Why do I talk about giving up bad habits? Because bad habits destroy both mind and body. A man with bad habits loses his mind and such a man is certainly an animal. Drinking destroys the mind. Drinking leads to intoxication, which destroys the mind. A drunk man walks unsteadily. He becomes a nuisance wherever he goes. He becomes ill-tempered and beats his wife and children. Aren't these bad habits? When someone is under deep stress or sorrow, or develops a mental illness and he starts blabbering nonsense, then don't you consider such a person to be under the influence of some evil spirit?

"It is absurd to talk about evil spirits and ghosts. People talk about them because they lack understanding. Stories are spread about ghosts having been sighted at night. Tell me, if there are ghosts where do they hide during the day? Why can't they be seen in daylight? When I first came to this Mangarh hill someone told me that it was a desolate hill and there was a genie here who had the company of many ghosts. I deliberately slept here alone at night. Kuriya had also warned me against it, wondering what they would be able to do in case of a mishap. I listened to none of these talks and slept well at night. I did not even have a bad dream at night. I had some sense in me and was able to drive away the doubts from my mind. Think, that I sealed my doubts in the pitcher of my intelligence. When there are no ghosts inside the mind then how can a ghost from outside devour you? The stories about ghosts are stories about false notions. Such talks should not be believed. You go to the extent of killing some poor women by declaring them witches. Why are the Bhopas angry with me? Ponder over this question. It is because these Bhopas deceive the poor and the innocent through their hocus-pocus magic. I oppose this because what they do is bogus and misleading. What they do makes no sense. It is actually wicked. Isn't it wrong to earn without doing any labour and misleading people? Is it wise to fall into the trap of such people and be misled by them?"

The seeds of wisdom were beginning to sprout among those who had been exposed to the discourses of Govind Guru. His words had removed doubts from the minds of many. Some others were now preparing to counter-question Govind Guru. They wanted to quiz him in the past but could not do so because they lacked the confidence to be sure of the basis of their doubts. They had thought it prudent to remain silent. But the more compelling reason was their extreme reverence for him. The adivasis had begun to see Govind Guru as a demi-god. Only those who had heard him the first time were still somewhat sceptical.

"Apply your mind to learn about awakening, which is akin to sagacity. A person's intelligence comes from the knowledge within him of right and wrong. The dust of ignorance and stupidity at times envelops awakening. Remove that dust and you can see the brightness of awakening. You may look to be wide-awake but you are actually sleeping because of your ignorance and stupidity. The brightness of awakening will wake you up. This will be awakening in real sense. This awakening comes from experiences both good and bad. It comes from giving up bad habits for good ones. It comes from brotherhood and sharing the joys and sorrows of others. It comes from understanding what lies beneath the sorrows and wants in life."

The congregation was listening to Govind Guru with rapt attention. They were spell bound by him and the expression on their faces suggested that they wanted to go on listening to him forever. Even the little children had given up their playful activities and seemed to come under his spell.

Govind Guru went on.

"The permanent workers of the Sampsabha obey a strict code that requires them to practise cleanliness, be teetotaller, give up meat-eating and the use of opium, refrain from cutting green trees, refuse to do forced labour, drink clean water after straining it, rise early, brush the teeth, after moving the bowels clean the hands by washing them thrice by applying the earth, take daily bath, keep the food covered, cause no harm to anyone and not to usurp the rights of anyone else. They have taken up the task of making the male members of each family a bhagat. Their activities are expanding. They are enthusiastic about their work. Women must also come forward. My appeal to all brothers, sisters and mothers is to actively participate in the Sampsabha activities, observe its rules and also inform other men and women about it. The more intelligent female members in each family should become members of the Sampsabha and also a bhagat at the dhooni. The couples, men and women, will sit together and make offerings to the dhooni and also look after the dhooni's eternal flame."

In order to drive home his point and remove any reservation that they might have, Govind Guru made five-seven couples sit right in front of the dhooni and addressed them directly. Some of the followers shouted in his support--

"Govind Guru ki Jai!"

"Guru Maharaj ki Jai!"

"Mahadev Baba ki Jai!"

The air around Mangarh echoed to the responding shouts from the rest of the assembled people.

The fair and the meeting ended after Govind Guru's discourse and the concluding slogans in his praise. The people who had assembled there started to return to their settlements. The socio-religious movement of Govind Guru was gradually taking a politico-economic shape.

The sun was rapidly going down the western horizon. These were the last days of the month of Kanwar (the last phase of the rainy season). The sky over Mangarh was absolutely clear. All around the Mangarh hill, as far as the eye could see, there was greenery and uneven hilly forests. Some of the special bhagats had stayed behind at Mangarh hill with Govind Guru, including Kuriya, Poonja, Deena and three-four other young men.

Govind Guru finished his evening prayer. Sitting near the burning dhooni he lit an incense stick and sat on a flat stone platform. The day had just ended. In the east, the full moon of Sharad Purnima had climbed up a little. Not many stars were visible in the sky because the moon was too bright. But a few stars right above the head were visible. On the northern sky the Great Bear and the Pole Star could be seen clearly. Some flakes of clouds that resembled the wings of partridge were slowly advancing from the western direction to the east.

At Mangarh, the air was still. But there was some movement of air in the atmosphere above because the clouds were floating towards the moon. The clouds tried to envelope the moon but their attempt failed because they were too thin and scattered to blank the moon. All they could do was dim the brightness of the full moon. After a while the partridge-wing like clouds sailed between the Mangarh hills and the moon to reach the eastern horizon. The moonlight had a very soothing effect. It was bright enough to illuminate a wide scenic area. What helped was that no fog or dust particles from a storm had polluted the *sharad puno* (full moon) sky that night.

Deena's eyes were stuck on the moon for a long time. Kuriya asked him, "Hey, Deena, what are you looking at in the moon?"

"I find the moon today fascinating. Like a properly baked swollen millet roti. The spots on the moon are like the flecks on the crust of the baked roti."

"Deena, you are a dope. Where does roti fit into the description of the moon? Haven't you heard and seen that there is a Neem tree on the moon and under it sits an old woman working on the spinning wheel." Poonja was talking about a myth handed down generations.

"Yes, yes. This is what I also wanted to say," Kuriya said in approval.

"But what do I know? I only know that I have cooked rotis in the prison. That is why I remembered rotis." Deena was subdued by what Kuriya and Poonja had said. Govind Guru's mind was somewhere else. From the valley towards Dungarpur came the roar of a tiger. The animals, birds and the reptiles in Mangarh hill and its neighbourhood were alerted. They had sent signals of caution to each other in their own languages.

Discussing the topic of awakening till late into the evening, Govind Guru and his companions slept on the flat bed of stones in Mangarh. Before he went to sleep, Deena had lit a small fire to keep the wild animals away. The Sharad Purnima night advanced. It had all become very quiet after the roar of the tiger and the initial tumult it had created among the animals.

Half the month of Jeth (last month of summer) had gone by without any pre-monsoon rain, though the month of Baisakh had seen some occasional showers. That day hot *loo* winds were blowing. No animal had come out of their hidings in the valleys and caves. By late afternoon, flocks of partridges were seen at some places. Deena thought of hunting the partridge. For a moment he had forgotten that he was now a recognised worker of the Sampsabha, which prohibits eating non-vegetarian food. As soon as he realised it the idea of hunting for the partridge vanished from his mind like a snake's reflexive withdrawal into its hole when it sees the peacock.

"Deena, you are not paying attention," Kuriya said, having assessed that Deena's mind had temporarily strayed when the Sampsabha's next strategy was being discussed seriously.

"Oh! No, nothing."

"But there is something," Poonja repeated Kuriya's question to him.

"Arre! Leave him. Why Deena, are you remembering the prison?" Doongar intervened.

Deena fell silent on the mention of prison. But Kuriya's forehead was furrowed. His eyes turned deep red. His right hand moved towards the lathi kept by his side. He tightened his grip over the lathi. Govind Guru knew well that an angry Kuriya loses control over himself and starts pacing up and down. To prevent such a situation and further obstructions in the discussion over the Sampsabha's next strategy, Govind Guru gently placed his right hand on Kuriya's left shoulder. Kuriya twice muttered within himself, "Jail-jail".

Govind Guru became his serious self and continued. "The Sampsabha groups have been formed in most of the villages and settlements in the Vagad region. Every child is familiar with our work. Everyone understands that the Sampsabha is the first and the most reliable organisation working for the adivasis. The workers of the Sampsabha are competent enough to ably resolve settlement disputes and sub-caste related issues. People are giving up the bad habits they had inherited over the centuries. We have used dhoonis, havans, and prayers to teach about good habits. Larceny and pilfering are disapproved. Cleanliness is being adopted as a way of life. Attention is being paid to eat healthily. The most important thing is that a large number of our brothers have got rid of the habit of drinking. It is really a deplorable addiction that is responsible for domestic violence and does nothing but cause destruction.

"Now our first job will be that all of us unite to oppose the opening of liquor shops at the instance of the British and in collusion with officials of the state. Our protest will be non-violent. There are two ways for achieving our aim. One, groups of local Sampsabha workers go round explaining to the liquor contactors that the adivasis have taken a pledge to give up the habit of drinking. Two, the Sampsabha units should ensure that if not all, at least the majority of adivasis in the village respect the rule of the Sampsabha, the foremost of which is to get rid of the habit of drinking. We have to accomplish this task in the next four months. The month of Aashadh (June–July) is ahead of us. People will be busy in ploughing and sowing. Therefore, this work has to be accelerated in the next fortnight that is to say by the next full moon day."

Selected Sampsabha workers were present at this meeting. All of them raised their hands in support of Govind Guru.

A meeting was held on a plateau near Aamaliya village situated at the base of the Mangarh hill. On the stone platform with Govind Guru were sitting Kuriya Bhagat, Poonja Dhira and two-three respected adivasis. The rest of the workers were sitting in the shade of a tree. The sun was still shining intensely over the Mangarh summit. The umbrella-like Jamun tree was laden with green raw fruits. After the rain in Aasadh, they will turn purple when their fruits ripen. The cuckoo was calling out its lover with its melodic sound. Flocks of green pigeons and parrots were frolicking on tree branches. Perched atop a tall branch, a peacock belted out its signature call four times to which many others of the species responded heartily.

"Oh, Guru Maharaj! This is a good omen. The peacock has called four times. It means that there will be good rain for four months from Aasadh (June–July) to Kanwar (September–October) months. If there is a good monsoon the employees of the state will have problem accessing us. We shall be able to complete our job easily." Sagatya Bhagat had interpreted the call of the peacock. He was a middle-aged man. His eyes sparkled with hope. Everyone present tried to look up beyond the thick branches. They could not spot the peacock, but they were all aware of its presence.

"Only today I saw the eggs laid by the sandpiper near the village fence. The eggs were placed at an elevation. It is true that we'll have good rains this time," Deepa Gameti said supporting Sagtya.

"Mahadev Baba should do just this. This is our prayer to him. Now, all of you rush to your respective areas to quickly start your Sampsabha assignments. Explain whatever we have decided and deliberated upon today. You, Kuriya, tell the youth what they have to do." Govind Guru concluded the meeting with these remarks.

By then the sun was receding fast and it was about to set. The shadows of the Mangarh hill were lengthening on the burning Aamaliya village.

Ditya, Galya, Bisanya, Hadu, Subana, Dagruya and Kadsa—all of them were young. They were enthusiastic for the Sampsabha mission. They had left their homes and had jumped at the opportunity to become fresh recruits of the Sampsabha. They were all dedicated followers of Govind Guru. They saw in him the image of their god, Mahadev Guru. In a matter of six-eight months they had completely devoted themselves to the Sampsabha. Ditya and Bisna had left their homes after quarrelling with their parents. By a coincidence all three of them were bachelors, while all the others were married who visited their villages frequently. This gave them more opportunities to explain the Sampsabha activities and aims to their families and others even as they remained in constant touch with their families and their villages.

But the bachelor trio did not return to their village once they had left it. Govind Guru had tried to explain to them several times that, "I don't want Sampsabha workers to leave their families. I want them to work for the Sampsabha wherever they are as that'll make our task easier. The Sampsabha work is not akin to becoming a Sanyasi who has to renounce the world, sever ties with his family and live in the forest. We work while living among our people. I have a family. Old dedicated workers like Poonja and Kuriya also visit their village and contact their people. Yes, Kuriya is a bachelor, but he has not uprooted himself from his village."

Ditya, Bisanya and Hadu had only one answer. People in their village will not be impressed if they went back to their village and started talking about something for their good. "It'll be like a prophet who is not honoured in his country!" This line of argument used to somewhat soften Govind Guru and he would say in the end, "Whatever your wish and that of Mahadev Baba!"

These enthusiastic half a dozen youth came from different sects of the adivasis, denoted by their surnames. Ditya Katara, Galya and Bisanya Damore, Hadu Meena, Suvana Kharadiya, Dagarya Singariya and Kadsa Dodal. But Govind Guru had succeeded to some extent through his message in support of the awakening movement in instilling the idea that at least in the Sampsabha there will be no discrimination on the basis of one's sub-caste and clan. All the adivasis face similar joys and sorrows. This idea he had planted deeply in the minds of all the workers. It was his dream to implant this idea firmly among the workers of the Sampsabha and to a large extent it appeared to be materialising.

Kuriya Bhagat briefed the youth separately. "The first task is to see that the liquor contractors move out of the village so that they cannot sell liquor. If they do not leave voluntarily, they'll have to be evicted by organising protest, involving the entire village. If anyone in a village helps or directly sells liquor we've to persuade him not to do so. We've to explain the harmful consequences on a person's health, mind and personal finances. The Sampsabha workers have propagated this idea extensively. But the need is to expand it further through persuasion."

Apart from asking them to work to erase the habit of drinking among the adivasis, Kuriya also entrusted another responsibility to the youth. "Awareness has to be spread in villages about the other principles of the Sampsabha also. We've to unite people to stop the entry of officials and employees of jagirdars, the state and the British governments into our villages. We've to explain that these people are behind most of our problems. These are the people who oppress the adivasis in many ways. It is these employees and officials who deprive us of our ancestral rights to the produce of the forest—fruits, vegetables, honey, gum, wood, leaves, grass etc. The British and the state rulers profit from these forest contractors while we suffer and bear losses. They are our enemies. They mislead the naïve adivasis by talking to them sweetly. They get close to us by deceitful methods or by pandering to our greed and then play with the honour of our sisters and daughters. Sometimes, they do these dirty things forcibly when they find their victim alone. Such wrong doings cannot be tolerated. Death is the best revenge for the perpetrators of such heinous acts."

"But Kuriya Kaka, the Guru denounces violence," Bisanya had no hesitation in interrupting Kuriya. Kuriya reacted sharply. "If someone misbehaves with our daughters and daughters-in-law should we worship him and accept him as our son-in-law?"

Bisanya was silent. He had shown some deference to Kuriya. What Kuriya had told him made more sense to him than what he had heard from Govind Guru. Galya, who was given to frivolity, joined the dialogue, "Yes, we shall worship such a person but it will be worship of a different form. It will be a worship of the type Kuriya Kaka has spoken of so that such an evil person either never repeats his misdeed or does not remain alive to repent."

"Yes. Kuriya Kaka, we shall break the legs and hands if any bastard who misbehaves, and if he dishonours our women we shall kill him and throw his body in a river so that nobody can find any sign of his existence." This observation by Hadu concluded this argument.

"Right. You have grasped the essential message. Go and get busy with your tasks," said Kuriya as he wound up his lecture which had taken place away from the presence of Govind Guru so that except for Kurita and the youths no one else had heard it.

Kuriya allocated villages to the youth in assigning them their responsibilities. Galya was asked to work in Bhukiya and Falwa villages. Deenya was to be active in Chikli and Shergarh. Bisanya was to go to the villages of Dalpura, Hathigala and Rohaniya. Similarly, Hadu was assigned Timbi Moti and Ghanganlai while Gatana and Santoliya were to be the field of activity of Subana. Sakora and Galiyakot were across the *Mahi* river so they were jointly assigned to Dagariya and Kadsa.

All these young men had understood their tasks and responsibilities as they left Aamaliya village, shouting a full-throated "Govind Guru ki Jai! Awareness for ever!"

After the Depawali festival, Govind Guru left Basiya with some prominent workers and arrived at Mangarh hill. Those who accompanied him included Poonji Dhira, Kuriya, Jeta, Bala, Lemba, Kalji, Jorji, Heerji, Galiya and few others.

According to a popular belief the Mangarh hill was the centre of a powerful kingdom of the adivasis in ancient times. Its old name was Makaniya Hill. It is said that in the *Haldighati* battle three Chauhan brothers of Chittorgarh—Mansingh, Darasingh and Maldarana—had helped Rana Pratap. Mansingh lost his two brothers in that battle. He became inclined towards asceticism because of the tragedy. Instead of returning to Chittorgarh from Haldighati, he arrived at this hill and began penance in the name of Lord Shiva. He built a small stone house to save himself from the elements. By and by, the adivasis of the neighbourhood got to know about him and started to visit him. They began to see him as a saint. The place where he said his prayers was the end of the boundary of the Santrampur state. The Santrampur ruler received the information that 'a Rajput from Chittorgarh named Mansingh was impersonating as a devotee of Lord Shiv. His real intention is to establish a kingdom of his own with the help of adivasis.' He saw it as a danger to himself. He sent a trusted spy and had Mansingh killed one night. People who visited him later did not believe that they were seeing his body. They thought of him as a highly spiritual person whose soul may have left his body. Since then the Makaniya Hill has been known as Mangarh. Govind Guru had constructed the dhooni about 200 yards from the original hut of Mansingh.

He held secret consultations here with some of his trusted lieutenants on the scope of the Sampsabha activities. Special attention was given to matters of prayers, community welfare and self defence.

"Today, the Sampsabha has a large number of workers in not only the entire state of Dungarpur but also Santrampur, Idar, Banswara, Mewar and Vijaynagar areas. What surprises me is that despite our numerical superiority over the area, the Rajputs with a few other communities, who are lesser in numbers, have been ruling over us for God knows how many years. Under their rule, we, the hungry and deprived people, are made to suffer atrocities almost everyday. The Raj does not care for our pains and sorrows. The British are a foreign community. The rajas and maharajas who rule over us dance to the tunes of the British. Our ancestral rights over our land, forests, hills, rivers and streams are being snatched away from us. They did not hesitate to arrest our Guru Maharaj even though he was innocent. The Sampsabha activities have been going on for some years now and there is awakening among the adivasis. But what is our lot? Our troubles have not gone. In my opinion we should prepare hit squads, we should get ready for violence..."

Kuriya was in a fit of frenzy and wanted to say more but Poonja stopped his flow to put his own point across. "Kuriya, you talk of violence repeatedly, but that is not easy. The Raj has an army of strong, powerful guns. They have the cavalry. The British are also ready to help them. With our bows and arrows we cannot confront the Raj directly."

"Agreed. But you'll concede that we are larger in numbers. We know the topography well. In the event of danger we can hide anywhere and when the opportunity strikes we can launch an attack on the enemy. If the Raj army is trapped in the valleys and narrow passes it will find it difficult to find a safe escape." Kuriya said to reinforce the point he had made.

"It is easier said than done, Kuriya! What you say is right but awakening has still not spread so widely nor has it become sufficiently strong. I've said it before also that bloodshed is not going to get us anywhere. We can inflict some losses on the Raj but in the end it might be difficult for us to win. Poonja is right that the rulers have well-equipped army, which has battle experience. We can get our problems sorted out by talking to Maharanas and Maharawals. Our real enemies are these British at whose behest the Raj commits atrocities on us. Things were not that bad before the British came. We must understand this that our fight is against a big power like the British who have taken control of even the rulers of the Pratap clan. The British rule over the entire country. The British army rushes to quell any trouble that may be started by the harassed people. We have heard a lot about how about 50 years ago the British had crushed a revolt by the people, which was joined by men in the cantonments in most parts of the country. With their power they were able to depose the emperor at Delhi. How can then we take them head-on? But if such a situation arises later we shall deal with it at that time. For the moment, our first task is to distribute the Sampsabha work among different groups."

Poonja occasionally nodded in approval of this statement by Govind Guru. Other workers were proud of the sagacity of their Guru. At first Kuriya was upset, but after listening in full to what Govind Guru had said about violence he agreed that no hasty step should be taken now.

"Why, Kuriya, if you have any doubts in your mind, let's hear them."

"I'm ready to wait for violence. Let's discuss ways to strengthen the Samnpsabha," Kuriya was brief in his response to Poonja. But his face betrayed an uneasiness, which he had temporarily suppressed. In a tense moment like this, Kuriya was in the habit of clutching his lathi tightly. This is precisely what he did.

With a smile on his face, Govind Guru was trying to read his mind. Kuriya was staring at a kite sitting on the stump of a tree. The bird was staring at a snake that hid itself in the root of a wild jujube tree clasping a writhing mouse or a small bird with its fangs. The ideas expressed by Govind Guru were fully endorsed by all, more out of reverence for him than by applying their judgement.

Selection of groups for different Sampsabha works was going to be a major task. The suitability of candidates for different jobs was considered at length. All the workers were dedicated to their tasks and were very loyal to the Sampsabha. It was deeply ingrained in their minds that whatever job is assigned to them will have to be carried out even if they had to face many dangers. They had experience, knew the area well and had influence over the adivasis.

Govind Guru had consulted all his associates before he took the decision on distribution of work. But decidedly, Poonja had played the most important role in it. There were two reasons for it—the original concept about the Sampsabha was his and the fact that he was three years older than Govind Guru, who had always preached respect for those who are senior in age. It was part of the social traditions he had inherited.

Because of influence of religious traditions over him, in the eyes of Govind Guru, the most important task before the Sampsabha was establishing the dhoonis, the holy fires with eternally lit lamp. Despite his extensive travels in the adivasi areas, familiarity with their joys and pains, acquaintance with their traditions and psychology, he had not jettisoned the concept of the original adivasi religion as a matter of belief, faith and trust. It is a different matter that the focal point in the banner that he had chosen for uniting the adivasis under the Sampsabha had the images of two symbols of nature, the sun and the moon.

In fact, Govind Guru's religious beliefs were strongly influenced by Swami Dayanand Saraswati. He was close to him for a long time during the Swami's visit to Udaipur. That was why the Vedic rituals of the Yajna was an important religious ritual for Govind Guru and establishing dhoonis was a reflection of it. To carry out this crucial job of setting up dhoonis was chosen Lembha Bhagat of Sundrav, who was not only a bhagat but was well versed in the art of masonry. He was good at building platforms, walls, roof, *bavan kund* (dhooni) and *deepalya* (place for the sacred light). Lembha Bhagat was pleased that he had got a job of his liking.

The work entailed a lot of activities that were part of preaching religion. Among them were remembering and creating new devotional songs and prayers, propagating the beliefs of the Sampsabha that included cleanliness in living, taking daily bath, wearing tulsi necklace, saying prayers with rosary, applying sandalwood tilak on the forehead, pouring ghee in the dhooni, lighting the lamp with ghee and offering coconut on special days, particularly the day of the full moon. From a constructive point of view these activities were designed to instil moral values for a better personality. The man in charge of this job was Jorji Bhagat of Bawari village.

The third important field of activity chosen was providing medical help to men and cattle. This was a facility much neglected in the adivasi region. If there were any practitioners of local medicines they were found in the towns and urban areas, beyond the reach of the adivasis, who had to depend for treatment of their illness on medicinal plants and their knowledge of the traditional ways of healthcare. The Sampsabha was opposed to superstitious ways of treatment. But the only alternative for the adivasis was to depend on natural herbs, plants and their self knowledge about treatment. Adopting and propagating this method could provide some relief to people. It was considered an essential part of their unfortunate life that they did not have any facility for the treatment of complicated and serious ailments.

But indigenous treatment for many everyday problems like bite by poisonous reptiles, light injuries, bleeding, seasonal ailments and those arising from carelessness or from insufficient precaution was possible with a little care. Often, an ordinary illness would take a serious turn, threatening life. Dealing with this problem was chosen as one of the activities of the Sampsabha and its responsibility was entrusted to Jeta Bhagat of Thali Talai. He had inherited from his elders the knowledge of the uses of natural herbs. Wherever he went he would collect medicinal plants and put them in a sack. He kept a large number of these medicines at his home for use at odd hours.

A good monsoon meant that there would be no shortage of drinking water and wherever farming was possible it assured water for irrigation in the Vagad region. But the *chchapanya* famine had convinced the people that there has to be a lasting source of water. Except for digging wells, no other alternative looked likely. At a constructive Sampsabha discussion on division of work, Kalji Bhima of Basiya had mooted the idea of digging wells. It was approved unanimously. He had acquired some knowledge from his father, Bhima, about spotting the place where ground water could be found. Most of the ground water sources are near rivers, streams and tanks. But if it does not rain for three-four years this source also dries up. It is not easy for most people to determine where to dig well in drought conditions. Only someone with experience would know. There is a particular kind of vegetation that grows on soil that has water below the surface. The growth of certain varieties of grass known as kans and patera is considered a sure sign of underground water.

This is what Kalji had learnt from his father. Kalji was considered an expert in pointing the exact spot for digging well. Before pointing the spot he would touch his nose with the first two fingers of his right hand as an omen, then ask an innocent boy to touch one of his fingers and then he will make some gestures to create the impression that he is finding out the exact spot where the well should be dug. This kind of exhibitionism did reinforce the belief that he has an inherited gift in locating the spot for ground water source. Hence, the task of selecting sites for digging wells and maintaining them was assigned to this native hydrologist.

Every worker of the Sampsabha was not a bhagat. Apart from observing the ceremonies of the bhagat tradition in the adivasi belt that were introduced by Sant Surmal and Mavji and then continued by Govind Guru, the bhagat had to strictly observe the Sampsabha rules, say his morning and evening prayers to God regularly and wear the rudraksha necklace. Jorji was given the task of propagating religious affairs and the rituals connected with prayers. This in itself was a big responsibility so it was separated from the task of anointing bhagats.

The institution of bhagats was useful in implementing the social reform agenda and its scope included eradicating bad habits and superstitious beliefs. Total prohibition was an important goal for the bhagats. This was a duty that could be performed only by one who was very active and enthusiastic towards the goal and was totally devoted to the Sampsabha. Actually, all the workers were eligible to perform this duty and anyone of them could have been picked up for this job. But Govind Guru and Poonja Dhira were assigning each job to the most suitable worker. The challenging task of appointing bhagats was given to Kuriya Danot. Govind Guru liked Kuriya no less than he did Poonja. Kuriya was hoping to be appointed to look after a defence or a fighting adivasi group.

But that was not to be. With his infectious enthusiasm, Kuriya had become very popular among the younger generation of adivasis. He was good at recruiting the youth for the adivasi defence squad. Govind Guru and Poonja worried that Kuriya was a little hot headed. Fearing he might unnecessarily create trouble, he was given the task of appointing bhagats that in the circumstances appeared to be a more important job for him. It was thought that Kuriya needed to soften his extreme opinion on the criterion for appointing bhagats and he also needed to think seriously before taking any decision or expressing his opinion. Nobody knew that inside Kuriya, a great adivasi character was taking shape. Kuriya had gladly accepted the responsibility given to him. But nobody was able to guess what was churning inside his mind.

Performing rituals for the departed was regarded as an independent work. This was how Govind Guru had looked at it. If the dead person was not a minor, the adivasi practice was to organise a feast after the death and immerse the ashes of the dead in any sacred river. The immersion of ashes at the confluence of the rivers Mahi, Jakham and Som was an important ritual performed at the annual Veneshwar Dham fair. Govind Guru was of the view that this ritual should be patterned on the lines of the Bundi Akhara.

The Bundi Akhara was set up by his Guru, Rajgiri Gosai. It was an important but not a big job. Yet, it was separated from other jobs and it was assigned to Bala Bhagat of Dokar village.

Thavara of Nava Gaon was good at spying. Lord Shiv used to be worshipped as the adivasi god in that region. People knew Narad Muni as a *khabarnawees* (informer) because his name used to figure prominently in the tales about Lord Ram and in the references to Ram and Shabari. It was in this background that Thavara had become famous as Narad in the area. Naturally, he was chosen to be in charge of the adivasi spy network.

It was an important function of the Sampsabha, a key instrument for solving problems of the adivasis. It required having an intermediary who could talk to the rulers and the role of that "envoy" was given to Galiya Bhagat of Vanda village.

Now remained the last but the most important job that had to be completed early. It was raising the defence squads, consisting of youth who were physically strong, courageous and enthusiastic and had a strong spirit of sacrifice in them. It was indeed a big task to select the right persons and develop their qualities to mould them for walking on the right path.

Poonja had drawn an outline in his mind about a trained police-like organisation. He had discussed the matter with Govind Guru on a number of occasions previously. Poonja knew a lot about the Mewar Bhil Corps. He had prepared a list of dozens of people who had served in the armed units of the Mewar Bhil Corps before they had retired at the age of 55 years. There was a list of those who retired annually and hailed from Dungarpur and Banswara states and the Bhomate area of the Mewar state. Poonja had thought of using the retired personnel of the Bhil Corps for training adivasi youth for the defence squads of the Sampsabha and render advice to it. When the division of Sampsabha work was being discussed, he had presented his detailed views on the subject before Govind Guru and other colleagues. The fervour that he showed for his plan both impressed and inspired those he addressed. On the recommendation of Govind Guru the Sampsabha appointed Poonja Dhira in charge of the adivasis' defence squad.

"For this job, some responsibility should also be entrusted to Thavara of Jkharkara. Shouldn't we take him into consideration? Thavara has worked a lot with Tantya Mama. He is a good marksman and a good guerrilla fighter," Kuriya had broken his long silence while addressing Govind Guru.

"Yes, Kuriya. You're right and thanks for reminding us about Thavara. Why has he not been seen for a long time?"

"About two months back he met me in Bhukiya village. He told me that he was preaching the Sampsabha principles vigorously in Jharkara and its nearby areas. He said, 'I shall certainly call Govind Guru to my village.' He is a Sampsabha worker and doing his job sincerely."

"Fellow bhagats! If all of you agree, let Thavara be appointed the chief assistant of Poonja in taking up the responsibility for the defence squads. His experience will be useful for that kind of work."

"Guruji, you and Kuriya are right. But I've a doubt in my mind. It is believed that during his association with Tantya Mama he committed many robberies and murders too. Maybe, the Jhabua police are looking for him. We can be in trouble because of such a man."

Hirji's comments took everyone by surprise. But Kuriya was quick in giving a measured response. "Thavara returned to village about ten years ago. Till date, no police force came searching for him. If someone does come, we shall see. The Tantya gang committed no sin. He fought for the rights of the adivasis. Sin was committed by the British who hanged him.

We have to fight the enemy determinedly. It'll not do to be hesitant, scared or be doubtful."

"Look Kuriya, no need to be upset over what Hirji said. It is better to remove one's doubts in time. If all of you agree, Thavara will share my burden in this task."

This resolution of Poonja, which Govind Guru had adopted as his on Kuriya's insistence, received unanimous support. The earnest manner in which Kuriya had reacted had also removed the doubts from the mind of Hirji.

It was the decision of the house that defence squads would be formed area-wise. Members of the defence squads would meet at an appointed place at least once in 15–20 days whenever they can free themselves from heir household duties to find time for the Sampsabha. As far as possible, the job of forming defence squads should have been completed before the coming full moon fair at Mangarh so that its volunteers could help with maintaining order in the fair. It would give the squad volunteers experience and also they would get to know people.

One of the squads would be that of five–seven armed youth who would carry guns in addition to bows and arrows. This group would guard Govind Guru. Until the time a group of committed youth could be tested and tried for full-time appointment in the defence squads, some youths would be chosen temporarily who would be changed according to our convenience. It was known to all that the Raj kept a sharp eye on the activities of Govind Guru and lest something untoward happens to him, the matter of providing him security was top priority for the Sampsabha.

Another important job of the adivasi defence squad would be to resist at local level the atrocities against adivasis that were witnessed almost daily. The state employees and those of the jagirdar who forced adivasis to do *begar* would be opposed. The defence squad would organise and unite people at a local level to successfully stop the forest department officials from preventing adivasis from collecting firewood, grass, and fruits and vegetation from the forest. It was the Sampsabha that would decide how much of levy should have been paid on the farm produce, and the defence squads would be informed about it in time so that the task of preventing oppression of the adivasis could be initiated.

The bhagats would enforce prohibition. But if contractors still tried to sell liquor or liquor shops were opened in the adivasi areas then the defence squads would strongly confront them and ensure that liquor shops were not opened in the adivasi areas. It would be for the defence squads to teach a lesson to the employees of the Raj or the jagirdar if they molested their women. A complaint about such activities would also be conveyed to the Darbar through the medium of the Sampsabha.

In case a situation arose that necessitated direct confrontation with the Raj, the defence squad members would quickly respond to the drumbeats, the *halkara dhol*, and would go to their posts and get ready for assault. The rest of the adivasis would come together, as was the tradition, and act on the advice of the Sampsabha workers. Poonja Dhira was asked to ensure that four big drums were placed at the dhooni site in Mangarh, which could be used whenever the need for giving a distress call arises.

The meeting for the allocation of the Sampsabha assignments and duties was held secretly, but the fact was that in no case could the presence of Govind Guru and his associates at Mangarh be kept a secret. This news had spread in the nearby areas by noon. The Sampsabha workers had to hold back a crowd of about 100–150 adivasis that had already arrived at Mangarh from reaching the meeting venue. The crowd waited to see their beloved leader. The meeting ended in the afternoon. The waiting adivasis went up to Govind Guru, touched his feet and sat around him. Since Govind Guru wanted to return to Basiya the same day, he spoke briefly, for less than an hour, to tell the assembled adivasis about the awakening campaign.

As Govind Guru got up to leave, Poonja Dhira asked bow and arrow-carrying youths from the nearby villages of Ambadara, Pothiwara, Gumanpura and Varet, five-seven in number, to accompany him for his protection. Poonja and Kuriya also went along with Govind Guru. Kalji, in any case, had to return to Basiya, so he too went with them. Other workers, briefed about their tasks and assignments, went their separate ways. The adivasis who had come there also headed back to their villages after full-throated cries to hail Govind Guru.

Basiya was about 25 miles from Mangarh, a distance that Govind Guru and his party, including his bodyguards, completed by late evening. Poonja and Kuriya had parted at the pathway at the point of entry to Basiya because they had to prepare for their assignments.

Some people from Suranta and Basiya villages, who knew that Govind Guru would return by late evening, had collected at the dhooni site in Basiya. Govind Guru spent some time in prayers at the dhooni and talked to the people who had come there. He then returned home where his wife and sons were anxiously waiting for him. He had his meals with his wife, talked to her for a while and went to sleep.

FOURTEEN

Changes with the march of time, though slow, were becoming noticeable in the adivasi belt. At an important Sampsabha meeting held in Amaliya village in the month of Jyesth, Kuriya Bhagat had, on instruction from Govind Guru, asked some youth to fan out to spread awareness about the ill effects of drinking and the harassment caused by the employees of the Raj and the Jagirdar. The performance of this group was reviewed from time to time. The progress on spreading the message of prohibition by Deepawali was especially encouraging. Govind Guru was constantly informed about the progress made in various areas of activities.

When he was at Basiya, Govind Guru had sent out a message that the youths given charge of the prohibition campaign at the Amaliya meeting and the bhagats assigned other tasks at the Mangarh meeting held after Deepawali had to reach Basiya on the second day after the Amavasya (the last day of the dark fortnight of a lunar month) in the month of Magshish. They had assembled at the dhooni site in Basiya before noon on the appointed day.

It was green all around the dhooni site at Chhani Magari. The site was part of a dense forest. The monsoon was normal that particular year. Crops were satisfactory. Rich jungle grass had grown all around. There were clusters of Mahua, Jamun, mango, wild fig, Dhak, Semal, neem and gum trees. There was a very thick growth of wild vegetation all along the narrow path that led up to Chhani Magari. To negotiate that path one had to constantly push these plants out of the way which also had a rich growth of shrubs of different varieties. Small wild plants had grown in the comparatively few free patches on the pathway. On the slope to the Magari were grass of different varieties like Kuri, Kodara and Barat which having ripened were shedding their seeds. This particular kind of grass becomes dry soon after the advent of winter, only to be revived at the next monsoon. There were also tender touch-me-not plants, which were not easily visible in the thick growth of vegetation all around. Even a soft touch of finger will wither these very sensitive plants but in the very next moment they will be revived fully.

The stream at the back of the Magari used to flow into a nearby natural lake, which was full of transparent water, making it easy to guess the depth of the lake. On the bank of the lake were flowering white ghetoola, a lotus like flower. At its mouth had spread a layer of water hyacinth. The wet soil of the stream was full of long patera grass.

Before the arrival of the workers and the bhagats, Govind Guru had had a bird's eye view of the scenic lake from the height of Chhani Magari. The sun had just risen. It was winter time, the breeze at that moment was a gentle cool. The sky was clear. The entire area was basking under a pleasant sun. It was the sunshine that gently caresses and exhilarates mankind and is found agreeable by both man and the kingdom of plants and vegetation, unlike the harsh winter. From a corner came the sound of a chorus by a group of chirping birds. Birds of different species, local as well migrant, were frolicking in the lake. In the middle of the lake was a playful pair of bright golden Brahminy duck. The darter was enjoying itself by frequently diving in the water. Chinese coots were swimming in small groups. Different types of ducks floating in the water stood out prominently. There were skylarks and many birds like pelican, cormorant, who created a rainbow with their green, golden and red beaks. Among the larger birds there were plenty of demoiselle crane with grey wings and one could barely take one's eye off the dart-headed goose. The carefree movements, joyous expressions and the playful acts by the birds had lent a pleasant atmosphere around the lake.

Govind Guru had held the first and the second meeting of the Sampsabha in Basiya and Suranta villages as a result of which everyone, right down to the last child, had become his follower. At Chhani Magari in Basiya men, women and children from these villages had assembled to see Govind Guru. After paying their obeisance at the dhooni they would touch his feet. He felt emotionally inspired. He thought to himself, "Despite my being born in the Banjara community, how much respect do these people bestow on me." From his seat on the platform, Govind Guru gave his blessings to all. When the bhagats and the young workers of the Sampsabha arrived there, he asked the men and women to return home with their children. Govind Guru asked some of his lieutenants to help the men and women out as they began to return home. He then signalled that the meeting be commenced with the decision on prohibition, taken at the Amaliya meeting, as the top agenda for discussion. Shouting 'Jai Guru Maharaj' the bhagats and the young workers sat at the plateau in front of Govind Guru.

"By the grace of Mahadev Baba and the blessings of our Guru Maharaj, the Sampsabha work is proceeding well. We have devoted bhagats. Considering the enthusiasm among the young workers, we can assure Govind Guru that we'll make faster progress. With the permission of our Guru, I'd like to ask the individual volunteers who campaigned for prohibition to talk and discuss their experiences in their areas." Looking reverentially towards Govind Guru, Poonja had opened the meeting proceedings. Govind Guru raised his hand as a gesture of hearty approval.

"As told by Kaka Kuriya, I went to Dalura, Hathigala and Rohaniya villages and talked to people there. No problems were encountered initially. There were no liquor shops in these villages but one liquor trader did sell liquor. I had a discussion with the *gametis* of the three villages. They agreed that nobody should buy the liquor being sold by the trader. But they did not agree to a ban on the consumption of homemade Mahua liquor. Gameti Modubhai of Rohaniya was specific: 'Drinking liquor made of the flower of Mahua tree is not a new tradition. What harm does it cause? A man feels relaxed if he takes a few drops of the Mahua liquor when he retires for the day after a day's hard labour. What's bad in it?' Modubhai himself is given to drinking Mahua liquor. The *gametis* and elders of the other two villages were well familiar with the name of Govind Guru and the Sampsabha. As soon as they heard these names, they agreed to introduce prohibition. The Panchayats of the two villages were called separately. Everyone agreed with the views expressed by their elders. Some young people were asked to maintain vigilance. Now nobody in Dalpura and Hathigala drinks. Yes, it cannot be denied that there might be an odd person, an addict, who may still be drinking on the sly. These two villages have many people who have great faith in Guru Maharaj. All of them extended cooperation in introducing prohibition. After a few months, the elders of Rohaniya and the *gametis* of Dalpura and Hathigala were able to persuade Modubhai to accept that drinking harms the body. He is past 60 years. He has constant pain in the stomach. A medical practitioner of the village had diagnosed it to his drinking habit, upon which Modubhai renounced drinking. There are a couple of alcoholics in his village; they are incorrigible."

"Bisanya, you have opened the meeting with encouraging news," Poonja patted Bisanya as he looked at the other youth workers. Satisfaction was writ large on the face of Govind Guru. Other workers too felt happy.

Galya was full of confidence as he began. "I went on my mission to persuade people not only in the villages entrusted to me, Bhukiya and Falwa, but I also went round neighbouring villages, Padola and Kahwada. In Kahwada, prohibition is already enforced because of the impact of Guruji's teachings. It required a little effort to persuade some people in Bhukiya, Falwa and Padola, but in the end they realised that as propagated by the Sampsabha, drinking was not a good habit. In Padola, Lemba Maharaj has constructed a dhooni next to the Than (religious place) of Mavji. For the last three–four months an eternal lamp is being lit there."

Hadu confirmed that prohibition was complete in Timbimoti and Ganganlai villages. According to him: "These villages were already familiar with the teachings of the Sampsabha and the awakening programme was proceeding well. That is why the majority of both elders and the youth were with me. Outside Timbimoti village there are some camps of the Mogiya community. They fight after drinking. A representative of the liquor trader visits them once in five or ten days to deliver liquor. With the help of some village elders I had several rounds of talks with the mukhiya of the Mogiyas. But even their women drink liquor. Some village youth thrashed the men of the liquor trader. After that no representative of the liquor trader visited the village. About two months ago, the Mogiyas shifted their camps from there voluntarily. I don't know where they have gone. In fact, I've not bothered to find out. I was concerned only with prohibition."

All the assembled workers were happy to note Hadu's self-confidence and determination. Govind Guru raised his hands to bless him. Hadu was quite proud of his success.

Subana said: "I liked the name Santloya, derived as it is from Sant (saint). But after I reached that village, I didn't like what I saw. The liquor contractor doesn't sell liquor there, but the consumption of Mahua is widespread. Every household in the village distils Mahua liquor. With two–four friends of mine from my village I visited Santloya many times and also spread the message of the Sampsabha.

"But nobody agreed to give up consuming Mahudi. The access to the village is also difficult. It may be necessary for a bhagat to visit the village. Yes, in Gatana people had agreed readily. The gameti there is the priest of Hirkuliya Baba. That good man has a great deal of influence in the village. He was very useful for my work. He knows Guruji and the Sampsabha very well. He summoned the village Panchayat and had the prohibition oath administered at the *Than* of Kirkuliya. Some years ago, a man from the village had drowned after drinking in excess. This had taught a lesson to people. Now the entire Gatana village is reformed."

Dagadya and Kadsa were assigned to work in the villages of Sakora and Galiyakot, across the river Mahi. The two had worked together hard. Kadsa gave an account of their work. "Galiyakot is a big village. It has a large population of non-adivasis. We can't count on our influence over them. We worked in villages and settlements which have only adivasi population. They buy liquor from the vendor in Galiyakot where they sell firewood, gum and catechu in the market. We tried to dissuade them from drinking by telling them that the liquor they purchase from the vendor is mixed with an ingredient that makes men impotent. This proved to be our ace. Our months of work there succeeded and now nobody drinks liquor sold by the vendor. Consumption of Mahua has also gone down. Some elders suffer from asthma and cannot sleep well unless they have had a few drinks. But they are not alcoholics. They eat in the evening, drink their quota of liquor, belch and go to sleep. Their family members say that if they don't have their dose of liquor they will cough all night and would thus disturb the sleep of the rest of the family. That is why we did not pursue with these people. Sakora is a small village. Some impact is visible after we visited and talked to people there a number of times. But consumption of Mahudi on a limited scale exists. With a little more persuasion it may be possible to totally rid the village of its consumption."

Lastly, it was Dinya's turn and he said that in the villages of Chikli and Shergarh prohibition was in force to a large extent because of the impact of Guru Maharaj's teachings. There were some who had to be talked to. Bands of youths have been formed in the two villages. Turning towards Poonja, Dinya said as he was concluding: "Poonja Baba, your men formed a defence squad of the youth, who have started to monitor prohibition also. We became good friends with them." Poonja's face lit up. Dinya went on: "I worked in the nearby villages, Debore, Navagaon and Dabla. There is complete prohibition in all these three villages. The villagers were one in telling the contractor that they would not allow the sale of liquor in their villages. I'm satisfied that the duty entrusted to me with confidence by Kuriya Bhagat I was able to discharge with full sincerity. It is now my heartfelt desire that I should be given more work."

With the happy tidings brought by Dinya the meeting of the young prohibition brigade came to a close.

"Tell us something that may have troubled someone or problems created by the employees of the Raj or the jagirdars." Poonja Bhagat had asked a question. It elicited no information about misdeed by the Sampsabha workers. It was a matter of great satisfaction for all. It may be that something untoward might have happened but for some unknown reason nobody talked about it. Govind Guru and other bhagats were proud of the performance of the youth brigade. It was also a matter of satisfaction for them that such an enthusiastic, energetic and capable bunch of youth will be taking over the role of future adivasi leaders.

After obtaining reports from the youth brigade about the jobs given to them, Govind Guru talked to the senior Sampsabha members about the distribution of work, as decided at its last meeting. Lemba Bhagat said that he has raised a group for establishing dhooni-dhams and dozens of people are playing an active role in it. After the Mangarh meeting, Lemba Bhagat had in the last one month constructed dhoonis in about 50 villages, teaching at least one adivasi in each of these villages how to look after the dhooni and keep the light burning in the earthen lamps there.

People began to show respect for the dhoonis established by him. Wherever the dhoonis were constructed, Lemba Bhagat had asked Jorji to come and explain the religious sanctity of the dhoonis. The religious rituals of the Sampsabha are being observed in these villages. At every dhooni site flutters a black and white flag bearing the image of the sun and the moon. People are getting familiar with the songs of the Sampsabha. Whenever an assembly takes place at the site of dhoonis, these songs are song melodiously to the accompaniment of drums and flutes. Apart from religious sentiments, a moral awareness is also taking place among these people. Jeta Bhagat went round villages to tell people about the herbs and plants that are useful in curing man and animal. Kuriya Maharaj appointed many bhagats in the villages, who go round to propagate the Sampsabha ideals. Some of the new bhagats gave up their household duties to work for social and religious awakening day and night.

Kalji Bhima gave his account. "I am able to tell about the spots where well can be dug for getting water. But in most places we encounter a rocky layer while digging the well. Penetrating that stony surface becomes a big problem. This work can be done easily by blasting gunpowder. But gunpowder is expensive and, besides, it cannot be procured easily. It is not necessary to dig deep for water near rivers and streams and the ground there is not hard. In summer it is easy to prepare beds for growing fruits and vegetables near such sites. People have already adopted this technique. But it is not a year-round facility."

"Kalji Bhagat, gunpowder will have to be used to remove the stone layer for constructing deep permanent wells. There is no other way. The defence squad of Poonjabhai will have rifles; won't it be necessary to have gunpowder to use them?"

"I've talked to the men who go round polishing and grinding weapons. They make rifles and pistols and also sell gunpowder. I'll get you some quantities of gunpowder." Poonja Dhira said. He was in agreement with what Kuriya had told Kalji Bhagat. He had given a very practical and useful suggestion, which was praised by all.

"Poonjabhai! In most of the villages that I toured for my assignment I met the members of the defence squads you have constituted. They are full of enthusiasm. Using the bow and arrow is part of their inheritance. I saw some of them carrying rifles also. Guru Maharaj, Poonja deserves to be patted for this work," Kuriya suggested to Govind Guru when he was talking to Poonja.

Govind Guru was well aware of the good progress made by Poonja in carrying out his assignment. He merely smiled. Nearly all the bhagats knew that Galiya Bhagat had used loud drum beating to propagate the Sampsabha ideals in villages. Although the Sampsabha ideals and principles were being preached for quite some time, the work done by Galiya Bhagat in the last one month was especially useful and deserving of high appreciation.

"I had four tom-toms placed at the dhooni at Mangarh and also arranged for them in fifteen villages situated on the slopes of the hills in far-flung areas. Drums are already in use in many villages for summoning people for singing prayers and religious songs. It'll be possible now to collect people whenever the need arises with the help of the call of the drum." Poonja Dhira gave this information during discussions on the defence squads.

The adivasis of the village had organised a community lunch near a pond for the workers and the bhagats who had taken part in the lengthy discussions and the review of the progress made in carrying out the various activities of the Sampsabha. While the feast was on, it was decided that with only a fortnight left for the Puno (Full Moon) festival at Mangarh's main dhooni, the Sampsabha workers and the bhagats should mount publicity to ensure that it was attended by as large a crowd of adivasis as possible. Shouting in praise of Govind Guru, everyone returned home after the meals.

Govind Guru was at home by afternoon. The sun was losing vits warmth. He spread himself on the cot in the inner courtyard of his hut, thinking about the future strategy of the Sampsabha.

The first rays of the sun hit the crowd of adivasis. Travelling long distances from Khairwada and Bhomat areas in the Udaipur state, Idar and Santrampur states of neighbouring Gujarat, and the states of Dungarpur, Banswara and Pratapgarh, the adivasis had arrived at Mangarh the previous night. Some arrived by morning from Sagwada, Garhi, Basiya and Bagidora. People from areas close to Mangarh were on their way. Govind Guru had arrived from Basiya with his family two days in advance. Kuriya, Kalji and Thavara Bhagat had come with him. The adivasis of Basiya, Suranta and other nearby areas arrived at the fair on its opening day, though Jeta Bhagat, Bala Bhagat, Lembaji, Jorji, Galiya and a few others had also arrived a day or two in advance. As for Poonja Dhira, he was already running a training camp for members of the defence squad at the Mangarh plateau. About half a dozen retired army personnel from Khairwada cantonment were fully occupied in the training camp, teaching their trade day and night. The large size of the crowd had enhanced the sense of merriment among the adivasi participants.

Govind Guru was never seen in such a happier mood! His impressive face, almost hypnotic, appeared to be shining with a divine power. The eternal light was burning at the dhooni site. The Sampsabha's white flag with its images of the sun and the moon fluttered in the air. Symbols and cords symbolising the preaching points of the Sampsabha in different colours were for the first time formally displayed on the eastern face of a large rock stone west of the dhooni site. The job was performed a day earlier under the direction of Govind Guru.

White represented peace; objects of nature were represented in the form of the sun and the moon; man and woman were represented by the white and red colours; more of red to represent power and the god of power, Lord Hanuman; green reflected prosperity; the emblems of awakening were trident, spear, conch, metal bangle, small necklace, the letter "Om" and a lit lamp. The sacrificial havan fire was lit at the crack of dawn at the dhooni under the supervision of the bhagats. Hundreds of volunteers were controlling the crowd. The devout were visiting the dhooni site in an orderly manner. They would come to the holy spot, pour ghee in the sacrificial fire, touch the feet of Govind Guru who sat nearby on a flat stone and receive his blessings, exit from the other end to join the fun and fair, laughing, joking, singing, dancing, gossiping, indulging in playful antics and talking merrily among family members and friends. The defence squad trained by Poonja Dhira was on alert to avoid the possibility of trouble being created by anti-social elements. Their trainers, the retired army personnel from the Khairwada cantonment, were keeping an eye over the entire arrangements at the fair with the help of the Sampsabha volunteers.

Men, women and children, all had come to participate in the fair. Despite their lack of resources, they had come attired in whatever they could find as their best. The women had silver bangles, coconut kasle, shellac bangles, gilt bhooriyas (big bangles), silver ghoogariwali bangari and silver kasli (hand jewellery). Their arms were covered with a silver ornament and large shellac bangles; they wore silver rings on their fingers or silver or gilt biti (ring). The back of their palms were adorned with silver ghoogriwala hathfool. A borala hung prominently on their foreheads and their wrists were covered with colourful bands. Their ankles were covered with jangling jwellery.Their ears were sparkling with a variety of ornaments, jhele, berle, or panriwale omania, dhimana or toti. A few wore gold ornaments but most wore silver nose rings, hansli around the neck, silver waistband, silver hankli, and cheap seer of artificial pearl.They also wore kandora made of silver around their waists. Their feet were adorned with kadla of silver or alluminium, brass ghoonghru and silver tore. The fingers in the feet had bichhiya (rings) on the big toe. The young women wore silver kondia or buttons. The married and virgins alike wore red loogras, red scarf, rati (brick coloured) kapadi (blouse), rati ghagra (long skirt).The widows wore most of these pieces of jewellery except borala. Men wore silver halli (neck ornament) kada (like bangle) around their wrists, bhooriyas around their arms, a silver waistband, silver or gold murki and jhele (ear-rings). Many had silver buttons on their waistcoat.

At different places on the plains of the Mangarh hills, adivasis from different settlements were performing their traditional dances. These dances included Gair, Gavari, Udniyana, Muriya, Hathjodia, Pagpasaniyana, Jalniyana, and Phadukchala. The special songs for each of these forms of dances were also being sung. The air was echoing to the beats of various adivasi percussion instruments and other instruments like jhanj, majira, khartal, thali (plate), matka (pitcher), mandal, dholki (drums) and flutes. The song that went with the Phadukchala dance went like this:

The black cuckoo'd love to be in the forest
And in the forest she'd stay long, feeding on the fruits.
On the fruits she'd feed and drink from the pond
And roost on the mango or mahua tree.
Who did she wait for?
Lo! Over there above the valley twinkles
The colorful crest of the groom's turban
Here comes the groom at last.

In executing the steps for the Gavari dance, the four main characters, the Rai, Buriya, Bhopa and the Pujari were exhibiting their skills well. Only men were participating in this dance, just as only women were taking part in the Udniyana dance. In the Muriya dance, young men and women, holding hands, were going round a couple that acted as the bride and the groom. At some place the story of Shiv and Parvati was being enacted in drama form, at another place mimicry, magic shows or physical feats were entertaining the crowd.

The young men and women who were strangers to each other were getting drawn to each other. It began with light conversation and introductions and blossomed into love climaxing in betrothal. The elder relatives helped in making matrimonial alliances. It was all very informal and relaxed. Songs in praise of saint Surmalji, Mavji and Govind Guru could also be heard. One of the most popular religious songs of the Sampsabha that was being sung was:

Live together in harmony as a unit, brethren
and go ahead hand in hand, brethren mine.
Brethren, sing God's glory and have faith in Him
and live together in harmony, brethren mine.

West of the dhooni, Kalua, the acrobat of Garhi village, was showing his skills. He had attracted a big crowd, walking on ten-foot tall poles. He held the top portion of the poles with his hands while he moved his feet that actually rested on wooden pieces stuck at a height of six or six-and-half feet up the bamboo poles. He was walking with perfect balance. Looking very tall, Kalua was an object of curiosity. Women and children appeared especially fascinated by his act.

"Oh you acrobat! Get down. If you fall the entire fair will get a bad name," Nagji Katara suddenly spoke from amidst the crowd that had gathered around him. Kalua's attention was momentarily distracted. He nearly lost his balance. Roopa, his 10 or 12 year daughter, cried out: "Bapu, please be careful!"

Kalua had fully restored his balance by now. After a while he threw the bamboo poles towards his right and left and jumped to the ground. His daughter had cautioned the crowd that the discarded bamboo poles were about to fall so that the spectators had cleared the area where they fell.

"Brother, if I lose my balance while performing my feat then what'll I do? My family will die of starvation. I've to get my daughter married." Kalua poured his heart out to Nagji.

Before Kalua had taken the walk on the tall poles, his daughter had climbed on one of the poles to do a spin. This was also a feat that fascinated many, seeing a little girl doing such a daring act. Kalua was middle-aged. Nagji had only warned him against the danger of slipping from the poles.

"You acrobat! Is it necessary to show your feat in the air? God has given us such a big piece of land on earth. It should be possible to show your deeds on land. That way, at least your life will not be in danger." Nagji was responding to Kalua.

"Oh brother! The land does no longer belong to God. The Raj controls all the land. We've only the air and the blue sky for us. That is why the feats are being performed up there." Kalua was baring his soul. The innocent eyes of Roopa were fixed on her father.

"This is the land of Mangarh. Not even a bird of the Raj can intrude here. You can perform as many deeds on this land as you like. Nobody is going to stop you." Gomana Damore replied plainly to the insinuation that was clear in the acrobat's remarks. Nagji looked quizzically at both the land and the sky after hearing Gomana.

Kalua the acrobat was winding up his show. Roopa spread a sheet on the floor and went round with folded hands. Some people took out small coins from their pockets and threw them on the sheet. The crowd dispersed and moved to other places in the fair. Roopa folded the sheet. Kalua gathered his gear and with his daughter headed for Kunda Ghati.

After watching the performance of the acrobat, Nagji Katara was going towards the dhooni when he met Manji Bhanat on the way. He was related to him from his father's side.

"Oh Kaka! You've also come to the fair?" He asked Manji as he hugged him. They had not met for years but Manji instantly recognised Nagji from his voice. Manji took his hand and said: "Son Nagji! You'll meet me here, I had no hope of it all. Actually, I'm not very fond of fairs and things. It is the Guruji's name that has drawn me here. I think he is an erudite saint, I shall have the privilege of seeing him in person and I may also be able to meet some relatives. You tell me, has anyone else from the village come?"

"No, no one else from the family has come. I've also heard the name of Guru Maharaj. But he talks big and I don't understand those talks. I've come only to enjoy the fair. Kaka, you've stopped coming to our village. You know my father died long ago due to a stomach ailment. My grandmother died at a ripe old age. My father did not live his full life, but that's the will of Bhole Nath. Kaka, you must sometimes come to look after us children. The two elderly maternal uncles have gone. You're the only elder in the family that I know well. Somehow you always used to attend weddings and such occasions. But you've not visited our village in a very long time." Nagji motioned Manji to sit next to him.

"Son Nagji. I used to come to the village to meet your aunt till she was alive. Now you're the only child in the third generation who likes me genuinely. Generally, relationships with older generation are buried under the weight of the new generation of relatives. Oh! Forget it. I shall make it a point to visit you on the first available opportunity. Tell me, how is your mother? She used to regard me as more than her

Devar (younger brother-in-law)." Manji, in sentimental mood, remembered Nagji's mother, Fatti.

"She is fine. She cries sitting alone whenever she remembers my father. She has got me a wife who is like goddess Lakshmi. Both of us look after our mother well. We're just three in the family. If we can't live happily together what other great achievement can we attain? She remembers you a lot whenever we discuss old days." Manji was pleased to hear this from Nagji as he recalled the jovial banter of those days between brother-in-law and sister-in-law, Nagji's mother.

"Let's go and have Guruji's darshan (see him)," Manji said as he took Nagji to the dhooni site.

The Sampsabha workers and the bhagats were addressing different groups of adivasis, preaching matters of religious and social reforms. Govind Guru would leave the dhooni site now and then address adivasis who had collected at different places. That big fair at Mangarh remained bustling throughout the day. As evening approached, the devout started to trek back home after shouting "Jai" to Govind Guru. It was getting cooler too. While the sun was going down, the full moon of Purnima was rising from the east. The fair ended. At the dhooni site Govind Guru was left with the prominent workers of the Sampsabha, the bhagats, members of the defence squad, the retired army personnel from the Khairwada cantonment and some volunteers. After his evening prayers, Govind Guru addressed them.

"On the occasion of this fair we've planted the Sampsabha flag and the statue of Bhairav Baba. According to our religious beliefs, God is formless, but Bhairav has his own importance. He's considered another form of Lord Shankar. One sect of my beloved Guruji, Rajgiriji Maharaj, was established in Bundi town in the Hadoti region. It is known as the Bundi Dashnami sect. Before coming into contact with Swami Dayanand, I'd lived with the Dashnami sect. The famous Lakreshwar Mahadev is close by. There I had worshipped the Bhairav form of Lord Mahadev upon receiving blessings from a sadhu. It was there that I realised the supernatural powers of meditation. I am talking about it because the bhagats and intelligent people understand the concept of the shapeless form of God but others who are not so intellectually endowed can easily place their faith in any statue. The statue of Bhairav Baba has been placed here to avoid that situation. The Bhairav statues can be placed at other dhooni sites and Dhams to arouse people's respect for religion.

"I have been saying it all along that the foreigners are more dangerous than the native rulers. They are hatching all the conspiracies against us. A cloth merchant of Surat is a friend of mine. He has sent me information that officials who work under the British have spread a rumour that I am opposing the foreign rule at the behest of Mahajans of the Jain community. The reason is supposed to be that after the foreigners introduced foreign textile and salt in the market, the Mahajans dealing in these trades have been badly hit. Tax has been imposed on the ordinary salt made from seawater, on the red salt from Sindh, and the salt produced from the dried waters of the lakes at Sambhar, Navan and Sujangarh. This has pushed the price of local salt and the foreigners are able to sell imported salt and increase their trade. The sale of local textile has also been affected because of the imported textile. The Mahajans dealing in the local salt and the textile trade are losing their business. They are upset with the British policies.

"I don't oppose foreign goods because that will benefit the local Mahajans. I oppose it because we become slaves if we depend on foreign goods. Apart from the trading class, others who are employed in this business also suffer. So I also oppose foreign goods. I believe in peace and non-violence. It's foreigners' propaganda that I'm influenced by the Jain sadhus because of my closeness with the Mahajans. I received my religious lessons from my Guru, Rajgiri Maharaj, and Swami Dayanand. I have nothing to do with the Jain religion. It is said that the Bombay Presidency government had spied upon me through the Agent in southern Rajputana, Hamilton. It is a matter of satisfaction for me that Hamilton has sent a correct report. It is believed he wrote that 'the following of the new faith created by Govind Guru is spreading very fast in the adivasi regions of Rajputana, Central India and Gujarat. So strongly has he succeeded in spreading the new faith that doubts have arisen in many minds who wonder how can he be worshiped as the founder of a new order when basically he was known among the locals as a Banjara who is neither well read nor is known to have performed any miracle.' Hamilton also accepted that 'Govind Guru has nothing to do with the Jain religion. He follows his own religion, the chief elements of which are dhooni, "havan" and good conduct and stresses the values of peace and non-violence.' Despite that, it is true that today all of you, me and the activities of the Sampsabha are being watched by British spies. Therefore, we need to be very cautious."

After Govind Guru's address, the bhagats and senior workers held discussions on the future activities of the Sampsabha.

Govind Guru and all the others were of the view that there will be no night halt at Mangarh. The bhagats and the senior workers had travelled on camels. They left for the destinations assigned to them for their specific work. The youth brigade marched on foot. Govind Guru, Kalji and four-five armed members of the defence squad left for Basiya on camels. Only two-four volunteers were left behind to look after the holy place at Mangarh. After the hectic activities of the day at the fair, the Mangarh hill had become very quiet. The noises of the normal night time activities in the forest could be heard, seen and felt in the velvety moonlight and the cool breeze.

FIFTEEN

Maharawal Vijay Singh had attained the age of 26 years by 1908. But the British administration had not given him the power to rule. A four-member Regent Council, presided by the Assistant Resident, was conducting the affairs of the Dungarpur state since 1898 when Maharawal Udai Singh had died and Vijay Singh was installed on the throne at a very young age.

As an adult, Vijay Singh was not happy with this arrangement. He was anxious to rule with the full powers. He had told the Assistant Resident about it many times. As a result, the Council had decided at its own level to allow him to sit on its meetings and express his views. The Maharawal's argument was that "in the 1857 mutiny the Dungarpur state had fully supported the British. How can the heir of such a state be denied his right to rule? It is unjust to do so." To avoid any adverse affect on relations between the Maharawal and the British government, the Assistant Resident had agreed to the new arrangement with the young Maharawal.

Hoping to get full powers to rule his state in the near future, Maharawal Vijay Singh kept a close watch on the activities in his state. He was getting information from different sources about the activities of Govind Guru and the Sampsabha. The Council too was not unaware of the unrest that was spreading among the adivasis. The Council's attention was concentrated on modernisation of the state where the biggest task was finding ways to enrich the state exchequer. The jagirdars were mainly responsible for the adivasis' protest over the *begar* system. It was because of the jagirdars that the adivasis' oppression in the name of *begar* had continued. The Council was not worried about the losses that the adivasis suffered on account of restrictions on the forest produce and the excise policies. Its concern on these two subjects was related to ways of increasing the state revenues. Similar was its attitude on the matter of levy on agricultural land. In the process of modernisation, the most important component was improving the administration and expansion of rail, postal and communication facilities. The progress on transport and communication facilities was considered more important for suppressing any possible rebellion than doing something in the interest of the people. The underprivileged adivasis were wary of such modernisation efforts.

Govind Guru and the activities of the Samp Sabha were the subjects of discussion at an important meeting of the Council in the Dungarpur Darbar. Considering the position of the adivasis, the AGG (Asstt. to the Governor General) in southern Rajputana had recently written a letter to the rulers of Mewar, Banswara, Pratapgarh and Dungarpur. It read like this:

"The tax burden on the adivasis has increased. The terror of *begar* has spread so much that villages after villages are being vacated. As a result the land is becoming fallow. You can well guess how adversely this affects the state revenues. Though the adivasis have been doing the *begar* service for a long time, now the teachings of Govind Guru have created an awakening in them and given them the confidence to oppose it. The religious and social reform programme of Govind Guru has drastically reduced the income from the sale of liquor. It simply means that the idea behind introducing the excise policy has proved to be a failure. As a result, it is impossible to collect the expected revenues. This is a matter of concern for both you and the British government. The income target from restricting the adivasis' right over forest produce also looks uncertain because under Govind Guru's inspiration the adivasis are opposing this policy.

"I'm sure that you'll not take this part of my letter in a different spirit but study it in the right spirit as I write with deep regret that the jagirdars keep a large portion of the agricultural crop that is taken as 'levy'. It adversely affects the state revenues. I understand that a similar situation prevails in regard to forest produce. A reason for this could be that the execution of these tasks has been mostly left to petty forest officials and their seniors have no control over them.

"Enhancing state revenues is the joint duty of the British government and the native states. It is true that the policies prepared in this regard have to be executed by the administration under you. But if the situation deteriorates then our cooperation and the arrangements for sharing of revenue will be obstructed and the cordiality in our mutual relations will come under stress. The subjects of native states are directly under your control.

"We'll continue to extend cooperation and render advice whenever the need arises. Please, pay attention to the provisions in the treaties between you and the Crown representatives, which will clarify matters. The situation is more serious in the states being run by the Council. I've the deepest respect for all you rulers and princes. The message I'm conveying to you through this letter is only my advice, which is based on some concrete information that I've received. You know well that the policy of the new Viceroy, Lord Minto, who replaced Lord Curzon, is very clear that there'll be no unnecessary British interference in the affairs of the native states.

"My request to all you Excellencies is, please review the situation regarding the adivasi land rights and correct the wrong that is being committed by the people who are under your obedience, the jagirdars, the landlords and the state employees. It is necessary to have the trust of the local chiefs for the sake of the loyalty of the subjects towards their ruler. Most of your subjects are adivasis, hence whatever I'm asking you to do to control the anti-Raj role of Govind Guru may be viewed as a well-intended advice. I can't talk at this stage about what other strategy will be useful for the purpose. It is my personal opinion that it'll be proper to adopt a sympathetic view about the genuine problems of the adivasis. There is no harm if for this purpose talks are held with Govind Guru or his representatives. But this also has to be decided by you.

If you think that he and his organisation are seditious and it'll be necessary to suppress them by force, then the British government will be ready to assist you in all manner, including ordering army action."

Assistant Resident Col A.T. Hume had read out the letter of AGG Trevor in the meeting of the Council. Maharawal Vijay Singh was surprised to find that the AGG, who looks after the entire Vagad and Mewar region, knew more about the developments in his state than him.

"Mr Colonel! You'd given me the responsibility for improving the administration in the Dungarpur state. I devoted night and day to accomplish this task. I recommended opening of excise and forest departments, which are directly under the control of the Council. The jagirdars have nothing to do with them. But to overcome any local problem that may arise, the officials of these departments have to seek the help of jagirdars and chiefs who are loyal to the Raj. The officials of the departments take all the decisions about implementing policy matters. Contracts for dealing in liquor and forest trade are awarded through an open process. The contract goes to the highest bidder in an open auction."

"But I've been receiving information that contracts for the two departments are awarded to people who are close to the jagirdars. I've, of course, not opposed it because our concern is revenue, not the person who gets the contract," Assistant Resident A.T. Hume said in response to the clarification that was given by a Council member, Rai Bahadur Shriram Dixit.

"Resident Saheb Bahadur, you may be aware that liquor contractors are from the Kalal community and the forest contractors are mainly those who trade in wood. All the Kalals are outsiders and only a handful of wood traders are local people. In such a situation, our jagirdars could not have known these contractors long. But after bagging a contract it is necessary to become friendly with the jagirdars in order to consolidate one's business. There can't be any objection to that. I admit there may be some drawbacks in our administration. There are many other reasons for the drop in the state's income, including the adivasi practice of preparing the homemade Mahua drink, which we find difficult to curb. Another reason is the prohibition campaign started by Govind Guru, which has reduced the sale of liquor at the contractors' shops. Theft of the forest produce is another reason. We have given wide powers to the jagirdars to deal with civil and criminal matters, but this matter needs more attention."

"I agree with the views of the Rai Bahadur. It'll not be possible to control sale of the forest produce and liquor unless activities of Govind Guru are curbed," intervened Maharawal Vijay Singh.

"Divan Saheb, you tell us what's the progress of land settlement?" Not paying much attention to what Vijay Singh had said, Assistant Resident Hume asked another member of the Council, Ganesh Ram, Divan of Dungarpur. Vijay Singh did not like it but he was satisfied with his participation in the Council meeting as an equal member though officially he was still to get his status as a full ruler.

"Mister Colonel! Everyone knows that I was entrusted the job of working on land reforms in 1903. With the help of assistants I've nearly completed the job. Three years ago, farmers were given good agricultural land on a ten-year contract. A good amount of lagan tax is being received from the flat fields. But most of the land in our area is hilly and adivasi farmers are deceitful in giving the true figures. They hide their produce at the time the levy is to be collected. To stop this we have the system of assessment of standing crops, but at the time of collecting the levy the farmer invents ways to show a poor crop. This has made it difficult to realise the levy fully. The followers of Govind Guru are misleading the adivasis by telling them that the levy is being procured in excess. It has become a big obstacle in procuring full levy."

Col Hume was satisfied with this explanation given by Divan Ganesh Ram.

Thakur Dalpat Singh, the fourth member of the Council, was slightly indisposed. His participation in the meeting was confined to grunts and nods in approval. Besides, he also thought it would not be proper for him to speak his mind when the Maharawal himself was present at the meeting. Dalpat Singh never lost any opportunity to show his loyalty and veneration for the Maharawal.

"What is your opinion about *baith begar* (labour without payment)? Can we lighten the burden it causes?" Col Hume was keen to know the views of the other members.

"Mister Colonel! I don't understand this talk about baith *begar* being a burden. This has been the traditional duty, almost a religion, of the subjects towards the rulers. It was never opposed in the past. It is Govind Guru who has incited the adivasis against baith *begar*.'

"In support of the Maharawal's views I'd like to say that we face no difficulty in collecting the Lagan and other taxes from non-adivasi farmers and traders in different commodities. The adivasis form the majority of our population and they're not as loyal to the Raj as members of other communities. After the 1857 mutiny and the anti-Raj activities of the Sampsabha and Govind Guru, the spirit of rebellion has spread among the adivasis. These people don't use their brains. They are stupid, illiterate and uncouth. Despite the legal ban, they sell forest wood. They cut forest grass for their use as well for sale. They collect catechu, gum, Mahua flowers and other forest fruits and roots, all illegally. In addition, they make and sell homemade liquor in defiance of our excise policy and in return contribute nothing to the Raj's exchequer. They commit theft, waylay people and rob them. Despite the ban by the Raj, the adivasis of some settlements extort money in the name of 'Bolai' from traders who pass through their areas. It gives a bad name to the Raj. Why should we be soft towards them when they defy the law with such impunity?

"Govind Guru is disrupting the ancient tradition while the Raj holds its grip over the adivasis with the help of the local area chiefs. He has started a drama for misleading the adivasis and spreading anti-Raj rumours with the help of workers and the bhagats of the Sampsabha. Under these circumstances if we give any concession to adivasis in one area it will be concluded that it was the result of the pressure from Govind Guru and his organisation. In my opinion it'll be wrong. It'll only give more importance to that fake sadhu.

"I'll say that this meeting should devote itself seriously to plan a strategy for curbing the activities of the Sampsabha and Govind Guru. At this juncture it will be dishonesty to talk of baith *begar* or concessions of any sort. The information that I receive suggests that the Sampsabha membership is increasing day-by-day and they are becoming more and more active. When Govind Guru had gone away from our state for four-five years there was peace in the area. Now after returning, he has been running his activities for the past one-two years from his camp at Basiya. He has kept a façade of dhooni and saying prayers. His real intention is to create unrest in the adivasi areas."

Col A.T Hume was listening to Dixit with great care. He was serious and did not betray any emotions while listening to Dixit. Perhaps, something deep was churning in his mind. He threw his glance towards Thakur Dalpat Singh, as though signalling him to speak something. And that turned out to be correct.

Thakur Dalpat Singh had taken his hint. He was an experienced, mature adult. He had participated in many such meetings in the Darbar of the previous Maharawal. He was made a member of the Council for this very reason. Speaking on the issue of *begar*, he said: "The *begar* practice in the Raj is not something out of the way. Colonel Saheb, I'm also a jagirdar. I used *begar* for our estate and have been enforcing it for the Darbar. The adivasis who do the *begar* work at the residence of jagirdars, Thakurs, rich businessmen, traders and senior officials. They are regularly paid for food, clothes and refreshments. Their medical expenses are also borne by those for whom they work. All these advantages that they receive in return for their services cannot be in any manner defined as *begar* or free forced labour. Govind Guru opposes this also. His attitude will only harm the adivasis. As for the *begar* taken at the time of work on projects of public interest, the Darbar and the jagirdars have no personal interest in these works which are executed in the interest of the people. These works relate to constructing wells, tanks, step-wells, dams, canals etc. The palaces and forts are necessary for running the administration and constructing them through *begar* ultimately serves people's interests. Those who render *begar* do get something in return and that helps them to eat, after all."

It was the maiden attempt by Thakur Dalpat Singh to present his views before a meeting of the Council. He had spoken with a lot of confidence. How much truth there was in his words is a different matter; but his speech sounded impressive. Col Hume and all others had listened to him with great attention.

"Thakur Saheb is right. *Begar* is an act of loyalty towards the Raj. Will the Darbar create a separate force of labourers for construction work?" There was a frown on his face as Maharawal Vijay Singh made this observation. It had the stamp of his feudal mind. But Col Hume again ignored his reaction and once more turned to Ganesh Ram: "Divanji, you may like to continue."

"Dixitji and Thakur Saheb have fully explained the *begar* situation. Dixitji has very rightly said that under today's circumstances the credit for any concession that may be granted will go to Govind Guru. It'll lead to mounting demands from the adivasis, and so will our problems. Accepting their demands would mean freeing them from the control of the administration. It'll unite all the adivasis and in future the Darbar will find it difficult to run the administration. I join Dixitji in saying that a strict watch be kept on Govind Guru and his men and their activities be checked. We can't afford to delay it anymore," Divan Ganesh Ram concluded.

"After listening to the considered views of you gentlemen I've no hesitation in saying that in the prevailing circumstances it'll not be proper to grant any concession to the adivasis in the matter of *begar*. I also endorse the view that curbing the activities of Govind Guru should be our priority. Failure to do so now will encourage adivasi uprisings everywhere. It has become necessary for us to consider the strategy for restricting his activities." Col Hume had clearly urged that the matter be considered more seriously.

"What's there to act? We must arrest him!"

Maharawal's impulsive response did not appear to please Col Hume as his face turned red. But he did not express his reaction in words as he tried to read the faces of the other members of the Council. He fixed his gaze at the portrait of former Maharawal Udai Singh which was hung on the wall opposite him. He was lost in deep thoughts.

There was silence in the conference room. It was broken by Col Hume: "Maharawal Saheb Bahadur, please pardon me and listen carefully to what I say. On the instigation of some people you had Govind Guru arrested earlier. What happened then? The adivasis came together to oppose it and he had to be freed without any condition. I admit that though you sat on the throne you were still a minor at that time. The decision was taken in your name by some ignorant advisers. It was a decision that affected the prestige of the state. It was taken without consulting the Council. Despite the fact that such a crucial decision should have been authorised by the Council, we did not say anything in order not to vitiate relations between the British government and the Dungarpur state. However, let's forget that. But I would respectfully like to give a piece of advice before this Council that in future you alone may have to take important decisions like the one taken by the Council today about Govind Guru. You'll have to make your moves very carefully. Most of the Dungarpur state is becoming a 'hot belt' because of the activities of Govind Guru. We can handle this if we adopt the correct strategy. May I request members of the Council to state their views on the subject again."

After the sombre observation by Col Hume the angry Maharawal Vijay Singh was forced to rethink about his hasty reaction. He was unable to look Col Hume in the eye. The Council members had given their silent approval for Col Hume's frank expression of views. The colonel was staring at the chandelier in the hall. A lizard had just been awarded for its patience, as it was finally able to pounce upon an insect on the wall. Col Hume had held his cigar in his fingers for a long time. He lit it, took a deep puff and blew rings into the air, which was filled with the aroma of tobacco. Takur Dalpat Singh took a few sips of water from a tumbler that was placed near him on a stool. Divan Ganesh Ram was rummaging through the papers in a file, apparently looking for some reference. Actually, he was hiding his embarrassment. He was an accessory with the Maharawal in the arrest and the subsequent release of Govind Guru, though he did have some reservations about his arrest. What embarrassed him was that Col Hume was aware that as the Divan he had a role in the arrest of Govind Guru.

"Mr Resident Saheb! As far as I know Govind Guru opposes violence. His main aim is to organise the adivasis to create awareness among them. His followers are able to instil this feeling among the adivasis that the path Govind Guru is showing will uplift them. That's why the adivasis flock to him. I agree that all this is not in the interest of the Raj. In this context, I'd like to say that some instances have come to light of adivasis manhandling forest employees when the forest produce had to be collected by force. The jagirdars started criminal proceedings against such elements and had them punished. Govind Guru had not opposed such action. This is an indication that Govind Guru does not believe in violence. We also know that he is deeply influenced by the ideas of Swami Dayananada Saraswati. That makes it clear that he does have some saintly qualities. If we arrest him, his peaceful demeanour can change. In my view, it'll not be proper to arrest him at this moment."

"Dixitji, I agree with your views against his arrest. We should send a powerful intermediary to meet Govind Guru, not as a representative of the Raj but one who can meet him in his individual capacity and read his mind. If we then gather the impression that he does not entertain thoughts of inciting people against the Raj we can start serious negotiations with him on the real problems of the adivasis. But we've to be careful that he or his associates don't get the impression that we are under any pressure to negotiate." Divan Ganesh Ram was replying to Dixit's observations.

"Resident Saheb, what Divanji says sounds appropriate. We have someone sensible in mind who can be an influential mediator. He was able to successfully sort out the previous problem with Govind Guru. That man is Seth Dalpatrai Mehta. He enjoys the trust of the Council and respects the Maharawal a great deal." This suggestion from Dixit won Col Hume's nod of approval, who looked at Thakur Dalpat Singh with anticipation. Dalpat Singh understood that the Resident wanted to know his mind. So he elaborated: "The main dispute between the Darbar and the adivasis is about *begar*, forest produce and Lagan. On each of these three issues, the views of Govind Guru clash with those of the Raj. How can then we proceed with negotiations?"

Winding up the discussions, Col Hume said: "It is finally decided that Govind Guru's arrest should be put off for the time being and Seth Mehta should be sent to him to know what's in his mind." This was seconded by all members of the Council. Maharawal Vijay Singh said nothing in support or opposition to this decision. Divan Ganesh Ram was satisfied that Col Hume had endorsed what he had said in support of the observations made by Dixit. He was no longer embarrassed. He also regained his confidence that had deserted him temporarily.

SIXTEEN

The horse carriage of Seth Dalpatrai Mehta stopped in front of the house of Govind Guru. People in the village knew Seth Mehta. He had sent relief material to Basiya during the *chchapanya* famine. He asked the villagers about their welfare and also asked them if Govind Guru was in the village. He knew that Govind Guru was at home, but he wanted to be doubly sure. He had come to Basiya for very important talks with Govind Guru. He sent the guard who had come with him to Govind Guru's house. The sight of the approaching armed guard startled Govind Guru. But when the guard conveyed the greetings on behalf of Seth Mehta, he was assured that all was well. He was relaxed as he came out of his hut to welcome Seth Mehta. The two, who were meeting after nearly a decade, hugged each other. Govind Guru's wife was busy with some domestic chores in the house. She realised that an important visitor was at the door.

Govind Guru and Seth Mehta reached the inner courtyard and sat on a string stool that she had placed there. Govind Guru had by then told her that Seth Mehta had mediated in the talks that had led to his release from the Dungarpur prison. Standing at the door of her hut, Govind Guru's wife made room in her veil to steal a glance at Seth Mehta who was wearing a white dhoti and a loose long coat. His head was covered with a colourful, stripped Mewari turban. A gold necklace hung above the coat. The pair of narrow, pointed shoes that he wore had beautiful embroidery work.

"She's my wife. She knows you by name, but this is the first time she is seeing you in person," Govind Guru said by way of introduction and continued, "This is Seth Dalpatrai Mehta. I've often spoken to you about him. He's very close to the Dungarpur Darbar. The whole state respects him. He has done a lot of good things for the people. A very kind and nice man."

"Maharaj, such high praise for a Bania is not good!" It was a traditionally modest response of the reticent Seth Mehta. Govind Guru's wife folded her hands in welcoming the Seth as she retreated into the hut. Seth Mehta was pleased to note that nobody else was around. His guard had also gone back to stand near the horse carriage.

"What brings you to the house of a poor man like me?" Govind Guru asked the Seth. Curiosity was writ large on his face but there was humility in his eyes.

"Maharaj, you are a Mahatma! You must be knowing everything. Nevertheless, I must inform you why I've been sent here by the Maharawal of Dungarpur." The mention of Maharawal alerted Govind Guru, though he didn't allow his discomfort to show on his face. But he could not control his curiosity as he politely asked: "Tell me Sethji, what's it?"

"Great Saint! I've deep respect for you in my heart. Please pardon me, but what I'm about to say is not my personal view. A few days ago the Darbar Council had met. The Maharawal, the Assistant Resident and the members of the Council think that some workers of the Sampsabha are openly opposing the policies of the Raj and for this they are inciting the adivasis at different places. I don't know how much truth is there in it. It is likely that your opponents had conveyed exaggerated facts to the Darbar, but the Darbar and the Council are convinced that all the anti-Raj activities are taking place at the instigation of Govind Guru. You are a saintly figure. But fingers will be raised at you if something unpleasant takes place tomorrow. I know very well that you've devoted your day and night for the welfare of the adivasis. I also know that it is necessary to resolve some of the problems of the adivasis. On moral ground I personally oppose the oppression of the adivasis in some of the jagirs. But I've to say that violence and agitation is no solution to any problem."

"The Maharawal is an adult now. But the Council is still competent to take decisions on state matters and the Council will do what the British want. Will you support the intrigues of the British?" Govind Guru was getting serious.

"I'm a local man. Why'll I support foreigners? It's not a question of foreigners interfering in running the affairs of a state. The point is that irrespective of what is happening, the people should live in peaceful conditions. We're fortunate that we've a native ruler when the British rule most parts of the country. Though the Resident is in charge of the Council, its other members are *desis*. The Maharawal will sooner or later get full powers of the ruler. It can be hoped that he'll pay attention to the interests of his subjects. You'll not like to see something untoward happen in our area before that time arrives to vitiate the atmosphere and create some ill feeling in his mind towards you, the Sampsabha and the adivasis. If something unfortunate does take place now it'll have an adverse effect on the interests of the adivasis in future.

"What does the Council want?" Govind Guru's mood was changing from serious to one of anger. Seth Mehta was worried that his talks might be derailed. Drawing from his vast experience, he chose his words carefully as he said: "You're a mahatma. You're not bound by the decisions of the Council. I'm present here as a well-wishing adviser. All that the Council wants is that there should be no disturbance during its tenure."

"The influential and devoted workers of the Sampsabha don't believe in disturbing the peace. They propagate awareness through peaceful means. The thought of violence can't enter the minds of devoted people. Only those become bhagats who are by nature good and believe in moral values. As for the young workers, they can be provoked only when an employee of the Raj, whether employed by the jagirdar or one of the departments, harasses an adivasi for no rhyme or reason. The adivasis accept it as part of their fate that they have to suffer certain miseries and problems like famine, hunger, floods and other disasters. But how can they put up with unjust acts inflicted on them on behalf of the Raj? This is true of not just adivasis, but all human beings. Can the Council do anything for the adivasis in such matters?"

"As far I know, Resident Hume will not like that the Council during its term under him takes any important decision about adivasi affairs. He would not like that a British official is seen as partisan in such a crucial matter. He would like that the matter is handled entirely by the native rulers. It's a separate matter that even then he may have an indirect role. It'll be pointless in my opinion to put up any proposal on adivasi grievances before the Council."

It appeared to Govind Guru that the words of Seth Dalpatrai would give no solace to the adivasis. But the way he presented his views made Govind Guru believe that he had no intention to play any mischief. He also felt that Seth Mehta had not come to him as an emissary of the Darbar or the Council. He was expressing his independent views and was speaking straight from the heart. During that conversation, Mehta had presented himself as a trustworthy adviser. A feeling of respect for him was growing in the mind of Govind Guru.

"You tell me, what should I do then?" Govind Guru asked out of curiosity.

"With utmost respect I'd like to say that during the rule of the Council you leave the state of Dungarpur. You're a wandering ascetic. Your work for the good of the human being will not be obstructed whether you live here or elsewhere. In any case, the tenure of the Council is not going to be long. Maharawal Vijay Singh is an adult now. There is no doubt that very soon he'll get his full rights to rule the state."

"All right, Sethji. I respect your advice. Please do tell the Maharawal and the Council members that violence will not be allowed under the leadership of any Sampsabha worker. But the work for the propagation of awareness among the adivasis will continue. Its main aim is to bring social improvements and create a spirit of devotion. The Council too owes it to the subjects that something is done to improve the economic conditions of the adivasis and prevent any unjust harm to them. As for your suggestion that I should leave this place, I'll consider it seriously. But I can't say anything on this matter right now. You came to meet me with an open mind and I thank you for that."

"Maharaj, I then take your leave. I'll urge the Maharawal and the Council members that the solution to the problems that can be tackled should favour the adivasis. I'll also tell them that Govind Guru listened to me carefully and is considering the proposal I made to him. Let me clarify again that I did not come to you as an envoy of anyone or to act as a mediator. I came to you because I respect you and feel close to you." Seth Mehta stood up from the string stool. With the movement of his body, the gold chain he was wearing over his coat began to swing. There was a shine on the face of Seth Mehta who was past his middle age. He looked happy at the outcome of his talks with Govind Guru, hopeful that he would accept his suggestion for voluntary exile. If that happens, his stock in the Dungarpur Darbar will go up further. He folded his hands before Govind Guru in veneration and came out where his coachman and the guard were waiting for him near his horse carriage. Some villagers had also assembled there by then. Women and children were looking at the carriage, the horse, the guard and the coachman with interest and some surprise. Now their attention was drawn towards Seth Mehta as he was entering the horse carriage. Govind Guru had seen him off at his hut. The horse carriage left Basiya village with Seth Mehta, raising dust in its trail along the unpaved path.

A week after this meeting between Govind Guru and Seth Mehta, Thavara Bhagat of Navagaon came to Basiya. By the time he reached the dhooni site it was dark. Govind Guru had completed his evening prayer and was talking to Kalji Bhagat and some villagers. On seeing Thavara he asked him excitedly: "Oh you bhagat, have you brought any special news?"

Shouting "Jai Guru Maharaj" he touched the feet of Govind Guru and folded his hands in respect towards the others who were around. They also replied to his greetings with 'Jai Guru Maharaj'. In the light from the eternal lamp at the dhooni that reflected on the face of Thavara, Govind Guru could read that he was worried. Getting up from the stone slab where he was sitting, Govind Guru put his right hand on Thavara's shoulders and escorted him to the rear of the dhooni. Pressing his hands on his shoulders, he asked him: "What's the matter, Thavara Bhagat? You looked worried."

"Guru Maharaj, the news is that Thakur Prithvi Singh of Pal Patta in the state of Idar has been committing atrocities on the Bhils and Garasiyas of his area. The Sampsabha has done good work in that area and there is awakening among the adivasis. As a result, the adivasis at many places have risen in revolt against the jagirdar. They've flatly refused to pay the lagan and do the *begar*. The Sampsabha workers talked to the jagirdar and asked him to fix a reasonable levy, but he refuses to listen. He is determined to fix an arbitrary levy on the Kharif produce. In some villages his musclemen have forcibly procured the levy. There are reports of some adivasis being beaten when the levy was forcibly procured. The news of such incidents has spread all over the jagir like the wild fire and the adivasis are getting impatient for starting an agitation. It is also said that Jagirdar Prithvi Singh has made full preparations to meet this situation. If the need arises, he can also get the army from the Maharawal of Idar."

Thavara Bhagat said it all in one breath. Kalji Bhagat, who was sitting at the dhooni site, was listening to all this. He was not able to hear every word but whatever bits reached his ears it was clear to him that Thavara Bhagat was talking to Govind Guru about the likelihood of some untoward incident. Meanwhile, Govind Guru called Kalji Bhagat: "It is quite late. Tell the village brethrens to go home and rest. And Kalji Bhagat, you stay here." Govind Guru's words were like command for the adivasis. On hearing him, they left the dhooni site, shouting "Jai Gurudev!" They did not know what was happening, so they accepted the command from their Guru quietly. The adivasis were descending down Chhani Magari while Govind Guru returned to his seat at the dhooni site with Thavara, asking him to sit next to him. Thavara was a little hesitant at first as he sat next to him. At another stone slab sat Kalji.

"What's the matter, Guru Maharaj? You look worried. Did Thavara Bhagat bring any bad news?"

"Thavara Bhai. Rising against the Thakur means violence in the whole of state. There will be the possibility of a clash between the adivasis and the state forces. It is absolutely important that such a situation is averted. We can't compromise on *begar*, but the levy issue can be resolved by talking to the Thakur. The adivasis should not do anything in haste. They'll have to think with a cool head and the workers and the bhagats of the Sampsabha will have to come forward to deal with the issue."

"Guru Maharaj, in the wake of mounting atrocities will the bhagats be able to advise the adivasis to bear it all quietly? Their influence will be reduced and they may be encouraging further atrocities if they plead for maintaining peace under the circumstances. We've to look for some other alternative," Thavara was quick to react to Govind Guru's suggestion.

"Thavara Bhai. Listen patiently to all that Guru Maharaj has to say. Is there a bigger man than him in our midst who can pull us out of our troubles?" Kalji Bhagat said intervening. Thavara looked at Govind Guru with expectation. There was more worry written on Govind Guru's face than Thavara's. Kalji was now anxious to know the full details.

"Thavara, what I'm saying is not against anyone's interest. You drew your conclusions without thinking over the matter. The action that we have to take to express the adivasis' dissatisfaction has to come under the leadership of experienced workers and the bhagats of the Sampsabha. Only then can the adivasis be organised to fight. If we don't act wisely now then our big fight will be weakened and there will be far too many leaders. We shall achieve nothing. Instead of resorting to violent rebellion everywhere we've to run an organised movement. After so many years, people have come to accept the Sampsabha as a force to reckon with. I know Thakur Prithvi Singh well. He's obstinate. We must inform the Maharawal of Idar that he doesn't want to talk about the problems of adivasis with the Sampsabha workers. The adivasis are the subjects of the Maharawal. I'm sure he'll pay attention to their problems. If it becomes necessary, I shall personally visit Pal Patta."

There was force in the voice of Govind Guru. Both Thavara and Kalji had listened to him attentively and understood very well what he said.

"Maharaj, it was my duty to convey to you the information that I had. It is for you to decide what's to be done about it." Thavara was seriously of the view that if Govind Guru visits Pal Patta then he will be able to quickly find a solution to the problems of the adivasis there.

The ninth day moon of the dark phase in the month of Margsheesh was visible over the southern sky. Its reflection could be seen in the lake below Chhani Magari. The gentle breeze was pushing weak ripples in the waters. A wolf stood near the bank of the lake. He drank water from the lake. A *titahari* (lapwing) gave out its loud "Tat-Tat-TTT-TTT" call to alert the other birds. There was commotion among the birds for a while. The wolf disappeared behind the tall and thick grass after drinking water. It was peaceful around the lake again. The moon was slipping towards the western horizon. Using the dim moonlight, Govind Guru and his two companions left the dhooni site for Basiya village. Kalji Bhagat took Thavara to his village, after the two had dropped Govind Guru at his home. Govind Guru was disturbed to hear about the plight of the adivasis in Pal Patta. It was already too late into the evening at the dhooni site. Despite his wife's pleadings, Govind Guru did not eat that evening. He had not paid attention to the fact that his wife would wait for him before she took her meals. She also slept on hungry stomach. The two sons had already gone to sleep. The courtyard was a bit cooler. Govind Guru lifted his cot from there and slept inside the hut. He kept thinking of Pal Patta till he fell asleep.

Following his routine, Govind Guru got up early the next day and left for Chhani Magari for his prayers and bath. He took a dip in the lake and went to the dhooni for morning prayers. Kalji Bhima, Thavara Bhagat and the adivasi devotees of Govind Guru had also assembled there for the morning prayers. Some people from Bedasa, Suranta and nearby areas had also arrived. Apart from the days of religious importance, whenever 100–200 people gathered at dhooni sites a session of prayers inevitably followed. The tradition was kept up that day. Before the start of the prayer session, Govind Guru had told Kalji Bhagat in the morning that he should send two camel riders to bring Poonja Dhira and Kuriya Bhagat to Chhani Magari as early as possible. Kalji had dispatched two men from Basiya on this mission.

Govind Guru used to compose bhajans. He had inspired other bhagats to do likewise. The main job of the bhagats was to spread awareness through prayers and religious songs. Govind Guru began his discourse at Chhani Magari with a couplet of Tulsidas.

"Compassion is at the root of dharma, just as pride is a basic sin; do not give up compassion as long as there is life in you," says Saint Tulsi Das.

Explaining the couplet, Govind Guru said: "Dharma is the way to God. Dharma creates respect for God. Dharma expands man's moral values and leads to destruction of tendencies of arrogance, hypocrisy and violence. It's the duty of all of us to obey the rules of the Sampsabha. All that the bhagats teach is part of the dharma. The saints have said that compassion is at the root of dharma. Tulsidasji has written the story of Lord Ram. These lines that describe compassion as the root of dharma are part of that story. It is, therefore, essential to believe in the feeling of compassion. Not cutting trees is an expression of compassion towards them. Not to harass a person by our actions, words or deeds is compassion towards mankind. Not to torture any other living being is compassion towards them. It makes the man's mind pure. Compassion can arise only in a pure mind. To talk about dharma without compassion is dishonesty. But God bestows His kindness on man when following the dharma man toils honestly and discharges his worldly duties with sincerity. The material fruits for labour cannot be obtained by sitting idle. A sage has said that honest work is the soul of managing the world that God has created.

Work plays a primary role in running the affairs of the world. It is the good conduct of the trees and plants in the forest that gives us fruits, roots and other vegetations. Mankind's existence depends on good upbringing of children from an early age.

"Today our adivasi brothers are suffering on many counts. Straying from the path of Dharma causes famine, floods and epidemics, which are nature's ways of showing God's fury. We are made to suffer atrocities by the Raj on account of our lack of awareness. Bad habits like drinking make people quarrelsome and make them sit idle at home instead of toiling to feed the family. A person with bad habits creates problems not only for self but also the family. We are suffering the hardships of the Kalyug, the epoch of bad times. The good times will follow if we truly follow the path of Dharma and awareness."

Keeping these thoughts in mind, Govind Guru had written a religious song, which he rendered during his discourse.

Break thy slumber Jambu![1]
The folk blow the trumpet and give thee a call
And the call echoes in the whole Jambu.
They call thee up again and again
Not to miss this opportunity.
The folk blow the trumpet and give thee a call
And it's thy turn to take heed of the call.
As Megadi is to get married at the end of Kali[2],
Music is on and the people are rejoicing.
The elderly and the wise tell us
That good people are getting united,
That the barriers of caste and class are breaking
And that Kali is on its last legs.
The elderly and the wise tell us
That the sinners are to perish sure and soon.
They are to assemble on the Mahude grounds
They are to assemble on the Ahude grounds.

---

1 Ancient name of the Indian sub-continent.

2 Name of the last Age in Indian mythology.

(The song carries a forecast by Govind Guru that the land of the adivasis will see a vast improvement during the Satyug, the epoch of good times. That age will bring respect to honest people belonging to a dozen communities and eighteen tribes.)

There is a popular ancient myth about Makna Elephant among the adivasis. Using this myth in forecasting the end of the sinners, Govind Guru composed another Bhajan, which also he sang at the dhooni site at Chhani Magari.

> Runs there a crushing wheel
> Crushing the witches and demonesses
> And sorecesses and the spirits evil.
> The oilmen thrush them down inside
> And the God send Makana Elephant
> Moves the staff to grind them.

(It means that there are bad people who mislead good people to serve their own interests. They build bad places like *Ahudawala Patod* to lure the superstitious and harass the innocent people. This is what happens in the Kalyug. To rid people of this curse, God has sent 'Makna Elephant' who helps to destroy all the sinners.)

Most adivasis were familiar with the myth of Makna Elephant. The listeners believed in the forecast made by Govind Guru about the Satyug. What they did not comprehend was the reference to the wedding of Megadi in the song. Some of them expressed their curiosity before Govind Guru, who then explained it thus: "The Marwar state had a saint, Hirji Bhati. He used to sing the tale of Megadi. When I was living in the company of Swami Dayanand in Udaipur I met Parma, one of the disciples of Sant Hirji. He was also a bhagat. We became friends. While relaxing, he used to sing songs about the discourses of Sant Hirji. According to Parma, once Lord Vishnu disguised himself as a Brahmin and went to the Ashram of Rishi Shrangi after he had heard praise about his adherence to truthfulness. Lord Vishnu in disguise asked for the hand of the Rishi's daughter. Rishi Shrangi told his wife about this request from the Brahmin guest. His wife discussed the marriage proposal with their daughter, Megadi, who willingly accepted it. Lord Vishnu went away, promising he will return for the marriage after four days. Lord Vishnu then sent word through Narad Muni to the Rishi that the Brahmin who met him was Lord Vishnu in disguise and when he spoke of 'four days' he was referring to the fourth age, the last phase of Kalyug. Parma Bhagat had also told me that God had blessed Megadi with immortality. She was to live till the end of Kalyug somewhere in the Jambu Khand, the adivasi region, where Lord Vishnu will be reborn in a different incarnation and marry her. I had included this reference in my song."

This explanation satisfied the curiosity of the adivasis. But a new doubt had arisen in the minds of Kalji and Thavara Bhagats. They looked at each other. Neither of them thought it necessary to convey their doubts to Govind Guru before his audience. At the end of the session of prayers and religious songs, the adivasis left the dhooni site after shouting the usual praise of Govind Guru.

It was then that Kalji and Thavara asked Govind Guru: "The adivasi region has always lived under the divine glory of God Bhole Nath. To end our sorrows, it is he who must be reborn here in the new age, not Lord Vishnu."

Govind Guru explained to them: "Despite both of you being bhagats neither of you knows that among the Triumvirate of Gods, Lord Brahma and Lord Shiv do not reincarnate. Only Lord Vishnu does. He was born in the Dwapar Yug (second age in the aeon) as Lord Ram, and as Lord Krishna in the

Treta Yug (third age). We are in Kalyug now and only Lord Vishnu will come in a new incarnation. This is the forecast that Sant Hirji had made.

"I want to say one thing more. We believe that God is formless, so we shall accept Sant Hirji's forecast in accordance with his sentiments and thoughts. By doing so, our faith in formless God will not be undermined. Look, everyone has his own beliefs. The saints will have faith in whatever form of God they perceive. We should not get into this tangle."

The camel rider who was sent by Kalji on instruction from Govind Guru to fetch Poonja Dhira returned the following day. He informed Govind Guru that he met Poonja Bhagat at Mangarh and found him busy training the defence squads. His message for you is: "I'm busy with the training. About half a dozen retired army personnel from Khairwada cantonment are here. The Poornamasi (full moon) fair at Mangarh is approaching. Preparations have to be made for that day in advance. Govind Guru will be arriving at the fair in two-four days. I'll meet him here. Besides, he has not told me what is the important task for which I'm needed." Poonja Bhagat had prayed for your welfare and asked me to convey his greatest regards to you".

Govind Guru remained silent after listening to the message brought by the camel rider. But he was gratified that Poonja Bhagat was discharging the task given to him with full responsibility and was also competent to take decisions on his own. Govind Guru was at his residence, sitting with a small group of people.

"Go son. Take some rest. You have travelled a long distance and must be tired," Govind Guru asked the camel rider, who touched his feet and left for his home. He was returning with an expression of satisfaction on his face for having been chosen to act as a messenger for Govind Guru.

A little while later a boy came panting. He looked shaken as he informed Govind Guru: "Kalji Bhagat's son has been bitten by a cobra. He had gone to Naharghati for grazing the goats. He has just been brought to the dhooni site in an unconscious state. Kalji, his wife and a few more people are with him. They want you there urgently." Hearing the news from the boy everyone who was sitting there stood up at once. Govind Guru went to his hut and came out with something wrapped in a coarse cloth. All of them rushed to the dhooni site.

Kalji's son was lying unconscious on a flat stone slab near the dhooni in Chhani Magari, surrounded by a crowd of 10–15 people. Kalji was standing near the boy, looking glum. His wife, Begali, was crying hoarse. As soon as they saw him climbing the stairs to the Magari, people hailed him and began to shout, "Guru Maharaj has come, Guru Maharaj has come." Kalji and others looked at Govind Guru with hope as he came nearer. He moved his hand over the head of Begali and tried to console her: "He'll be all right. If he doesn't, then it is God's will."

"Kalji and Patji, bring at once water from the well that you two brothers are digging," Govind Guru said, signalling Patji.

"Guru Maharaj, there is no water in the well yet."

"Do what I say at once. Patji, take along a rope and a bucket. Don't delay." The people around were surprised to hear their dear Guru asking for water from a well that had not been dug deep enough to have water. They knew that their Guru was a great soul. But they did not expect him to perform a miracle. "Hurry up, Patji," came a chorus from the crowd. Patji ran towards the well, about half a mile away, with a rope and a bucket in his hands. Govind Guru sat in front of the *Guru ki Dhooni*, the largest of the nine dhoonis at the sacred spot in Chhani Magari. He had already examined the pulse of the boy. He closed his eyes in meditation. He picked up the holy ash from the dhooni and smeared it on the forehead of the boy. Begali who was sitting close by looked stunned. She kept looking at Govind Guru. It was not clear if she did it in a state of shock or in the hope that Govind Guru would be able to save her son.

Water had apparently leaked into the well from some tiny source. There was enough water to drown the bucket. A surprised Patji filled his bucked with that water. Everyone was surprised to see him return with a bucket of water. Govind Guru poured the water in a Tumbi (hollowed dry gourd) which was filled to the half level. He mixed the powder of medicinal plants he had brought with him in the water and poured the liquid mixture over the boy and also put a few drops into his mouth. The snake had bitten in the calf of the boy's right leg. The fangs had left visible marks on the leg. Govind Guru had carried a pocket-knife in his waistcoat. When he made an incision on the boy's legs blood started to ooze out. He asked everyone to move to one side as he bent himself and went into a sitting Yogic posture. He sucked the blood that came out from the incision he had made and then threw it out from his mouth. He repeated it many times. Then he gargled his mouth two or three times with the water that was stored in the hollowed gourd. He sent for some fresh Neem tree leaves, heating them over firewood and then placing them over the bleeding spot on the boy's leg. He then tied a bandage over the wound. In the meanwhile he also recited what sounded like Mantras and examined the boy's pulse again. Govind Guru looked grave as though he was saying something to himself. Begali was still sitting stunned, her eyes glued to Govind Guru. Kalji was sitting with his hands clutching his forehead. His gaze was fixed on the floor. The other adivasis were watching it all quietly. The sun appeared to be moving fast towards the western horizon. The air was a bit cool. A cuckoo sitting on a dense mango tree was singing its signature tune.

"Did anyone see the snake?" At last Govind Guru had broken his spell of silence. Everyone looked at everyone else.

Another boy, Anatya, was also grazing the goat along with Kalji's son, Amalya, at Nahar Ghati. He recalled: "When Amalya cried I went near him and found him next to tall dense grass. He said to me, 'I've been bitten by an insect. You go and see what was it'. I then searched in the grass and at a distance I saw a black snake moving away fast. I chased it with my lathi but it escaped into the crevices in the stone. I repeatedly shouted, 'A snake has bitten Amalya.' A crowd of herdsmen gathered there on the hill. A little later his parents also arrived."

After listening to this eyewitness account from Anatya, Govind Guru asked him again: "So, two-three hours might have lapsed before this child was brought here?" Kalji lifted his head, removed his hands from his forehead and said: "Yes, Guru Maharaj, it must have taken that much time." Begali was still sitting paralysed.

"Shall I call Jeta Bhagat?" Thavara sought permission of Govind Guru to summon the person who knew about the herbs and the roots used for the treatment of snakebite. He looked worried. Govind Guru was battling within himself between hope and despair. Outwardly he looked serene.

"A person bitten by a cobra usually dies. It's difficult to feel his pulse. The Pran (Life Force) goes out of the rest of the body and concentrates on the Brihm-Randhra (centre of the Pran, i.e., area below the opening at the top of the skull). There are hopes of revival as long as life hangs there. There's no need to call Jeta Bhagat now. In any case, Thali Talai is far from here and it's not certain that he's in the village." Govind Guru had turned down Thavara's suggestion. A few others had proposed that Bhopas and village exorcist may be summoned. But nobody supported this idea. The better informed knew that Govind Guru did not approve of exorcism and hocus-pocus.

The sun was about to set. The chill was increasing. By now a large crowd had gathered at Chhani Magari. A *sonchiri* (baya weaver) was seen flying to the right of the place where Amalya was lying. "It's a good omen," said someone. Some faces lit up with hope. Govind Guru was quiet. After listening to the reply of Govind Guru, it occurred to Thavara that Govind Guru was no less qualified than Jeta Bhagat in treating various diseases and injuries.

Just when the sun was about to hide behind a hill, the body of Amalya stirred a little. Govind Guru took his pulse and smiled. He said: "Look, this boy's life-force is re-entering other parts of his body from the Brihm-Randhra. If he'd not been treated in time his life would've gone forever."

The joy of the parents of Amalya can only be guessed. Govind Guru had treated snakebite. Those present there thought he had performed a miracle. The entire air in Chhani Magari echoed to the cries in exultation of Govind Guru.

"Take him home. He'll resume speaking a little later," said Govind Guru as he handed the mixture of herbs placed between two 'tendu' leaves in the hands of Kalji. He further instructed him: "Don't give him anything to eat or drink tonight." He called for a bowl from the dhooni site and poured into it the water with the dried herb mixture and told him: "Give him one dose after every two hours. He'll be all right by morning. A person bitten by a snake suffers in pain for a moment and then he slowly slips into unconsciousness. It is said that a scorpion bite makes a man cry but the snake bite induces sleep."

Some were of the view that till he regains total consciousness Amalya should be left under the care of Guru Maharaj. Kalji was a trusted disciple of Govind Guru. His faith in Govind Guru was supreme. Obeying the instructions from Govind Guru, he took help of a couple of youth to take his son home. The crowd at the dhooni site was dispersing, but some had stayed back. One of them was Thavara.

Govind Guru was very pleased with the successful treatment of Kalji's son. Silently, he expressed his gratitude to God. That evening he took longer to finish his prayers.

Overnight, news had spread that Govind Guru had brought a dead boy to life and also had a dry well filled with water. After that night, Govind Guru came to be known as the Miracle Baba (mendicant).

By next morning, it also came to be believed that havans, the lighting of sacred fire, at the dhooni site helps bring in the rain. That was not all. People were telling each other: "We knew it all along that he's a miracle saint. During his stay in Udaipur, he had rid the Maharana of an incurable disease."

As the talk of Govind Guru's miraculous powers circulated around, the camel rider who was dispatched by Kalji returned to Basiya around noon along with Kuriya Bhagat. Hearing the summons from Govind Guru, Kuriya, who was at Sagwada, had immediately agreed to go to Basiya.

Govind Guru discussed the situation in the Palpatta area with Kuriya Bhagat. The influence, the authority and the leadership of Govind Guru during the Sampsabha agitation that was initiated by him for the adivasis in the regions of Vagad, Mewar and the nearby Gujarat areas, was unquestionable. But he used to consult his faithful colleagues before taking any crucial decision on matters relating to the agitation. Though all the prominent workers and the bhagats were equally dear to him, Poonja Dhira and Kuriya Danot were nearest to him. Like Govind Guru, they were the founder members of the Sampsabha. Poonja Bhagat was not able to reach Basiya because of his preoccupation with the training of the defence squads. Govind Guru had to restrict his consultation with Kuriya on the situation in Palpatta. Kuriya was of the view that senior functionaries of the Sampsabha should intervene immediately, though that will not be possible before the Punyo fair, which was just four or five days away. Govind Guru was keen that before that Kuriya should visit Palpatta at least once. Govind Guru and Kuriya were still in serious discussions over the issue when Kalji appeared with his son Amalya. The boy had fully recovered. He touched the feet of Govind Guru. Kalji was looking at Govind Guru with the expression of immense gratitude. Thavara had also come with him. After paying his respects to Govind Guru, Kalji asked his son to return home. Kalji and Thavara had learnt that Kuriya was back in Basiya. Kuriya had gone straight to Govind Guru's home.

Govind Guru consulted Kalji and Thavara also on whether or not to send Kuriya to Palpatta before the fair. Kalji and Thavara knew well that Kuriya is a hotheaded person. It will be difficult to restrain him if he loses his temper during talks with the jagirdar. After their mutual consultation and dialogue, the duo was unanimous in saying that Kuriya should not be sent there straightaway in view of the oncoming Punyo fair at Mangarh. After the fair, Govind Guru himself should go to Palpatta. The problem before the adivasis at Palpatta was not a simple one. Finally, it was decided that the visit to Palpatta should be put off till after the fair.

The news of Govind Guru being a miracle saint kept circulating throughout the day. A crowd of adivasis from nearby areas had started to gather at Chhani Magari right from early morning. It was a crowd of men, women and children. People were arriving at the dhooni site bringing with them dozens of people who suffered from multiple diseases. If someone was an asthma patient, another could be a paralytic, a third person could be suffering from chronic stomach pain or headache, while some were mentally ill. Govind Guru was receiving information about these visitors at his home where he was discussing the Palpatta situation.

Discussions over, Govind Guru reached the dhooni site at Chhani Magari. What he saw there gave him an immense sense of contentment that people had so much faith in him. But he also worried what would happen to the awareness campaign if he was accepted as a miracle saint.

He began his address to the crowd. "I am not a miracle saint. Kalji's son was bitten by a snake. That can be cured and I was able to do so successfully. The God was kind and the boy was all right. Treatment of curable diseases is possible. But one has to go to the right person. God has to be trusted for the treatment of incurable diseases. It is superstitious to talk of miracles. You believe in sorcery and witchcraft because of superstition. Only the Vaids, Hakims and those who know about herbs and medicinal plants should be approached for cure."

Govind Guru and Kuriya Bhagat distributed medicines, all procured from the forests, for stomachache, severe headache and indigestion. People took them because they implicitly trusted the quality of these medicines. They also took instructions on diet and various dos and don'ts to be observed by patients. Govind Guru and Kuriya Bhagat had no medicine for the cure of an incurable disease like paralysis. Family members of people with such diseases were persuaded to return home with trust in God's power. The crowd was melting away after bowing their head at the dhooni, touching the feet of Govind Guru and smearing the holy ash on their forehead. Despite the enlightening discourse of Govind Guru, he was being seen more and more as a miracle saint. Those who were discerning recalled the messages propagated in the awareness campaign and were able to understand what Govind Guru was saying.

The Dungarpur darbar had started to spy on Govind Guru after it was found that the talks between him and Seth Dalpatrai Mehta had brought no change in his views. In the previous year's fair organised at Mangarh on Kartik Purnima (full moon day of last rainy season) the presence of some gun-carrying youth had created a serious situation. Maharawal Vijay Singh informed Assistant Resident Hume in a letter, who was staying at Udaipur, about it. Col Hume asked the members of the Council and the Maharawal that a vulnerable worker in Govind Guru's organisation be picked up to act as an informer for the Raj. "Such a person can be lured by different temptations. With the help of such a spy and other sources, who may include trusted men of the jagirdar, a strict watch must be kept over the activities of Govind Guru. Any adivasi who keeps a firearm without licence should be arrested, his arms seized and criminal proceedings started against him."

Though the Sampsabha had not developed a well-organised capacity for gathering intelligence even then all the important news used to reach Govind Guru. An incomplete version of the steps that the administration proposed against him had reached him. He thought it prudent to go out of the Dungarpur state for a few days. It would be in line with the advice that Seth Dalpatrai Mehta had given him and, besides, it had become necessary for him to visit Palpatta. The original plan was that Govind Guru would leave for Palpatta just after the Poornima fair at Mangarh, but he decided to advance his visit in view of the news about the Raj spying on his movements.

One day Govind Guru took Kalji with him and mounting a camel before dawn, he left Basiya for Palpatta. He wanted to enter the Idar state territory before sunrise. It was a deliberate decision not to take any member of the defence squad with them. Govind Guru would ride a camel only when he had to reach somewhere quickly; normally he preferred to walk.

SEVENTEEN

After deliberations with his chief adviser, John Atlee, Viceroy Minto sent a telegram in February 1909 to certain native rulers in accordance with an established practice. The Mewar region of Rajputana was under the Viceroy's scrutiny because of rising unrest among the adivasis. Because of this reason, the Maharana of Mewar was an important figure for him. The viceroy sent him a telegram.

"Maharana Saheb Bahadur, please accept greetings from the highest British Crown representative in India. Yours and our interests are common in the Indian states. The rebellion by adivasis is a danger for both you and the British Raj. For a long time relations between you and us have been cordial. We want our relations to be closer, taking them to a more friendly level. We must prepare a future strategy for improving economy and military cooperation. Only by doing this can we present an example of our competence and power in our respective areas. We do hope that we shall meet soon. Best wishes."

The AGG was instructed that he was not to add any explanation to the text of the telegram, which should be handed over to the Maharana in its original form. The AGG found it a little strange because he was the all-powerful figure on behalf of the British in the state of Mewar. He was the sole authorised link between the British Raj and the Maharana. He felt his status would be adversely affected because of the nature of instructions for him contained in the telegram. He had to swallow his pride as he carried the message of the telegram to the Maharana.

The telegram sent by Lord Minto arrived at a time when the Indian National Congress had completed two decades of its existence. The Congress leaders were not able to do much beyond passing resolutions and presenting their demands to the British rulers and meeting them in delegations. The Congress had adopted a policy of loyal opposition and a politics of appeasement for seeking the blessings of the British rulers. Such a leadership of the party was called liberal and dovish. It led to the emergence of militant, hawkish leadership. Among the fronrank hard-line Congress leaders were Lala Lajpatrai, Bipinchandra Pal and Bal Gangadhar Tilak. The slogan "Swaraj (self rule) is our birth right" was coined by Tilak, a member of this trinity. These leaders were gaining in popularity. As a result of the harsh policies of Viceroy Lord Curzon unrest was rising in British India. Seeds had been sown for an armed rebellion. The interference of Political Agents in the states had increased a great deal. That is why even the native rulers were also getting restless within themselves, although it was impossible to see anti-British feelings taking roots in their hearts and minds. The British wanted to be friendly with the native rulers so that they could deal with the rebellion in their areas with the help of state armies. They had imagined that this would also help them in suppressing the anti-British atmosphere as well as the widespread unrest in the country.

As a result, the British adopted a policy of "subordinate rule" in 1906. In 1905, Lord Minto had replaced Lord Curzon and was instrumental in seeing this policy introduced within a year of becoming the Viceroy.

The new British policy was not to put pressure on them but to befriend the native state rulers and get their cooperation by reducing unnecessary interference in their affairs.

Communication facilities were being extended fast in India of those days. The Viceroy was able to keep himself in direct touch with his assistants like the AGG with the help of telegrams. Through these assistants, telegrams were also being directly sent to the native rulers and the Viceroy was also able to receive telegrams from them directly.

Maharana Fateh Singh replied to the Viceroy's telegram at once. "Dear Viceroy, we have just received your telegram. We send greetings to you and we express our gratitude to you. We have always respected the British Raj and their representatives have likewise shown their respect to us. We need hardly remind you that the diamond jubilee of Queen Victoria was celebrated with great pomp and show in the capital of Mewar, Udaipur. The British Crown had honoured us on the occasion with the title of GCSI. We can never forget this honour bestowed upon us by the British Raj. We shall gladly do whatever we have to because of the profound sentiments of equality that guide our mutual relations. You are cordially invited to the capital of Mewar. Please do accept our request. Greetings and with best wishes—His Highness Maharajdhiraj GCSI, OCOI, Maharana Mewar."

The Viceroy's telegram had pleased the Maharana. He recalled the fact that in the years 1892–94 serious differences had arisen between Maharana Fateh Singh and two British officials, the Resident in Mewar, Col Michaels, and the land revenue official, Wingate, over the matter of running a mail cart train between Chittorgarh and Udaipur.

It was the reason why Maharana Fateh Singh had stayed away from the Delhi Durbar the British had organised in Delhi in 1902, though he had taken the plea that he was unwell. The British government took a serious view of it, sure that he had faked his illness. Two doctors were sent to examine the Maharana, who took it as an insult. The Viceroy, aware of the past controversy, had welcomed the cooperative attitude of the present Maharana.

Relations between the Mewar rulers and the adivasis had lost the cordiality that had existed since the days of Maharana Pratap. The tradition of the adivasis applying blood on the forehead of the ruler at the time of coronation, a tradition that indicated the respect the adivasis had for the Maharana, was still maintained but was now reduced to a mere formality. With the adivasi unrest spreading in the states of Dungarpur, Banswara, Soonth, Idar etc, and also in the Mewar state, Maharana Fateh

Singh had felt that there might arise an occasion for seeking the help of the British. This was the biggest reason for the "telegram politics" between the Maharana and the British. It was also the reason behind the Viceroy's immediate acceptance of the invitation of the Mewar Maharana to visit Udaipur.

The Viceroy, Lord Minto, arrived in Udaipur on a visit in November 1909, travelling by train from Delhi to Chittorgarh and then in a mail cart to Udaipur. The mail cart was a shuttle service with two carriages.

AGG Trevor and other British officials were present at the Udaipur station to welcome the Viceroy. On behalf of the Maharana had come a state minister, Shyamji Krishna Verma, and a royal welcome guard. The Viceroy received an enthusiastic welcome upon his arrival in Udaipur.

The city of Udaipur was bedecked in honour of the Viceroy nearly on the same scale as at the time of the diamond jubilee celebrations of Queen Victoria. By November, the season of flowers does begin. Despite spring being months ahead, there was fragrance of the rose around the city of lakes, Udaipur. Every road and crossing through which the Viceroy was to travel was decorated tastefully. All the roads were cleaned, welcome arches were put up everywhere with buntings and colourful flags and smartly dressed security guards were positioned at important places.

The Viceroy was taken to the Jug Niwas Palace in a specially decorated royal horse carriage. All arrangements were made for his comfortable stay. Maharana Fateh Singh himself received him at the Jug Niwas Palace. He was offered bouquets and girls in traditional Rajput dresses applied sandalwood mixed red 'tilak' on his head. The Viceroy was ecstatic with the kind of welcome he received.

The Maharana of Udaipur had specially invited the Maharawals of Dungarpur and Banswara, Vijay Singh and Shambhu Singh respectively, along with other rulers and jagirdars on the occasion of the Viceroy's visit. All of them were present when the Viceroy was welcomed at the Jug Niwas Palace. They also welcomed him with bouquets.

The welcome ceremonies over, the Viceroy had tea and snacks with the Maharana in a palace room that was earmarked for his stay and then decided to take some rest. He came out of his room a little before sunset to find that the AGG and the prime minister of Mewar were waiting for him. The Maharana hosted a banquet for him at night.

All arrangements for the dinner in the open lawn behind the Darbar Hall was complete. The jagirdars of Mewar, the British officials, and specially invited Maharawals of Dungarpur and Banswara were already there. The Viceroy took a walk with Maharana Fateh Singh on the terrace of the palace, from where he viewed the enchanting sight of sunset. The sun had gone down behind a hill in the Aravali ranges. The air was getting to be a bit cool, but it was still pleasant. The Jug Niwas Palace was in the middle of the picturesque Pichola Lake, which was full of water. Standing on the terrace of the palace, the Viceroy felt overwhelmed and proud.

With the help of an interpreter, secret parleys were held between the Maharana and the Viceroy. Usually, the Viceroy's assistant, the AGG, would join in a discussion between the two. It was the first instance when the AGG had to stay out of the discussion.

The Viceroy was even more pleased by the fireworks that were on display in his honour by the side of the Pichola Lake.

Around 8 o'clock Maharana Fateh Singh and Viceroy Minto arrived for dinner from the palace terrace and were greeted by the assembly of VIPs and others. The two of them were seated side by side in two identical but artistically designed wooden thrones. The rulers of Dungarpur and Banswara were also seated next to them, but their thrones looked artistically less appealing. At a table nearby sat the AGG and two other British officials, one of whom was the Assistant Resident of Dungarpur, Col Hume. The jagirdars, who were privileged to be invited, and officials of the state were seated separately some distance away. Since the Viceroy had come without his wife, the Maharani, consort of the Maharawal, and other women dignitaries had not been invited to the dinner.

Liquor was always an inseparable part of such a banquet. The guests were being treated to foreign liquor. The jagirdars and the state officials were restrained in the intake of their liquor so that they did not become too inebriated and lose control over themselves. The guests were chattering in small groups. A large variety of vegetarian and non-vegetarian dishes had been prepared for the guests.

"Lord Viceroy, Sir, everything is fine in the state of Udaipur. There was some trouble from the adivasis. Its main reason was the arrogance of landlords. We adopted a two-pronged strategy. One, we successfully crushed the activities of the mischief-makers with the combined power of the state and the army help provided by you. Two, we opened a direct dialogue with the chiefs of the adivasis to restore peace. By the grace of Eklingji (God), everything is smooth now." Maharana Fateh Singh broke a silence that had descended a while ago.

"Oh! I am glad to hear that. And how are you Mister Dungarpur?" Lord Minto asked, turning to Maharawal Vijay Singh. Maharana Udaipur had briefly mentioned the adivasi unrest in the Dungarpur state during his private conversation with the Viceroy. The Viceroy had kept that brief in his mind. The Viceroy wanted to know things in more detail from the Maharawal of Dungarpur. Since he was still a regent prince, Maharawal Vijay Singh was flattered by the attention he had received from the Viceroy.

"Yes, Viceroy Saheb Bahadur. There is one Govind Banjara who comes from our own area. He is a very conceited man, busying himself in misleading the illiterate Bhil and Meena adivasis, provoking them against us. We had arrested him some time ago. He has a few followers. There was some opposition to his arrest. Since we didn't want the situation to go out of control, we let him off after cautioning him. Actually, that was the time of an acute famine in not only Dungarpur state but also the entire Vagad region. We had released Govind Banjara to ensure that his arrest did not add fuel to fire among the famine-stricken people. The fear of our might led him to leave this area and migrate to the state of Santrampur. We're in touch with the ruler there. The Banjara did not create any trouble in that area. But he has since returned to his village and has resumed instigating the adivasis. He has formed an organisation by the name of Sampsabha. Though he talks of religion and piety, he opposes Lagan on agricultural land, restrictions on forest produce by the state and the practice of *begar* on construction projects. All this opens up the possibilities of an Adivasi stir."

"So, what've you done to counter that?" The Viceroy wanted to know. The AGG who was sitting at the next table was listening to the conversation keenly. He wanted to participate in the conversation but decided to remain quiet fearing Viceroy's disapproval.

"He was exiled a few days ago. He has gone away somewhere but we shall keep a strict vigil over him if he returns to the state. We've also made sure that some of our informers in his group keep updating us about his movements," said the Dungarpur Maharawal as he took a sip from his glass.

The Viceroy was listening to him with attention. He said: "Um, it is all right. But he can still create problems for you."

"Yes, Lord Saheb. Govind likes to be called a Guru. He is known in the region as Govind Guru. His popularity is increasing. He is in exile now, but it can't be denied that he may return and resume his activities in our area. In such a case we shall certainly need the help of the Maharana Hazoor and you." Worry was clearly writ on the face of Maharawal Vijay Singh when he said this.

AGG Trevor and Col Hume did not like that the Council, which is headed by Col Hume, was still in charge of running the affairs of the Dungarpur state but the Viceroy was discussing matters with the Maharawal, not Hume. The arrest of Govind Guru, his release and his subsequent exile, all were acts for which the Maharawal had not taken the Council's permission. The two British officials were slightly tense.

In the meanwhile, the Viceroy had finished his first peg. Seeing that, the other three quickly did likewise, gulping their drinks. The royal servants, standing at a distance, were watching and brought another round of drinks. All except Maharana

Fateh Singh accepted the fresh round of pegs. The Maharana was not fond of drinking. He had taken a peg as a formal duty.

"Tell us something about Banswara, gentleman." The Viceroy had turned to Maharawal Shambhu Singh as he cut half a portion of kebab with a fork and put it in his mouth.

"Sir, Viceroy. Everything is fine but for the activities of Govind Banjara which are spreading in our areas also. The place he has chosen as the centre of his activities, the Mangarh hills, is in Banswara state. He has influence in the nearby areas. His prohibition campaign has slashed the income of the state. We are also not able to take full control of the forest produce. We face difficulty in realising tax on agriculture."

"Yes, Lord Saheb, our revenues have also been affected because of Govind," Maharawal Vijay Singh chipped in, intervening on behalf of the ruler of Banswara. The Viceroy did not approve of this interjection. He looked sharply at Maharana Fateh Singh, who read his mind but said nothing. The Viceroy's disapproving looks had somewhat reduced the tension that was brewing in the minds of AGG Trevor and Col Hume.

Before Maharawal Vijay Singh could say anything more, the Viceroy stopped him and said: "That's all right, but please let the Banswara ruler finish what he is saying." The Dungarpur Maharawal was embarrassed and fell into silence. The Banswara Maharawal then resumed. "Lord, Sir, the Jhabua areas in the nearby central Indian province is also a fortress of adivasis. Troubles have become common there. That's why chances of rebellion in Banswara always exist, especially since trouble had taken place in the border areas previously."

"Yes, I realise that," Lord Minto reacted. By now the Viceroy had looked a little jaded. "Another round, perhaps?" Maharana Mewar inquired.

"No, thanks. Let's have dinner. The dinner guests enjoyed the sumptuous meal that had been spread before them."

After dinner, the Viceroy held lengthy discussions in his room with the Mewar Maharana, the two Maharawals, the AGG and Col Hume. These talks with the three rulers in the Mewar and Vagad region were open and held in an informal atmosphere. The Viceroy encouraged the AGG and the Assistant Resident of Dungarpur to participate in the discussions without hesitation. The change in the attitude of the Viceroy pleased the AGG and Col Hume. The subjects discussed related to defence, boosting economy with improved state revenues and analysing the causes for unrest among the adivasis. It was a satisfactory dialogue for all the participants. The AGG and the three rulers expressed their gratitude to the Viceroy. Despite a daylong journey and his busy schedule in the city, there was neither any sign of fatigue on the Viceroy's face, nor did his behaviour give such an indication. But it was quite late in the evening. The Viceroy acceded to the suggestions of his guests to retire. That night all of them slept well.

Next day, another formal meeting was due at the Mewar Raj Durbar after breakfast. Viceroy Minto was given the most respectable seat, next to the Mewar Maharana. The AGG, Maharawals Vijay Singh and Shambhu Singh, the jagirdars of the Mewar state and Raj officials sat in their designated seats.

The previous evening's discussions and the information that he had gathered from other sources were enough for the Viceroy to satisfy his queries about the situation in the Mewar state and the states of Banswara and Dungarpur. At the morning meeting, the Viceroy, the three rulers and some of the jagirdars more or less raised the same issues about which the Viceroy had already gathered some information. Before he arrived in Udaipur, the Viceroy had studied the old reports and correspondence relating to the Vagad region and the Bhaumat area of the Mewar state. Lord Minto had also gone through the reports sent by his previous assistants (AGG) and tried to verify them through other reliable soures. In brief, he was fully prepared for his Udaipur visit. He began his address before the meeting.

"The Mewar Maharana Saheb, the Maharawals of Banswara and Dungarpur who pay obeisance to the Mewar dynasty, all officials of the Mewar state and the jagirdars present here, to all of you I want to inform on behalf of the British Crown that the British policy towards the native rulers has always been one of treating them with respect. During the time of the

Company also these relations were marked by friendliness. Most of the rulers had helped the British government in crushing the Sepoy Mutiny, except some misguided soldiers of the cantonments and others who had been led astray by them, rulers and jagirdars who had proved to be incompetent and unpopular. I concede that some of the policies introduced by officials during the Company rule might have been faulty. But the British have come to India with a mission. In this spirit a lot has been done. I also accept that the East India Company was a commercial company. The British Raj had replaced the East India Company because the British government was seriously of the view that under no circumstances the interests of the native rulers should be undermined and unrest should not spread among their subjects. It was a decision that was fully in support of the native rulers.

"The subordinate officers of the British Raj have expertise in running administrative affairs. We want the native states to make full use of that. In the past, the economic policies adopted on our advice led to increase in revenues of native states. It is a living proof with which all of you are familiar."

The three rulers, the jagirdars and some officials, nodded their heads in approval. AGG Trevor liked what he heard from the Viceroy.

The Viceroy continued his address. "Here I would like to clarify that the British Crown desires that you must immediately implement a new plan for land settlement to bolster the coffers of the state. The Lagan system based on crop yields has possibilities of disabuse. The farmer and the revenue collecting officials try to serve their interests as a result of which the state is denied the anticipated income. That's why I'd like to advise that the Lagan amount be settled according to the land area so that a fixed amount accrues to the state exchequer. You should also have full control over the manufacture of liquor. It is a good source of income. A similar policy is necessary for the forest produce.

"The previous Viceroy, Lord Curzon, had appointed a famine control commission under the chairmanship of Anthony McDonald. In its report, the commission had prepared a three-point programme, which had given priority to suspension of recovery of land-related taxes, immediate opening of relief works and financial aid to farmers for buying seeds and cattle. This kind of help is a must during famine for retaining your subjects' faith and loyalty and to ensure that mischief makers do not exploit the situation on account of any anger or misery."

A wave of cheer greeted this statement of the Viceroy. Everyone liked the stress on retaining the "loyalty" of subjects. Lord Minto had expressed his agreement with the policy of Lord Curzon so that the native rulers get the message that despite some changes there was continuity in the well-considered British policies.

In conclusion, Lord Minto said: "The British Raj believes in friendly and respectful relations with you. Your pain is our pain. We shall always be ready to render any help that you may seek. On this occasion I also announce on behalf of the British Crown the handing over of the full powers of the regent to the Dungarpur Maharawal, Vijay Singh."

The meeting greeted this announcement with thunderous cheers and full-throated "Jais" of the Viceroy. The happiness of Maharawal Vijay Singh knew no bounds.

"I express my gratitude for the presence of you all and pray to God for your continued prosperity."

A visibly delighted Maharana Fateh Singh thanked the Viceroy for his visit to Udaipur and unveiling the policies of the British Raj.

EIGHTEEN

Lusariya was the first village in the state of Idar where Govind Guru addressed the adivasis. The camel fed on the branches of an acacia tree. The dawn had still not broken. After a short rest he left and arrived at the next village, Bhilora. Govind Guru and Kalji Bhagat completed their morning chores of bath and prayers. The camel got some much-needed rest. Bhilora had a dhooni. The villagers knew Govind Guru well because he had already visited the village once. They welcomed him heartily in their midst. He stayed at the dhooni site. The news of his arrival in the village had spread over a wide area, attracting the adivasis from the nearby villages of Rojada and Kanadar. Govind Guru was happy to see that a large crowd had gathered in no time. He realised that the Sampsabha was doing well in this area also. One of the important Sampsabha workers who lived in a corner of Kanadar village ran across the forest to meet Govind Guru as soon as he learnt about his arrival in Bhilora. A few days ago at a meeting of workers of the Sampsabha he had presented a resolution that Govind Guru should be immediately called in order to face the threat from the Thakur of Palpatta. That idea was already in his mind. He told Govind Guru about the problems of Palpatta.

"Our demands are not so unreasonable that Thakur Prithvi Singh can't meet them. The adivasis have not refused to pay the legitimate taxes and levy to the government. The Thakur is an obstinate fellow. He arbitrarily wants to burden the adivasis. That's why the situation has deteriorated. Once or twice he talked to adivasi representatives but an agreement was not possible. Now he is irritated by the very mention of the Sampsabha and avers 'I'll not talk to the bhagats.' Reliable information is that he has told a trusted gameti of his that 'if I compromise with the bhagats then they may become very unreasonable in future and harass me all the time.' He wants to talk only to the *gametis* and the traditional chiefs so that the influence of the Sampsabha in his jagir is restricted."

Govind Guru wanted to assess the situation thoroughly before he took any step. For days together he travelled with Kalji and Soma Bhai in the villages of the Palpatta jagir—Chittariya, Gadi, Valeta, Jinjori, Jayala, Masota, Limdi, Chithori, Chitrodi, Parvat, Chorimada, Kanadar, Kodiyada etc. He established dhoonis in each of these villages—Bhilora and Chittariya already had dhoonis. Drinking was rampant in these villages. With the efforts of the Sampsabha workers, the adivasis had reduced distilling the Mahua liquor in their homes, but the jagirdar of Palpatta had invited Kalals, the liquor traders, and given them contracts to sell their ware in the villages. The Kalals had engaged some adivasis on a daily wage basis to sell liquor. There had been clashes between some of the more enthusiastic Sampsabha workers and the employees of the Kalals. The sale of liquor had been a good source of revenue for the jagirdar and the state. But because of opposition by the Sampsabha workers this income began to shrink. That's why the jagirdar wanted to control the activities of the Sampsabha. But he did not see it prudent to do so in the Pal Thikana area because of the presence and influence of Govind Guru.

Ramjibhai Manglaji Parmar, the gameti of Chittarya village, commanded a great deal of influence over the adivasis in his area. He was also trusted by the jagirdar. He used to mediate in adivasis' disputes, usually in the jagirdar's fort. But he had no vested interest in getting close to the jagirdar. All he was interested in was that he should be able to command great influence in his village and its nearby areas. Somaji Bhagat and some Sampsabha workers had requested Ramjibhai Manglaji many times that he would earn more fame if he used his influence for the good of the villagers by becoming a worker of the Sampsabha. But under no condition was he prepared to damage his relations with Jagirdar Prithvi Singh.The two of them got along well. Balota, Kodiyada and Laxmanpura had a good population of the Patels. Chittarya had about a dozen Rajput families. The rest of the jagir was dominated by adivasis, most of them belonging to the Bhil, Garasiya and Meena communities. Though Thakur Prithvi Singh did not have moral flaws in his character, he was an obstinate fellow, very clever and cunning. In order to rule over the adivasis, he had won over some mukhiyas who became his trusted lieutenants.

Govind Guru started an intensive tour of the villages. He used to familiarise adivasis with the teachings of the Sampsabha to stir among them awareness and the spirit of devotion. The Sampsabha workers were creating a new image of a clean adivasi leadership. As a consequence, the influence of the traditional adivasi chiefs and the *gametis* had begun to wane. Possibilities were emerging of a division and confrontation between the old and new leadership of the adivasis. Govind Guru was worried about such a prospect. He held secret parleys with Kalji, Somabhai and a couple of experienced workers at the dhooni site in Bhilora. It was decided to call a meeting of all workers and bhagats of the Sampsabha in the jagir to discuss various problems and mull over the future strategy of the Sampsabha. On Somaji's suggestion, the *Thaan* of Hirkuliya Baba on the banks of the Hathmati river was fixed as the venue for the meeting. This spot was between Bhilora and Kanadar villages by the side of the river. It was almost in the middle of the Palpatta jagir and was surrounded by dense forest. The date fixed for the meeting was the Ekadshi in the month of *Paush* (high winter season). In the nearby Doongri a youth was singing while grazing goats:

How fascinating is the kohl
Filled in her pretty eyes!
How beautifully hangs down
the tassle of her bodice!
Tassel O! Don't move please
along with the breeze

and let me see this bewitching beauty
to my heart's content.
(The breeze stops blowing.
The gratified youth murmured:)
Thanks, Wind kind! I am leaving now.
Move now the way thou wish.

Govind Guru was amused to hear the song. Kalji said: "Why Maharaj, isn't it the way of the youth?"

"Yes, Kalji Bhagat. I had become old even in my youth. Anyway, let's forget these things." Govind Guru had again turned thoughtful. Somji's attention was somewhere else. Despite the seriousness on his face, what captivated the other workers present was Govind Guru's attractive and impressive appearance. His peppered hair on the head and white moustache, the Rudraksha necklace around his neck that hung over his white tunic with buttoned collar. Fifty-one-year-old Govind Guru's personality was more mature than his age. Very polite, with a hypnotic voice, sharp in intellect and a mind as transparent as the glass.

Govind Guru held the meeting with the Sampsabha bhagats and workers at Hirkuliya. Among the issues that were discussed with urgency included the matter of the levy and Lagan.

He dwelt on the importance of propagating the Sampsabha aims and its rules before the workers. He said: "First make the organisation strong, only then will it be proper to talk about our problems here with the Thakur."

Following his instructions, the employees of Thakur Prithvi Singh had decided that the levy on this year's Rabi crop was to be procured in full. There was every possibility of opposition to this wherever the influence of the bhagats was strong. In the past also those who had come to collect the levy had to return empty handed from such villages. In the villages where the adivasis were scared of the jagirdar, arrangements were made for forcible procurement of Lagan and the levy on Rabi crops. For some places, it was decided that the procurement should be on the basis of the actual production and if there was any shortfall in procurement, it could be met at the time of the next crop.

After the meeting at Hirculia, Govind Guru toured the area, during which he was kept informed about the developments. The central theme in his addresses and his main advice was that unless the Sampsabha organisation was strengthened further and awareness reached more people, it would be harmful to embark on any protest agitation. His biggest worry was the unseen battle for the leadership between the adivasi chiefs and the *gametis* on one side and the Sampsabha workers and bhagats on the other. Wherever he went, he had these two groups of people sit together to thrash out issues. He succeeded to a great extent in sorting out the question of egos and doubts over the future events that had agitated the *gametis* and the adivasi chiefs. Many of the chiefs and *gametis* became Sampsabha workers. The influence of the chiefs and *gametis* who were lackeys of the Thakur started to decline. It came to be believed that those who do not oppose the Thakur's oppression of the adivasis are not sincere to the adivasis. It was also being said in whispering tones that anti-adivasi behaviour would lead to excommunication from both the community and the clan after a decision taken at a meeting of the clans and the sub-castes. Nobody ever wanted to raise his voice against Govind Guru though he never used strong words in his addresses or meetings.

Thakur Prithvi Singh was making his moves cleverly. With the help of his employees he was keeping a close watch over the activities of Govind Guru. He wanted to take the right step at the right time. Despite his obstinate nature, he had the experience to use guile to rule over people. He was waiting for the right moment. Time was moving fast, but Govind Guru believed in moving at a slow pace with courage and understanding.

The nature of adivasi oppression in southern Rajputana and its nearby areas and in Gujarat was similar. With the intervention of the British government, restrictions had long been placed on the *Bolai* tax on the traders passing through the adivasi areas and the *Rakhvali* tax on non-adivasis for providing protection. The new excise and forest policies had struck at the root of the traditional rights of the adivasis. But despite stiff opposition by the Sampsabha, the practice of *begar* had continued. The state governments had no intention to scrap this tradition. The minions of the Raj looked at the adivasis with contempt. But Palpatta jagir had some other problems too: the dishonest practices of the middlemen and village heads during the procurement of levy and Lagan, the unnecessary interference by the Sisodia brothers, Raghubir Singh and Naval Singh, who were lackeys of Thakur Prithvi Singh, in revenue matters, and making it compulsory to get permission for using produce from the mahua tree grown in domestic premises and farmlands. The prominent adivasis of the jagir had submitted a written memorandum to the Idar Maharawal against the unjust policies of Thakur Prithvi Singh. Among the prominent signatories were Nanama Kodhar, Soma Pandor, Kala Devji, Jeeva Kharadi and Sankala Dhoola. The henchmen of the jagirdar had threatened to involve them in a criminal case. They were respectable figures of the area and also active workers of the Sampsabha. The threat they had received was another reason for turning the wrath of the adivasis of the area on the Thakur. Govind Guru and his associates were trying to deal with these problems, by understanding them, analysing them and then preparing a strategy to counter them.

Govind Guru established a dhooni at Rojada village and also put up the flag and signs to denote that the place was to be used for propagating religious and devotional activities. He also set up his temporary headquarters at the dhooni site, where appeared during the course of his wanderings for preaching the Sampsabha ideals, Dharmabhai Bodar. Govind Guru was surrounded by Somaji Bhagat, Kalji and many other workers. Somaji introduced Dharmabhai to all. Govind Guru was happy to note that Dharmajibhai had devoted himself totally to the work of the Sampsabha after leaving his family. Govind Guru heaped praises on him on his face. Dharmabhai was quite delighted. But he had a regret in his mind. He had toured many villages in the past year or year and a half, propagating the Sampsabha ideals and teachings to the people in order to evoke awareness among them, but despite hundreds of efforts he had no influence over the people in his own village of Laksmanpura. Even his son did not listen to him. He had, therefore, no love for his village.

A Bhopa from Chittariya village had come to repose total trust in Govind Guru, whom he regarded as a great saint. He was a devotee of Asapuri Mata. Her spirit used to visit him, but after coming in contact with Govind Guru and listening to the reformist songs of the Sampsabha the visit of the spirit stopped. This change made him feel better and his mind had peace. He used to go round villages, wearing a red-coloured loose garment. He would sing religious songs devoted to Asapuri Mata to earn his living. It also helped him gather information from the villages he visited, which he would then pass on to Govind Guru.

Out of the blue he appeared at the Rojada dhooni. He hit his body with the iron chain he had on his shoulder and shouted "Jai Mata Mai ki! Jai Guru Maharaj ki!" He knew Somabhai well. He had heard the name of Dharma Bhagat but perhaps he had never seen him. If he had, he had forgotten his face. He used to update Govind Guru about the situation in Laxmanpura. After a bit of small talk, he told Govind Guru: "Guru Maharaj, the adivasis in the entire region have high regards for the bhagats, but they don't have the same opinion about the lone bhagat of Laxmanpura, Dharmabhai. Is something wrong with Dharmabhai?" Dharmabahi appeared distressed to hear this. The Bhopa did not know that Dharmabhai was in the audience. Govind Guru calmly told the Bhopa as he looked at Dharmabhai: "This is Dharma Bhagat in person!"

The Bhopa was embarrassed. But he was a much experienced person and excelled in ready-wit. He immediately took control of the situation. "Guru Maharaj, I gather information secretly but I speak openly. Even if Dharma Bhagat is sitting here why should I hesitate? I'm saying what I saw and heard."

"That is fine. But tell us why do the people in the village not like Dharmabhai?" Govind Guru was not ignorant, but he asked the question to know something more from the Bhopa.

"The truth is that the head of the Patels, Jassubhai and the village gameti, both are sycophants of the jagirdar. That's why they don't follow your teachings and also don't respect Dharmabhai, though I know that there is nothing wrong with Dharmabhai." He tried to suppress whatever he had heard about the flaw in Dharmabhai and continued: "They realise that the jagirdar will be angry if they follow the bhagats. This has helped the Laxmanpura adivasis in one respect at least. They have got the fertile land of Dharvah."

"Bhopa, that is all right, but the question is: will they be able to retain the land long? Those who oppose me don't know this secret." Dharmabhai was upset after listening to the Bhopa, but he had composed himself and looked at Govind Guru.

"Dharmabhai, you don't worry. There is a vast territory for Sampsabha activities. As for your village, we'd like the adivasis to adopt the path that benefits them most."

At an informal meeting that day, Govind Guru decided at the request of Soma Bhagat that the bhagats, the workers, the *gametis* and other influential people should meet under the aegis of Sampsabha at the dhooni site of Rojada on the new moon day of the month of Magh (January–February). Somaji and Dharmabhai Bhagats and other workers sent their messengers to convey this decision in different villages.

The Bhopa of Chittaria one day told Govind Guru that the village barber, Kajoda, was acting as spy and transmitting news to the jagirdar about all the activities that take place at the dhooni site after dusk, including the prayers and the devotional songs that are sung here, the discussions held, the propagation of the social reform agenda and the progress of the awareness campaign. He comes here on the pretext of participating in the prayers and to show that he venerates you. Then in the morning he visits the Thakur in his fort and conveys all the news while massaging his head. Of course, his family has been serving the Thikana, the landlord's family, for long. That is why nobody suspects that he is a spy.

"What secret conspiracy are we hatching that his spying can do us any harm? We don't keep anything hidden within ourselves. We are open in our discussions. It's good that our ideals and teachings are reaching the Thakur's fort. In a way, isn't Kajodi the barber serving our interests?"

"No, Guru Maharaj. Barbers are a wretched community. They have a habit of carrying tales. It's possible that he had been exaggerating the news that he transmits. I think his coming and going at the dhooni should be banned." After listening to the Bhopa, Govind Guru only said: "The dhooni is open to all."

"We don't want to stop anyone from coming here. We work for the welfare of mankind through the dhooni; hence all are welcome here. Yes, the Sampsabha activities are limited to the interests of the adivasis. If anyone who is dedicated to the welfare and well being of the adivasis wants to become a Sampsabha bhagat or a worker we welcome him. So, forget about that barber. Follow the path of piety and good conduct in mind, words and action. God will be kind to all."

The adivasis of Rojada and its nearby villages would remain busy through the day in farming, or some other vocation involving hard labour. After their evening meals they would assemble at the dhooni site to hear the discourses of Govind Guru. The devotees would pray and sing religious songs to the accompaniment of a large number of instruments like drums, flute, pitcher, cymbals and Ektara, the one-string indigenous guitar. The teachings of the Sampsabha were incorporated into the traditional religious songs that were sung regularly. These religious activities would continue all night on special occasions, but normally they would conclude by late evening so that the devotees could rest before starting their next day's grind in the morning. If the devotees found that something they had heard in the discourse was in the interest of wider mankind, they would discuss it the whole day. Directly or verbally the awareness campaign was progressing well and so was the religious and spiritual counsel of Govind Guru, the teachings of the Sampsabha, devotional songs and the knowledge about the significance of the dhooni sites.

One afternoon, two youths astride a camel reached the Rojada dhooni site. They had come with a message from Poonja Dhira for Govind Guru. They tied the camel to a tree branch a little away from the dhooni and came to Govind Guru. "Guru Maharaj ki Jai", they shouted in greetings and sought the blessings of Govind Guru as they touched his feet. They introduced themselves as members of the defence squad. Govind Guru asked the two to sit near him as he returned their greetings affectionately. "The Sampsabha work is progressing well and awareness is spreading," the two men gave this reassuring news to him. One of the two then read out the message sent by Poonja Bhagat. "Guru Maharaj, Poonja Kaka has sent his salutations with folded hands."

"Yes, son, speak on," Govind Guru was keen to listen to the message.

"Poonja Kaka has asked us to tell you that all three members of your family are well, hale and hearty. No need to worry about them. Guru Maharaj! On Poonja Kaka's instructions we went to Basiya village. We met the Kaki Mother. She's absolutely fine. Your two sons, Aru and Amaru, who are like brothers to us, face no problems. They've sought your love and blessing." Hearing about his family Govind Guru was momentarily lost in memories. When he had left Basiya for the Palpatta jagir area, Amru was down with fever. He had recovered, but Govind Guru was worried about a relapse because the boy was physically weak. Hearing that he was in fine fettle brought some comfort to Govind Guru. He had not seen the faces of his wife and sons for a long time. He was so much preoccupied with the Sampsabha work that he had not personally inquired after his family, though he did get information about the Sampsabha activities in the Dungarpur, Banswara and Khairwada areas. No matter how much one may be devoted to serving humanity, one can't be totally unconcerned about one's own family. There is no alternative to emotional ties. In the clean slate of memories in his heart,

Govind Guru simultaneously saw the picture of his dear wife and two sons.

The youth continued. "All the bhagats and Sampsabha workers are doing their jobs as assigned by you. There is no shortcoming there. The special message that Poonja Kaka has sent is to ask you if there is need to form a defence squad in the Palpatta area? If you say yes, he is ready to come personally to complete the job."

"No, there is no need for it here," Govind Guru reacted brusquely. The talk of defence squad had jolted him back from the corridor of memories of his family.

"All right, Guru Maharaj! We shall deliver your reply to Poonja Kaka." That was the end of the defence squad proposal for Palpatta. In fact, right from the beginning Govind Guru was not in favour of the defence squads. It was a different matter that he had not been able to say that openly. He believed in taking everyone along.

"Poonja Kaka has also sent another important message. Elaborate arrangements were made and publicity was organised on a large scale for last year's Punyo fair at Mangarh. All bhagats and workers wanted that you should return to Mangarh as early as possible after completing your work in Palpatta. We wished you were with us. We missed you because of your engagements here."

The mention of Mangrah brought its geography before his eyes. He wanted to leave for Basiya and Mangarh at once, see his wife and children and talk to the bhagats and workers, see the sacred dhooni-dham. Despite his wish, none of this was possible at that moment. The problems of adivasis that had brought him to Palpatta had remained unresolved. There was also the need to strengthen the Sampsabha. The jagirdar will not talk about solving the problems of the adivasis unless the influence of local bhagats and workers of the Sampsabha spreads in the Palpatta area.

"Give my blessings to all the bhagats and workers. Tell Poonja Bhagat about the situation here. Tell him it'll take time. The responsibility for organising the Punyo fair has always rested with Poonja Bhagat and his associates. Convey my congratulations to them for successfully organising last year's fair. The load of hard work is always on the shoulders of energetic young men like you and the team there. Inform the people of Basiya that I shall return there soon." Govind Guru dictated his message to the two young men. He made arrangements for their dinner at the dhooni site, gave his blessing to them while saying goodbye to them. He kept looking at the two men till they had disappeared behind the hills. He was not simply staring at the youth but was lost in the deep recess of his memories.

The first large meeting of the Sampsabha bhagats, workers, social reformers and other influential triabals of the area began near the headquarters of the Palpatta jagir at the dhooni-dham in Rojada village. The venue was previously known as Rojada ki Magari but now it had become locally famous as the dhooni-dham. In the month of Baisakh, the forest full of palash trees turns red with its flowers. The name and fame of Govind Guru had similarly spread all over Palpatta, the most important and biggest jagir in the state of Idar. This was not an illusion but evidence of how far awareness had expanded, a reality that pointed to a better future. The more active local adivasis had started arriving at the dhooni site from early morning. The eastern horizon was covered with the clouds carrying winter rains. The sun was visible only a little after its rise. But daylight had broken. By late in the morning a big crowd had gathered. The invitations had gone out to a limited number of adivasi representatives, but a few curious friends had accompanied each one of them. The adivasis had come in large numbers from the neighbouring villages of Kanadar, Bhiloda and Posina. About a dozen youth from Laxmanpura had quietly slipped out from their village to hear and see Govind Guru and the bhagats at Rojada. Govind Guru's reputation as a miracle saint had spread in the nearby villages. As such, a couple of families had come with mentally ill patients. Darling of the adivasis, Govind Guru addressed jointly the invited and those who were present there on their own. His message was: engage in mass awareness campaign keeping in mind the message of piety and the social reform agenda. His discourse was brief. Then he asked most of the crowd to return home as he had things to discuss with the people he had invited. They obeyed the Guru and left. He told those who had come with mentally ill patients: "Go and bow before the dhooni, smear the holy ash on the forehead and trust in God."

He then discussed Sampsabha matters with the bhagats, workers, *gametis* and those who were engaged in social reform work. The discussions were open and frank. The earlier fears that tension might creep in between the Sampsabha bhagats and the traditional adivasi *gametis* over the latter's role as the traditional local leaders were gone. The misunderstandings between them, which were of psychological nature, were removed. all were convinced that all of them had to work together for the common good of the adivasis. The point of discussion in the meeting was the problems of the adivasis in the Palpatta jagir and finding a solution for them. The unanimous view was that a couple of representatives should be sent to probe the mind of Thakur Prithvi Singh about the problems. The Thakur's fort was not very far from Rojada. Soma Bhagat and Kalji were sent to the Thakur with a message from Govind Guru.

The deliberations continued in the meanwhile, as everyone was keen to know the Thakur's reaction. On their return they said that they had a satisfactory dialogue with the Thakur. He had told them: "The adivasis are the subjects of the Raj. To look after their welfare is my job. Why should I wish them ill? Only some people are engaged in instigating them against me and the Raj. Is it possible to expect any good by using coercive methods against the Raj? If the adivasis adopt the right path, I'm ready to solve their problems, which are minor in nature. Govind Guru is a saintly figure. I respect him. But I'll not talk to any bhagat of the Sampsabha as I don't know any of them.

Mutual trust is necessary to solve any bilateral problem. I am ready to talk to the *gametis*."

The Thakur was confident that even if some of the *gametis* were outwardly identified with the Sampsabha, the majority of them were still loyal to him. That was his illusion. The reality was changing. After talking to the Sampsabha activists, Govind Guru decided that it would be best to start a dialogue with the jagirdar before the Holi festival. It was also decided that only the *gametis* who had reposed full faith in the Sampsabha would join in the dialogue. They were already invited to the meeting at Rojada. The decisions were taken unanimously. Kajodi, the barber from Chittariya, was frequently seen coming and going with a bucket of water and a lota (vessel), ostensibly to give water to the thirsty. The meeting ended after daylong deliberations. The expressions on the faces said it had been a successful gathering.

After the evening prayers, Govind Guru was sitting at the Rojada dhooni, talking to Kalji, Somaji, Dharmabhai and two-three persons from Rojada village. The sky was turning grey. The *mavatha* (winter clouds) seen in the morning dispersed without pouring rain. It saved the Rabi crop from any damage. It was a bitterly cold evening of the month of Magh (January–February). Sitting by the side of open fire, Govind Guru continued talking to the bhagats till late in the evening.

News had reached Thakur Prithvi Singh that the adivasis of Laxmanpura had taken part in the meeting called by Govind Guru in Rojada. He was looking for an excuse and he found it. The greedy eyes of the Patels were set on the fertile land of Dravah. Some followers of Jassubhai Patel had poisoned the Thakur's ears. Jassubhai himself had visited the fort two-three days after the Rojada Panchayat meeting. He told the Thakur that the adivasi youth of Laxmanpura had gone to Rojada on receiving a clandestine signal from Dharmabhai. The adivasis were hoping to reap a good Rabi harvest when employees of Thakur Prithvi Singh arrived there. They delivered a message from the Thakur to Pitarbhai Bhanat, the gameti of the adivasis: "The adivasis shall not harvest the crop in the fields at Darvah." The words left Pitarbhai stunned. Others who heard this message were no less shocked. Accompanied by the gameti, Pitarbhai, the adivasis of the village went to Mukhiya Jassubhai Patel's house. He was sitting outside his house alone, drawing at his hookah. There was no clue of what was going through his mind.

"Mukhiya, we've been informed by the jagirdar's men that Thakur Saheb has ordered that no adivasi will harvest the crop at Darvah fields. We toiled hard to clear that land and made it cultivable. And that too on your and Thakur Saheb's insistence. We had not demanded that. What has changed so suddenly? We're not able to understand anything." Hearing this from Pitarbhai, Mukhiya Patel pretended to be surprised. The Thakur's men had deliberately avoided taking Jassubhai Patel into confidence.

"I too have no idea. We shall have to find out why this order was given. Thakur Saheb had voluntarily bestowed this favour on you. He had also talked about giving financial assistance. I remember very well what he said at the village Panchayat. Thakur Saheb is a kind soul. It's not possible that he goes back on his own word. Something must have happened. Since it's an order from Thakur Saheb harvesting will have to stop. I have been with you in all your troubles. Pitarbhai, let me come with you. We shall together find out from Thakur Saheb what is the matter." He spoke the last sentence while looking at Pitarbhai. The stunned adivasis thought he had offered them their last hope.

"We had somehow managed to gather wheat and pea seeds. After taking the maize crop, we spent day and night in clearing the land of wild growth so that we could sow this crop in time. It is highly unjust to give such an order when the crop, raised with our toil, is ready for harvesting. It places us in deep trouble," a middle-aged adivasi in the crowd spoke up.

"All right! I understand your problem. Am I a stranger to you? Let's us meet Thakur Saheb. You have patience. Now you go to your homes. Pitarbhai, you sit here while I get ready," Jassubhai said as he entered his house after telling his farmhand.

"Keep the bullock-cart ready. We've to go to Chittaria." The farmhand, who had worked for years on Patel's land, was an adivasi. He spiritedly ran through the threshold of the house and headed for the cattle pen adjoining the fence as Patel kept observing him carefully. Some of the young adivasis were returning with a sullen mood. Others stood silently outside the house. A whisper of "this is injustice" was frequently heard.

When Pitarbhai called on him, Jassubhai Patel was wearing a dhoti and a *bundi* (waistcoat). He did not have the turban on his head. As he neared the threshold of his house he found a restless Pitarbhai. He did not sit on the cot even when Jassubhai asked him to. The aroma of the tobacco in the hookah was wafting through the corner of Jassubhai's house. Jassubhai retreated to the house and came back, wearing a freshly washed Angrakhi waistcoat and white Gujarati turban. He adjusted the turban with his hands, lifted the hookah, took a deep puff and then blew the smoke. "Let's go, or else we shall be late in returning," he said as he came out of the house. Pitarbhai was behind him. The farmhand was placing the yoke on the bullock's shoulder. Next moment he fixed the leather harness at the two ends of the yoke. This bullock cart was not used for carrying grain and fodder and so looked like a smaller Tonga. The cart was known as *saggar* with its two wheels covered with wooden planks. It could seat four men, apart from the coachman. The cart was well secured with iron nails. Patel's *saggar* left Laxmanpura for Chittaria. The adivasi men, women and children at the village square watched intently as it moved along raising a trail of dust.

Jassubhai Patel and Pitarbhai Bhanat returned late at night. The Patel families were asleep comfortably. Unaware of the problems of their elders, the adivasi children were also fast asleep. The restless women were half awake in their huts. The elders, the middle-aged and the young were sitting at the village square waiting for the mukhiya and the gameti. As soon as Jassubhai's Saggar stopped outside his house, all eyes turned to it. It was the dark fortnight of the month of Magh (January–February), but there was enough light to provide some visibility. The faces could be recognised from close distance. But the expressions on the faces could be read only partially. The strong winds of the daytime had stopped but it was quite cold. There was a bit of mist too in the air.

"Things didn't go right," Jassubhai said in soft tones as he stepped out of his bullock cart before a small gathering of adivasis. Pitarbhai was so dejected that he could not utter a word.

"Mukhiya, what happened? Tell us," a middle-aged person asked intensely.

"Sit down, all of you. I'll tell you the whole story," said Jassubhai as he moved away from his house towards the square where a crowd was waiting for him. Hearing his voice, some who were half-asleep also came to the square. The adivasi women in the village stood with their ears glued to the windows and doors of their huts, waiting to hear the news.

Jassubhai began: "What should not have happened did happen. Even I did not have a clue about it. The thing is that defying the wish and hope of the Thakur Saheb, many young men of our village went to attend the Sampsabha Panchayat called by Govind Banjara in Rojada. It was like hitting your leg with your axe, inflicting injury to yourself. With what expectations did they go there? Thakur Saheb is well informed about what happens in this area. It was decided the other day in the presence of Tahkur Saheb that no one would get involved with the Sampsabha bhagats. Why did then our men attend the Rojada Panchayat? Thakur Saheb was upset about it. And his anger is justified. You can't clap with one hand. If you commit a mistake, how can you expect someone else to suffer for it?"

The adivasis were paralysed after they heard Jassubhai. They started looking at each other. Most of them joined in protest: "We do not know anything about when and who went to the Rojada Panchayat." An elderly person intervened: "It's, then, they and the families of those who went to the Panchayat that should suffer. Why are all the adivasis of the village being punished? Pitarjibhai, why don't you say something?"

"Jassubhai is right. It's our fault and..."

Pitarbhai wanted to say something else but Jassubhai cut him short to reply to the elderly person. "Baba, we had told Thakur Saheb precisely what you said. But he was annoyed and said, 'When we had talked about the Darvah fields being collectively given to the adivasis, then it became a collective responsibility for all to see that nothing that vitiated our word should happen'. Thakur Saheb first refused to talk. Ask Pitarbhai. It was because of me that at least he heard what we had to say and we learnt the reality. I folded my hands before him for your sake, but what could Thakur Saheb do when things had gone wrong? One thing more that Thakur Saheb said: 'I never go back on my word. The adivasis have betrayed their trust in the Raj, therefore I can't help but take my word back'. Thakur Saheb is a kind man but I know how he reacts when something goes wrong. Why Pitarbhai, isn't it true?"

Pitarbhai nodded his head and added, "Yes, Patel, it is true."

The adivasis were thoroughly disappointed to hear Jassubhai Patel and Pitarbhai. They started to look at each other with suspicion. The only question that was in the minds of all of them was: "Who are the villains because of whom we have to face this hour of sorrow?"

One or two young men who had attended the Rojada Panchayat were present there. They remained silent. They did not think it proper to open their mouths at that moment. They quietly slipped out without anyone noticing them.

"Now go and sleep. We shall wait to face tomorrow," Jassubhai said as he entered his house. Stricken with grief as though a young family member had died, the adivasis silently trekked back to their homes. They could not sleep for the rest of the night.

Next day, the adivasis called their Panchayat at the Barkadev site. The purpose of the meeting was to identify the youth who had attended the Rojada Panchayat. The previous evening Pitarbhai had sent word about the morning Panchayat. Everyone expected the Panchayat to take a decision on the Darvah land. Almost all the adivasis in the village were present at the Panchayat.

Pitarjibhai, the gameti, began his address to the Panchayat: "The lads who went to Rojada should step aside voluntarily." The previous night the youth, who had attended the Rojada Panchayat, had decided that if asked they would tell all, hide nothing.

In response to Pitarbahai's call, about a dozen young men who were sitting in different rows stood up simultaneously. They said in unison: "We did go to Rojada, but the Panchayat should listen to us fully. We'll then accept any decision that it takes."

Though Pitarjibhai, the elders and the middle-aged were very much aggrieved, they had the momentary satisfaction that the Rojada youth had instantly responded to the call to identify themselves.

Pitarjibhai asked the youth: "If you have anything to say, you can present your case before the Panchayat."

"We had gone merely to satisfy our curiosity to hear Govind Banjara and his companions. The Panchayat had attracted a big crowd. We had gone there only to see the event. We didn't talk to anyone there. We didn't even stay there long," said one on behalf of all the youh who had attended the Rojada Panchayat.

"Then, why didn't you tell us before leaving?" an elderly man asked.

"We didn't go there to participate in the Panchayat. We had gone to the low hills along the cluster of villages. There we learnt that a Panchayat had been called at Rojada, which was attracting people from far and wide. We went there out of curiosity. We had no definite purpose behind it. We did no wrong. We were like the other spectators who had reached there from nearby villages. What sin did we commit? This is making mountain out of a molehill. We're ready to tell the truth anywhere." The youth gave an explanation and sat down, and so did his other friends.

Nobody doubted the veracity of the youth's statement, but the panchayat wondered if it would serve any purpose to tell all that to Thakur. He had already announced his decision.

"For whatever reason these lads went to the Panchayat, they were responsible for depriving us of our land. Who will make up for this loss?" a middle-aged man asked in anger.

"They did commit a mistake," said another middle-aged man in support. Pitarbhai and many others agreed with this view.

"Then they have to suffer punishment," Pitarbhai announced the Panchayat's decision. The youth and their families protested strongly against this. But all others endorsed the decision announced by Pitarbhai. The Panchayat was divided into two groups.

"We don't accept the decision of this Panchayat," said the band of youth who had gone to Rojada as their family members started to leave. Pitarbhai and others tried to pacify them but in vain. In view of the split in the Panchayat, Pitarbhai withheld the decision on the punishment.

For the Patel community the rift among the adivasis was a topic of daylong conversation. They were quite pleased with it. What gladdened their hearts more was that the Darvah land had slipped out of the hands of the adivasis. The news reached Thakur, who too was happy. He had feared that the question of land might unite the adivasis in a rebellion and they might join the organisation of Govind Banjara. The 50–60 adivasi houses of Laxmanpura consisted of Damor, Parmar, Ninama, Bhana, Bodar and Garasiya sub-castes. Damors used to call themselves Meenas also. All the youths who had attended the Rojada Panchayat were Garasiyas. The Garasiyas formed a group of their own.

When he heard that the jagirdar had betrayed the adivasis of Laxmanpura, Govind Guru was very distressed and upset but he did not let that be converted into visible anger. Dharmabhai Bhagat was very worried about the situation in his village. He thought it was time he went to the village and talked to people there. He was sure the Garasiyas would support him. With Govind Guru's permission he took Kalji Bhagat with him and reached Laxmanpura. The Garasiyas welcomed him and after talking to him they agreed that they would follow the path shown by Govind Guru and the Sampsabha. There were only four–five Bodar adivasi families. They were also influenced by Dharmabhai and Kalji Bhagat. Dharmabhai's son, who was his family's only male child, realised that it was wrong to have opposed his father. For the first time Dharmabhai was satisfied that at least his being a bhagat had made some impression in his village. The Patels did not get to know what transpired between Dharmabhai and Kalji and the Garasiyas and Bodars, but they did get a hint that the Garasiyas were getting associated with the Sampsabha. This was what they had feared after the split in the adivasi Panchayat.

The jagirdar of Palpatta, the Thakur handed over the standing rich Rabi crop raised by the toil of the adivasis to the Patels on the basis of one-fourth share in the crop. Jassubhai divided the crop into different sections for the Patel families. The adivasis' crops became the property of the Patels. Before harvesting the crop, the Patels had decided that whatever extra hand they needed would be hired from the adivasis who did not belong to the Garasiya and Bodar sub-castes. The Garasiyas and Bodars had no means of livelihood left. One or two members of their families went to Vijaynagar and Idar in search of job.

The crop at Darvah was ripe with wheat, peas and mustard. The adivasis had no jobs. Some of them were employed as farmhands by the Patels. But on the whole, the adivasis faced a serious question of finding a livelihood. Now that the situation had gone out of their control, they decided collectively that they should establish direct contact with Govind Guru since he was going to talk to the Thakur on the problems of the adivasis of the Palpatta area. The son of Dharmabhai Bhagat was sent to Govind Guru. He came back and delivered the short message from Govind Guru: "Follow the rules of the Sampsabha. The problem of the adivasis of Laxmanpura will be included in the talks with the jagirdar."

Next day, Govind Guru sent Dharmabhai, Kalji and Soma, all bhagats, to Laxmanpura. They collected all the adivasis and explained to them that a way out would be found if all of them remained united and followed the path shown by Govind Guru. On the same day a programme of devotional songs of the Sampsabha was organised at the *Than* of Barkadev, which was attended by men, women and children. The Patel families ignored it. They had trust in the jagirdar and they had already got the crops at Darvah.

A dim glow was spreading from the eternal light kept at the lamp room at the newly established dhooni near the Barkadev *Than* in Laxmanpura. The adivasis were caught ruminating over the uncertainties of future.

Suddenly, news flashed that the body of a man was found in the Kanadar forest. People rushed there from the villages of Kanadar, Laxmanpura, Chittariya, Bhilora, Rojada and Posina. The body had marks from a sharp-edged weapon. There was a big wound in the head and a lot of blood was splattered on the body and the ground around it. Despite the body being mutilated it did not take long to recognise it. It was that of Dharmabhai Bhagat. It sent a wave of shock amidst all. The news was immediately sent to Govind Guru. He came rushing with Somaji and Kalji Bhagats. They were all shaken to see Dharma Bhagat lying dead.

"This is incredible! Murder of a bhagat!" They said in disbelief.

One of the Laxmanpura Patels immediately conveyed the news to the jagirdar. He dispatched a horse rider to the Maharawal at Idar. Thakur Prithvi Singh also sent a message to the Maharawal: "A special bhagat of Govind Banjara has been murdered. Please send the *kotwal* (city police officer) immediately for investigations to find out who the culprits were. If it is delayed, the adivasis can resort to violence."

The jagirdar sent one of his men to the murder spot to tell the people that the Idar police station had been informed. "The police will arrive soon to nab the culprits," the man assured the shocked villagers.

The crowd near the body of Dharma Bhagat kept swelling. Mangalya, who was crying inconsolably at the loss of his father, was later paralysed with grief as he sat near the body. His eyes had turned stony. It was feared that he might go insane. Govind Guru and Kalji tried to console him by putting their arms around him, but Mangalya was neither able to hear anything nor did he feel consoled. He became unconscious. Govind Guru had brought his *kamandal*, the water pot used by the ascetics.

It had water in it. He sprinkled the holy water on Mangalya and on his forehead. Mangalya regained consciousness after a while. The people around looked at Govind Guru with amazement. As for the murder there were as many different versions about it as the number of mouths around! But the whisper most heard was that "whoever committed the murder it is sure that he did it at the behest of the jagirdar with the help of Patels". But nobody was willing to say it openly. A little later a voice was heard, loud and clear: "The Patels of Laxmanpura were secretly nursing ill-will against Dharmabhai because of the Sampsabha. The murder has been committed by the Patels." Another person joined him: "Pick up the body and take it to the front of the house of Jassubhai Patel. He'll have to pay *mautana* (compensation for death)."

"Yes, yes. Do this." The words echoed loud. "Either Patel Jassubhai presents the murderer or he'll have to agree to pay compensation." The amount of compensation was to be fixed by the *gametis* of the local adivasis and other panchas (village council members) of the village. The compensation amount was to be paid either by the accused or the principal suspect. The local custom was that if neither of this was done then the body would be buried in the compound of the murderer or the family of the suspected murderer and the house would be set on fire.

Govind Guru, Kalji, Somaji and other discerning people tried to pacify the crowd. They knew that the talk of *mautana* would spread trouble. First, it was not proper to demand compensation by levelling a serious charge without any proof. Secondly, the jagirdar would support the Patels. That would make the matter more complicated and there was every possibility of violence and bloodshed. The important thing was that the demand for compensation for the murder of a bhagat was against the principles of the Sampsabha.

Following a request from Kalji and Somaji, Govind Guru raised his hand and expressing his deepest sorrow, said loudly: "All of you listen to me carefully, please. The murder of Dharmabhai is a matter of great sorrow for all of us. It is a sin committed by a heartless person. But to talk of compensation for the murder of a bhagat is not justified by any standards. It's natural for all us to be angry over such a death. But we should not allow anger to make us lose our senses. We've to act prudently. We'd want that the police investigate and find out who that heartless murderer is. We'll also try to find out the criminal. Such a sinner can neither descend from above nor can he hide below the earth. The jagirdar has sent word that police have been informed about the crime. We must keep patience. It will help no one if the anger over the murder of the bhagat leads to violence."

There was something in the voice of Govind Guru that touched people. They had faith in him. They saw him as a great saint who to some extent possessed the power to perform miracles. The biggest thing in his favour was that he was working for the well-being of the adivasis. His words had a soothing effect and calmed the atmosphere.

People started mulling over the motives behind the murder and the person who could have committed the crime. Govind Guru and all others who had collected there squatted around the body and discussed that issue. Two-three rough towels were tied together to cover the body, the wounds on it and the blood that had splattered around the body.

By afternoon, two policemen, including the Idar police inspector, Pathan Gafar Ali, came on a camel to inspect the murder scene. The police officer was experienced enough to realise the gravity of the situation. Looking suitably glum and folding his hands before the crowd, he went towards the body, removed the rough towels and started to examine the various parts of the body, especially the hands, the neck and the feet. The sepoys who had come with him then covered the body again. He paced up and down to inspect the murder spot, looking pensive as he gave his first reaction: "There are no signs of a fight. It appears to be a brutal killing. It has to be a case of enmity." He asked people about the character of the deceased. Their reply in one voice was: "He was a bhagat. He never did any harm to anyone. What enmity can anyone have with a person who treads the religious path?"

"I think the murder must have been committed at night," the inspector told his subordinate.

"Yes, Sir. Rigor mortis has set in but the body does not appear to be very stiff. The 'post matam' report will give an idea about the time of the murder."

"How many times have I told you it is 'post mortem', not 'post matam'? You've been working with me for so long; you've seen many dead bodies. Learn to speak English correctly.'

"Sir, I learnt Urdu from you. You can ask anything, but it will take time before I understand the foreigner's language."

The two policemen had talked in low tones, beyond the earshot of the people around. In British India, the laws of evidence, the Criminal Procedure Code and the Indian Penal Code, had been introduced years ago. Later, the states had accepted these laws with some amendments. According to the Criminal Procedure Code, a post mortem is compulsory in the event of an unnatural death. But the Idar state had made a concession that the post mortem would not be necessary if the cause of the death becomes clear during the course of initial investigations following the first information report and the panchas concur with the conclusion. Since it was concluded that it was a case of suspected murder, Inspector Gafar Ali completed the formalities with the consent of the panchas. He had heard the name of Govind Guru, but he was seeing him for the first time. He assured Govind Guru and others who were present there that he would be able to catch the culprit soon.

The Kanadar forest was about one-and-a-half or two *kos* from Laxmanpura. The body of Dharmabhai was put on a bier made of dry wood collected from the forest. He was buried at the rear of his hut where the earth was stony. His last rites were well attended. The Patels of the village were also present, as was Govind Guru himself.

The police tried hard to unravel the mystery behind the murder. The inspector went round the whole area, making inquiries from dozens of people. At last, Inspector Gafar Ali arrested two adivasi youths of Laxmanpura. After interrogation, the two confessed to the crime. During investigations, the two youths were detained in the Thakur's fort.

According to the Inspector, twenty-four youths of Laxmanpura had gone to Rojada Panchayat on the call of the murdered as a result of which the adivasis of Darvah village were not allowed to harvest the crop. Greatly angered by this, they had murdered Dharmabhai. The adivasis in the village did not stomach this explanation. They were willing to concede that the murder was committed by the two youths, but they were sure that behind it was the hand of the jagirdar or the Patels acting at his behest. Govind Guru also thought so. As a result of this, a wave of resentment was building up among the adivasis against the jagirdar.

Following the murder of Dharma Bhagat, Govind Guru announced that the pace of the Sampsabha activities should be boosted. Govind Guru and other workers decided that time had come for a decisive battle with the jagirdar. No half concessions would be sought from him. In order to ensure unity among the adivasis and create a spirit of awareness among them, the bhagats and the workers toured the villages in the estate. They set up dhoonis at prominent places. At the site of old dhoonis flags were put up. Govind Guru himself toured a lot. The number of new bhagats started to climb up. The young workers became more enthusiastic about the Sampsabha activities. The bhagats began to attract people in hundreds. Govind Guru, identified with the hopes and beliefs of the adivasis, drew huge crowds wherever he went. At the dhooni sites, religious songs of the Sampsabha became a regular evening feature. The invigorated activities of the Sampsabha were acquiring the shape of an adivasi movement, which was primarily aimed against the jagirdar of Palpatta but it was also against the policies of the Idar state and its attitude towards the adivasis.

One morning Govind Guru asked Pitarbhai: "Why did Thakur Prithvi Singh suddenly dispossess the adivasis of Laxmanpura of the land with its ripening rich crop?"

Pitarbhai narrated the story in chronological form.

Between Chittariya and Laxmanpura there is a large plateau with forest all around it. The adivasis of Chittaria have some farming land, which is enough to feed them. Laxmanpura has a population of the Patels. It has some good fertile flat land with black soil. The land yields a good crop of paddy, cotton, sugarcane, etc. All the fertile land is owned by the Patels. Being landless, the adivasis of Laxmanpura have been living in pitiable conditions. There are forests around, but because of restrictions on collecting forest produce, they have no sources to meet the needs for their food and other requirements. If they steal something from the forests, they stand the risk of being arrested. It has been common to see them facing criminal charges and being confined to the Thakur's fort after arrest. They are tortured in many ways, like being made to sit with their arms round their knees, whip-lashed, humiliated and asked to do free labour for months. The adivasis have no other alternative but to be landless labourer at Patel farms. The Patel farmer asks them to do all the farming, from sowing, tilling, and weeding to reaping. At the time of threshing they are be paid daily wages, and something extra in cash or kind may also be given to the farm workers who are retained on yearly basis. But the women and minor members of their families are compelled to work without payment.

Darvah in Laxmanpura was a forest spread on a levelled ground extending about 200 sq acres. It had mainly Palash trees but also some jujube trees, interspersed with some *thoor* (a kind of cactus) and Naagphani, the prickly pear. The Patels played a dirty trick on the adivasis. They enticed them into clearing the forest and make the land cultivable. After consulting his community, the chief of the Patels, Jassubhai, advised Thakur Prithvi Singh that in order to make the Darvah forest land cultivable the adivasis could be duped into believing that the land that they cleared would be handed over to them. It would have two advantages. One, the adivasis would clear the forest land, increase the size of the land available for agricultural in the jagir which would also make more land available for the levy. This would boost the income of the jagir and the state. Two, it would stop the theft of wood, catechu, gum, roots and fruits by the adivasis. Thakur Prithvi Singh jumped at the idea. He sent a message that he would be visiting Laxmanpura and talk to adivasis about something of their interest. Thakur Prithvi Singh had visited Laxmanpura several times but only for the sake of Patels. He would talk to them and return. On a couple of occasions he had dinner with them ,too. This time the visit was specially to meet the adivasis, who looked forward to it quite eagerly. The adivasi men, women and children assembled at the village square with great expectations.

Lead by the Patels' chief, Jassubhai, and the gameti of the adivasis, Pitarbhai Bhanat, the prominent adivasis of the village welcomed Thakur Prithvi Singh at the village entrance. The Patels also attended the Panchayat held at the village chaupal, the assembly place. The adivasi women came with their children. The Patel women were watching it all from their terraces. Only the Patel males were present at the chaupal.

"It's a matter of our good fortune that the landlord of the area, Thakur Saheb, is visiting us. The adivasi brothers count on their labour as their only source of income. Thakur Saheb is a kindly person. The Patels and the adivasis in the village have always lived in harmony. We employ the adivasi brothers in our homes and fields as labourers. We think we pay them adequate wages. We also do not have big farms and our sources of income are limited. That's why despite the wages that we pay their lives remain hard. If they had a permanent source of income, they could lead a better life. The adivasi brothers are faithful and dutiful subjects of Thakur Saheb. I'll request Thakur Saheb on behalf of the entire village that he should consider this issue and take some steps to improve the economic conditions of the adivasi." This is how Jassubhai Patel initiated the proceedings of the panchayat.

Most of the people present nodded in agreement with him. A ray of hope emerged among the adivasis. Fired by hope, they were intently looking at Jassubhai and Thakur Prithvi Singh. Jassubhai wore a white Gujarati turban, a flowing tunic and a dulangi dhoti to cover the lower portion of his body. He had crossed 60 years but he was quite healthy for his age. He had ordinary but sturdy leather shoes on his feet. Other Patels were also attired more or less in the same fashion. Thakur Prithvi Singh had come riding a horse, which was tethered outside Jassubhai's house. The horseman had also come with him and he was busy running his hands over the neck, shoulder and calves of the horse while it was enjoying its meal of grass. The horse looked strong in built, in contrast the horseman was weak in physique. The horseman belonged to the Daroga community, who were traditionally retainers of the Thakur. The horse, tied not very far from the assembled crowd, was as much a centre of attraction for the adivasis as the Thakur.

It was the beginning of the month of Jeth. It was the early afternoon. The sun was losing its intensity but it was still warm. The Panchayat was being held under the umbrella-shaped mango tree at the chaupal. The elderly Thakur was sitting on a cot, covered with a mattress and a pillow. He was attired in a brown *achkan* and a white dhoti. His pointed leather shoes were embroidered with blue and golden thread. His face reflected his noble moorings. The wheatish-coloured Thakur kept a handlebar moustache. A Patel youth filled a hookah with tobacco and placed it by his side. As Jassubhai spoke, the Thakur drew a few puffs at the hookah and placed it for a little while on the ground. The mouth of the long pipe of the hookah was on his right. The adivasis who came there had covered the lower portion of their body with dirty clothes. Some of them had also carried coarse towels, which were either flung across the shoulders or tied to the head. The women wore clothes of different colours and had managed somehow to cover their entire body. As could be expected, the children, dark and emaciated, were half-naked as usual.

While Jassubhai was addressing the crowd, a bird, that was sitting on a branch of mango tree, dropped its excrement upon his shoulder. Jassubhai wiped his shoulder clean with his finger and then rubbed the dirty finger on the lower portion of his dhoti. He growled at the tree branch and continued to speak. The adivasi women and children found the bird's dropping its excrement on his shoulder highly entertaining. Men were in a sombre mood and paid no attention to the incident. From the mouth of an adivasi youth came a strange shrill noise as he clapped his hands. At this the flock of hundreds of birds on the tree branches flew away. Most of the birds were parrots. Right above where Jassubhai was standing and delivering his speech, was a parrot eating the flesh of a mango. Perhaps it was the parrot that dropped the excrement. Thakur Prithvi Singh's eyes were, however, fixed on an adivasi youth who had not taken away his eyes from the handle and the sheath of the sword hanging from the Thakur's waist. Meanwhile, the tobacco in the hookah was lit and Thakur Prithvi Singh drew a long puff and blew the smoke away, filling the air with the aroma of the tobacco.

After Jassubhai, two–three Patels expressed their views, which were almost identical to his views. The adivasi gameti, Pitarbhai, said only this much at the instance of Jassubhai: "We shall be fortunate if Thakur Saheb says and does something in our interest. He is our bread-giver. If he doesn't look after us then who else in this wide world will? Ram (the God) is already angry with us, now at least the Raj should not." Jassubhai folded his hands before the jagirdar and requested him to give his blessings to the entire village. Adjusting the handle of the sword, the Thakur began his address.

"All subjects are equal for the ruler. A man has to live the kind of life that is written in his destiny. Nobody can change his destiny. I'm the jagirdar of the state and all of you are its subjects. Some adivasis of the area have been misled into neglecting Raj Bhakti (loyalty to the ruler) and are learning a different type of bhakti (faith). We should all have faith in devotion to God, but rebellion and anti-state activities under the pretext of following bhakti can't be tolerated. Some villagers have been reluctant to give the levy crop, saying its burden is too much for them to bear. But is it for the Raj or any Tom, Dick and Harry to decide how much levy has to be procured? When the Raj treats all its people as equals then every person must have equal respect for the Raj. Now, who's this Govind Banjara whom some people accept as their 'Guru'? What has he got to do with our area? Should the people here accept what I say or listen to an outsider who doesn't even belong to your caste? What good will he do for you? I've learnt that a person from Laxmanpura, Dharmabhai Bodar, has joined that Banjara's class and instead of looking after his family, he wanders here and there posing as a mendicant. How long will he survive by begging for food? One has to put in hard labour to fill the stomach."

The words of the Thakur had brought furrows on the forehead of the adivasis who were listening to him. An adivasi elder got up with folded hands and said: "You're the master, God for us. Why do you talk like this? We're your subjects. Which one of us has been short in loyalty? What wrong have we done? We survive by working at the Patel families. If Dharmabhai has become a bhagat, how can we be blamed for it? We had even warned him against joining the new-fangled organisation. But he did not listen to us. Instead, he started to give us sermons. When that did not make any impression on us, he left the village. His wife died many years ago. He has a young son who survives by doing hard labour. There is friction between the father and the son. Dharmabhai visits the village sometimes. This time he hasn't been here for more than a year." The elder person was Gomajilalji Ninama.

Jassubhai asked him to be quiet, telling him: "Yes, you Gomaji Baba! Thakur Saheb has come to our village to listen to our problems. You listen to him fully."

Thakur Prithvi Singh was happy within himself when he heard from the elderly person that Govind had little influence, at least, in Laxmanpura. One man from the village had become a bhagat but could not do anything. The Thakur resumed his address:

"You'll regret if you allow yourselves to be influenced by Govind Banjara or his bhagats. I'm satisfied that the adivasis of this village are on the right path and I must tell you that this is the reason why I am inclined to favour you. Now I'll talk about something that'll benefit you."

The moment he mentioned "benefit", all the adivasis looked expectantly at Thakur Prithvi Singh. They looked sombre. One or two Patels looked a little perturbed. The Palpatta jagirdar continued: "The land in the Darvah forest in the village is flat and has silky smooth black soil. There is a portion with gravel near the waterway (nullah) but it is not stony. Except for the land near the plateau at the Pal, which is flooded by the monsoon rainwater, and the land near the waterway, the rest of the land is fertile. This forest has no big trees except mainly 'Dhak' trees and some *thoor* and prickly pear plants. If this forest is cleared, we can have fertile land on which we can grow any good cash crop. Our adivasi brothers can do this job because they've no work. If they clear the forest then in return for that job I can give this land on a community basis to the adivasis of the village for cultivation in the monsoon season. You'll be compensated for your labour after just one crop. If you continue to be loyal to the Raj, I can consider paying you money for the land that you clear."

Faces in the Patel community fell after hearing the last sentence. Jassubhai didn't expect the Thakur to make an announcement in the village Panchayat meeting about payment of cash. He too looked worried. In the minds of the adivasis a hope swelled that they would finally have a source of permanent income. To own land was the biggest joy for them. They joined in shouting praise of the Thakur.

Raising his hands in a gesture of blessings, the Thakur acknowledged the greetings. He stole a glance at Jassubhai who was sitting in a plain cot next to him. Their eyes exchanged secret messages. Suddenly, the lines of worry disappeared from the face of Jassubhai. He smiled within himself. The other Patels were sitting behind him on the ground.

The adivasi gameti, Pitarbhai Bhanat, was sitting right below the Thakur. He was thinking that it would be a matter of great pride for him if the Thakur made fertile land available to the adivasis during his tenure as the gameti. The clever Thakur Prithvi Singh was reading his face. Like Jassubhai, the jagirdar had known the adivasis' gameti Pitarbhai Bhanat for some time. He looked at Pitarbhai and said: "Pitarbhai, what would you like to say on behalf of the adivasis?"

"Oh, the bread-giver! You're everything for us. Your command is our compliance. You know our problems well. Earning our bread is our biggest problem. If this problem can be met even partially, not only we but also our future generations will sing your praises. And while we are at it, let me also say about Govind Maharaj. We assure you that none of us adivasis will have anything to do with him when you're trying to do so much for us."

After listening to Pitarbhai, something bothered the Thakur. It was all right, he thought, that the adivasis would stay away from Govind Banjara, but why did he add the suffix 'Maharaj' with Govind's name? His worry vanished quickly when he realised that Pitarbhai was after all a trusted man of Jassubhai.

It was decided at the Panchayat that the work for cleaning the forest will begin immediately. The residents of Laxmanpura bade an affectionate goodbye to Thakur Prithvi Singh. The adivasis looked optimistic and enthusiastic. The sunset was still some hours away. The daylong hot *loo* winds had stopped. Thakur Prithvi Singh was riding his horse back from the village, leaving a trail of dust behind.

Thakur Prithvi Singh was back in his fort in Chittariya from Laxmanpura. After saying goodbye to the Thakur, Pitarbhai, the gameti, accompanied Jassubhai to the Darvah forest, which was adjacent to the habitable area of the village. They had a bird's eye view of the forest. They looked at the vacant land between Palash trees. The season for the shower of flaming red flowers on the tree was over. Fresh buds were sprouting after the autumn into flowers.

"Pal Pitarbhai! The earth is lovely and totally black. You can raise any crop on it. It'll grow like *gaundara* (a kind of grass that grows very thick) but will yield gold."

"Why, Patel? Are your intentions honest?"

"Hey, what're you talking about? It was my suggestion to the jagirdar. The adivasis in my village go hungry, how can I see this? You should all get to work. I repeat the land will yield gold upon gold."

"What do we do with the gold? It is enough that we earn sufficiently to have two square meals a day. If everything goes well, the adivasis of this village will sing your praises and that of the jagirdar. May I ask you a question? It is a secret that I am sharing with you. Don't talk about it to anyone else. I can't even talk about it with anyone else. So after listening to my secret conversation, keep it all as a secret."

"Yes, you speak up. What's is it? Today is a very auspicious day for you. What's it that has entered your mind? Hurry up, out with it."

"The thing is that all the adivasis in the jagir are fed up with the Thakur. Compared to other states, a higher levy is procured from here. People are fed up of rendering *begar*. The adivasis are facing false charges and they are in addition harassed by the jagirdar's men. Because of these problems, a large number of adivasis have come to regard Govind Guru as an agent of deliverance. You'll agree to this much that compared to other farmers, on the question of levy the adivasis are subjected to discrimination. In our village the adivasis do not have land, so there is no question of their contributing to the levy procurement, but in other areas they do have to give levy.

"An important thing that I want to talk about is: how has the Thakur suddenly turned soft on us adivasis after a long history of ill-treating us? Is there a trick behind it?"

Jassubhai was taken aback by Pitarbhai's observations. He wondered if Pitarbhai had understood the secret eye message the Thakur and he had exchanged during the Panchayat meeting. Though he felt unease he kept it to himself as he quickly replied:

"Look, Pitarbhai. You're a gameti. You're an experienced man. You're close to me, and closer to the jagirdar. All three of us have often talked about our joys and sorrows and shared secrets. It amazes me that such a preposterous idea could even enter your intelligent mind!"

"If I don't tell what's in my mind to my brother, who else will I turn to? If I'd kept it quietly in my stomach, it would have caused ulcer. If it's baseless and isn't liked by you, I take it all back to swallow it and banish the thought altogether. But was only wondering if the Thakur entertained the kind of designs that I visualised in my mind."

"I know Thakur Prithvi Singhji better than you. I tell you this because there's a doubt in your mind. I agree that it's not unexpected that certain doubts will enter your mind, considering the situation that already exists or is developing in the village. I also know it well that Thakur Saheb is no paragon of charity and truth. He may be stubborn but I don't think he is deceitful. Briefly, you should understand this that the adivasis will cultivate the forestland that they clear, but won't the jagirdar have the right over the wood from the trees that will be cut? He'll sell that to contractors. It'll bolster the Raj revenue. Thakur Prithvi Singh thinks ahead. Half the income from the wood will go to the jagir's exchequer and the rest will go the Idar Darbar. This should please both the Maharawal and the jagirdar. The labour put in for clearing the land will yield fruits in the shape of plentiful crops for you adivasis. The wood will be sold through the contract system. The contractor will also make some money. Doesn't it benefit all? So, why should anyone, even if that is Thakur Saheb, entertain any different ideas?"

The explanation given by Jassubhai cleared the doubts that had arisen in the mind of Pitarbhai. Both of them returned to their homes. Pitarbhai talked to the adivasis the same evening. They agreed to clear the forestland. Promising to start the work next morning, they went to sleep peacefully. It was after years that the adivasis of Laxmanpura had slept so contentedly.

Next day, the adivasi men and women were at the Darvah forestland before the crack of dawn. They took their various implements, pickaxe, shovel, chopper, and got busy clearing the forest of its growth of wild trees and plants. The Palash trees fell one after the other. It was tougher to uproot the growth of *thoor*, prickly pear and wild jujube. There were some catechu and *dhaunk* trees which were also hard to cut because their wood was green and slippery.

The forest trees and other vegetations had traditionally been a useful source for the adivasi. In fact, their lives had depended on these trees and vegetations. But things had changed now. The forest policy of the government and the laws had ended the adivasis' right over the forest produce.

It was strange and ironical that the very forest the adivasis had loved so much for centuries and for which they had given their blood, was being destroyed for their better future! One reason for the change was that what was required today was not forest but land that could be cultivated permanently. The adivasis who were working in the forest were not thinking about who would get how much land. Their only obsession was who could clear the maximum area of the forest.

Laxmanpura had only about a dozen Patel households while there were 50–60 adivasis households. The entire families of the adivasis, men, women, young and old, and children, all were working to clear the forest. From dawn to dusk they worked. Some enthusiastic youth worked all through the night.

The operation to clear the land brought misery to the animals living in the Darvah forest. As the trees and bushes began to be cut, these animals looked for the safer parts of the forest. But the safe area was also getting smaller and smaller. The animals then looked beyond the forest for their habitat. All these animals, bears, hyenas, deer, rabbits, fox and wild cats, all ran towards the hills of Rojada Kanadar for shelter. Some migrated to the forest around the Pal plateau. The birds flew to the trees in distant areas. Snakes and reptiles were running in all directions though most had preferred to stay in the safety of their burrows. The Patel families watched with curiosity the constant felling of trees with loud crackling thuds, the fast disappearances of thick bushes and the sight of hapless wild animals running for their lives. In the hearts and minds of the adivasis there was only one thought: clear the forest area as fast as possible and as much of the area as possible.

Those were the last days of the month of Jeth. Most of the forest was cleared. The adivasis did this work in the midst of the fierce summer sun and the hot *loo* winds. The top skin on the naked shoulders and the back of the adivasis looked scabby because of the intense heat. There were blisters in the hands of all the workers. Their skins turned darker. They did not get adequate nourishment to compensate for the extra hard labour they were putting in. Their physical weakness was reflected on their faces. Despite all this, they were full of zeal and hope for a better future. The employees of the forest contractor used to visit the area occasionally. They chopped the trees in pieces, including the branches and the trunk, and stored them in separate piles. The thin debris from the branches and bushes of *thoor* and nagphani (varieties of cactus) were burnt. On surface, the forest looked almost clean, but the hard and challenging part was removing the roots. It could not be possible.

The month of Jeth ended. Two-four days of Asadh (June–July) also passed. Possibilities of rainfall were emerging. It rained heavily in the first week of Asadh. The faces of the adivasis lit up. All their time had gone in clearing the forest. It was not possible for them to have completed the pre-sowing exercises on the land they had cleared. A fragrance of freshness from the wet earth and the virgin land filled the air. It was not the time for sowing cotton or sugarcane. Besides, their seeds were expensive. The land required further preparations for paddy.

The unanimous decision was to sow maize which, in any case, was the most favourite crop of the adivasis. The adivasis of Laxmanpura did collective farming on the land that they had cleared in the forest. The maize crop turned out to be better than expected. The rain in the season was also just right for the maize crop.

As promised by him, the jagirdar did not impose levy on the adivasis. Some of the adivasis who had taken loans from the Patels were able to clear them. It was after a long period that the adivasis of the village looked so happy. The Patels were jealous. They eyed the crop raised by the adivasis. They were not concerned about how much labour had gone into clearing the forestland.

Pitarbhai narrated the full story of the Darvah land to Govind Guru. He then added, "The adivasis were allowed to grow the next crop also. But then came to the surface the conspiracy between Thakur Prithvi Singh and the Patels of the village. They needed only an excuse. Merely because two–four lads from the village had participated in your Panchayat, the Thakur took away this year's ripe crop?"

News of the increasing activities of the Sampsabha was reaching the ruler of the Idar state. One day he sent word to Govind Guru that the Maharawal wanted to meet him or one of his representatives to know about the problems of the adivasis. Govind Guru sent Kalji and Soma Bhagat to meet the Maharawal with a message for him: "The first job should be to clarify the situation by finding out if the jagirdar had a role in the murder of Dharma Bhagat."

A few days later, the Maharawal replied. "I've had full inquiry conduced into the murder of Dharma Bhagat. The Thakur of Palpatta or anyone of his men have nothing to do with this murder. The two drunken murderers were upset over the question of Darvah land and then in a fit of drunken rage they committed the crime. The ruler of Idar is sensitive to the joys and sorrows of his subjects and has all the sympathies for them. I'm sending a separate message to the jagirdar of Palpatta, Thakur Prithvi Singh, for solving the problems of the adivasis."

His message also carried the assurance: The Darvah land at Laxmanpura will be distributed among the adivasis of the village. They'll also be given lease permanently, provided they agree to give the levy regularly.

The message from the ruler of Idar created hope among the Sampsabha workers and Govind Guru. They were now willing to talk to the jagirdar. There was pressure on the jagirdar too, from both the Maharawal and the Sampsabha agitation. At last, there were talks between Thakur Prithvi Singh and a delegation consisting of Govind Guru, Kalji, Soma Bhagat and two-three other workers. The talks were held in a cordial atmosphere in Prithvi Singh's fort in Chittarya. The talks were successful. The two sides reached an agreement.

The Thakur had to reverse his decision disallowing the adivasis to harvest the Darvah crops on account of the Sampsabha agitation, the murder of Dharmabhai and pressure from the Maharawal. It was decided that the ripening Rabi crop will be handed back to the Laxmanpura adivasis.

The Palpatta Thakur, Prithvi Singh had his clerk prepare two copies of this agreement as a written deed. Handing over one copy to Govind Guru, the jagirdar told him and his associates: "It should not be publicised in a manner that it sends a message that these concessions were given under pressure from the agitating Sampsabha. I accepted this agreement because I care for the good of the subjects and all of you know that."

The Thakur celebrated the agreement with the customary tradition of offering jaggery. After leaving the Thakur's fort, Govind Guru and his associates headed straight for the dhooni at Rojada, where a large number of bhagats and other workers were waiting for them. Govind Guru broke the news of agreement to them, much to their happiness. They shouted "Jais" of Govind Guru. He explained to them that the agreement in the form of a deed will be kept in the safe custody of Somaji Bhagat. He requested the assembly to convey the news about the agreement to the people in their villages. It was 20 February 1910.

Next day, Govind Guru left the dhooni site for Basiya after advising Somabhai to be patient and peaceful while moving about in connection with the Sampsabha activities. He was personally happy with the Palpatta agreement. He had silently thanked God that his mission to Palpatta had succeeded. But while he was happy he was also saddened by the murder of Dharmabhai. The eyes of all the bhagats, Sampsabha workers and the adivasis present there were moist as they said good-bye with a heavy heart to their beloved well-wisher, Govind Guru.

NINETEEN

The Delhi Durbar in honour of King George V was held in 1911. Like other rulers in the country, the Maharana of Mewar was also invited. As soon as Kesari Singh Barhat got to know that the Maharana would be leaving for Delhi to attend the Durbar he lost no time in writing 13 couplets under the series *Chetavani ra Chungtya* (warning) and tried to have it delivered to the Maharana. But Maharana Fateh Singh had left Udaipur to board the train at Chanderia near Chittorgarh. Kesari Singh Barhat dispatched a special messenger who was able to present the couplets, written on a piece of paper, to the Maharana when the latter had entered his coach.

The couplets brilliantly captured the fame and bravery of Mewar. Some of these lines were:

Ghan ghaliya ghamsan, Raan sada rahiya nidar (A)
Fenkanta furmaan, halchal kim Fatmal huve (AA)

(Many battles have been fought on the soil of Mewar, but the Maharana was always dauntless. Oh, Fateh Singh! Today how have you become so disturbed by merely looking at a *Shahi* [royal] letter?)

Nariyand sah najran,jhuk karsi sarsi jikan (A)
Pasrailo kim paan, paan chhatan tharo Fata (AA)

(It is easy for some to bow their head while presenting their gifts they have brought, because this has been a tradition in their families, but Oh, Maharana Fateh Singh! How can you

> extend your hand for presenting the gift when you have to carry your sword?)
>
> *Sir Jukhiya ah Shah,singashan jin saamhne (A)*
> *Ralno pagat raah,phabe kim tone Fatan (AA)*
>
> (Oh Fateh Singh! How will it befit you to sit in a row below the Durbar when many kings have bowed their heads in respect before the Mewar throne which you occupy today?)

Maharana Fateh Singh quickly reacted to these couplets after reading them. "Had I read these couplets when I was still in Udaipur I'd not have left. But I'm now on way to Delhi. We shall see in Delhi what's to be done." The special messenger returned to Udaipur from Chanderia. Maharana Fateh Singh was on his way to Delhi. During the journey he read the couples written by Kesari Singh many times. The lines had left a deep impression on the Maharana, who was reminded of the greatness of Mewar. Despite arriving in Delhi, he did not attend the Durbar.

After the 1909 visit of the Viceroy, Lord Minto, to Udaipur the bitterness between the House of Mewar and the British that had cropped up due to certain old disputes had ended. These disputes were: the controversy over the Udaipur–Chittorgarh Mail Cart service, the transfer of Political Agent Col Miles, the appointment of Rai Bahadur Pannalal Mehta by the British as the prime minister of Mewar and his subsequent removal from the post due to opposition from the Maharana, the inclusion of Shyamji Krishna Verma in the Maharaja-Sabha (Princes' Council) and seeking local army for the defence of the British Empire. Maharana Fateh Singh wanted to re-establish the glory of the House of Mewar that had been achieved during the time of Maharana Pratap. Maharana Fateh Singh was a man of self esteem. He wanted that there should be no unnecessary British interference in his administration. But at the same time he did not want to antagonise the British needlessly.

After he was removed from the post of Political Agent in Mewar due to pressure from Maharana Fateh Singh, Col Miles wrote in his diary: "Two centuries ago, Mewar was the only Rajput state which had refused to give its daughters to Delhi. Today, it is the only state that has refused to contribute army for the British Empire."

As an administrator it was difficult for the Viceroy to ignore Maharana Fateh Singh, especially at such an important time as the visit of King George V and the Queen to Delhi for the Durbar. The British officials were surprised to note that after arriving in Delhi, Maharana Fateh Singh did not attend the Durbar. The Viceroy, Lord Hardinge consulted his trusted officials. Till then the British government had accorded highest status, among the native rulers, to the potentates of the states of Hyderabad, Mysore, Baroda and Kashmir. To this list was added the Maharana of Udaipur at the 1911 Delhi Durbar which was held in honour of King George V. Each of these five rulers was lodged near the King's camp. It was also decided to honour Maharana Fateh Singh with the title "RULER-IN-WAITING". This honour entitles the recipient ruler to be among the first to meet the British King. In the order of the ceremonial procession taken out during the big festivities organised on the occasion, the elephant carrying the Maharana of Mewar was to follow just behind the Baroda ruler. This in itself was a matter of honour. Despite all this, Maharana Fateh Singh took part neither in the ceremonial procession nor the Durbar. He was awarded the title of GCIE in absentia.

The situation of the rulers of Banswara and Dungarpur was very different. Maharawal Shambhu Singh of Banswara and Maharawal Vijay Singh of Dungarpur attended the Delhi Durbar flaunting great respect for the British. Vijay Singh was granted full powers to rule in 1909. Maharawal Shambhu Singh was given the powers in 1906 but, holding him incompetent, the British had entrusted the administrative powers to the Council headed by the Assistant Political Agent.

A day after the Durbar ceremonies, these two Maharawals called on the Viceroy, Lord Hardinge. They told him about the activities of the Sampsabha under the leadership of Govind

Guru. They had included the Idar ruler, Daulat Singh Rathore, in the talks they had with the Viceroy. All the three Maharawals betrayed extreme anxiety about the anti-state activities of Govind Guru that had gathered pace considerably. Led by the Sampsabha workers, the adivasis were openly opposing the state policies and orders. The three were unanimous in expressing the fear that if the adivasis in their territories, who mainly belonged to the Bhil, Meena and Garasiya communities, rebelled against the state it will be difficult to contain it.

The Viceroy assured them that the British government took the matter seriously. "The elements that can create disorder and unrest should be kept under strict vigil and stern action must be taken against them. If there is a possibility of the situation going out of control somewhere, we can think of sending the army. You should keep your police and security forces ready and be prepared to meet any situation. I shall issue the necessary instructions on my own to the AGG and other British officials. You should remain loyal to the Crown. You have my best wishes. I also thank you for participating in an important ceremony. You can now return reassured to your states." He bade them farewell.

TWENTY

Late in the evening, the adivasis had gathered at the dhooni of Amaliya village, which was situated in the Mangarh hill valley. The month of Kartik Purnima (full moon day of last rainy season) had begun. For a month before and after the Diwali festival, the place used to echo till late everyday to the adivasi Hida folk tunes. Carrying Ektara, a one-string guitar, in his hand, Haliya Bhagat began singing the strains of Hida folksong at the dhooni site.

Haun...Aey...Hee...Doo...
Haun...Aey...Hee...Doo...
Haun...Aey...Hee...Doo...
Haun...Aey...Hee...Doo...

The crowd joined him in singing. After playing the first strains, Haliya narrated the Hida story in the folk song form.

Sadan was the ruler of Ujjain city. His son's name was Harisan. The son's stepmother forced the ruler to exile Harisan to the forest for 12 years while her own son, Raj Bhanwar, was installed on the throne. Obeying the orders of his father, Harisan, who had disguised himself as a mendicant, was on his way to the forest.

Hungry and thirsty for many days, he reached Navinagari. He arrived at the door of Lali, a Brahmin widow, who respectfully asked Harisan, the disguised mendicant, to sit on the cot. She offered him a jug of water to drink. It was noon time when the blistering heat is at its peak. He felt better after drinking water.

"Mai (mother), I'm hungry. May God bless you if you could spare a few morsels of food?" Harisan could not resist asking her, having been hungry for many days. He had felt a nearness to the Brahmin woman as he spoke of his hunger. The woman was greatly rejoiced to be addressed as "Mai". She immediately cooked two rotis and served them to Harisan with buttermilk. Harisan had lost his mother years ago. After a long time he felt that sitting with that Brahmin woman was like sitting with his mother. After finishing his meals when he got up to take her leave, he found tears in the eyes of the widowed Lali. He asked her why was she crying. "Son, I've lost two sons of mine who looked like you."

On further probing, Harisan was told: "The ruler of this city has kept a tiger as a pet, who is fed human flesh everyday. On the orders of the king, everyday a man is sent to the tiger's den. I lost my two sons because of this practice. Today is the turn of my third and only surviving son. He'll be killed today. I'm a widow. If I lose my third son I'll be totally helpless."

The Brahmin woman was crying loudly as she spoke these words. The widow's love for her sons and their tragedies moved Harisan. He thought to himself, "I've none in the world to worry for me. Despite being the prince, my father has turned me away. I don't know what sin I committed in my previous life that I've to suffer this pain. Why shouldn't I do something for this Brahmin woman?" He worked out a plan. "If I succeed I'll be able to save the Brahmin woman's son; if I fail in my plan I'll still be able to save her son by sacrificing my life."

Harisan asked the Brahmin woman to bring some wheat flour and poison. He took this to the forest where the king had kept his pet tiger. He mixed the poison in the flour and made a human effigy out of it. He hid himself near the effigy with a sword in his hand. The tiger came at night and thinking that there was a man ready to be devoured he ate it at once. The tiger then went to the river to drink water. The poison had started its effect on the tiger, who began to writhe and shake. Finding an opportunity, prince Harisan killed the tiger.

As soon as he started to walk back after cleaning his bloodstained sword in the river water, the eyes of a princess fell on him. She had come to wash her clothes which had become dirty due to menstruation. Looking at such a handsome man as Harisan, she became pregnant. She returned to her palace. After nine months she delivered a baby boy. The king, keen to ensure that his daughter does not get a bad name for being an unwed mother, ordered that the newly-born child be carried by two female servants to the forest and be buried somewhere. The female servants set out to obey the orders. A sense of pity kindled in their hearts. They left the child in a pit and told the king that they have buried the child. A little later a woman potter, Nani, out on her donkey to collect clay, arrived near the pit. While digging the earth she saw the child who was crying in the pit. She brought the child home. She was childless. She raised the child with great love and affection. She called him Vagudiya.

"Jai Bhole Nath!" the listeners to the story shouted loudly. Haliya Bhagat explained that a song is not complete without receiving an encore and a story is worthless without visible signs of receiving appreciation. He then resumed the story of Vagudiya.

When he grew up, Vagudiya used to take the potter woman's donkey for grazing to a forest named Hadliya Maal. The sixteen Umraos (nobles) of the state had also employed Vagudiya to graze their donkeys. He would graze the donkeys in the forest and then take them for drinking water to a nearby lake by the side of which was a banyan tree. He used to swing under the tree, tying a rope to the branches, and play the flute. The 24 daughters of the 16 Umraos and the king of that state used to have their bath in the same lake. All of them were very young and beautiful. They requested Vagudiya to let them ride his swing. But he refused. When the girls insisted he asked them to form separate groups and collect green teak wood, the trunk of 'Saler' tree, garland of mango leaves and bamboo. Placing all these things together under a Mandap (canopy) that he erected, Vagudiya took the hands of each one of the 24 girls by turns and took the traditional rounds of a wedding ceremony. After that he took them one-by-one for a ride on the swing while playing melodious tunes on the flute. After some years, the girls turned adults.

The king and the Umraos sent for Pundits, astrologers, from different places to find the match for their daughters. They asked the astrologers to fix the auspicious time for the wedding of their daughters. None of the astrologers was able to find the auspicious time for the wedding of any of the girls. The king demanded that the astrologers must fix the time for the wedding, no matter what.

The head cook of the king called the astrologers for meals. The worried astrologers had lost their appetite. The cook also knew astrology. But the king did not think much of his talent as an astrologer. The cook consulted his own almanac and told the astrologers: All the 24 girls have been married in their childhood.

The astrologers told this to the ruler and the Umraos, who were upset when they heard it but they had no other alternative but to perform the *gauna* ceremony (sending the bride to the groom's family) of their daughters. The king found out through his spies that Vagudiya was the man the daughters were married to. The *gauna* ceremony of all the 24 girls was performed half-heartedly. The girls accompanied Vagudiya, crying and sobbing.

Vagudiya began to live in the deserted forest near the Hangariya lake in separate huts with his wives. For 12 years none of them had conceived. They were leading miserable lives. Vagudiya could not bear to see the plight of his wives. One day he slipped out and started living in a hut, which he had constructed near the bank of a river in Kajali forest. One day he found the statue of Lord Mahadev in a bush. He prayed before the idol for 12 years but it was all in vain.

"What no fruits for praying before Bhole Nath? This is certainly strange," remarked elderly Dharji as others joined him.

"Dharji Kaka. Listen further." Haliya then continued with the story.

"One day some fishermen came for fishing at the river. One of them was called Kala who had seven wives. All of them were childless. He was also a devotee of Lord Mahadev, but was not blessed with children. He caught fish and started to hit them on the idol of Lord Mahadev in a fit of rage. Upon this Lord Mahadev appeared in person and told him: 'Don't throw dead fish on me. I shall fulfil your wish.' The fisherman said: 'I want children.' 'Your wish will be granted,' Lord Mahadev blessed him. The fisherman went away.

Vagudiya was watching all this. He picked up a heavy piece of stone from the bank of the river and before he could throw it on the idol, Lord Mahavir appeared before him and said: 'Don't hit me with the stone. I'll fulfil your wish.' He then added: 'All your 24 wives will be blessed with a son each. A sadhu will beg to take away your eldest son. He'll then kill him and eat him.'

Vagudiya left the Kajali forest to return to his abode where his wives were living in privation. He began to live with them again. All his wives bore him a son each. Vagudiya called his eldest son Bhoj. He was very handsome. Exactly a year later a sadhu came on his round of seeking alms. Deceiving both Vagudiya and his wives, he took away Bhoj with him. In that moment of confusion, Vagudiya had forgotten the warning that Lord Mahadev had given him.

The impostor sadhu of Santuvan kept the child in his hut and saw him grow up. He had a galloping mare by the name of 'Boli Baseri.' Bhoj used to look after the mare. When Bhoj grew up, the fake sadhu hatched a plan to devour him. But by then Bhoj had somehow learnt that the so-called sadhu was a cannibal. One day the sadhu heated oil in a big cauldron and when it started to boil asked Bhoj to go round it five times. This made Bhoj suspicious. He asked the sadhu about the exact way he wanted him to go round the cauldron. The sadhu led Bhoj in going round the cauldron with boiling oil. Just when their fifth round was to end, Bhoj threw the cannibal sadhu into the boiling oil, who died a painful death."

"Bhagat Baba, this was a great act by Bhoj. Jai Bhole Nath!" said Sukha, a youth, while expressing happiness over the death of the sadhu. All other joined him in shouting "Jai Bhole Nath."

Haliya Bhagat then resumed the narration.

After some years Vagudiya died due to old age. Soon all his 24 wives also died due to the shock of losing their husband.

One day dark clouds appeared in the sky. It rained heavily. Rivers and streams were in spate. Jelunar had to cross the flooded river, but she found it impossible. She swallowed her pride and requested Bhoj to get her across the river. He agreed after extracting a promise that she would marry him. She gave her word at the temple of a local goddess, Havadi-Madri. Bhoj swam through the overflowing river to take her and her herd of cows to the other bank.

"I've heard the Hida song many times. But this love story about Bhoj and Jelunar I'm hearing for the first time, Haliya Bhagat," Dhanji exclaimed.

"Yes, Kaka! The thing is that the Hida songs and tales are sung and told in many forms. I'm recounting the story in the form that I've heard. I'm not a storywriter who is free to give a twist to a story."

"Dhanji Baba! You've gone senile. The story that Haliya Kaka is narrating sounds interesting. Let him complete." It was young Nandu who had interjected. His face was full of curiosity. Nandu was a growing adolescent.

"Why son, are the seeds of love sprouting in your mind? Who is the girl that is pulling you towards her?" one of the elders in the audience teased Nandu, who was embarrassed but kept quiet.

"Bhagat! Carry on with the story," said another elder. Before he resumed the story, Haliya Bhagat sang the opening strains of a song.

Hun…Aey…Hee…Doo…
Hun…Aey…Hee…Doo…

Others joined in a chorus, repeating the opening stanza of the song. A couple of listeners were yawning. But they were ready to hear the story in full. The story then proceeded.

Days passed by. Bhoj headed for Malwa with his brothers. The daughter of King Hunda Vajuda, Jelunar, had grown up into a young woman. She had never told anyone about the promise of marriage she had given to Kunwar Bhoj. Astrologers were summoned to determine the auspicious time for her marriage. After consulting their almanac, they said: "In the Malwa region ruled by Rana Diwan live 24 Gujars whose chief is Bhoja. He is a bachelor; all others are married. Jelunar must marry him, according to the almanac."

King Hunda Vajuda sent a Brahmin to chief Bhoja with the customary coconut and an auspicious thread, the gift that precedes marriage. Trying to contact Bhoja, the Brahmin lost his way in the middle and, instead, landed at the palace of Rana Diwan. The Pandit handed him the auspicious pre-nuptial gifts of coconut and the thread he had brought.

"Oh Bhole Nath, what did you do? It was treachery, Kaka!" Young Sukha, who was enjoying the story, could not contain his surprise as he spoke to the narrator. The growing adolescent Nandu felt a little jolted inside him.

"There are many twists in the story. You keep listening attentively. An important thing after every twist is that in the end Mahadev Baba destroys the evil." These words from Haliya Bhagat brought Nandu back to the reality of his surroundings. The story moves to the next stage.

Rana Diwan had come to know that Jelunar had promised to marry Bhoj. Yet, he wanted to marry her. Jelunar became worried as soon as she realised that instead of Bhoj she will be married to Rana Diwan. As the day of her wedding approached nearer, Bhoj and his brothers also got to know about the marriage of Jelunar to Rana Diwan. On the day of the wedding, the elaborate wedding procession of Rana Diwan reached in front of the palace of Hunda Vajuda. Behind them came the procession of Bhoj with his brothers riding the mare, Boli Baseri. From the latticed window of the palace Jelunar saw Bhoja. She was delighted.

At the ornamental arched gateway the two wedding processions came face to face. Both Rana Diwan and Chief Bhoj were adamant about marrying Jelunar. King Hunda Vajuda realised at this stage that he had been deceived. Rana Diwan was a powerful king and it was not possible for Hunda Vajuda to refuse to marry his daughter to him. Chief Bhoja claimed that the auspicious pre-nuptial gift of coconut and thread that the Pandit had brought from Hunda Vajuda were meant for him, but Rana Diwan had cheated him and accepted the gifts by pretending to be Bhoja. At last Chief Bhoj suggested to Hunda Vajuda: "Why not ask princess Jelunar who she wants to marry?"

"The Pandit who brought the auspicious pre-nuptial gifts from Jelunar's father had decided my wedding with Jelunar. Now what is there to decide? She'll have to be married to me. If it is not done with consent, I'll carry her forcibly. You'll be responsible for any ridicule and insult that it brings upon you." Rana Diwan had presented his case forcefully before Hunda Vajuda, who was utterly confused.

At last Jelunar herself intervened in order to avoid any bloodshed and end the controversy. She said: "I've blisters on my fingers. That's why instead of holding Rana Diwan's hands and going round the sacred fire under the *mandap* (canopy) I'll hold the double-edged sword of Chief Bhoj while taking the wedding rounds with Rana Diwan." Before uttering these words, Jelunar had signalled something to Chief Bhoj, who remained silent.

On the other hand, Rana Diwan was very happy. "She'll go round the sacred fire with me. This is what wedding is about. What difference does it make that she walks with the sword of Bhoj. If it solves the dispute, what's wrong in it?" He agreed with Jelunar's idea.

Rana Diwan was now returning with his bride, Jelunar. The king had earlier given a respectful send off to Chief Bhoj and his wedding party. Rana Diwan's wedding party was to pass through the temporary camp of Bhoj's party. The princess bride requested Rana Diwan: "Now that I'm married to you, if you give me an opportunity to meet Bhoj I'll be grateful to you all my life. You already know about the promise I had made to marry him. I could not honour my word. That's why I want to seek Bhoj's pardon. Please, grant this much wish of mine."

Rana Diwan gave his consent to Jelunar.

The evening had descended. It was getting dark. The wedding party had stopped in a part of the forest, close to which was a thatched-hut settlement of the Gujars. Dressed in her bridal clothes, Jelunar went there to meet Chief Bhoj. For her safety, Rana Diwan himself and three-four armed youths shadowed her. The mare Boli Baseri was standing in front of one of the huts. Chief Bhoj, dressed as a bridegroom, was standing next to it. He had already sent all his brothers with their families to safer places. The moment the bride came near him, he jumped with her on the mare and was galloping at lightening speed through the familiar route deep into the forest. Rana Diwan had no chance to stop them. He was overcome by a deep sense of remorse and frustration.

"Jai Bhole Nath! Fantastic! Haliya Bhagat you have recounted an excellent story." Everyone present nodded in agreement. Sukha smiled looking at Nandu. Dharji put his hand on Nandu's shoulders and said: "Why son, are you happy now?" Nandu was blushing.

TWENTY ONE

Mangarh hills became the centre of the Sampsabha activities under the leadership of Govind Guru, who had shifted his family to the dhooni site. News about all the awareness campaigns by the Sampsabha bhagats, workers and the youth front in the states of Mewar, Dungarpur, Kushalgarh, Idar and Santrampur used to reach him there regularly. Bearing their pain and abject poverty, the adivasis had pinned great hopes on the Sampsabha movement. Thousands of adivasis participated in the 1912 Kartik Purnima (full moon day of the last month of rainy season) fair. They were more enthused by the spirit of awareness that had permeated their community than the festivities of the fair. All the Sampsabha bhagats and workers were present at the fair. Many of them informed Govind Guru that some jagirdars and liquor contractors had sent hired men to destroy the dhoonis in various places. It was being alleged that "the meetings for prayers and discourses at the dhooni sites are being used for preaching prohibition and other anti-Raj activities. This has affected the sale at liquor shops run by contractors. The adivasis have also started to defiantly gather firewood, gum, catechu, roots, fruits and plants." All this has been fed to the Darbar. The men behind the propaganda were jagirdar's acolytes, forest employees and the liquor contractors.

The destruction of the dhoonis was widely resented by the adivasis. They beat up men who were sent to destroy the dhoonis whenever they had advance information about their destructive missions. If the dhooni sites did not remain safe there was every possibility of incitement of large-scale violence. Govind Guru was disturbed about these events. He delivered an unambiguous message to the workers that destruction of the dhoonis will not be tolerated under any circumstances.

Thavara Bhagat brought a specific bit of information to the notice of Govind Guru and other bhagats. "At some places, jagirdars and the police have been harassing the adivasis after the introduction of the 'Criminal Tribes Act' during the days of the *chchapanya* famine in the states. The innocents are being summoned to the police stations and posts. They are being tortured and arrested after false charges of theft and robbery are slapped on them. In order to lower their morale, the Sampsabha workers are also summoned to the police stations, asked irrelevant questions and are detained till late in the night." Many bhagats and workers recalled their own experiences to support Thavara's statement. When the law relating to "criminal tribes" was being promulgated in the states, Govind Guru was not aware that in order to suppress dissent, this law will be used not only against people indulged in criminal activities but also innocent persons. He took a serious note of the news that the Criminal Tribe Act was being used to harass the Sampsabha bhagats and workers. He announced: "Such incidents should be opposed jointly by us all." He prepared a declaration which said:

"I request all the rulers in the Vagad region with folded hands that I have adopted the route of piety for the well being of human beings. I am a disciple of the respected Guru Rajgiri Gosai. I learnt the lesson of worship from him. It is an extension of the cult of worship started by Sant Surmaldas. I have no other mission in my life other than the development of human being and cultivating virtues in them. All you rulers have always respected ancient scriptures and the teachings of saints and the holy men. I have also believed in those values and have been asking my followers to observe them. I talk of welfare and well being of all. But I pay special attention to the adivasis in the Vagad region because they are poor, deprived and ignorant. My main work has been religious in nature and spreading social awareness, which are not anti-Raj activities. I had established the Sampsabha, which is primarily a religious organisation, for this very purpose. It has nothing to do with any other philosophy. Some people who do not believe in religion and God spread rumours that the Sampsabha is an anti-Raj body. It is totally baseless. The lesson I give to my followers is: work hard and honestly let everyone be wise through awareness and cultivate moral values, follow the path of religion to practice pious traditions, adopt swadeshi (indigenous products) and get rid of the harmful habit of drinking. I have also been urging them not to believe in superstitions.

"The Creator of this planet has no form and on this earth rulers like you are the protectors of your subjects. You know everything about 'dharma'. You are also familiar with the pains and sorrows of your subjects. You are all in all and are kind to your people, but my soul is hurt when those who are subservient to you, Jagirdar, Thakur, police, forest officials, officials of the excise department and other subordinate officers, act tyrannical towards them. I listen to the oppressed and console them by asking them to have faith in God and everything will turn out right.

"Why are then the Raj employees destroying our dhoonis? The dhoonis are sacred places, used only for religious rituals. I am greatly saddened when I hear that kind of news. Worshiping and praying at the dhoonis does good to all. To damage them is an act of sacrilege. How can someone like you who believes in 'dharma' tolerate that such a sin is committed under your rule? It brings you a bad name. I have been inspired by Swami Dayananad Saraswati. As a result I support swadeshi. I disapprove of interference by the British in your state for this reason. I am sure you will agree with this view.

"Another request that I have to make is that the 'criminal tribe' law was enacted by the British. This law is in force in those parts of the country that are directly under their rule. A person from any community can commit a crime. I can concede that the majority of people in some communities are engaged in criminal activities. But the Bhil, Meena and Garasiya communities in the Vagad region were never associated with crime. They have been working honestly for their living. Is it a crime if they take some forest produce to fill their stomachs? They have been doing it for generations. You have to give an exemption for using the forest produce. But they are held criminals and punished. This is injustice.

"I heartily endorse the view that those who commit acts of stealing or other crimes should be given sever punishment. But what kind of a law it is that every adivasi has to appear before the police? It is injustice to implement in your territories a law made by the British. You are the custodians of the state that is why I am pleading before you.

"The third thing I wish to tell you is that I and our bhagats have been working to get the adivasis rid of their drinking habit. The jagirdars and the liquor contractors oppose this commendable work of ours. Even in the villages where prohibition has been accepted, the employees of the contractor are selling liquor. You know it very well that drinking harms both the mind and the body. I am sure you accept that fact. I request you to tell the contractors through the jagirdars that their employees should stop that. Only happy subjects are a loyal lot. The ruler is the bread provider of the subjects. If he does not take care of his subjects who are like his sons then who else will? I am a sadhu, so I talk only of the good of man. This has been my message to all. You are considered God's incarnation in the form of the ruler of the subjects. You should always think of the welfare of your subjects in that spirit.

"Just as the children become unruly if they receive no attention, similarly ignoring the interests of the subjects distances them from the ruler. If the ruler expects loyalty from his subjects then the subjects also want the trust of the ruler. You must have heard the proverb, 'As the King, so are the subjects'. Every good ruler wants to see his subjects happy and prosperous. As a good ruler you must protect the interests of your subjects. I do hope you will seriously pay attention to my petition. May God always keep you happy."

Poonja Dhira was writing these words being spoken by Govind Guru. Other bhagats and workers were quietly watching and listening to the duo. Kuriya Bhagat appeared to be somewhat disturbed. He got up many times and walked around before returning to his seat. Govind Guru gave him an occasional smile.

The politely worded declaration that spoke of the pains and sorrows of the adivasis was sent through messengers to the Mewar Maharana and the Maharawals of Dungarpur, Banswara, Pratapgarh, Kushalgarh, Idar and Santrampur. The fire started by the Sampsabha was alive among the workers and the bhagats who had assembled at the Mangarh hill on that cool full moon night.

The rulers in the Vagad region neither responded to the declaration sent to them by Govind Guru nor did they think of taking any action on it. The incidents of damaging the dhoonis during the night or the quiet part of the day by the Raj employees continued. Govind Guru used to receive information about these incidents from Thavara Bhagat and other sources. Employees of the jagirdars and the police were obstructing the awareness campaigns, discourses at the dhooni and the programmes of prayers and religious songs. People were being stopped from going to the dhoonis. They were also receiving all kinds of threats.

The police announced in the whole area that "under the pretext of religious programmes of prayers and discourses anti-Raj activities are being encouraged at the dhoonis. The disciples of Govind Guru are inciting the naive adivasis to indulge in violence. If anyone is seen to be participating in these activities at the dhoonis the police will add his name in the black list. The person thus listed can be prosecuted for treason any time."

The jagirdars were circulating a similar message in their areas and the liquor contractors followed suit. The rulers of Banswara, Dungarpur, Idar and Santrampur endorsed this dubious police initiative. They did so because the movement started by Govind Guru was fast becoming a challenge for them. They felt the very foundation of their thrones shaken. Their spies had fed them the information that "though Govind Guru has not announced it, in his mind he entertains the idea of a separate state for the adivasis'. The news brought by the spies had the Banswara Council and the Maharawals of the four states extremely worried. During the Delhi Durbar these rulers had already taken the Viceroy's permission for mounting an offensive against Govind Guru's movement. Coming together, these four rulers prepared a joint strategy to suppress Govind Guru's movement.

Orders had reached senior police officers, inspectors, Divans and other officials that 'strict vigil be kept on Govind Guru and his disciples. To know the activities and the routine of the bhagats informers may be appointed. As far as possible these spies should be hired from the adivasi communities by offering them some temptation. The information they feed can be relied upon and nobody would know who our spies are. Extra funds are being made available at police stations for this work'. The jagirdars and the Thikanedars were also asked to be vigilant about the activities of the Sampsabha in their areas. Officials particularly of the excise, forest and salt departments were also ordered to convey all the relevant information of the area to the Darbar (ruler). Special directives were sent to the jagirdars that they should contact the *gametis* (tribal chiefs) and influential people of the area who are loyal to the Raj and through them people should be told that "Govind Guru is bent upon revolting against the Raj. He is a fake saint. He wants to be the ruler of the adivasis. His virtues and religious devotion are a sham. It should also be emphasised that real saints don't raise a family. He has collected a lot of money that is offered at the dhooni sites. He is gathering money for his future generations. His talk of welfare for the adivasis is humbug. He is no miracle sadhu but he knows how to use his cleverness to mislead the gullible adivasis. The dharma that he advocates is not the traditional dharma of the adivasis. The adivasis have been traditionally worshiping Lord Shankar, Mother Parvati and folk gods. From the formless God, Govind Banjara, the self-styled Guru, has floated his own religion. It is contrary to the basic religious beliefs of the adivasis. He is himself from another community. How can he do any good to the local adivasis?"

The police prepared a secret plan of its own, according to which, in order to create fissures among the adivasis, the task of destroying the dhoonis would be assigned to the drunkards and the criminal and mischievous elements among the adivasis, especially the youth. Attractive baits would be thrown at them. If the activities of these people incited the adivasis, a few among the youth who damaged the dhoonis would be arrested and later released with further allurement so that they remained quiet and did not disclose the secret after their release. Policemen in plain clothes would be sent to different areas to find out about the fresh activities of the Sampsabha workers.

Govind Guru was profoundly sorry to hear about the sacrilege of the sacred dhooni sites. He was worried that his declaration had failed to move the state officials into action. On the other hand, it led to increasing incidents of damage to the dhoonis.

In the entire Vagad region over 100 dhoonis had been set up in different villages. The white flags on the dhooni-dhams were visible from afar. At every dhooni-dham at least one bhagat used to be present every evening who would address the congregation on awareness campaign. The dhooni-dhams had become the centres of awareness among the adivasis. Big drums are placed at all the dhooni-dhams, which was used whenever it became necessary to send a special message to the adivasis in different parts of the area. Keeping a big drum in the villages was an old practice.

Govind Guru's movement had spread far and wide. People had come to regard him as an incarnation of the Muktidata (liberator). In his humble and mild personality people saw God. Govind Guru and the Sampsabha activists enjoyed their work. They had begun to feel that they would be the vehicles for a change from bad times to good times for the adivasis. After the end of the Palpatta controversy a new spirit of enthusiasm had filled the bhagats and the workers because of the success of Govind Guru's efforts. The zeal of the young had to be seen to be believed. With this ground reality and mental frame how was it possible that anyone associated with such a movement would tolerate any act of sacrilege against the centres of awareness?

Govind Guru discussed the matter of protecting the dhoonis with the bhagats and Sampsabha workers at Mangarh hill. The previous two years had seen a big push in the number of bhagats, who included Dharji, Surji, Haliya, Gajja, Kodar, Khuma, Ramla, Bebaria, Vala, Kaliya, Meha, Partabiya, Jala, Bhura, Chamna, Bijjiya, Kanji, Ranji, Tarasiya and Sumbha. In addition to these, most of the bhagats of earlier days were also present. Apart from the bhagats the meeting was attended by hundreds of workers.

Among the most spirited appeared to be the armed youth brigade rised by Poonja Dhira. Some among those present looked sad because of the news about damage to the dhoonis, but most of them appeared to be more eager to see a swift counter action. Govind Guru scanned the faces of his colleagues carefully. The adivasis had come to nurse a religious fervour about the dhoonis. What worried him was the act of sacrilege by the Raj employees on the one hand and on the other the possibility of retaliatory violence by the provoked adivasis.

"Dhooni-dhams are our centres of awakening. The acts of destruction and damage at these places are deplorable and a matter of worry. We should take up the matter directly with the rulers of Dungarpur, Banswara and Idar." Poonja Dhira's words had suddenly enlivened the otherwise calm atmosphere.

"You prepared a declaration on Guru Maharaj's bidding. What happened to it?" asked an agitated Kuriya Bhagat. The concerned but silent faces of most of the youth seemed to reflect Kuriya's mind. The bhagats and the elderly workers whispered into each other's ears. Poonja Dhira's eyes were stuck at his beloved Guru's face. As was his habit, Kuriya was squeezing the top of his lathi with his right hand.

"It's pointless now to genuflect before the Maharawal or anyone else. You can no longer use fair means to achieve the ends." This was a loud warning from Chamna Bhagat.

A youth sitting in the back rows shouted: "We shall defend the dhoonis. Sampsabha ki Jai! Guru Maharaj ki Jai!"

The loud cries echoed off the nearby Kunda hill. The stillness of Mangarh had been broken. The birds sitting on tree branches started to flutter their wings. A few of them flew from one to another branch. It was the day following the night of the full moon in the month of Paush; the first day of the dark fortnight of the month of Magh (January–February). The sky was clear. In a matter of an hour, the rising moon had ascended high above the eastern horizon. Planet Mercury appeared tiny next to the Moon. The Pole Star was shining bright in the northern hemisphere and looking at the Great Bear, the seven stars, it was difficult to believe that by the end of the night it will complete half a circle round it. The lustre of the bright moon-lit night had enveloped the hills of Mangarh like a big transparent sheet of cold. To save themselves from the bitter cold the Sampsabha workers had arranged burning firewood at different places. The temperature difference created by the fire was converting the cold breeze into a caressing one. Occasionally, sparks will fly from the burning wood with a crackling noise. The bronze face of Govind Guru reflected a godly glow. After the cheering he had received from the youth his eyes had radiated a special sparkle. His personality looked holier with his bellowing white tunic, his dulangi dhoti and the Rudraskha necklace in his neck. He would often appear with folded hands and that is how he appeared at that moment.

Sitting on the thick, trunk-like branch of a Palash tree an owl was looking at the Sampsabha meeting with its roving eyes. Dina Bhagat threw a stone at him, asking: "Oh! Why are you staring at us? In the name of the king throw a crumpled straw into a well."

The owl took to wings. There was an old belief that during a conversation no one's name should be mentioned if an owl is sighted. The owl picks up that person's name and repeats it frequently, raising danger to that person's life. The owl picks up a straw with his beak and repeating that name he then throws that straw into a well. The time it takes for the straw to rot in the well will determine the time it will take for the person to meet his doom."

Some people felt obliged to Dina in their hearts for driving away the owl. All of them had the same premonition about the owl. Ancient beliefs have very deep roots. The physical effect of a curse presents itself soon. Most superstitions are not in the interest of mankind. But there are some beliefs that don't go away. The one about the owl was one such.

Govind Guru smiled at Dina's conduct. Dina was a simple person who knew nothing about worldly affairs except cooking rotis in the Dungarpur prison. Today he was a Sampsabha Bhagat. He had become cautious, wise and brave. Govind Guru was pleased to see this transformation in the life of Dina. Pious people have a correspondingly high emotional attachment. The organisation they establish may not look very efficient. But it does progress, though slowly and in a natural way. Govind Guru was satisfied that he had formed such an organisation where members are honest at every step and are occupied in their tasks day and night. Looking at the eternal lamp at the Mangarh Dhooni, Govind Guru turned sombre for a moment. He appeared to be lost in deep thoughts.

Kuriya Bhagat was staring at the rising flames from the fire in the midst of the moon-lit icy cold night. He turned over the wood in the fire. The flames rose high. The roar of a tiger reverberated through the Kunda valley.

"You need to think harder if it is a complicated matter and cannot be easily comprehended. The destruction at dhooni-dhams is intolerable. Their protection is our first duty." Kalji had again broken the silence, as he looked at Govind Guru.

"Poonja, you tell us. What's your plan for protecting the dhooni-dhams?" Poonja thought over for some time and replied: "All the bhagats are present here. Also, the old workers of the Sampsabha. It'll be better to take the step after consulting all of them."

"Yes, Guru Maharaj, there are over one thousand members of the defence squad of the Sampsabha youth brigade. They can be asked to guard the dhooni-dhams. But I personally think that any local person can be put on guard duty. The defence squad has been trained to repulse any serious attack and if necessary launch a counter-attack. Their training will be wasted if they are put on guard duty."

"When time for war comes, whether in the shape of defence or offence, we shall all have to unite to put up a strong front. For the moment our priority is to protect the dhooni-dhams. I think the duty for guarding the dhooni-dhams should be entrusted to the defence squads in villages wherever the youth have been trained. Where there is no trained defence squad, it'll be better that the local villagers take turns in guarding the dhoonis." Kuriya Bhagat expressed this opinion after taking a cue from Govind Guru.

"Any other brother wants to suggest something else?" Govind Guru asked the audience. Kalji and Mema Bhagats consented with the suggestion of Kuriya. The other few bhagats left it to Govind Guru to take a decision on the matter.

Talking over the matter with his colleagues, Govind Guru expressed his opinion. "Our people have to face many problems. We worry about them. The Sampsabha has many responsibilities. The Raj is not listening to us. On the other hand, the representatives of the Raj are out provoking us. We've to protect the dhooni-dhams at all costs. We've to forcefully oppose the activities of the Raj which are designed to damage the dhooni-dhams. If we can't protect the dhooni-dhams how can we then solve the many problems of the adivasis? I'd like that Poonja Bhagat continues the task of strengthening our defence squad without any hindrance. At least one member from each village represented here should go back to the village and collect people and hand over the task of guarding the dhooni-dhams to them. This job should be completed under the leadership of a bhagat. At the same time, the awareness campaign has to be taken to its final stage. We don't believe in violence and direct fight. But the Sampsabha has to oppose every wrong act. If a sinner is found damaging a dhooni-dham he should be caught and the panchayat will have to award him punishment." Govind Guru's remarks were greeted by Kuriya with shouts of 'Jais'. Others joined him.

Continuing, Govind Guru said: "But this job has to be done very tactfully. Even when catching someone red handed, there has to be no recourse to violence. It is likely that the person who desecrates the dhoonis is an adivasi who has been committing this crime either due to some allurement offered to him or has been misled by someone. If this turns out to be the case we must find a way to counter it. After gathering the full facts, the next move should be made at the level of panchayat. We'd not like our opponents to benefit by misinterpreting the action that we take.

"Now, for the other jobs of the Sampsabha. Thanks to our teachings, most of the adivasis have given up drinking. This is the happy result of the hard work done under the leadership of Kuriya and Jorji bhagats and others. This job has to be taken further. People will now have to be made aware that all the land, forests and hills are the creation of God. He alone has the rights on them. The rajas and maharajas are there for the protection and well being of the subjects. They have no right to rule if they oppress the subjects or do something against their interest. They were not always the rulers. The adivasi society was independent in ancient times. Their society used to be run by their own chiefs. The chiefs used to elect a ruler. It was our rule. The Rajputs established their kingdoms by exploiting the ignorance and natural simplicity of the adivasis. Coming under the influence of the British, they are oppressing the adivasi subjects. We've to oppose it.

"We must restore our ancestral right to land and forests given to us by God. We've no other alternative for our livelihood. For the welfare of the entire village and safety of non-adivasis, the *gametis* used to collect 'protection money'. To provide safety in the routes used by the traders they used to collect 'Bolai'. On orders from the Raj, the *gametis* have stopped these practices. At the root of this order was the fact that some *gametis* used these collections to serve their own ends. The native rulers have heavily taxed the tobacco and 'Amal' (opium) productions at the behest of the British. It has ceased to be profitable. We didn't oppose it because this kind of farming produced narcotic substances. At least, we did obey one order of the Raj! Our people earn their livelihood by the dint of their hard work. We don't believe in earning through coercive ways. It's bad enough that our brothers are forced to offer *begar*. It's inhuman. We opposed it right from the beginning, but this injustice continues. It's the duty, the dharma, of all Sampsabha bhagats and workers to spread awareness against *begar*. Some of us are afraid of the people from the Raj. Our organisation has become big. The efforts of the Sampsabha have brought awareness among people. A feeling of unity has also grown among them. They understand the reasons behind their pains and sorrows.

"We've already discussed a lot the issue of criminal tribe. In the beginning this law was brought to deal with the criminals. Now it is being used to frighten Sampsabha workers and other innocent people. This point was also made in the declaration that we had sent to the Maharawal.

"No attention was paid to our declaration. It is an insult. It has hurt me to see that they did not listen to something that a sadhu like me had to say. But we must have patience. We collectively oppose the anti-adivasi policies of the Raj. But our opposition must be limited to creating awareness among the adivasis against injustice. All you brothers have to take special care to see that during this work nothing is done that leads to violence, unrest or riots."

Govind Guru's hut was about 15–20 steps from the dhooni site. It was made of walls of loose stone and a roof of wood and dried grass and leaves. Govind Guru's wife, Gani, their two sons, Aru and Amru, and Poonja's daughter, Kamali, were sitting inside the hut, all listening attentively to Govind Guru. Poonja had no time to think that his daughter had grown up and had to be married. Kamali had started to take part in Sampsabha activities with Gani. She used to work for spreading awareness among the women. Most of the time she was with Gani. She had not been to her village for a long time. What was there in the village for her? Her father was busy in the Sampsabha activities day and night. Her elder brother was busy looking after his wife, children and attending to farming duties.

Govind Guru bade farewell to the assembled crowd after that fruitful discussion, asking them to be more intensely active in the Sampsabha work. He stood up with folded hands and made his way to his hut. All others also dispersed. Poonja Dhira with a dozen members of his defence squad stayed back. There were a few huts towards the Kunda valley on the Mangarh plateau. That is where the defence squad members went.

It was past midnight and there was absolute silence all around. Govind Guru spread himself on a flat board in a corner of the hut. His wife, children and Kamali were presently fast asleep in another room.

Govind Guru did not sleep well. He came out of the hut. The ghee in the burning lamp in the lamp room of the dhooni was low. He filled the lamp with ghee. The flame in the lamp rose high. The fire was not radiating much heat because there was not enough wood in it. Only the embers were burning lowly. He sat near a heap of embers. Poonja Bhagat was also unable to sleep well. He returned to the dhooni.

"Come, Poonja Bhai. Sit." Govind Guru invited him as he saw him coming. Poonja sat on the other side of the heap of embers. There were a few pieces of wood. He thrust them into the fire. The flames started leaping at once. The two had some relief from the cold.

That night Govind Guru composed a song.

In Jhalod is my high altar
In Dahod, my lamp of light
White men, listen!
I defy to abide by any of thy decrees
Godhara has my peers
and Ahamedabad, all my associates

My throne is in Delhi
and my book of law in Beneshwar
In Mangarh have I my holy hearth for worship
White men, listen!
I defy to abide by any of thy decrees
The entire Jambu is my battlefield
Mangarh my shelter
And my strength as well
our own commune would reign over our region
White men, listen!
I defy to abide by any of thy decrees.

Govind Guru considered the Vagad state as the Jambu (mythological name of a region) region. He regarded the British, whom he called *Bhuretiyas*, his enemy because of them that the native rulers had adopted anti-adivasi policies. Mangarh had already become the central point of the awareness movement. Delhi was the centre of power of the British. The song that he composed suggested that Delhi was the ultimate destination of Govind Guru, that is to say end the British rule. His dream was that in future the adivasis should be ruled by their Panchayat. His thinking was concentrated on finding ways to rid the adivasis of all their difficulties. But never did he entertain the ambition to rule by himself.

Poonja Bhagat had an inkling of what was going on in Govind Guru's mind. Poonja also believed that it was possible to confront the native rulers. They are not in a position to face the organised resistance of the adivasis. The examples of Rishabdev and Palpatta agreements were before him. But the British were a powerful ruling power. They had well-trained and well-equipped army. It will be difficult for the adivasis to engage them in a direct fight. The retired soldiers of the Mewar Bhil Corps used to feed him information about the state of preparedness of the British army. Listening to the new composition of Govind Guru, Poonja Bhagat said to himself that for the first time Govind Guru has challenged the throne in Delhi through his song. But how will this challenge succeed?

Poonja was a very sound person. He kept this question to himself. Govind Guru had no clue about the query that Poonja had in his mind.

Govind Guru felt somewhat light after he had sung for Poonja the song he had composed. After a while, the two of them went to sleep in different corners in the room.

As assistant to Poonja Dhira, Thavara from Jharkara was busy enthusiastically training the defence squad. An informal division of duties had taken place in the natural course among Poonja, Thavara and the retired soldiers of Khairwada.

Either by touring himself or through his messengers, Poonja was for a long time encouraging the youth to join the Sampsabha. The retired soldiers were preparing these Sampsabha youth psychologically and training them how to hit the target with rifles and bow and arrow. Whenever he had the time, Thavara used to impart them the tricks of guerrilla warfare. Taking one by surprise in attack, escaping secretly, what to tell or not to tell if caught, how to behave with colleagues, how to identify a suspect—these were some of the things he was teaching. He would take groups of defence squad to inaccessible areas in the hills and the forest. He was training them how to clandestinely negotiate through the hills, ravines, valleys, rivers, streams and thick forests, how to alter the route if danger lurks ahead, how to convey messages by imitating different birds. Recalling his association with Tantya Mama, Thavara was faithfully passing on the tips he had learnt during his association with him. For all this he had plenty of energy, time and inspiration.

One day he was sitting alone, looking a little sad, on a hill in Mangarh after he had listened to the discourse of Govind Guru. Memories of Tantya Mama kept haunting him. He had fought well, shoulder to shoulder with Tantya Mama for the sake of adivasis. After Tantya was hanged, Thavara like other associates of his had changed his style for the adivasi struggle and its strategy. The time for armed struggle had gone with Tantya Mama. While training the defence squad these days, his mind would wander back to the days of Tantya Mama, his war strategy, his deportment, his organisational capacity, his love for the downtrodden, the weak and the oppressed and the powerless adivasis. He began to see the real-life image of Tantya Mama in front of his eyes. He recalled the incident when Tantya Mama, posing as a barber, had cut the nose of a police inspector who had been specially deputed by the ruler of Holkar dynasty to arrest him, dead or alive. He thought to himself, "How different are the personalities of Tantya and Govind Guru." A thought kept coming back to him repeatedly that what was needed to fight the battle for adivasis was daredevilry and spunk not timidity and cowardice. Fighting the cunning and intrigues of the Raj successfully is possible not by being nice but by being clever, astute and bold. The discourses can spread awareness only up to a point. It is necessary to take some active steps on the ground to challenge the Raj. How will submissiveness work when the Raj is adding to the atmosphere of oppression, coercion and fear under the pretext of introducing new laws everyday? Thavara was undoubtedly loyal to Govind Guru, but remembering Tantya he began to feel that there is something lacking in the Sampsabha leadership.

Moti, a member of the defence squad happened to be around. He had observed that some kind of conflict was going on inside Thavara. It was getting dark. Coming from behind him, he suddenly put his hands on Thavara's shoulders. A startled Thavara turned around to see what had happened. "Arre, Moti, it's you. I nearly got frightened," Thavara said.

"Brother Thavara, we've no need to be afraid here in the hills. All this area is ours. How can there be any room for suspicion, much less fear, when no outsider can reach here," Moti told him as he sat next to him.

Thavara recalled the moment when he had met Tantya for the first time in a forest. He did get frightened when he saw Tantya.

"What's the matter? You're looking very glum today. I saw that change in your face after Govind Guru had finished his discourse. You did not even eat your meals today."

"No. Moti, there is nothing wrong. I don't know why I didn't feel hungry today."

"Are you feeling unwell?"

"No, I'm feeling well. It's all right, buddy. I've been remembering Tantya Mama today. My mind is a little restless. He was a very courageous man. The bastards had caught him deceptively and wrenched his neck like a rabbit. If they had fought him face-to-face he'd have shown them that he was not made of clay and would have fought like a brave man."

"Are you any lesser brave? You also fought many battles with him. And that's what you're teaching us. We shall together fight Tantya-type war."

"Who listens to us?"

"You're right, brother Thavara. Guru Maharaj is a great saint, but he's not like your Tantya."

"Let's do one thing. Let's discuss this with Poonja Kaka. If he agrees we can create a reign of terror in the Raj after slaying a few tyrants. Then only will these oppressive rulers and jagirdars listen to us."

Agreeing with Moti's proposal, Thavara accompanied him to Poonja Dhira. Thavara was becoming more restless.

"Poonja Kaka, Thavara Bhai is somewhat agitated." It was Moti's opening gambit.

"What is it? Thavara has been working with great ardour. Has something new cropped up today? Thavara, You tell us, what's the matter?"

"Just like that, my mind went back to Tantya Mama. Actually, the thing is that despite our hard work, our fight has not come out in its true form. These dhooni-dhams, sacred fires, coconuts, eternal lamp and plain talks, how much can they help us in mitigating our problems? I'm not able to understand anything. I didn't wish to talk about this to you, but when Moti insisted then I decided why not come out with it. But I assure you that whatever work you had assigned to me I did sincerely and shall continue to do so. You know it how sincerely I'm involved in the Sampsabha activities."

"Thavara, I've often heard about Tantya Mama from you. But it's only today that I've realised that you still nurture his principles. You know that Guruji has lit the fire of awareness through long years of sacrifice and leading an ascetic life. We should be able to gather its fruits soon. Look, Thavara. All mukhiyas are not alike. I agree that there is an ocean of difference between the personalities of Govind Guru and Tantya. It'll be wrong if you weigh them on the same scale. Guruji Maharaj is our chief. You know that the path that Tantya Mama had adopted was, after all, violent. Guru Maharaj is a saintly man. If we had adopted violent ways the awareness campaign would not have succeeded in reaching where it has today. It's better to ponder and act with patience. That's what all of us are doing. That's why the path we've chosen appears to be the right one. The work assigned to you and me by Guru Maharaj will ultimately prepare us for the day when it'll be impossible to put off a battle. I'll say that you continue to follow the path shown by Guru Maharaj. Don't entertain any other idea in your mind. Look, we've reached this stage after years of hard work and sacrifices. Sometimes, there is a clash with Kuriya over this matter and he finally understands that every man has his own ideas. Those ideas can be discussed. Such a discussion should be encouraged. But the important thing is that it should never be let out that there are any differences between certain bhagats and workers."

Kalji Bhagat had arrived there a little earlier. He had listened to this dialogue, but had kept mum. After listening to the sane and effective advice of Poonja Dhira, both Thavara and Moti became silent.

TWENTY TWO

Kamali was in a playful, joyous mood in the company of her friends. These young girls belonged to the villages Amaliya and Dhalariya which were at the foothills of the Mangarh hill. The morning sunshine of the month of Phagun had spread over the plateau of Mangarh. The cold spell had started to wane after the Makar Sakranti festival. The month of Phagun is famous for its customary Gair dance, which could be seen performed all over the area to the accompaniment of various instruments like drums, tambourine, cymbals, flute and plates.

"Come, let's dance the Gair," suggested Pano of Amaliya.

"Only we girls will perform the dance?" asked another girl.

"You're right. The Gair dance is not complete without boys. But if there're no boys around let us girls perform the dance," replied Pano. Her friends supported her and they clasped their hands together to start the dance. Just when they were taking the initial steps in the dance by forming a ring, Kamali said, "First, look there." She had pointed in the direction of the Sampsabha defence squad youths, about two furlongs away at the other end of the plateau. All of them were carrying rifles and bows and arrows.

"You mean we should be firing rifles," another friend said in amazement.

"Look, what's in my hands."

"It's a sling, Kamali."

"If those lads can shoot with rifles can't we play with the sling?"

"Kamali, why are you talking of rifles and slings when the

Holi festivities are in the air? I can't understand anything," asked another one out of mild curiosity.

"All you lasses lend me your ears. One day after the evening prayers at the dhooni, Guru Maharaj told my father and Kuriya Kaka that there was a possibility that we have to fight the white men (British). Kuriya Kaka was repeatedly stressing on the need for a fight."

"Kamali, our ancestors fought many wars with the Raj and the police. Who are these white men? Do you know? Have you ever seen them?" another curious friend had asked.

"The white men are believed to be foreigners. Guru Maharaj once told the Kaki Gani that these white men have come to our country to rule over us. Guru Maharaj and other bhagats also call them foreigners. Their complexion and build is different from ours."

"Have you ever seen the white men?" Pano asked Kamali.

"My father had gone to the market in Dungarpur to buy certain things for my brother's wedding. That's about four–five years ago. I had accompanied father to Dungarpur. When we were returning after seeing the king's palace from outside, I saw two white men riding horses."

"Tell me quickly. How did they look?" Mangli of Dhalriya could hardly contain her inquisitiveness.

"I'll tell you. The horses were tall. The two foreigners who mounted on them were red in complexion. They wore tunic that clung tightly to their body up to their neck. There was something tight fitting on their feet also. The skin on their hands and face was visible. They had luxurious drooping moustaches, not like the Thakur's. One of them had a black beard at the chin. They had cat-like eyes. Their heads were covered with caps. They were taller than our men. To me it appeared that they were taller than the Thakurs and the Pathans. They got off the horses in front of us at the gate of the palace. Their boots reached their calves. For a while all the eyes, my father's, mine and others who were around, were stuck on them. I found them very frightening."

After hearing this description, all the girl friends of Kamali looked at her with astonishment.

"Do all the foreigners look like them?"

Satisfying Pano's curiosity, Kamali said: "Just as we're all of the same complexion and height and wear the same kind of clothes, all the other foreigners should also look like those two white men."

"Yes, you're right. People of one race will look alike. Just as there are many species of animals, there must be human beings on this earth who look different from each other."

"The white men don't live anywhere near us. Then what enmity can we have with them that takes it to the stage of a fight?" Mangli wanted to know.

"You lasses know nothing beyond homes and forests. Haven't you ever listened to discourses by Guru Maharaj and other bhagats? Pano, Guru Maharaj himself had once given a discourse at your village dhooni. I didn't attend it, but I do know about it."

"Yes, I was in that panchayat. One or two of the lasses here were also present. Guru Maharaj had asked some people there to work for awareness. He had preached about Sampsabha, dhoonis, devotion, prohibition, etc. But I can't remember what he talked about the foreigners. I could not have sat through the entire Panchayat like a Gameti Baba. I have to perform hundreds of chores. I left the Panchayat for one of these chores. If you tell about what happened there how will it belittle you?" Pano, upset by Kamali's allegation that she knew "nothing", had replied to her and at the same time had expressed her desire to know more about the foreigners.

"All right. Why get upset? I've been living with Guru Baba (Govind Guru) and Guru Ma (his wife) and my father is a Bhagat-like figure. I'll tell you whatever I've heard or learnt from them about the foreigners. This much you know that our ancestors were never stopped from collecting forest produce like wood, fruits, roots and plants, glue, catechu, grass. The foreigners had the Rajas impose a ban on our collection of these forest produce. Now the contractors pay money to the Rajas for these things. The liquor contractors go against the preaching of the Guru on prohibition and destroy our men by selling liquor to them. Guru Baba and the bhagats oppose the system of *begar*, under which the jagirdar and officials of the Raj force adivasis to render free labour. The foreigners are angry over it. It was because of them that Guru Maharaj was thrown into the Dungarpur prison. Broadly, these are the issues that have turned us against the Raj and the British. Won't we all have to unite and fight to redress them?"

"Kamali, you've become profound!" Mangali, Pano and a few others pronounced.

"This is all due to the company of Guru Maharaj, my father and the bhagats. All of us must work under the guidance of the Sampsabha for spreading awareness among our people. Now, do you understand the talk about the rifle and the sling?"

After this enlightening dialogue among the bunch of girls led by Poonja Dhira's talented daughter, Kamali, they started to practice hurling small stone pieces tied to the sling. The Gair dance had easily given way to a competition in hurling stone from the sling. The girls would pick up pebbles and hurl them with the sling in the direction of the Kunda valley. The practice went on, though hurling with the sling was not something new for them. It was a practice that had been handed down to them for generations. The sling has been used for centuries to shoo away animals like blue bull, pigs and antelope that damage crops and birds that pick the grain from the crops. A piece of stone hurled by Managli shot past the stream in the Kunda valley and hit a herd of pigs. The startled pigs disappeared in the tall grass. Kamali took some pieces of stone the size of a berry and hurled the stony missiles in the sling with all her force. Looking at her face it appeared that she did aim to throw the stony missiles towards the Kunda valley, but because of her carelessness she lost her grip on one end of the sling, or perhaps she did so deliberately. The stone pieces fell not in the Kunda valley but among the defence squad youth who were doing their training routine. One piece hit Nandu Damore on his back. The other pieces did not hit anyone in particular. A furious Nandu looked around, obviously at pain after receiving the hit from the sling. He saw the bunch of girls. The lovelorn bachelor's eyes were able to spot the mischievous Kamali. The two had been drawn to each other for some time. It was a love that was so far confined to communication through their eyes rather than meeting and talking to each other. Nandu was sharpening the iron tip of his arrow on the stone ground. He started to rub his back where he was hit. He rather enjoyed Kamali's mischief without speaking about it. Other youth remained busy with their training routine, dismissing the sling episode as an accident.

The sun was getting strong. Govind Guru and Poonja Bhagat were talking to each other sitting on a string cot placed under the shadows of the hut that was a little distance away from the dhooni. They were fully engrossed in their conversation. The youth brigade and other devotees had prepared the daily meal of rotis and saag (vegetable) at the dhooni.

"Daughter Kamali, come here! Tell Guru Maharaj the rotis have been baked. Call everyone for meals," Govind Guru's wife, Gani, called out. Before Kamali could reach them, Govind Guru and Poonja Bhagat had got up as soon as they heard Gani's call. Poonja Dhira then yelled: "The youth brigade, come and have your meals. Daughter Kamali and your friends be ready with the *pattals*, the leaf-plates, and rotis."

Nandu had a desire in his heart that Kamali should serve him roti and saag. Kamali herself had entertained a similar thought in her heart. It was a happy coincidence that Poonja Bhagat had unwittingly said something that both of them had wished in their hearts. Had Poonja Dhira not called the youth for the meals would the secret cravings of Nandu and Kamali for each other have remained confined to their hearts? Both of them were around 18–20 years. It was difficult to guess which one was elder or younger. Youth does not last long among the poor and the toiling classes. Because of lack of physical comfort their youth quickly reaches the middle age in appearance and then old age. Irrespective of how long the old age may last, death starts knocking at the door early. The youth in Nandu and Kamali was at its peak that yearned to be expressed through the language of love. Physical contact is the medium for establishing the emotional bond that both of them needed. They had so far had the pleasure of expressing their love only through their eyes.

Kamali and her friends started to place the plates of the big leaves in front of Govind Guru, Poonja Bhagat and the youth from the defence squad. When Kamali was putting the plate on the ground in front of Nandu her fingers touched Nandu's. An electric current of pleasure passed through her entire body. For a second, Nandu stared at Kamali. She ran in and quickly returned with two rotis of maize, which she placed on his plate as she disappeared again to bring the dry *kachri* vegetable dish. Nandu told her: "Don't give me so much. There are others who've to eat. You've to look after everyone."

Kamali did not like it. She said to herself: "I've to look after only you." She went past other youth sitting in a row while serving food to them. In between she stole glances at Nandu who was paying more attention to her than his meals.

The sun started to mellow. The cuckoo perched on the Jamun tree was sending out its lyrical cry. Kamali's friends had gone back to their villages, promising to return in the evening. She had told them: "Come back when it is still daylight. We'll have the Gair dance." Pano, Mangali and other girls thought that since they had agreed to Kamali's suggestion for practising sling throwing, she had reciprocated the gesture by agreeing to the Gair dance. In the afternoon, Kamali collected jasmine flowers and took them to the Guru Ma's (Gani's) hut. Govind Guru's sons, Aru and Amaru, aged eight and ten, respectively, were playing the game of *pitthu* outside the hut. "Mai (mother), please make a garland out of these flowers that'll adorn my hair," Kamali requested Gani.

"Why, Kamali, for the first time you've talked about adornment. You always talked only about awareness. Is there something special today?" Kamali looked very coy. She covered her quietly smiling face with her palm. The cool Phagun breeze was forcing its entry through the door into the hut.

"No, nothing special, Mai! I was thinking of the approaching Holi season. I feel like doing the Gair dance."

"Your friends have gone. Who'll you dance with?"

"They're coming back soon."

"But there has to be a male partner for the Gair dance."

"Mai, you tell my father that some of the boys from the squad he's training in shooting rifle and bow and arrow should join us in the dance."

"Right. Let your friends come, then I'll talk to him," Govind Guru's wife scrutinised Kamali's face as she spoke. Slim, swarthy, with a beautiful round face, bright eyes and above them natural black brows, that was Kamali. In her red ghagara (skirt) and yellow *odhani* (scarf), Kamali looked a beauty. Virgins don't cover their head with the *odhani*. Her long and thick black hair reached right up to her waist. Her hair was tied with a silver thread. Gani made a *gajra* (garland) of the jasmine flowers and lovingly fixed it in her hair. Kamali looked like a decorated bride even with only this limited adornment. Gani remembered her own young days. She also looked like Kamali. She was widowed just a few years after her marriage. She had danced only once with her husband in the camp of her Banjara community. The song sung at the dance echoed in her heart.

Chamcham chamke choondi Binjaara re Binjaara re
Aa thodo so mhare sang naach le Binjaara re...
(O My Partner *Banjaara,*
Look At My Glittering Scarf
Come And Dance With Me,
O My Partner *Banjaara*!)

Gani thought to herself. "I'm lucky to have received the kindness of Govind Guru who married a widow like me and made me a happily married woman." She then returned to the present from her nostalgic trip to her younger days. She kissed Kamali on the forehead as she said: "Daughter, how quickly have you grown up! Nobody seems to have noticed it. Your Guru Maharaj and father are so much engrossed in the awareness movement that they've no time to look after the children. Let me find a nice young lad for you." The dark complexioned face of a bashful Kamali turned red on hearing these words from Guru Mai. She hugged Gani. For the first time after coming of age she felt the love of a mother. Her heart was soaked under a shower of motherly love. Her eyes turned moist with happiness. Her mind went back to her childhood when she had lost her mother due to high fever. She felt she had found her mother again.

The Gair dance began in the afternoon and ended a little before dusk. The young men carried swords and sticks and the young women carried handkerchiefs in their hands as they danced to the beats of drums and Thali. Hand in hand they danced with gay abandon. Enjoying it in the audience were Govind Guru, Poonja Bhagat and Gani. Kamali and Nandu were the happiest pair dancing. They were at the threshold of their adult life and saw visions of a beautiful future together. The dance of love continued in their hearts long after the Gair had ended.

Poonja Bhagat sent the members of the defence squad at Mangarh hill to their villages to celebrate Holi. That left only Govind Guru and his family and Poonja Dhira at Mangarh hill, not counting the steady stream of devotees who came everyday in the morning and evening. Yes, Kamali too was there. She had looked morose right from morning on the day of Holi festival. In the afternoon, Pano from Amaliya village came to meet her with another girl. "Kamali is lonely here. We'll celebrate Holi in our village in the evening. Why don't you send Kamali with us," they requested Guru Mother, Gani.

Pano also assured Gani: "Kamali need not return home at night. She can sleep in our house. In any case, she has to have her dinner with us."

Apart from Gani, Govind Guru and Poonja Bhagat had got to know Pano since she had been frequently visiting Kamali. They also knew that Pano was a special niece of Haliya Bhagat. Gani told Govind Guru about Pano's request. At first he hesitated about allowing a young girl to go to another village and that too for the night. He, however, thought that a young female visitor in a village which is home to bhagats will encounter no problem. Keeping that in mind Govind Guru talked to Poonja Dhira about letting Kamali go to Amaliya village. Poonja Dhira was not going to say no to Govind Guru. He understood that Govind Guru had agreed. He then thought that while Kamali should be allowed to go to Amaliya for the sake of her happiness, why shouldn't he too visit the village. Poonja Dhira was a full-fledged bhagat, totally dedicated to the Sampsabha. Because of his long association with Govind Guru he too had acquired many qualities of the 'sadhus'. Therefore, it didn't suit him to be seen at festivals and celebrations. After pondering over the matter he prepared himself mentally to send Kamali to Amaliya village. What influenced his decision was the fact that Govind Guru's wife is like mother to Kamali, though the father of a young girl does have some worries for her.

While letting Kamali go to Amaliya, Govind Guru said to Pano: "Daughter, make sure that Kamali sleeps at Haliya Bhagat's house."

On the way to Amaliya from Mangarh, Pano joked a lot with Kamali. She asked Kamali: "Why, Kamali, tell me honestly. What's it between you and Nandu?"

"How did such an idea enter your mind, Pano?" she reacted with surprise. But her surprise was mixed with shyness. Pano got the hint. Pano knew a lot more; in fact, she knew everything about the amorous interest between Nandu and Kamali. Nandu, after all, was Pano's cousin. It was only this morning on the occasion of Holi that Nandu had confessed before Pano his love for Kamali. He had been trying since early in the day to get

Pano to somehow bring Kamali to Amaliya from Mangarh for the Gair dance and the Holi bonfire. When Pano wanted to know the reason for his request, he confessed about his love for Kamali. Pano had begun to understand these things. The spark of love was burning within herself too. After all, it is that age. Pano was pleased to find that her cousin had fallen in love with a beautiful, talented and wise girl. She had gone to Mangarh keeping all this in mind. Pano told Kamali the entire story on the way to the village. Kamali's shyness had disappeared. She became quite open in talking to Pano, though she did not discuss Nandu with her. She did not need to ask her anything about Nandu who was everywhere, all the time in front of her eyes and had become part of her heart and soul. She was lost in the dream of becoming his life partner. Nandu was slightly darker than Kamali. Round faced with a flat nose, a broad forehead, eyes full of innocence and a sprouting moustache that indicated the onset of adulthood. The slim Nandu was a boy of average height. Thanks to daily exercise, his body looked well-built with broad shoulders, bulging chest and arms with rippling muscles.

Standing on the path to Amaliya, Nandu was waiting for the moment when Kamali comes with Pano and he is able to hide with her somewhere outside the village where he could see her to his heart's content. When he saw Kamali coming from a distance, the shy Nandu ran away from her towards the village square. He busied himself in doing the odd chores for preparing the Holi bonfire in the evening. He wanted that Kamali should see him at work so that she realised he was hard working and full of energy.

The Holi *Thamm*, the holy pile of wood, had been stocked a month in advance, as was the custom. The *Thamm* was prepared of a eight–ten foot long green branch from the Semal tree. On the day of Holi smaller pieces of wood and dung cakes had been placed around the main pile. The Holi fire was lit at dusk. The ceremonies of burning and worshiping at the holy fire were supervised by Haliya Bhagat. The village elders stood a little distance away from the burning fire. Young men and women went round the burning fire, singing the Holi song.

Stay a day or two more, sister Holi
Sister Holi, stay a day or two more
Do stay at least today and tomorrow, sister Holi.
(But Sister Holi has gone away today itself.)

Old man Dharji and a couple of other contemporaries of his were keenly watching the rising flames of the fire. Dharji noted: "The burning wood and dung cakes are inclining towards the east and so are the flames. It's a good omen. It'll be a good year."

The rest of the crowd, which had also observed the direction in which flame was flowing, was happy to hear Dharji's forecast. After the ritual of burning the holy fire was completed, one of the young men pulled out a smouldering piece of wood with the help of some of his friends and ran with it towards the stream. His friends followed him. Following the custom, some of them threw fistful of soil at the smouldering piece, which extinguished the fire altogether. After allowing the burnt piece of wood to cool, it was brought back to the original place where the Holi fire was lit. It symbolised that Prahalad's aunt, Holika, had been reduced to ashes. The pieces of wet wood that were left half-burnt symbolised the fact that the ascetic Prahalad had stayed alive.

Most of the elders returned to their homes after the end of the Holi ceremonies.

It was time for the young to sing and dance the traditional Gair. Nandu was suitably dressed for the occasion. He wore a silver bracelet, a ring in his ears and a beautiful waistcoat. Kamali also arrived there dressed like a bride. She wore some shellac bangles on her arms as well as gilt bangles. She also wore bell-shaped pendants. A silver band hung from her waist. Another silver thread was tied to her hair while a black decorative knot swayed from her pigtail. Her skirt was crimson red and her *odhani*, the long scarf, was yellow with red polka dots. Her *odhani* hung across one side of her shoulders. She had tucked it into her waist while dancing. The blouse that covered her bosom and stomach had a string of silver buttons. The ambers were still burning at the site of Holi. Under the open skies of the full moon the young dancers, hand in hand, danced with frenzy. In a manner, there was something special the way Nandu and Kamali held their hands. Only Pano was privy to its secret. Finally, curtains came down on the Holi ceremony. With it ended the first part of the full moon phase of the month of Phagun. Pano took Kamali to her house for meals. One of the items she served was *lapsi* of sweet rice with mahua flowers.

Around the uneven ground where Holi bonfire was lit were 10–12 houses of the adivasis. Rest of the families lived in their scattered hamlets. On a slope to the west of the dhooni, situated on the hillock, was the hut of Haliya Bhagat which was built with stone walls with a sturdy roof of thin bricks. In the courtyard was a thick Mahua tree and around it hedges and fences of *thoor* and nagphani (cactus). For the protection of the courtyard and the hut was a gate made of logs of acacia tree tied with a rough string of wild grass and placed at the entrance.

As instructed by Govind Guru, Pano took Kamali to Haliya Kaka's house to spend the night. To save them from a possible attack by wild animal on the way, Nandu and another youth, Sukha, accompanied the two girls to the house of Haliya Bhagat. Pano pushed the wooden gate and entered the courtyard. The other three followed her.

"Haliya Kaka! Please come out," shouted Pano.

"Who's there?"

"Me, Pano."

"I'm coming, daughter. Why've you come so late? Is everything all right?" he asked as he came out. In the moonlight he was able to recognise Nandu and Sukha.

"What's the matter, you boys? And who's this girl with you?"

"Jai Guru Maharaj!" Nandu greeted Haliya.

"This is Kamali, daughter of Poonja Baba," said Pano introducing Kamali.

"Oh daughter, you are here and at this time? Is everything all right at Mangarh?" Haliya Bhagat asked as he moved his hand over her head in a gesture of affection.

"Yes, Kaka! All is well. I came here today with Pano to watch the Holi festival," said Kamali as she touched his feet.

"Guru Mai, Baba and Guru Maharaj let Kamali come to our village on my invitation. They said that she should spend the night at your place. In the morning I'll take her to Mangarh. Kaka, I've served her dinner. She'll only spend the night at your place. Now, we must leave," Pano said all this in one breath.

"Oh daughter! What difference does it make whether she eats at your place or mine? All right, it's dark now. You must return." The three of them left. Haliya patted Kamali with his right hand on her shoulders as he returned inside the hut. Kamali and Nandu kept looking at each other as the two went separate ways. Pano could barely contain her knowing smile. Sukha took it all nonchalantly. He knew nothing about a budding romance.

Pano lived near the village square. Nandu and Sukha left her there. Nandu also lived in Pano's neighbourhood. He entered his house and immediately came out to drop Sukha at his house, overruling Sukha's objection. Sukha lived some distance away from the dhooni amidst a cluster of three–four huts. When they were passing the dhooni, Nandu told Sukha: "You go and rest, Sukha. I'll attend to the dhooni." Sukha had worked hard at home the whole day. He had weaved the string rope for the cot and also prepared the frame for the cot after chopping branches off an acacia tree. He returned home and hit the sack at once.

During the brief moment he had gone inside his hut before seeing off Sukha, Nandu had told his family that he would spend the night guarding the dhooni. So engrossed was he in dancing with Kamali that he had forgotten to play his flute. He played with the drum for a while and then he was lost in dancing while holding Kamali's hands. He had the urge to play his flute in the full moon night right after he had left Kamali at Haliya Kaka's house.

It was very quiet at the dhooni in Amaliya village. The moon was ascending in the middle of the sky, scattering a milky shine on the hills, the huts of Amaliya, the trees and the green crops of barley, gram, peas and linseed. Dew drops were glistening at the tip of the grass and vegetation that had grown around the dhooni. Nandu paid respects at the dhooni. He saw the eternal lamp lit in the special room. The lamp was full with ghee. A little while ago someone had filled it. But he poured ghee into it and adjusted the wick in the lamp. He then sat on a stone slab and took out his flute which he had stuck to his waist. He blew hard into the flute to remove dust particles in it. Then he wiped the flute with the towel that he had slung around his neck. Placing his lips on the mouth of the flute he started to play a tune. It was a long *alap* (prelude) in which he played the full octave very rapidly. He did not have the theoretical knowledge of the musical scale. It was not possible for him to acquire this knowledge and, besides, he did not need it. Playing the flute was his centuries old inheritance. It came naturally to him to play the right melody in the right season. He played the flute from his heart. That night he was inspired by his soul. The soothing musical notes from his flute were wafted by the silver waves of moonlight that floated past the holes in Haliya Bhagat's hut to reach the ears of Kamali.

Kamali did not know who was playing the flute or where the sound was coming from. All she felt was that someone was pouring the sweet tones of the flute into her ears. She thought it was the first time in her life that she had heard such a captivating tune from the flute. She thought she was dreaming. The flute had helped Nandu immerse deeply into the feeling of love. There was a sensuous feeling in every single pour in his body. Was it Nandu who was playing such enchanting musical notes on the flute or was it a love-God! Was it the Kanhiya (Beloved) of Radha? And his Radha did not even know who was playing the flute! The Radha-Kanhiya love story had become a legend. Nandu and Kamali's love story was a present-day reality.

The full moon was gliding fast towards the western horizon. The glow of the moonlight was waning. The morning star was rising in the eastern horizon while the other stars were disappearing. The Pole Star on the north looked still. Its eyes were fixed on planet earth as though like the invisible Prahald (the chief mythological character of Holi) at the sites of the Holi bonfire, it was looking for his memories.

Nandu stopped his flute recital after playing it for a long while. He had wallowed in the ambience of gentle cool breeze of the month of Phagun. His heart was filled with extreme pleasure. The night was entering its fourth phase. He quietly got up from the dhooni and headed home. His feet were aching after the hectic rounds of the Gair dance the previous day. His entire body was tired. But he did not feel all this for the rest of the night as he immediately passed into deep sleep. He had a sweet dream.

Kamali kept turning in her sleep the whole night. She could not understand why she was unable to sleep soundly. Was it because she was sleeping in an unknown place, or was it the haunting effect of the flute she had heard, or was it the sweet memories of Nandu? The physical strain of the Gair dance had left her too tired and then there was this confusion in her mind. At last an imaginary touch of Nandu's hand made her sleep. Towards the end of the night she also saw the same dream that Nandu had.

TWENTY THREE

In the forests of the Vagad region the Palash tree branches were laden with profusion of flowers, red like the burning flames, as though the entire forest had been set on fire. The fields were barren. The tiny plants of the Chait month had blossomed into full-grown plants. Here and there in the forest the yellow laburnum flowers were hiding in the womb of the tree branches. The long teak tree looked like the forest guards. The thick trees of tamarind, mahua, sares, banyan, peepul, kamun and mango stood solemnly quiet. Warm weather was approaching.

The feudal and colonial face was getting uglier and uglier for the adivasis. The rigorous implementation of the policy introduced years ago to restrict collection of forest produce had forced the adivasi communities to shift to agriculture. In the first decade of the 20th century the native states had completed the targets for land settlements. Under this policy the adivasis too were given some land for cultivation, but with strict conditions for recovery of the Lagan because the Rabi crop was expected to be particularly good. The adivasis were not able to get adequate returns for the amount of labour they put in. After the ban on the distillation of Mahua liquor in homes and introduction of new excise laws that allowed sale of liquor only through contractors, income from excise revenues became the principal source of enriching the coffers of the native states. The income from this source increased twice to thrice.

But for the last five or six years the situation had begun to change. The long prohibition campaign of Govind Guru had begun to succeed with a drop in liquor sales. This was the reason why men of the jagirdars and the police along with the employees of the liquor contractors were increasingly found to be behind the instances of causing destruction at the dhoonis.

The prohibition campaign of the Sampsabha workers had a wide impact. For example, three years ago the Banswara state had consumed 18,749 gallons of liquor, which so far in 1913 was reduced to mere 5154 gallons. The yearly decline in excise income had worried the state governments, the jagirdars and the liquor contractors. That is why they were inciting the adivasis against the teachings of the Sampsabha and resorting to destruction at the dhooni-dhams. They started to lure the adivasis back to their drinking habits by propagating the so-called benefits of consuming liquor sold by the contractors.

On the other hand, the Sampsabha Bhagats and workers, inspired by Govind Guru, started touring the areas extensively to guard the dhooni-dhams. It was not possible for isolated opponents of the Sampsabha movement to cast an evil eye on the dhooni-dhams. But a situation of confrontation between the Raj and the adivasis was developing fast. The area where trouble had spread also included the districts of Panchmahals and Khera in the British-ruled Bombay Presidency. The British officials were receiving information from every corner of the region. In this connection, the Political agent in southern Rajputana sent a telegram to the Mewar Resident.

"The movement started by Govind Guru has a direct and adverse impact on the liquor contractors. They and their agents are trying their best to save themselves from economic ruin. Undoubtedly, they have gone to the extent of using the wrong methods. They are forcing the adivasis to revert to their old addiction."

The state officials, jagirdars and their employees intensified the harassment of the adivasis over the issues of land tax, forest produce, *begar* and excise income. The jagirdars formed their own policing force, which was used to commit atrocities against the adivasis. The AGG of Rajputana wrote a letter to the secretary to the foreign and political departments of the Government of India about the Jagir Police of the Banswara state.

"Jagir Police is creating difficulties. In a state like Banswara, which is largely under the control of the jagirdars and where the Darbar is comparatively weaker, the income to the state's exchequer has started to shrink because of the jagirdar's arbitrary methods. It has been difficult for the state to raise its own police to deal with any challenge that may arise anytime. The jagirdars have created their own armed police. The Jagir Police can have a limited role where it may be needed to contain any local disturbance by the adivasis and in cases of robbery, looting, and the aftermath of a natural disaster like last year's scarcity. But it will create problems if it takes up duties such as collecting the Lagan and other taxes, execution of warrants of arrests, ordering *begar* and summoning the services of the adivasis to act as messengers. All this has become part and parcel of the feudal system, which will be weakened slowly. It is important to remember that the power of the local jagirdars cannot be wished away. The power of the jagirdars to decide on criminal cases was taken away during the reign of the British-appointed Council. The prominent jagirdars were given the limited powers of a magistrate under the jurisdiction of 'criminal courts' of the darbar. The fact is that today the jagirdars are using all the criminal and civil powers to decide all matters. Only the cases in which the disputes between the two parties related to the government land reach the darbar courts."

The Political Agent's letter to the Mewar Resident also said: "The seeds sown by Govind Guru have started to grow. The adivasis are now becoming aware of the fact that the Raj always looked down upon them and behaved inhumanly with them. Mentally, they have started to compare themselves with the social status of non-adivasis. The Raj does not pay as much attention to their problems as other communities. Last year Banswara had received 55 inches of rain, which yielded good crops of pulses and oil seed. Yet dissatisfaction among the adivasis has grown because of the feudal practices like *begar* and lagan. Instances of the Sampsabha bhagats and workers being implicated by the police in false cases of robbery, plunder and theft have also come to light. Not only this, almost everyday there are many instances of the flags at dhooni-dhams, the places of worship, being uprooted by the jagirdars to disrupt the awareness campaign of the Sampsabha. The adivasis who attend the Sampsabha discourses are being exiled from their areas of traditional habitat. These circumstances are creating the possibility of the adivasis rising in revolt." The Agent's letter concluded with a suggestion: "We must take a concrete decision about all these problems before it is too late."

Sitting at his Mangarh dhooni-dham, Govind Guru was regularly receiving timely information about all the important events and happenings in their areas from the members of the spy network that was established under the leadership of Thavara. One day Thavara himself arrived there when Govind Guru and Poonja Bhagat were seriously discussing how to prevent the possibility of a confrontation that was building up. Despite all the vigilance by the adivasis, the incidents of damage and desecration of their holy places by feudal elements were increasing.

"Jai Guru Maharaj!" said Thavara in greeting.

"Come, Thavara Bhagat! What news have you brought?" Govind Guru asked him gently as Poonja Dhira and Thavara Bhagat hugged each other. Both of them sat on the stony ground in front of Govind Guru, who was sitting on a cot. It was almost noon. Under the shade of Govind Guru's hut, where all three of them were sitting, they were comforted by a mild breeze blowing across.

"You must be receiving all the news, and besides the bhagats and others keep coming here. It's been a long time, so I thought let me go and meet the Guru…"

"First, tell me did you have your meal?" Govind Guru affectionately asked him before he could continue.

"I met Haliya Bhagat of Amaliya village before coming here. I had my meal there."

"Now go on."

"Guru Maharaj, our guards are posted at all dhooni-dhams. A bhagat is present at every dhooni almost all the time. The problem is that all the dhoonis have been constructed away from the inhabited areas. I understand very well that being far from the inhabited areas ensures their sanctity. But it's not possible to depute someone on guard duty with a lathi, day and night. The adivasis in the village have their household duties. It's enough that they assemble at the time of prayers and songs. Now, this entire month will go in weddings and marriages. Either people are going out with wedding parties or if they are receiving wedding parties. They don't have the time to attend to the dhooni-dham affairs. Yes, they do visit the dhoonis to pay their obeisance. Another thing. The awareness campaign is on with full steam. This has made the jagirdars jealous. The liquor contractors are raging with anger. Pretending to arrest the criminals, the police arrive at the dhooni-dhams and then insult bhagats by asking them irrelevant questions. While doing so, sometimes the angry police officers uproot the dhooni flags and throw them away. By the time the villagers arrive, they run away on their camels. They also issue a threat: "The names of those who assemble at the dhoonis are being included in the black list of rebels so that no-one should go there. Some people are scared of the police behaviour. But it is generating fury in most of them. Now, you must have heard the story about Falva village..."

"No. I've hard nothing about Falva village. You tell me." Poonja Dhira was curious after listening to Thavara. He looked at Govind Guru, who only nodded. That was a clear sign of approval. But neither Poonja nor Thavara was sure if this nod was to suggest that he knew the Falva story or the eagerness to know the details of what had happened there. Thavar continued.

"Two men of the contractor uprooted and tore the dhooni flag there. They smashed the lamp and extinguished the eternal light. Some local boys who had learnt about the incident beat up the men, who were released after being warned never to venture back into the village. When the contractors learnt about the incident he approached the village Thakur, who then had the boys arrested by the police. The parents of the boys begged before the gameti, Bhairu, who went to the jagirdar. The boys were made to apologise. It is said that the Thakur also imposed and recovered some fine and it was only then that the gameti was able to get the boys out on bail with the assurance that they'll never repeat their mistake."

"The contractor's men were at fault. Did the gameti speak the truth before the Thakur?" Govind Guru wanted to know.

"It's said the gameti abused the boys. He also threatened them before the Thakur that he'll not come to their rescue if in future they repeat their crime and they should be sure of harsher punishment. Two–three days after the incident, Kuriya Bhagat arrived in Falva village. He got to know the truth about the incident after making inquiries in the village. Kuriya Bhagat and Gameti Bhairu had a heated exchange. The gameti sided with the contractors instead of the villagers. The gameti took no steps on his own against the mischief committed at the dhooni-dham. As a result most of the villagers turned against him. Kuriya Bhagat called the village panchayat at the dhooni. The gameti realised that he might be humiliated at the panchayat so he avoided it. The panchayat elected Hirji Bhagat of Falva as its chief. All this was accomplished under the leadership of Kuriya Bhagat. The villagers were divided into two groups. After the arrival of Kuriya Bhagat in the village, the gameti went to the Thakur and poisoned his ears against him."

"Was Kuriya all alone?"

"No, he had a group of five–six boys with him. One or two of them carried rifles." Poonja was glad to hear that. Govind Guru looked worried.

"In the presence of Kuriya another flag was hoisted at the dhooni the same day. The eternal lamp is burning there again." Govind Guru was relieved. He looked relaxed.

"Where's Kuriya Bhagat now?" Govind Guru asked as he remembered Kuriya. He had been receiving news about him. But now he was anxious to meet him.

"According to my information, he left Falva village, saying that he would be going to Mal Dungar and Chikli Vadra. We've to find where is he now." Thavara spoke with confidence. His spy network was strong. His men were spread all over. He also had about a dozen camel riders who collected information from distant areas.

"It's said there was trouble at Mundari village also. Do you've any information about it?" Poonja Dhira and Govind Guru knew this much that the day after Holi, that is 'doolhandi', the day colour is thrown, there was a clash between the camping members of the Sansi community and the Bhils of the village. When the inebriated Sansis created a ruckus the bhagats at the dhooni sent some youth to their camp. The Sansis clashed with them. Poonja wanted full information about the incident.

"I didn't hear anything about it. Had it been a big incident I'd have heard about it. It's likely that the matter was sorted out after a meeting."

"Yes, I'd like to say one thing about this matter. And that is that the Sansis, Kanjars and Mogias are nomadic tribes. They get drunk and indulge in violence. Drinking is a bad habit. Some adivasis also join them, which spoils the atmosphere. It's against our prohibition campaign. We can't stop them from drinking. But it's not right to have their camps near our areas, especially near the inhabited areas. They are meat eaters and hunt for wild animals, which is also against our religion. It's wrong to commit those sins near our inhabited areas. They commit another sin, and that is their habit of stealing. They go out for committing such crimes, but the police suspect us and harass us. Therefore, there should be an announcement that such nomadic people will not be allowed to stay near our inhabited areas."

Poonja Dhira and Thavara Bhagat nodded their heads in agreement with the suggestion of Govind Guru. Poonja Bhagat added: "Yes, Guru. You've said the right thing. People must be cautioned about it."

It was afternoon by the time they had finished their confabulations. The shadows of the trees were lengthening.

A beehive was hanging from a branch of the Jamun tree near the dhooni. The bees were buzzing below it. Kamali, who was practising with the sling at some distance, came running. She was out of breath as she said: "Guru Baba, there's a cobra couple, entwined with their fangs open." She pointed in the direction where her friends were standing.

"Don't be afraid, daughter. Call your friends here. And listen don't trouble the cobra couple. They are representative of Lord Mahadev. It's auspicious to see them."

Kamali cried out to Pano and called all her friends. Nandu and the young members of the defence squad were busy gossiping under the shade of a tree in another corner of the plateau. Their attention was drawn by the commotion among the girls. They ran towards the corner where the cobra couple was spotted. Nandu shouted and sought to know from Pano about the fuss over the cobra couple.

"Boys, don't mess with the cobra couple," Poonja Bhagat yelled at the youth.

"No, Baba! We'll only see the cobra," one of the youth assured Poonja Bhagat. By the time the young men reached near the cobra couple they had untwined themselves and had slithered back into the grass to disappear altogether.

Govind Guru resumed his conversation. Nandu called Pano, who reached there holding Kamali's hands. Nandu was staring at Kamali.

"Hey, brother Nandu! Why did you call me?"

"Pano, did you see the cobra couple?"

"Yes, all us girls did see them. That's why Kamali had rushed to call Guru Baba and her father."

"I've seen snakes many times but never a couple. Were they quarrelling?"

"How was I to know? They were in a tight clasp."

"Were they striking their fangs at each other?"

"No." Pano said emphatically. Hearing this, Nandu stole a glance at Kamali, who smiled.

For Govind Guru, the burning eternal lamps at dhooni-dhams were the source of energy for the Sampsabha movement and the white flag, symbol of awareness. All the followers of Govind Guru held these symbols in high esteem, equal to the regard they had for him. That is why none of them was ready to accept any mischief with these symbols. Govind Guru decided that he will himself tour the main villages in the area to assess the arrangements for the security of the dhooni-dhams. He advised his trusted and dear colleague, Poonja, that he should not leave Mangarh in his absence and must keep a sufficient strength of the defence squad with him. He told Thavara Bhagat: "Today is Saturday. By Monday I'll reach Basiya. Send a message to Kuriya that he too should reach there by Monday." Thavara then left on his errand.

After two days, camels were brought from Amaliya village. Govind Guru left for Basiya with his wife and two children. Poonja Bhagat sent four armed young men on two camels with him for his and his family's protection. Kamali stayed back at Mangarh with her father. Her eyes had turned moist as she bade farewell to Govind Guru's wife, Gani. She kept staring at the Govind Guru family as they faded from sight and the Mangarh hill.

Accompanied by Kuriya, Thavara also reached Basiya. Govind Guru was discussing Sampsabha matters with the workers at dhooni-dham situated at Chhani Magari. He also learnt about the developments in the area from the two bhagats. Thavara told him: "Perfect arrangements have been made for the protection of dhooni-dhams. Armed members of the defence squad have been posted everywhere. No one will dare look at the dhooni-dhams." Kuriya informed him that he found the awareness campaign was doing well in all the areas he had toured. He said with great confidence: "Guru Maharaj, the adivasi community will rise as one at your signal. Women have also started to grasp the significance of awareness. They'll not lag behind. The young are zealously engaged in Sampsabha activities."

Govind Guru and all the bhagats were aware that there was a great resentment against the Raj in villages where levy was enforced during the Rabi harvest. There was a danger that the employees of the Raj and the jagirdar may be assaulted in such areas. The prohibition campaign was in full swing in the Vagad region with the help of teachings of Govind Guru and the bhagats and workers of the Sampsabha. The dhooni-dhams looked fairly safe now. The villages where the Sampsabha influence was widespread it had become difficult for the Jagirdar to force any adivasi to do *begar*. The biggest problem for the adivasis was the restriction on the forest produce imposed by the British government. These restrictions were being enforced with strictness by the governments in the Indian states. It was a big challenge for the Sampsabha. For Govind Guru it was a matter of deep concern.

A crucial decision was taken following the discussions at the Chhani Magari with the bhagats. "When the government has abrogated the ancestral rights of the adivasis and despite our pleadings it has shown no interest in our deteriorating economic condition then we've no other alternative but to forcibly snatch our rights over the forest produce. We've always tried to avoid violence and confrontation. We've never believed in bloodshed. We've been forced to stealthily collect firewood, catechu, glue, tendu leaves, grass, roots and fruits. With the Raj increasing its vigilance even this may no longer be possible. On the other hand, the British and the Darbar are cutting forest trees on a large scale for use in construction work. Not just that, the expensive teak and 'dhaunk' wood is being exported to Britain. If the forests are continued to be destroyed like this our sole source of livelihood on this earth will vanish."

After listening to these words from Govind Guru, Kuriya realised that some sparks from the fire that was long burning within him had started to fly from the voice of Govind Guru. Heaving a sigh that showed his restlessness, he asked: "So, Guru Maharaj! What should we do now?"

"A counter move."

"Violence?"

"No."

"Guru Maharaj, don't beat about the bush. Be unambiguous," Kuriya had suddenly lost his cool.

Kuriya respected Govind Guru a lot. Even when he disagreed with him over something he would keep it to himself. He never talked about any differences with Govind Guru before anyone. He had been associated with the Sampsabha for a long time. He was one of the senior most bhagats. The qualities of powerful leadership had taken deep roots in him. He betrayed no signs of ego and ambition. If he had any desire and aim it was to see the awareness campaign of the Sampsabha, which was being sustained day and night by its workers, reach the stage where it can help the adivasis launch a decisive battle against their oppression. Seeing the red face of Kuriya, Thavara and Kalji Bhagats wanted to intervene but they kept quiet out of deference for Govind Guru, who took the matters in his hand.

"Kuriya, I know you since your childhood. We've together nursed the plant of the Sampsabha. Today it has spread densely like the Banyan tree. We've kindled the lamp of awareness through the medium of Sampsabha. Today, there's no dearth of people who will walk with us shoulder to shoulder. If I order the Halkaro (beating of the big drum) all the adivasis of the Vagad region will collect at one point. The fire that burns in you kindles in the hearts of all of us. Don't mind my words, Kuriya. For me, you and Poonja are not just bhagats but like my brothers. This much everyone understands. You often talk of violence. Violence means attack. We shall be held guilty of attack. The moral responsibility of violence will be ours. It has to be seen if that will solve our problems. Even if we order violence, what'll be its result? We had discussed the issue once earlier also. Our main fight is essentially with the British. They've a big and well-armed army even though we may be numerically superior to them many times over. Violence will prove like crackers. I want the fire from the awareness campaign to hit like the gunfire. The feudal-British nexus should be frightened of the Sampsabha strength even before they get the occasion to fire their guns. We shall see if we ever reach the stage of helplessness. That's why I don't talk of violence. What I'm talking about is counter measures. What it means is that we'll have to take back our rights with the same force with which they were taken away from us. This force means that the adivasis enter the forests in their areas en mass and collect the forest produce. The forest department staff and the employees of the jagirdar will be outnumbered. They'll not be in a position to oppose our move. This is the season for gum and catechu. We'll also know what counter moves the Raj makes."

Kalji and Thavara heartily endorsed Govind Guru's views. Despite some reservations, Kuriya too came around to accept Govind Guru's view. Thavara had a message sent across to different adivasi belts about the strategy unfolded by Govind Guru on collecting the forest produce.

The Raj had given the contract for collecting catechu and gum from the forests in the hilly areas of Khairwada, Kotda and Pahada in the Udaipur state to baniyas (traders) of Khairwada. To help them collect the produce, the baniyas had called the adivasis of the Kathodi community from area of the Panchmahals district in the Bombay Presidency. As instructed by Govind Guru, the local Bhils, Meenas and Garasiyas had also started collecting the forest produce independently. The contractors tried to create a situation of confrontation between the local adivasis and the Kathodi adivasis so that the latter could continue with their collection from the forest and the local adivasis could be thrown out. The adivasis from the two sides called a Panchayat to ensure peace between them. The *gametis* decided that the Kathodi adivasis will get similar work in their own area. What was the use of getting into an altercation in an unfamiliar land for the benefit of the contractor? The local adivasis had told them about their economic hardship. Govind Guru's influence did extend to the Panchmahals also. The Kathodi adivasis forsake the contractors and went back. The contractors then proposed that the local adivasis be employed for working in the forest. But it was turned down. That marked the end of the contract system for collecting the forest produce. The baniyas withdrew themselves from the contract job. No one else took the forest contract. The Raj had to suffer financial losses as a result. The Maharana of Mewar did not think it proper at that stage to start an army action against the adivasis.

Tension spread in Dungarpur, Banswara, Idar and Soonth states where the adivasis were not able to earn sufficiently. There were both overt and covert attempts to collect the forest produce. In all, the collection of catechu and gum depended on local conditions. The adivasis were not going to trade in the forest produce, after all. Their interest was to collect enough to meet their personal needs.

None of the states decided to use the army for suppressing the adivasis' counter action for fear that it might revive their agitation for restoring their forest rights. But some cases of intimidation and violence against employees of the forest department were registered with the police. Only in a few cases the adivasis were named but no arrest was possible. After the police had learnt about the decision taken at the Chhani Magari about the adivasis' counter strategy, criminal charges of inciting and looting of forest produce were levelled against Govind Guru, Kalji, Thavara and Kuriya also. The collection of gum and catechu from the Raj areas was held a serious crime of robbery and looting. The police described it as a gross violation of the law. It was done to put pressure on Govind Guru. When Govind Guru and the bhagats got wind of the police move they thought their arrest was imminent. As a result all of them became more alert. Govind Guru left for Rojada village in the Idar state.

TWENTY FOUR

In the first week of October, Govind Guru reached Kahvada, a village near Mangarh, from Rojada. He had sent prior intimation about it and summoned some of the special bhagats, including Kuriya, Poonja, Kalji, Mema and Thavara. From Rojada itself came Somaji with half a dozen young disciples. Villagers from nearby areas also collected there. At the Kahvada meeting it was decided that an assembly as large as possible be ensured at the Poornima fair in the month of Margsheesh. Hukka Gameti of Falvania had arranged for the transmission of this information in the area with Halkaro Padyo, the beating of the big drums. It was part of a well-conceived strategy that a message should also go out that an epidemic will break out after Diwali. Those who reach Mangarh will be saved from the disease; others will suffer. Govind Guru and his companions reached Mangarh. They had sent messengers to bring their families also to Mangarh. While at Mangarh, Govind Guru intensified his efforts to gather the adivasis from Dungarpur, Banswara, Idar, Soonth, Kadana, Panchmahals, Khairwada, Kotada and other hilly areas. The Halkaro drums were beaten everywhere in these areas to signify that the adivasi community must arrive at Mangarh before the fair for starting a decisive battle. Posts of armed men of the defence squad were established at *tekaris* (strategic points) on the Mangarh hill.

The Mangarh fair was a regular feature on the day of Poornima (full moon). But the message from Govind Guru that had been widely circulated in the area had caused a lot of worry to the Maharawal of Banswara. After consulting Maharawal

Shambhu Singh, Yuvraj Chandravir Singh sent a letter to the Udaipur-based Political Resident about the possibility of a rebellion led by Govind Guru and asked for army help. The Maharawals of Dungarpur, Idar, Soonth (Santrampur) states sent telegrams and special envoys to the British officials. The district collector of the Panchmahals also expressed concern. The biggest danger from Govind Guru's planned action was to the states of Dungarpur, Banswara, Idar and Soonth. The rulers of these states saw it as the sounding of the bugle of adivasis' revolt, led by Govind Guru, against the Rajput rule. It was thought to be precursor to the advent of adivasi rule.

On a request from the Maharawal of Banswara, Lt-Col J.L. Kaye, Political Agent in southern Rajputana, sent a telegram to all the states before October 18 that Govind Guru must be arrested. His associate, Poonja Dhira, should also be detained. Govind Guru already anticipated such action by the Raj. He began to live under heavy protection. All around the dhooni site at Mangarh were posted defence squad men, armed with rifles and swords, on twenty-four hour vigil. One of the messages that Govind Guru had sent through the Halkaro Padyo was that those arriving at Mangarh should bring enough food to last till the day of the fair. There was a touch of cold in the weather. The heat of agitation was, on the other hand, rising at Mangarh.

On October 30, the Police Inspector at Soonth sent Jamadar Yusuf Khan and sepoy Gul Mohammed on a spying mission to Mangarh. A day after they reached there the adivasis beat them up. Yusuf Khan died and Gul Mohammed was taken hostage. The group of adivasis on their way to Mangarh from the Soonth state attacked the Pratapnagar fort. Assessing danger approaching him, the Maharawal of Soonth sent telegrams to the British Commissioners at Godhara and Ahmedabad, saying that thousands of adivasis were gathering outside his fort and were about to launch an attack. They were going to loot the capital. Therefore, the army help be dispatched at once. The attack on Pratapnagar fort had taken place on November 1. No one had the time to celebrate the Dipawali of 1913. There was turmoil in all the native states in the Vagad region. All the rulers had sought urgent help. The British officials were keenly watching the situation.

Following the Halkaro Padyo announcement hundreds of adivasis in Banswara, Dungarpur, Idar, Soonth and Mewar areas, led by the Sampsabha workers and bhagats, were marching towards Mangarh. They were armed with swords, bows and arrows, axes and lathis. The leading bhagats had already arrived at Mangarh, escorted by the members of the defence squad. At the security posts established around Mangarh the rifle-carrying members of the defence squad had already been appointed. The Mangarh hill had become the secure but unannounced fortress of the adivasis. Thousands of adivasis from all over the Vagad region, especially those from the Bhil and Meena communities, had assembled at the Mangarh plateau by the first week of November.

By the time the British officials received the telegram from the Maharawal of Soonth, a crowd of adivasis had left for Mangarh after attacking the Pratapnagar fort in the Soonth state. The General Officer Commanding of the 5th Mahu Division sent information to the Army Chief on 6 November 1913 that the adivasis of the Soonth state had gone out of control. They had declared an open revolt against the Raj and were collecting in large numbers at Soonth. After obtaining permission from the British government, the Army Chief had kept a company of machine gun-equipped infantrymen of the Indian Army ready for any mission at a moment's notice. He had another company of 104 Welsley Rifles ready as a reserve force. The AGG in southern Rajputana sent a telegram to the government of India, based on information received from the British officers in the Bombay Presidency and other sources:

"Adivasis from all over the area are gathering at the strategically located Mangarh hill at the tri-junction of the boundaries of the states of Banswara, Dungarpur and Soonth. A large number of armed adivasis have already arrived there. Reports sent previously from time to time have mentioned the social, economic and religious grounds that led to the adivasi unrest. Some of the grounds are justified and the problem could have been resolved through dialogue, but for some reason it was not possible. The principal figure of the adivasi unrest, Govind Guru, used to talk about social and religious reforms. For the last few years he has converted his awareness campaign into a pure political movement. He has declared support for rebellion against the native rulers. The situation has become explosive. It has become necessary to immediately remove the adivasi siege of Mangarh. The job has to be accomplished without any further loss of time. Therefore, we must provide whatever army assistance that we can to the native rulers."

The political and foreign department of the Government of India gave its approval to the suggestion from the AGG. It was also agreed that two companies equiped with machine guns should be sent on mules to Banswara via Namli, and from there to Mangarh. Army reinforcements should be sent via the Dahod route also if British officers demanded more help. The soldiers at Mahu, Baroda, Ahmedabad and Khairwada cantonments were alerted to be ready to suppress the adivasis' rebellion.

On November 8, the Commandant of the Mewar Bhil Corps, J.P. Stockley left for Mangarh with two armed companies. On November 11 he had reached Bhukiya village, three km from Mangarh. An armed company of the 104 Welsley Rifles from Baroda division, under the command of Major Bailey, had reached Soonth Road at 9.45 in the morning on November 12. The same evening, a detachment of the 7th Rajput Regiment (Ahmedabad), armed with machine guns, also reached Soonth Road. Besides the British army, the Maharawals of Banswara, Dungarpur, Soonth and Idar had also sent their armies, which had arrived near Mangarh by the morning of November 12 to suppress the rebellion. Thakur Bhim Singh of Kadana and the Garhi Jagirdar, Rao Himmat Singh, had arrived to lead the native armies. A cavalry unit of the Mewar state had also arrived at Ambadara.

Looking at the mobilisation of the army, the adivasis stopped coming in large groups and instead started to arrive in smaller groups at Mangarh after the first week of November. The adivasis who came from the side of Garhi and Bagidora abandoned the Bhukiya route and took an alternative but difficult course through the hills and forests to dodge the army. After November 12, women and children had also started to gather at Mangarh for taking part in the fair. Though the fair was due only on the 17th, Govind Guru had announced that the participants, including women and children, should reach the dhooni at Mangarh ahead of that date.

To guide the army units reach Mangarh for launching Operation Mangarh, the Commissioner of the Northern Division, R.P. Barrow had got a route chart prepared and handed it over to all the army commanders before they left the cantonments.

Another incident took place in the meanwhile. Commissioner Barrow had arrived with a mounted unit close to Baramata village near Mangarh on November 10 for reconnaissance. The adivasis, who outnumbered him heavily, stopped his further march and he had to return. Barrow thought that Operation Mangarh would be adversely affected if he clashed with the adivasis.

This incident was the basis of a message from the Commissioner to British officers engaged in the army action: "The adivasis seem to have made up their mind for confrontation. It does not appear that they will be deterred by the sight of the army. It will be better to make a last attempt at easing the situation by talking to Govind Guru."

Most of the army units that were headed for Mangarh from the cantonments between 6 and 12 November chose to camp at the dhooni-dhams that they found on the way. The temporary messes that were opened there cooked both vegetarian and non-vegetarian food. They desecrated the dhoonis and tore the religious flags at Sampsabhas offices. Seeing this, the henchmen of the jagirdars also caused destruction at dhooni-dhams. Most of the bhagats, workers of the Sampsabha and the defence squad had gone to Mangarh, so there was no arrangement for the security of dhooni-dhams. Govind Guru was deeply hurt by these activities.

As soon as he reached Ambadara, Comdt. Stockley had stopped the gameti of Ambadara, Nanji, who was on way to Mangarh. He sent a message to Govind Guru through him: "There will be no army action if Govind Guru leaves Mangarh." An assurance was also given that the agricultural tax will be reduced to ₹1.25 per plough and the practice of baith *begar* will be scrapped. Govind Guru turned down the request and stopped Nanji from returning to Ambadara. A swarm of adivasis was moving towards Mangarh, but nobody was allowed to descend down the hill. If somebody expressed a desire to go, the orders from Govind Guru were to fasten the person's feet to a piece of wood and also ties his hands and then throw him on the ground. This was done to stop anyone from acting as spy. He had discussed the matter with his trusted bhagats. It was decided that if anyone brought a message from the British and something constructive is found in it then the messenger would not be detained at Mangarh but would be sent back with the reply.

Around this time, a messenger arrived at Mangarh with a signed letter from the Political Agent of Revakantha, Hudson. He translated the letter written in English into Hindi. "Please send a deligation of your trusted representatives down to Ambadara so that the British officers could start talks for an agreement." This was on November 12.

TWENTY FIVE

At the Nahar Magri valley Dalli of Amaliya was grazing her goats. Above at the Magra, Ranger Kisan Singh was on duty with two guards of the forest department. He was in charge of the forests in Amaliya, Dhalariya and Ambadara. Subedar Liaqat Khan of Khairwada cantonment, who was a friend of Kisan Singh, had left the army camp at Ambadara telling his officers: "I'm going to collect information about the area from my friend, Ranger Kisan Singh."

Sensing no danger since the adivasis of the area had gone to Mangarh on Govind Guru's call, Liaqat Khan mounted his horse and travelled alone to meet Kisan Singh. On the way he saw Dalli grazing the goats.

She was a young and somewhat plump girl, her youth in full bloom. The only daughter of Panchya, she was brought up with a lot of love and care despite all the wants in the life of her parents. Panchya had betrothed her to Hariya of Kunda village, which was situated on the west of Mangarh, directly opposite to Amaliya village. Her father had put a caveat: after marrying Dalli, her husband will live with them as the "house son-in-law".

Dalli had first seen her would be husband at the village market in Bhukiya. Their wedding was fixed for the next auspicious *Akha Teej*. Panchya and his wife were very happy that their dark complexioned daughter had found a wheatish complexioned groom. He was a hard working youth. Dalli had seen the thickset body of her would be life partner, his bulging muscles and his wide chest. She was struck by the sparkling brown eyes of her soon-to-be husband and the innocence on his round face. She had dreams in her eyes and the expectation of receiving lots of love from her suitor. They had two or three meetings during which they got to know each other better.

Their wedding day was about a month away. Sitting under a Semal tree in the valley of Nahar Magra, Dalli was watching her herd of goats. But her mind wandered off to the king of her heart, Hariya. From her love-struck mind emerged spontaneously a love ditty.

> A garden did I lay in my home for you only, Hariya
> Which alien tree did thou love to perch on?

"No, it's not a good song. My Hariya's mind cannot stray towards another woman." She had reasoned all by herself. Sitting alone she had gone deep into the lyrics of the song.

The birds sitting on the tree flapped their wings. It diverted her attention from the love song that was echoing in her heart to the fluttering birds. She did not find any parrot named Hariya among them. From the stream by the side of the valley a grey shrike flew to her right. Dalli was delighted, as it was a good omen. A brown rabbit dashed to the root of the tree and seeing Dalli it scurried behind the bushes. The grey shrike did a reverse dive and flew in the opposite direction, which made Dalli uneasy.

It was getting to be afternoon. There was a slight chill in the air and a mild breeze. About 20 steps ahead was a stony ground where a flock of partridges was pecking at its food. She suddenly remembered, "Hariya is extraordinary with the sling. If he were here he'd have killed the partridges and I'd have roasted them in the fire. With salt and pepper we'd have enjoyed eating that great dish. Then, Hariya would have played the flute and I'd have danced. My friends would've then come to know that we, two lovers, are frolicking in the river of love."

All of sudden it occurred to her that she had not collected the firewood for the day. She had forgotten everything else when she was dreaming of Hariya.

Dalli, who was resting her back on the tree trunk, got up and started to collect firewood. She tied the wood in a bundle and returned where she was sitting under the tree. She looked at the grazing goats. She was quite at ease with herself when she saw that the herd of the goats was intact. Right above the stream a hawk had pounced upon its prey.

"You lass, you have cut wood in the forest?" Dalli was startled to hear someone shouting behind her. Confused, she pulled herself together and looked back. She saw two stocky youth in the uniform of forest guards. They had lathis in their hands.

As she was hoisting the bundle of firewood on her head, one of the two guards caught hold of her pigtail and pushed her. She fell to the ground. She had tied the bundle of firewood with the cloth she had used to cover her head. The cord, which held the bundle together, snapped and the firewood lay scattered on the ground when she fell.

Dalli had heard many tales about the way wild animals attack, but this was her first experience of attack by a "wild human". The ground being stony, she had received injury on her forehead. She held her forehead in her hand and gathering enough courage she tried to escape from there.

"You thief! You're destroying the forest and now you want to escape," said the second forest guard as he held her by the hand.

"Okay, she made a mistake. Let's take her to the Saheb (officer). He'll pardon her." The first guard had chosen these words of sympathy to entice her. The second guard looked at her with a mischievous smile. There was commotion in the herd of goats. They gathered near and looked at Dalli. The eyes of the meek animals reflected both sympathy and anger.

"My dear friend has come! Do something to please him," Ranger Kisan Singh had told his employees.

"There'll be no need to run around for that. I've just returned after sighting a sweet round 'forest fairy' grazing goats by the side of the stream. Go and catch her and by the time you bring her here I'll be 'ready'." Subedar Liaqat had made the task of the forest guards easier. The two guards went straight looking for Dalli.

"Kisan Singh! How did you manage to get this liquor that has the flavour of both fennel and cardamom? It's not very bitter in taste and causes only a little of burning sensation but it gives a kick after just a few first sips." The Subedar gulped a couple of neat pegs, without mixing water in his liquor.

"It's a rare liquor from the house of Thakur of Asgarh. Don't think it is cheap country liquor. Pour some water in your drink and then enjoy it slowly. You'll remember for a long time what a good time you had with the superb liquor served by your friend."

"Who has so much time, friend? I've to return. If I'm unsteady after the drinks my horse will go out of control. Let me have only that much that will be sufficient for enjoying that forest fairy." By then he had consumed a quarter of the bottle. The liquor was strong. It began to show its effect.

"Are your servants dead? They haven't come back yet."

"They must be on their way. Why do you worry? It is possible that the damsel may have gone back from the forest with her goats."

"How is that possible? Only a short while ago I saw her." He was barely able to speak coherently as his lecherous eyes were pining for the sight of Dalli. His nerves were getting taut.

The two forest guards were keeping a vigil outside the teakwood and tiled roof forest Rest House. In the verandah, Ranger Kisan Singh was waiting for his turn. Subedar Liaqat came out of the room adjusting his clothes. There were a few fresh bloodstains on his clothes.

Kisan Singh went into the room and immediately rushed out.

"She is unconscious. Her pulse is running. But is she going to die?"

"The bitch was unwilling. I tied her hands with her own clothes to the frame of the cot as I had her. She was a real virgin. It was tough in the beginning but when she calmed a little it became thoroughly enjoyable. There was some blood. It always happens in the first instance. There is fun in doing it with force. You don't worry. I've untied her hands. She'll be all right in a moment. Slap any charge on her. The bitch will not then open her mouth." Thus instructing Kisan Singh, Subedar Liaquat sat on a bench. There was a crude smile on his face.

The two forest guards had brought Dalli to the Rest House. Liaquat Ali was getting restless in his room and had sent Kisan Singh outside to look for the guards. Kisan Singh was anxiously waiting for them. He was afraid that the two might return empty handed. Seeing them with Dalli he heaved a sigh of relief. He also had the satisfaction of discovering that the girl was really a 'forest fairy' with a figure as perfect as the Subedar had described! "She might have been born in any family, but she is meant for the enjoyment of people like us."

"The big Saheb is sitting inside. No need to be afraid or show any hesitation. You've stolen wood. Accept your guilt. The Saheb is a good man. He'll pardon you. Yes, just do something to please him for a while." Kisan Singh had thus tutored Dalli as he sent her into Liaqat Ali's room. When she stepped into the room he was waiting for her like a wild animal ready to pounce upon its prey. He shut the door behind her at once.

Dalli shouted and shrieked. She resisted bravely, pushing the Subedar with all her force. She hit him on his chest with her feet. She yelled for her parents. She called out to Hariya: "Save me from this beast!"

When Dalli was screaming the birds perched on the trees around the Rest House cried as they took off in a hurry. The peacocks hollered angrily. The sun had quietly gone down the western horizon shrouded in a haze.

The enraged Subedar slapped Dalli hard on her face. He flung her on the wall and like the sheaf of paddy thrust her against the cot. A wolf was mercilessly trampling upon a kid.

When the goats had tired of waiting for Dalli they withdrew themselves to the courtyard of Panchya's hut. Their eyes were moist. None of the goat kids suckled their mother that evening.

Dalli's father kept searching for his darling daughter the whole night.

Next morning, the body of Dalli was found in mud near the nullah that flowed below the Nahar Magari. The rising sun had kept itself hidden for a long time in the shadows of clouds.

Kunda village was not very far from Amaliya. Despite the zigzag path that led to it, it was only two to three miles away. Somebody informed Hariya, "Your fiancé, the girl you're betrothed to, was killed last night by some wild animal!"

Hariya could hardly bear to hear this heart broken news. He turned into stone. He felt the earth below him was shaking and the sky had fallen on his head. Before the news reached her parents, he took three-four friends of his and rushed to Amaliya.

Panchya had brought his daughter's mud smeared body, carrying it on his shoulders, to his hut. The crying mother clung to her daughter's body. The inconsolable Panchya had almost gone crazy and had started talking nonsensically. Hariya was finding it hard to see their grief but had somehow kept himself composed. He wiped the mud from Dalli's face with his towel and touched it with his shaking hand.

"Whatever has happened has happened. It's all God's wish. Don't disrespect this body. Prepare for the last rites," gathering courage, an elderly person said.

People had assumed that Dalli was killed by a wild animal. But at the time her body was being washed, there was a whisper among the women. "There are signs of injuries on her neck and scratches all over her body. There are signs of man's bite on her breasts and injuries below."

"The animal would have injured her and might have even eaten her, but would not have dishonoured her like this. Even the ghost with the back-to-front feet would have shown some mercy," said one person in the crowd.

The whispering among the women had by now turned into solid information. Hariya was furious with rage but he restrained himself from showing it. He did not allow the turmoil inside him to surface.

He lit the funeral pyre of Dalli.

The last rites over, he headed straight for the nullah at Nahar Magra with his friends.

They located the spot where Dalli's body was found. They saw no signs of the presence of tiger, leopard, bear or any other wild animal. There was no trace of Dalli's footmarks. But they did see some footmarks that suggested movement of two men. Entangled in a bush nearby was Dalli's scarf.

As soon as Hariya touched that piece of cloth a big electric shock went through his body. He felt as though Dalli's spirit had taken liquid form and was being transfused into his blood. He shut his eyes and tied Dalli's cloth tightly around his forehead and clinched his fists. His steps automatically ascended towards Nahar Magara. His friends were still searching for some more clues near the nullah.

In the verandah at the Rest House, Hariya saw a forest guard on duty. Ranger Kisan Singh and the other forest guard were missing since morning. The guard at the Rest House was scared as Hariya's burning eyes turned to him inquiringly. He suspected that something was wrong. His guilt was troubling him. He tried to run away.

"Don't run. Tell me everything honestly," Hariya shouted at him.

The forest guard now knew for sure that something was indeed amiss. He ran towards the back of the Rest House. Hariya chased him and caught hold of him.

"You bastard, didn't I tell you to tell me honestly what happened?" Hariya roared. The forest guard was terror-struck. He was shaking like a mouse in the mouth of a wild cat.

"I did nothing," the shaken guard managed to say.

"Who did it? That's all you need to tell me."

"On the order of the Ranger, me and another employee had brought her here. She had stolen firewood."

"If it was a theft you should've taken away the firewood from her. Why did you have to touch her?"

"I'm not a party to the sin. The security officer..."

"Quick! Out with the name," Hariya cut him short.

"Subedar Liaqat Ali."

"Where's he?"

"Ambadara."

Hariya had the information he was seeking. He was still withholding his anger from exploding. But inside him a hurricane of revenge was raging intensely. He was a man who believed in hitting the target. Hariya pushed the forest guard hard, knocking him to the ground. Anticipating another blow from him, he started to yell. His shouts attracted the friends of Hariya to the spot.

"Let's go to Ambadara!" said Hariya. His friends understood what was in his mind.

The band led by Hariya could not find Subedar Liaqat in the big gathering of men from the British Army and the sepoys of the native states. Hariya and his friends had come to Ambadara village, posing as relatives, in search of the Subedar.

The group that Hariya led knew well that Govind Guru was going to preside over an adivasis' panchayat at Mangarh where a fair will also be held. Some of the members of his group were familiar with the messages of Govind Guru and the bhagats that they had heard at Kunda and other places. They also knew about the awareness campaign, though none of them was directly associated with the Sampsabha movement.

They decided to head for Mangarh.

TWENTY SIX

Lakha Jeevan Banjara of Batakwada was a distant relative of Govind Guru. But more than that he was a friend of his. Muniya Teja was a Bhil from Galagaradu. He had not joined the Sampsabha but was sympathetic to the movement started by Govind Guru. Because of his respect for Govind Guru whenever an occasion arose he was eager to help him. Dalpatrai Mehta was, of course, a well-known rich man of Dungarpur.

Before the army could reach Ambadara, Govind Guru had sent a message to these three.

"This is from Mangarh hills. I'm doing fine. The blessings of this Guru are with you all three. My followers will attend the fair, under the aegis of Sampsabha, to be held here at the next full moon day. The adivasi brothers will assemble here at the appointed place at this hill, bringing their tales of sorrow and pain. I'm a sadhu who believes in peace and non-violence. Mutual talks and dialogues can find solutions to all problems. For the past many years, I and my disciples have been honestly living by the code of awareness. My bhagats were expecting some relief from the Raj. Their anxieties are increasing. Lest they do something unexpected, the Rajas must take some timely steps for the betterment of the adivasis. I've sent letters to all the rulers. None of them has sent a reply. This has upset my disciples. All you three gentlemen are in touch with the Darbar of Dungarpur. Please acquaint him with the situation here. Come here as soon as you receive this message. Leave whatever chores you were performing to rush here."

The three gentlemen hastened to Mangarh in response to the emotional appeal in Govind Guru's message. Before he set off, Seth Dalpatrai had left a small message for the Maharawal of Dungarpur that he was going to Mangarh on a "very important mission" and shall present himself before the Darbar on his return.

Govind Guru asked Poonja Dhira to write a letter for starting talks with the British officers. A three-member delegation was sent to Ambadara with the letter and a brief on the situation. The letter's text was as follows.

"I built a hut in my village Basiya where I lived with my family and the adivasi community of Bhils and Meenas etc. who knew nothing about the Creator. I showed them the path of Truth and Dharma. I taught them many things like worship of God, refrain from stealing, illicit relations with women, deceit etc. I advised them not to bear ill will against others and show equal respect for all by treating them as the children of their father. I advocated farming for livelihood and asked them not to trust magicians of any sort and to see that they stay away from them. I'd taught them to establish dhoonis and pray there. To my followers I tell the following: wear the Rudraksha garland, tie a yellow turban on your head, do not possess arms like sword, rifle, bow and arrow, instead carry *chimta* (tongs), bathe and clean the body every morning and do not kill any animal. They accepted my teaching so much and found them so easy to follow that the number of my followers went up by leaps and bounds. Today there are between two to three lakhs of them. This cult has expanded. But the employees of the Raj misled their masters by telling them that I am a fake sadhu and that I am looting the people. Because of their ego and pride the rulers did not bother to know the truth. The ruler of Dungarpur unexpectedly arrested me and sent me to prison. He threatened me and seized my property, asking me to leave this cult. But God protects the truth. Therefore, He helped me come out of prison in five days. I left my village because of acute harassment and came to live in this dense and dangerous forest. I have come here with my disciples to save my life and my Dharma.

"Our festival will last another one and a half month and seven days. We are sitting here peacefully, praying to God. My place is on the boundary between two states. We have sufficient water and eatables here. That attracts my followers to come here on the full moon day and show their respect for me. I have buried my love for worldly attachments. I am confined to myself here. Yet, my followers are being harassed. You should be cautious and considerate about what you do. We have God on our side; you have power. We pursue the truth; you are attached to worldly affairs.

"I do not approve of those who eat pork or beef, drink alcohol, are greedy, crafty, liars, adulterous and believe in slandering or have some other vice. These adivasis are poor creatures of the earth. They till the land and raise a small crop over it. For me a little of alms is enough and I accept that happily. I do not want anything else from anyone. I take from those who give voluntarily. The police inspectors of Idar and Lunavada and the uncle of the Darbar asked me for bribe. When I refused they said they will defecate in my dhoonis, slaughter chicken or goat and insult our religious flag. After this threat they came to arrest me and out of fear I hid myself in the hills of Mangarh. I am not going to attack or kill or loot anyone. I am busy in my devotion. No Raj allowed me to live in the plains. They want to sully my reputation and abuse my religion. I have taken shelter in this hill for the sake of my self respect and security. Be afraid of God. Everyone has to die. Believe in the spirit of compassion and piety. I am Guru to the poor adivasis. A Guru has to do three things: advancement of the disciples, give the Guru Mantra and preach to the disciples. I do not indulge in any fraud. Today you are very powerful. It is my request to you please do not use a big hammer to swat an ant. Sooner or later everyone has to go. The people who come to this world must go one day. The divine world looks after the saintly. If you continue to torment me then I shall fight till my last breath. I trust you will find a way to end our sufferings."

On the evening of November 12 the designated delegation reached the British officials at Ambadara village with the letter from Govind Guru. The two sides did talk. The British officials included Hudson, Hamilton and Stockley. The British officials said they had sympathies for the reformist movement of Govind

Guru. But collecting adivasis in such a large number amounted to treason. First these adivasis should evacuate Mangarh and return to their villages then only the talks for resolving the issues could begin. Govind Guru had made it clear to the delegation that the adivasis would not leave Mangarh till their demands were accepted. As a result the talks broke down.

The British officials handed over a letter to Govind Guru's delegation. The letter said: "We have received your application. We were pleased to learn that the adivasis have given up drinking and other bad habits, including stealing and robbing and adopted the path of religion. We shall not force you to resume drinking and other aforementioned bad habits. We shall direct every state that they should not force you to commit any of these sins. But the assembly of such a large number of people with arms at one place will not be tolerated. If you want to worship, you can do so anywhere, but we cannot approve of your gatherings. Tomorrow we shall send our army to the hills. Therefore, you are requested to descend from the hills by tomorrow afternoon or if anyone stays behind he should not put up a fight. If he does so, he will be killed."

Govind Guru had not included any of his active bhagats in the delegation for two reasons. One, he wanted the delegation to be composed of those respectable people who could negotiate while they sympathised with his movement. Two, he feared that the British officials will arrest any of his special bhagats who went to meet them as part of the delegation.

Dalpat Rai Mehta gave a detailed account of the talks that the delegation had with the British officials and the attempts made to reach an agreement.

"Please have faith in God. If you permit, we three will approach the Maharawal of Dungarpur to impress upon him the need for him to intervene and contact the other Maharanas and Maharawals in the Vagad area, who in turn can ask the British officials to diffuse the situation of confrontation. It can avoid the chances of any unpleasant incident."

Mehta's words were seconded by Lakha Jeevan and Muniya Teja Gala.

"Yes, that'll be the right thing to do," Poonja was succinct.

"The army has come very close and you're asking someone whose voice does not count to speak to the Maharawal of Dungarpur to resolve the problem. Anyway, whatever the wish of Guru Maharaj!" Kuriya commented. He wanted to say something more but did not want to in the presence of Seth Mehta and others.

"All right. You people keep trying at your level and if something important crops up then do send a message to me. I pray to God that may He grant some wisdom to army officers."

Govind Guru bade a respectable farewell to Seth Dalpatrai Mehta, Lakha Jeevan and Muniya Teja from Mangarh.

Govind Guru was disappointed to receive the threatening letter from the British officials. He was upset over the obduracy of the British. He told the adivasis' assembly at Mangarh: "The British have not accepted our demands and are threatening to kill us. We should not be scared of their threats. Instead of bullets, water will flow from the barrel of their guns. All of you should be confident and be ready for the confrontation."

For the ordinary adivasi, Govind Guru was a miracle saint. The assembled adivasis concurred with him. They were also sure that the British army, which had arrived down below the hills in large numbers, was hesitant to climb up. It meant that they were afraid of the prowess of Guru Maharaj.

Along with the peace efforts the British were also preparing their army for an attack. The possibilities of an imminent assault on the adivasis' assembly at Mangarh were increasing. From early morning on November 13, the men of the British and native army had blocked the movement of the adivasis to the Mangarh hill. Without the permission of Govind Guru the adivasis did not want to create a situation of confrontation. Hence, they just assembled on the hillocks around Mangarh. Govind Guru still wanted an agreement to be reached. For this purpose he had another letter written by Poonja Dhira on November 14.

"I am sitting at my old dhooni with our flag. I depend on the food sent by others. I neither indulge in stealing nor do I advise my disciples to do so. If they do not obey me then it is pointless being their Guru. You have been misled. You are not illiterate and you should not allow yourself to be deluded by others. The world is destructive. All we need to live is some food and clothes to cover our bodies. Why have you come here with such a big army? Fearing that they and their women will be humiliated the Bhils and Meenas have escaped towards the hills. They have been forced to drink and eat meat. Me Guru too was insulted. Our misfortune does not allow us to settle anywhere. Our answer is no if you ask us if we ever committed the crime of stealing and murder. We have done nothing but worship. We are a simple people right from birth. We are not clever like the baniyas (traders). We spend our life doing farming and collecting the forest produce, all within the bounds of the law. We are ordinary people of the world who have migrated to the hills because our religion is being destroyed. The main followers of my sect are Ghota Giriji, Salan Giriji and Raj Giriji. You can seek information whether it is a new religion or one that has spread in the world. The adivasis accept me as their Guru and I have my followers. I have created this cult after inquiring about their religious traditions. The followers have come to see their Guru. If it is feared that anyone might indulge in some act of deceit he can be made honour bound not to do so with the intervention of the village chief. The sinner will suffer the consequences. Your actions determine the fruits that you receive. We are not going to establish a rule with our might for the sake of some worldly pleasure. Please shoot us if I or any of my disciples descend from the hill to rob a village. I have full confidence in the world that lives in our dhoonis. My disciples are a contended lot. They share whatever they get. If they get clothes they wear them. If not, they sit near the fire to keep their bodies warm. They are not immoral. They have given up all the bad habits. The mighty should not misuse their power. Please do not destroy our faith. You rule the country. There is no justice in this Kalyug, the age of darkness. The sins will surround you one day. Do not use force. Do not torment people. A fire is burning in our hearts.

You are wise. We have the Guru mantra. Please trust the words of a Guru. Sooner or later we have to die. But do not kill our religion."

The rulers of Banswara, Dungarpur, Soonth and Idar were getting anxious over the delay by the British officials in attacking the adivasis who had well fortified themselves at Mangarh. These feudal lords were repeatedly asking the officials to crush the adivasis.

The British officials, as before, said in reply to the letter from Govind Guru that there cannot be any talks for an agreement if the adivasis did not get out of Mangarh. The letter that Govind Guru had sent on November 14 was milder in tone than the previous one from him. That had made the British feel sure that Govind Guru will surrender after seeing that he had been surrounded on all sides. The stubbornness of the British led Govind Guru, the bhagats and the Sampsabha workers to entrench themselves more forcefully at Mangarh to face the British onslaught.

After leaving Mangarh, Dalpatrai Mehta met the Maharawal of Dungarpur to give him an account of the talks between Govind Guru and the army officers.

"Excellency, I had met Govind Banjara at Mangarh without seeking your permission, for which I seek your pardon. But I had sent a message for you which I trust must have reached you in time."

"We did get your message. Tell me, Sethji, what made you take the trouble of coming to the Darbar today?" There was a hint of a taunt in the tone of Maharawal Vijay Singh as he replied to the polite words of Seth Mehta with a counter question. Seth Mehta was a much experienced man. He had detected the annoyance in the Maharawal's question.

"Salutations! I've always been the recipient of your kindness and shall continue to receive it till the end of my life. The situation at Mangarh is deteriorating fast. The British officials want that Govind Banjara should leave the Mangarh hill with his followers and the assembly of adivasis there should be dispersed. On the other hand Govind Banjara and his main followers want an honourable agreement to be reached so that they are vindicated. As for Govind, regardless of what you might hear about him from anyone, I as a person you trust, may submit that the saintly inclined Govind Banjara holds you in high esteem. Before I left, he had told me, 'Please request the Darbar that he should collect the correct information and take a decision in the interest of his subjects'. Knowing that you have good relations with the Maharaja of Banswara, he also told me that your subjects will be 'greatly obliged to you if you could talk to the ruler of Banswara for accepting the demands of the adivasis and thus eliminate the chances of bloodshed."

Mehta had obviously exaggerated the words of Govind Guru. He knew in his heart that when the British forces are closing in on the tribals' assembly they will not listen to any native ruler. He was also well aware that the rulers of Dungarpur and Banswara had little influence over the British. He had chosen words that were expected to come out of the mouth of a rich and intelligent man like him when speaking to a ruler. Yet, he did expect the Maharawal to play some useful role. It was part of his diplomacy when he used the word *Banjara* for Govind Guru. He did respect Govind Guru in his heart. He wanted a solution to be found that satisfied the Govind Guru-led Sampsabha and thus a possible confrontation between the army and the adivasis was averted.

The understanding of the situation by Maharawal Vijay Singh was limited to the fact that when the British officers are camping with their army at Ambadara to protect the Indian states in the Vagad region, they will be competent enough to ward off the challenge from the adivasis who had gathered at Mangarh. He had also come to believe that the hero of the adivasis, Govind Banjara has openly declared that he is bent upon creating an adivasis' kingdom. That is why he did not want to discuss the proposal from Seth Mehta. But he did need Seth Mehta, so in the end he only said this much: "Sethji, we shall see."

Seth Mehta had understood that it will be pointless to expect anything from the Maharawal. It was a disappointed Seth Mehta who sought the Maharawal's leave and left the Darbar.

Seth Mehta could not sleep for many days. He had sent no good or bad news to Govind Guru, contrary to the promise he had made.

For the Dungarpur Maharawal Vijay Singh everyday was proving to be too burdensome. He consulted Divan Ganesh Ram and wrote a letter about the seriousness of the situation to the Political Agent in southern Rajputana.

"The delay in quietening the Bhils and Meenas is adversely affecting the situation. They are praying in groups that the British army will be defeated and Baba Govind will be victorious. Guru Baba has divine powers. The attack is being delayed because the Sahebs (British) are scared to attack Baba. Please take some effective steps otherwise these rebels will create problems not only here but also in Mewar and Idar. Pardon me for writing this letter, but I cannot miss this occasion to send important information to you. The adivasis of Limarvada are creating difficulties for me. I am doing all I can to keep them quiet."

The feudal lords lacked adequate strength to quell the adivasis' rebellion. They had, in fact, sought British help to crush the rebellion. The British had their own interests in protecting them. They did not want to see their control over any part of India become loose. The victory of the adivasis' rebellion will mean that the government has lost its hold over the adivasi areas. For the British government the adverse economic consequences from such a situation were obvious. A key factor for the British was the likelihood of the end of income from the forests. Army action in the native states was not a new experience for the British. It was part of their old colonial policy. It was these interventions that had led the British to tighten their grip over the native states.

During the course of the day on November 15, Major Bailey, the commander of the assembled army detachments, held two rounds of consultations at the Ambadara army camp with J.P. Stockley, Commandant of the Mewar Bhil Corps, Capt. Ayscough, commandant of the 7th Rajput, and the Company Commander of the Regiment about the strategy for the army action. All the army detachments had reached Ambadara. They discussed the route chart for Operation Mangarh, prepared by the Northern Division. On November 16, Major Bailey sent Stockley and Ayscough for a reconnaissance of the routes to Mangarh. After receiving their report he mounted on his horse and left with one army detachment for Pratapnagar in Soonth state where the Commissioner of the Northern Division was already camping. The two officers discussed Operation Mangarh with each other. The Commissioner ordered that on November 17, Mangarh should be evacuated with the help of army action and Govind Guru and Poonja Dhira be arrested and brought before him. Major Bailey returned to Ambadara and gave a detailed briefing on Operation Mangarh to all the officers in charge of various detachments and battalion commanders and the soldiers under them.

"With the consent of the Great Crown we have assembled here to implement the instructions of the British government, the supreme administrator in India. All of you know that the adivasis of the area have defied the administration of the native states. Despite our efforts to make them understand, the principal actors of the rebellion have not listened to us. This is a revolt against the British government. We are left with no alternative but to launch an army action. The rebels have assembled in thousands at the Mangarh hill. They've also gathered at the hillocks situated below Mangarh. We've to stop them from reaching Mangarh. The main action has to take place at the Mangarh hill itself. The officers in charge of different detachments have been briefed about the routes up the hill. You've to make your moves on instructions from these officers. Some of the rebels have traditional weapons. They're neither experienced nor trained to confront an army action. We've modern weapons and ammunition in appropriate quantities."

In the two companies of the Mewar Bhil Corps most of the soldiers belonged to the Bhil, Meena and Garasiya communities. Turning to them directly, Major Bailey said: "We don't want unnecessary bloodshed. We also don't want any of our soldiers killed. But such a possibility exists in an armed clash. We'll have to adopt safety tactics till we arrive at the hill. Our job will be smoother then. We've to keep in mind that if we encounter any adivasi on the way, he's not to be harassed or harmed in any way because that will further provoke the adivasis. We have to reach the hill safely."

Major Bailey's words were listened with rapt attention and understood by all officers and soldiers. For the officers and soldiers of the native armies this was a novel experience. They were also present at the Ambadara army camp. It was after dusk that Major Bailey had addressed the mixed army of British and native detachments. The air was turning cooler. The sepoys had left for their mess for their evening meals.

Ambadara village looked nearly empty. Except for a few old, infirm, women and children none was left behind in the village. The remaining villagers were scared and had locked themselves in their huts. They had never seen before such a large gethering of army with its equipment. The army camp was only a little distance from the village. Each company and unit had its own distinctive camp. In addition there was cavalry. There was also a large army of mules for carrying equipment and rations for the army.

The 14th day moon in the Magshirsh (Second Month of Winter) was climbing up the sky. The scenic beauty of the Mangarh hill and its surroundings was intact, only the circumstances were very different. The pressure of the oppressive army was casting its shadows over all that was natural, simple, innocent, open and pure. The wild jackal sounded muffled; the bark of the dogs in the village hinted that something improbable was likely. The Mahua trees were silently shedding tears.

At 4 am on November 17, a company of 104 Welsley Rifles and two companies of Mewar Bhil Corps set off for the Mangarh hill, south of the army camp. It took them an hour to reach there. Taking another route, the recce group appointed by Major Bailey also arrived there a little later. The three companies and the recce group jointly covered a distance of two miles by 6 am. Half an hour later, the difficult route leading to the southern slope of Mangarh was inspected again.

As a preparation for the assault strategy, Major Bailey asked various units to take up positions. The 40 armed soldiers under Mr Longley, the police superintendent of the Panchmahals district was asked to proceed to the south-western valley below Mangarh; the cavalrymen under the Thakur of Baria were asked to take up position in the valley east of Mangarh where it met another valley; the 100 cavalry men of the Banswara state were sent to the plateau north-east of Mangarh and the uneven ground located towards east; the police from the Soonth state was dispatched to the southern slope of Mangarh with cavalry from Mewar assisting it. The Thakur of Garhi was asked to take position with his army unit on the ascent to the hill by taking the narrow path at the other end of the southern slope. The 7th Rajput Regiments' companies and the army of the Dungarpur state were instructed to be behind the Mewar Bhil Corps and Welsley Rifles where they will be directly under the command of Bailey.

Two detachments each, one under the Bhil Corps commandant, J.P. Stockley and the other from the 104 Welsley Rifles were to launch the assault under the command of Capt Peterson.

After surveying the difficult southern slope route, Capt Stockley moved ahead with his men as advised by the recce group. After covering the difficult southern route, Capt Stockley divided the army detachment into two groups for reaching Mangarh. One group was to attack from the left. But the main assault was to come from the second group. At exactly 7 am Capt Stockley quietly moved up with his men from the side of the nullah, taking the narrow south-east route. At the two ends of the hill above, 200–300 armed adivasis were keeping a vigil. Thick trees covered the nullah. The adivasis could not see the movement of the army from their position on top. Stockley had covered three-fourths of the hill climb to Mangarh with his men. The second assault detachment was being commanded by Capt Peterson. He had the full company of 104 Welsley Rifles. He headed for the meeting point at Mangarh hill, taking the narrow southern route by the side of the hill slope. At the top of the hill there was a group of rifle-carrying members of the Sampsabha defence squad. But that group too could not spot the men Peterson was moving with because of the dense forest around. The Sampsabha armed group was still under the misconception that the British, scared of the massive gathering of the adivasis, were camping at Ambadara and would eventually settle for an agreement.

TWENTY SEVEN

The Sampsabha workers, bhagats and adivasi devotees, many of whom women and children, who had come to participate in the fair had lost contact with the area below the hill. There was no movement of ordinary visitors to the fair on the hill above. The talks on agreement had failed. But Govind Guru had no news about the army siege. He had assumed that the army was still camping near Ambadara village. In the absence of any communication from Govind Guru, the groups of adivasis below the hill were in a state of mental uncertainty. Despite an atmosphere of tension and apprehension, they were singing songs in praise of Govind Guru and the Sampsabha, hopeful of victory for the adivasis. There was a noticeably less enthusiasm in the fair this year. But the ritual of lighting the holy fire and offerings by the devotees at the dhooni had started early in the morning. Unmindful of the prevailing tension, Govind Guru was blessing his disciples. In between, Poonja Dhira, Kuriya Bhagat and other companions were talking to him about the developing situation.

Simple minded and unfamiliar with the ways of the world, Kamali knew nothing about the movement of the army. She had stayed close to the dhooni when on the previous evening she found that the usual air of excitement was missing at the fair. Since early morning she and her close friends were helping Guru Ma, Gani, in the routine chores at the dhooni. Her eyes were searching for Nandu. But he was not to be seen anywhere. The previous evening, Poonja Dhira had posted him on duty along with a company of the defence squad at one of the security posts at the hill. Kamali did not know about this. Nandu and his friends were vigilantly guarding the post. Poonja Dhira had explained to them well what was expected of the defence squad in case of any unexpected development.

Like any other day, the sun was up on time. The shy sunshine of early morning had begun to spread. Dewdrops were gleaming on the small grass and vegetations. Flocks of frolicking early morning birds were flying in the westerly direction. The air was still. The fire lit in the open by the men on guard duty at the dhooni-dham had extinguished, but a few sparks could be seen smouldering under the ashes. The thick, tall trees in the Mangarh hill and the valley below stood motionless. An owl sitting on the branch of a Palash tree was staring at the dhooni with its round eyes.

Govind Guru and Poonja Bhagat were conversing in low whispers near the dhooni. Suddenly, Thavara of Jharkara came to them and said: "Guru Maharaj, if you agree I can launch a surprise attack at the Ambadara army camp with the rifle-carrying youth of the defence squad. I'm conversant with guerrilla warfare tactics. I had learnt it from Tantya Mama at Jhabua."

"No, don't do any such thing. I trust your bravery. Poonja will tell you what and when something has to be done," Govind Guru lost no time in telling him.

"Son Thavara, you take a round of the hill to enquire after the defence squad members who are on guard duty at the security posts," ordered Poonja. Thavara left immediately in obedience. Two–three youths, who were waiting for him a little distance away from the dhooni, also went along with him.

A panting Madho Nai (barber) of Amaliya came to Govind Guru, running in from south of the plateau. He was carrying an empty lota. He was also screaming as he said: "Guru Maharaj, I had gone near the nullah to ease myself. There I saw the firangi (British) army."

"Poonja, he can be right! We could have been betrayed. It is likely that the British army is stealthily advancing towards us. You go and find out."

Govind Guru also spoke to Kuriya who was standing nearby: "Kuriya, you alert the men at the posts and ask them to fortify themselves. If any army is sighted it should be challenged and asked to stop. But we should not be the first one to fire the initial shot or aim the arrow at them."

Govind Guru had spoken loudly so that people around the dhooni could hear them. There was commotion among them. They were all looking at Govind Guru.

Poonja Bhagat returned soon with the news confirmed and told Govind Guru: "Guru, the British army has climbed the hill from the southern side. We had anticipated that and only two–three days ago we had built a five-foot high wall of stone there. Rifle-carrying members of the defence squad members are already entrenched there. It will be difficult for the army to climb up the hill from any other direction. But we are vigilant."

Lines of worry were clearly visible on Poonja's forehead.

"Where's Kuriya?"

"He was running towards the direction of the British army."

"Call him back at once."

"I'll send someone just now. I think..."

"I'll listen to that later. First do what I've said."

"Yes, Guru Maharaj," Poonja replied as he looked around. He summoned a youth and sent him to bring Kuriya.

"Now tell me, Poonja."

"The British force will attack us. We should immediately announce that women, the elder people and children should move in the northerly direction."

"Yes. Do it at once."

"Maharaj, it's better that you make the announcement so that people obey instantly and move to safety." After listening to Poonja it occurred to Govind Guru that for the first time the self-confidence of Poonja had become shaky. Without any further loss of time, Govind Guru announced: "The elderly and the women should immediately move with children towards the north. There should be no pandemonium. After reaching there they should hide behind rocks and trees. The British army is advancing. There is a possibility of a war. I'll try to avert the danger. To ensure that there is no panic or chaos, the Sampsabha volunteers should escort them to safety and return."

The orders from Govind Guru were obeyed, but panic was inevitable. Some women insisted that they be allowed to stay close to the dhooni, but they were dissuaded by the volunteers to shift to the designated place for safety. With about a dozen of her friends, Kamali remained with Guru Maharaj and Poonja Bhagat. Sending his wife, Gani and sons to the safe place, Govind Guru had asked her to take care of the women. Gani wanted Kamali to come with her. But Kamali refused. She did not want to leave Govind Guru and her father. Apart from affection for her father and Guru Maharaj, there was Nandu in her heart. She did not want to stay away from him in this hour of crisis. She knew that he was bound to be around somewhere amidst the crowd of men.

Summoned by Govind Guru, Kuriya had come rushing in. Govind Guru and hundreds of bhagats and volunteers had surrounded the dhooni.

Kuriya sounded frenzied as he spoke: "Guru Maharaj, the British are upon our chest. They have reached the other side of the stonewall fortification. The defence squad and our other armed men are awaiting your orders. The British army is about to attack. If we don't fight now then when will we?"

"Be calm, Kuriya. In the hour of danger, we must think coolly. We'll repulse them, but we'll not be the one to start the war. God Bhole Nath and Bhairav Baba will look after us all."

"They are climbing the hill stealthily. Cheats! If they had announced that they were coming we'd have stopped them from climbing up the hill," Kuriya said furiously.

"Yes, yes. I had already said that the British army should've been taken by surprise with an attack from hideouts in Ambadara. Now there is a big crowd here. The casualties on this plateau can be high," said Thavara of Jharkara, as his mind went back to Tantya Mama.

"All of you accept me as the Guru?" Govind Guru asked seriously. Despite showing patience he looked deeply worried.

"Yes, Guru Maharaj! Can there be any doubt about that? Why do you ask this question?" It was a question asked unanimously.

"All right then! No arguments at this critical moment. Those of you who have a warrant of arrest against them will not come before the British army. Poonja, Kuriya and Kalji, you remain here. Soma Bhai and Jorji, take some volunteers and go towards the fortification. Return the fire at once if the British open fire when see you enter the area."

Kamali and her friends were watching and listening to all this. They were carrying slings in their arms. They stepped out and collected stone pebbles from the stony ground in the makeshift bags made out of their *odhnis* (scarf).

Everyone at the security posts set up by the adivasis at Mangarh, the youth of the defence squad, the Sampsabha bhagats and volunteers, others who were assigned different duties, all became alert to the impending attack. Except bhagats all the others carried at least one of their traditional arms, be it bow and arrow, axe or even a lathi. A few could be seen with muzzle loading guns and swords.

Now and then the crowd will burst into hurrahs for Govind Guru.

Capt Stockley was not able to sight the size of the crowd that had assembled behind the fortified wall put up by the adivasis at the Mangarh plateau. For a better assessment of the crowd, he climbed up a rock. He estimated that it was a mob of between 25,000 and 30,000. He got a fuller view of the hills with the help of a binocular and concluded that breaking through the two fortified walls would lead to a direct confrontation with the crowd.

From the loud shouts hailing Govind Guru that reached his ears he guessed that the assembled people would be ready to do anything on receiving a signal from Govind Guru. They saw Govind Guru as a miracle saint and also subscribed to the misleading belief that he could prevent the inevitable. Considering the physical features around the Mangarh plateau and the mindset of the adivasis, he felt that the British army could suffer heavy casualties in the event of a direct clash even though the adivasis too may be killed in large numbers.

Capt Stockley consulted Capt Peterson. Both of them knew well that the most important principle of a military attack is that victory should come with the minimum possible losses to the army. The two officers were certain that the adivasis with their traditional arms will be no match for the modern arms and weapons of the well-trained and experienced army. Nevertheless, they did not want any of their men killed. It was not going to be a war between two nations. The level chosen for the military response to quell an internal mass rebellion was adequate. Capt Stockley shared his belief with Major Bailey that it will be easier to arrest the rebel leaders of the adivasis if the crowd at Mangarh gave up its belief in Govind Guru's so-called miracle powers.

Since his detachment was not very far behind Major Bailey's, Stockley went up to him. The Thakur of Devgarh Baria with his native army men was with Bailey. After listening to Stockley's plan, the Baria Thakur spelt the strategy: "Throw some blood or the flesh of an animal in the dhooni and spread the rumour that the dhooni was desecrated in the presence of Govind Guru. It'll serve the purpose that the Captain wants."

"It's not possible now. If someone is sent for this job he is sure to be lynched. We can't take this risk," Major Bailey scolded the Thakur, who was acutely embarrassed at his humiliation but was in no position to react.

"I understand that Govind Guru has spread this disinformation that no one need fear our riffles and machine guns because instead of the bullets water will come out of their barrels. If it's true then a fire can be shot at one of the rebels to demolish this falsehood and also ruin the image of that fake saint."

"Yes, that's true. The shooting can serve our purpose," Capt Stockley agreed. But he added: "We've little time at our disposal. The decision has to be taken at once because the rebels have come to know about the location of our armies. We must take action before they make their move."

Capt Stockley immediately returned to his detachment. He had a brief conversation with Capt Peterson and then ordered his men:

"Demolish the wall."

The wall at Mangarh was built by placing large boulders, one upon another. It was undoubtedly a thick wall, but after all it was just a pile of stones. Some of the soldiers started to remove the stones at one end. With a view to warding off a possible attack, Capt Stockley positioned two detachments armed with rifles and machine guns to the right of the wall and left of the rock. He then announced a warning to the adivasis.

"I order you to disperse immediately or else you'll be roasted by fire from the rifles."

Without waiting for a response from the adivasis, Capt Stockley ordered the army detachments:

"Fire!"

Ratatat…tat…rattat…

"Fire!"

Taratar…taratar…

"Fire!"

Tartar…tartar…tartar…tartar…

Govind Guru did not expect the army to so suddenly start firing. Hearing the rattle of the firing, he got up from his position at the dhooni and ran towards the area which had come under fire. Poonja and other bhagats were with him. Some members of the defence squad were also with them for their security. On Poonja's request, they stopped Govind Guru from heading into the shower of bullets. When he did not stop, they surrounded him. A couple of defence squad members were hit by bullets and fell to the ground. Poonja and other members of the defence squad lifted Govind Guru and brought him to a safe place by the side of his hut near the dhooni. After leaving Govind Guru in the custody of the defence squad members, Poonja made an announcement. "Since we've been attacked, start the counter attack at once."

Govind Guru was not able to lift his eyes from the dhooni. It was difficult to guess what was going on in his mind. Suddenly the lines from a song he had composed came out of his mouth.

Mangarh is our dhooni.
White men, listen!
I defy to abide by any of thy decrees.

He smeared the ash from the dhooni on his forehead. He reviewed the unexpected development at the Mangarh plateau.

"These British have annoyed us a lot. Oh, You of the Blue Umbrella, please extend Your hand of protection over us. Jai Bhole Nath! Jai Bhairav Baba!" The words had come out loudly from deep inside Govind Guru. He felt as if the *maru* drum was beating inside him and from the background was coming the sound *dhoomal*. He was visualising the intensity of the war.

Kalji Bhagat shouted at the top of his voice. "Govind Guru ki Jai!" The crowd that had assembled at the dhooni site repeated it with equal zeal.

Guru Maharaj ki Jai!
Guru Maharaj ki Jai!
Baba Bhole Nath ki Jai!
Baba Bhole Nath ki Jai!

The adivasis who had gathered at different places in Mangarh joined in shouting the "Jais" to Govind Guru and Bhole Nath. The shouts echoed around the hills.

The walls could not be demolished completely. That was done deliberately to provide cover to the soldiers. On the other side of the wall, members of the adivasis' defence squad were going down one by one under a hail of bullets from the machine guns and rifles. From their safe height on the rock, the army marksmen were taking direct shots at them; others were behind the safety of the half-demolished walls. The front rows of the Sampsabha defence squad faced the bullets directly but none of the British army member was hurt because of protection provided by the high rock and the half-demolished wall. The armed men under the command of Capt Stockley and Capt Peterson were also firing indiscriminately not only at the defence squad members but also into the crowd of adivasis that had assembled at the Mangarh plateau.

Kalji Bhagat recalled something that Thavara of Jharkara had once told him. He now realised the importance of those words. While standing about 50 steps away from the fortified wall, Kalji was giving instructions to a group of youth to attack the soldiers north of the Kunda valley. A bullet hit Bisniya, who was standing next to him, in his thigh. He fell to the ground crying in pain. A colleague of his, Hadu, quickly lifted him on his shoulders and as he ran towards the west for safety bullets rained on him, piercing his body. Writhing in pain, both of them fell unconscious. Looking at these two near dead bodies Kalji asked the youth to quickly carry out his orders. They headed stealthily down the slope of the Kunda valley behind the British front lines and launched their attack with stones and bows and arrows. Stockley was taken by surprise. An arrow struck a soldier in the hip and he fell to the ground moaning. Hearing his cry, Stockley pointed at the youths and ordered his men to fire at them.

"Roast all these wild monkeys!"

The youths were behind the rocks. They crawled to the valley down below where there was a shield of thick trees, bushes and rocks. They were protected from British bullets but they were not in a position to attack their enemies. They had zest for fight, but were helpless as it was difficult to do so. Subana was the leader of that small group of adivasi fighters.

A group of 15–20 adivasi women, carrying axes and stone and shouting "Jais" of Guru Maharaj, moved from the northern side of the plateau to the southern end, which was the main target of the British attack. Ahead of them were lying men coiling under pain; some unconscious and dead bodies or injured were soaked in blood. Lemba and Jeta Bhagats had a hard time preventing this group of women from advancing further.

Sugani of Dhalariya village was the leader of this group of women. She shouted at the top of her voice: "What's the point of our living if our men are dying. In this hour of danger we've no fear for our lives. We'll do whatever we can." She was extremely agitated.

Capt Stockley was watching all this with his binoculars. He apprehended that a large number of adivasis are being killed. In such circumstances, a group of adivasis could attack from any direction. It will be a hand-to-hand combat situation. He signalled towards the adivasi women and ordered firing. A bullet pierced through the shoulders of Jeta Bhagat who was standing as a shield for the women. He slumped there. Bullets also hit some of the women. There was utter confusion among the women as they ran for safety. There were a few trees, which provided them a corner to hide themselves. Carrying an axe in her hand, Sugani bravely stood alone. A rifleman fired at her, it hit her head. Straggling and blood-soaked she fell dead. Lemba ran like a mad man to the dhooni site, past the dead and the wounded.

Amidst the mayhem, Thavara of Nava Gaon was shouting at Jorji Bhagat: "Guru Maharaj didn't let me go down the hill when the time was right, else I'd have brought all the information about the plans and plots that were hatched by the British army. If I had done that none of this would have taken place."

"Brother bhagat, who can prevent the inevitable? Did Guru Maharaj want to see all that's happening here? Whatever he did was for the good of us all. What's the use of hair-splitting now? Perhaps Bhole Nath wanted this," Jorji Bhagat replied.

At that moment a bullet came whizzing past and struck him in the stomach, opening a flood of warm blood. He tried to steady himself by clutching at his stomach. But he had begun to stagger. He managed to speak a few words: "Thavara Bhai, these butchers have done great injustice. The One with the Blue Umbrella is watching all this silently."

Jorji's intestines had burst. A lot of blood had flown. "Jai Guru Maharaj...Jai Bhole Nath..." He shouted as he fell unconscious.

Hearing Jorji's cry, Mema Bhagat broke through the crowd and arrived there. He hugged Jorji and began to sob uncontrollably, hurling abuses at the British. The bhagats were a close-knit group. But Mema was very attached to Jorji.

"Brave bhagat, get up! I'll not let you go like this!" said Mema shaking Jorji violently even as he clung to his nearly dead body. Thavara could not bear to witness this scene. As he tried to comfort Mema, he made an unsuccessful attempt to separate him from Jorji. Thavara moved away even as he looked restless.

The south-east flank of the adivasis had become disarrayed. Many of the defence squad youth deployed there had been killed. The rest had positioned themselves behind the rocks and trees in the north-west direction and started to open fire from their archaic rifles. The incessant hail of bullets from the British forces did not allow the time these rifles of the adivasis needed for reloading ammunition. The situation for using swords, axes and lathis in hand-to-hand fight had not arisen. These weapons of the adivasis proved to be useless. The adivasis with bows and arrows were bearing the brunt. But the British forces were behind a shelter and they wore helmets and bullet-proof jackets, which had rendered the adivasis' counter attack with bullets and bows and arrows harmless. Slowly and slowly, they started to move towards the west-north direction behind the main hill. Thavara of Jharkara fired a bullet from behind a big rock and it hit the turban of one of the soldiers who was in the front formation under Stockley. He was not hurt. But an arrow from the bow of Nandu, standing behind a tree, hit another soldier in the leg. He cried in pain as he slumped to the ground. A bullet from the rifle of a defence squad member hit a rifleman in the front formation, who was actually Stockley's gunman. That was enough for Stockley to lose his cool.

"A lot of your men have been killed. Leave at once or else all of you will be roasted alive," Stockley threatened through the megaphone.

But where could the men run to? In the west and north were sharp slopes. To the south-west was the deep Kunda valley. Positioned in the south-east were the British and princely state forces. To overcome these handicaps the adivasis had built a fortification, but that had failed. The action by the army was like the sudden ambush attack by barbaric killers on a flock of free animals. There was pandemonium among the crowd of adivasis. Kalji Bhagat shouted.

"The British are firing indiscriminately. So try and hide wherever you are."

Rushing past the heap of dead bodies, Kuriya was headed for the Kunda valley. He grabbed a bow and arrow from a youth and hurled it at Stockley. It struck a soldier on his shoulders. Stockley ordered one of his soldiers to fire at Kuriya. The soldier fired and the bullet went grazing past Kuriya's left shoulder. He hid himself in the valley. The injured Kuriya held the bow in his hand. A highly agitated Kuriya was abusing the British.

From behind the huts of the defence squad, Kamali and her friends were propelling stones from their sling. With dead bodies all around and the chaos of people running for safety, her eyes were searching for Nandu. She spotted Nandu behind a tree, darting an arrow. For a better look at him, she moved from her secure position behind the wall of the hut. A bullet hit her stomach. She screamed and rolled on to the ground. Hearing her cry, Nandu ran towards her only to be caught in a hail of bullets. He was hit in the temple. He fell before he could reach Kamali. Soaked heavily in blood, Nandu breathed his last within a few moments. Kamali was unconscious, a stream of blood coming out of her stomach. At last when she became conscious for a brief moment she was heard asking for "N…an…du!"

As soon as Pano learnt that Kamali had been hit she ran towards her. Haliya Bhagat followed her. He fell on the way when he hit a stone. Thavara of Jharkara, a bow in hand, came to help him stand. Before Peterson could order his soldier to aim at Thavara, his experienced hands shot an arrow that hit the soldier in the shoulder. The soldier could not hold the rifle that was in his hand. Meanwhile, the army detachment kept on firing under orders from Stockley. One bullet hit Pano in her left leg. She fell. Govind Guru was watching it.

"You cannibals! You've killed many innocent people. You didn't spare the unarmed, elderly, women and the innocent children," shouted Govind Guru as he ran towards the martyred.

Govind Guru was facing an intense inner conflict. What a tragic end of a long struggle that was started with the help of Sampsabha and had progressed to an important stage! Such a mass murder of the bhagats, workers and innumerable followers! It had never occurred to him that the eternal lamp of awareness would be extinguished in a flash by the storm created by an oppressive and tyrannical army. Poonja was near him but his eyes were searching, unsuccessfully, for the other bhagats and workers in the blood-soaked plateau and in the chaotic scenes of people running helter-skelter after the army attack. Memories of words spoken by Kuriya Bhagat haunted him. The sound of "Attack! Attack!" kept reverberating through his ears. He was in a state of deep shock but gathered enough courage to compose himself. In those difficult moments all kinds of thoughts were churning in his mind. "Finally, did I prove to be the only person responsible for such an unnecessary end of so many innocent lives?" This was an uncomfortable thought that had stuck deep in his mind. He felt as though a poisonous prickly plant had spread all over his heart and its thorns were hurting his entire body. The focal point of this inner conflict appeared to be balancing the feeling for penance with the reality of the treacherous attack by the army.

It was the morning after the full moon day of the month of Aghan (November). The sun appeared reluctant to rise with a weary sunshine. Even the chill in the morning air was dissipating. The animals who climbed to the Mangarh plateau every morning were nowhere to be seen. The trees and vegetation around the plateau were in a state of shock. Not a single bird was in sight. Kites and vultures were flying very high in the sky. A tiny floating cloud appeared in front of the sun, its shadow resting for a few moments on a corner of Mangarh. The cloud sailed along; the sun was fully shining again.

The fire that had earlier slowed in Govind Guru's heart at the dhooni was ignited again. His attention was concentrated on the eternal flame from the lamp. His mind wandered from the scenes of piles of dead bodies and pandemonium that he had witnessed to those groups of the brave who were attacking the British like burning arrows carrying the fire of the dhooni. Thavara of Jharkara was leading the group of the young adivasi fighters. This courageous young man, an expert in guerrilla warfare, was showing his bravery in his first experience of a face-to-face combat.

Govind Guru realised the force of the collective strength of the Sampsabha warriors. He felt as though an unseen power was inspiring them to go for a decisive battle.

"Jai Bhole Nath! Jai Bhairav Baba!" Govind Guru shouted loudly. His normally calm face looked agitated for the first time. There was fire in his eyes that normally reflected only love. His forehead that radiated a divinely feeling was for the first time lined with worries.

> We're human beings
> We've started a movement for the rights of human beings
> We'll live with honour
> We'll die with respect!
> Brave Bhagats,
> This is a fight of generations
> The fight will continue
> Yes,
> The decisive battle…

Govind Guru had given his clarion call.

The adivasis were fighting unmindful of the continuous shower of bullets. After the call of Govind Guru, the fighting bhagats, the Sampsabha volunteers and Poonja Dhira's defence squad, all were filled with renewed zeal. Just as the swift current of a river in spate washes away all the obstacles on the way, the adivasi warriors, unmindful of the threat to their lives and carrying only their traditional weapons, had kept engaged the feudal and colonial forces who were armed with modern weapons.

Capt Stockley and Major Bailey were confounded by the boundless enthusiasm of the adivasis for continuing the fight. The jagirdar of Baria, the commander of the native armies, and the Thakur of Garhi had hidden themselves.

Mangli, a friend of Kamali, had taken over the leadership of the band of women warriors after re-igniting their spirits. She had recovered from the shock of the death of her friend Kamali and Pano. Following Govind Guru's call, she had put together a new group of women warriors and lifted their morale. Their weapons were slings and axe. A few had bows and arrows. They were fighting like true female warriors.

Inspired by the lusty shouts of "Jai Bhole Nath" and "Jai Guru Maharaj" that pierced the skies, the adivasi warriors had gathered all their courage for a final showdown with the might of the British forces.

"Major, we've lost some of our men! We must order the machine gun fire," Capt Stockley almost shouted at Major Bailey. Capt Stockley was shaking like a tree leaf.

"Yes, Capt. They belong to barbaric and uncivilised communities. Wild people! They've no fear of death. Hundreds of them have been killed but still they insist on carrying on the fight. It's absolutely necessary to catch their leader, or else they'll attack us from any direction."

"Machine gun!"

"Fire…fire…fire…" Capt Stockley had ordered Subedar Liaqat Ali of the Mewar Bhil Corps.

The group led by Hariya, engaged in a hide-and-seek war from a cluster of wild sandalwood shrubs, had long been looking for Liaqat Ali. Hariya and his companions knew that the man the British officer had asked to open machine gun fire was the same Liaqat Ali who was guilty of dishonouring Dalli. But, at that moment, they could contain the storm of revenge within them.

The machine guns had started their incessant shower of bullets. Thavara, the adivasi fighter, was riddled with bullets. Roaring like a wounded lion, he fell to the ground.

A little distance away, the women's group led by Mangli was face to face with the British army, hitting the enemy with the shots from their slings and arrows.

The frightened native forces led by the Thakurs of Baria and Garhi ran for cover behind the rocks. The two Thakurs had failed to restore the morale of their men. Major Bailey and Capt Stockley looked in vain for the two Thakurs.

"Step up the firing!" Major Bailey ordered. He said to himself, "Undoubtedly, it was Capt Stockley who insisted that we bring the machine guns, I was hoping to win this battle only with rifles. Without the machine guns it would have been like a fight between two nations and we'd have suffered heavy losses".

The rattle of the machine gun was continuing. In the meanwhile, Mangli too became a martyr. Her last words were: "Jai Guru Maharaj!"

At last time came for the dance of death by the tiring machine gun fire to stop. Major Bailey then ordered arrest of the leaders of the adivasis. Govind Guru, Poonja Dhira and other bhagats and volunteers were rounded up.

The army that carried out Operation Mangarh thought everything was under their control finally. The army detachments were busy arresting the adivasi leaders while the machine guns were silent. Subedar Liaqat Ali was proud of his bravery. He was satisfied that he had come up to the expectation of his officer, Capt Stockley, in carrying out his orders. He had begun to dream of medals and promotions.

"You wolf in the disguise of a human! Now even the God above can't save you!" Roaring like a lion Hariya chopped his neck with one swift but surprise attack from his axe. His head hanging, his body fell on the machine gun. His hand and feet were quavering in convulsion. The machine gun was smeared red with his blood. Seconds later, Subedar Liaqat Ali was lying dead on the ground; his eyes wide open like a ghost.

The British officers were aghast at the sight. By this time the Thakurs of Baria and Garhi had also appeared on the scene with some of their men.

"We made a mistake in assuming that the fight had ended," was all that Major Bailey managed to say in suppressed tone.

"It's brutal," Capt Stockley said shaking his head. His legs were trembling. It looked as though he had lost the war.

"Trace him and kill! But be alert!" he shouted.

A hail of bullets followed the direction in which Hariya had escaped. The firing was aimless. Hariya was as swift as the flash of lightening and disappeared from sight.

"Dalli…!I've taken your revenge!"

The loud cry of Hariya that came from the valley down below was audible over a wide area. He had won his Mahabharat.

"You butchers! Today you control the sinful science of Kalyug, the evil era. You've the power that was made possible by that kind of wicked science. You can hunt the oppressed, poor and helpless humans. But think. We are fighting for our rights. It is not a fight for our lives but for our future dynasties. Our ancestors had also fought for our land. The ignorant children of today will progress in future with awakening. God may not be taking care of us now. But He is the custodian of truth and Dharma. Our movement is in accordance with the wishes of God. We are not fighting for humans but the creation of God. This is the creation of the gods of forests, the offspring of the forests among whom are we the humans, the animals, birds, trees and vegetation. These are all the good children of God. You are the evil children of mother Earth. God will never forgive you. These are the words of Govind Guru. May my and my bhagats' curse visit you."

The words were flowing from the deep recess in the mind of Govind Guru.

Govind Guru's personality had spread like the banyan tree. On the branches of that tree in the shape of the Sampsabha organisation the bhagats and other followers were growing like abundant leaves. Like the falling tree leaves in autumn, the followers of Govind Guru were laying down their lives in the holy fire ignited by war for the pride of the adivasis. Govind Guru was thinking about the spring that must come after autumn. There will be fresh shoots of the trees and the Sampsabha members will bloom like the blazing red flowers of the flame of the forest tree. They will kindle a new fire for the protection of the forests.

"Tragic memories are the progenitors of sweet dreams." This was a firm belief in the mind of Govind Guru.

He was physically under the control of the British, but his mind and spirit were traversing the path of freedom...He was aware that right now there was nothing but darkness around him. But he was also convinced that no matter how frightening and intense the darkness of the night it invariably carries in its womb the light of the dawn.

The expression on Govind Guru's face was that of one hopelessly caught in a whirlpool. But he was still hopeful of swimming through smoothly as in a calm river. He took pride that he was on the track shown by Tantya Mama and Jorji Bhagat, a path on which all worthy native sons must tread.

Surrounded as he was by the army at the height of the Mangarh hill, the worthy son of the forest, Govind Guru, cast his eyes around the uneven terrain around him. It was an area that had the capacity to nurture simple lives and provide a bond between human beings and other living creatures.

The point at the Mangarh plateau where the army held Govind Guru stood a dense mahua tree, which despite being old was very green. Its ample shadow was spreading under it. Govind Guru's face radiated in the sunlight that penetrated through the rich leafy and tall branches of the tree and reached out to the thick trunk. His face shone bright like a lamp that keeps burning in the midst of a storm. His face reflected a strong fire of resistance. The invisible current of adivasi awakening could be felt in the atmosphere of Mangarh hill with the help of the eternal lamps at dhooni sites.

Surrounded by the army, the arrested adivasi warriors were being taken down the hill from Mangarh to the temporary cantonment at Ambadara. Back at Mangarh, amidst the piles of bodies of the martyrs, the wicks in the lamps that were kept in the various lamp rooms had extinguished. But they were still hot. The fire at Govind Guru's dhooni had also been doused but there were sparkles underneath the ash.

During the battle at Mangarh, Kuriya had slipped and fallen down the Kunda valley when he was trying to take position behind a rock. He was carrying a bow and arrow. From the height of Mangarh he had shot an arrow at a white vulture that was hovering over the Kunda valley. The straggling vulture had dropped in the valley. Shouting at the top of his voice, Kuriya did a "Halkara": 'Fight'. The Kunda valley echoed with that one word!

Hearing Kuriya, Govind Guru felt as though the river of hope inside him had suddenly swollen. His fists, tied behind him, clenched automatically. He wanted to raise his right hand in a gesture of blessing, but he was helpless.

He lifted his head. He turned his neck in the direction from where had come Kuriya's call. His lips quivered as though he wanted to say, "Oh brother Kuriya! We are not born of the same mother but, nursed in the lap of Mother dhooni, we are equal bhagats. The virtues and the glory of devotion of sadhus like me belong to you too. You're now my right hand. You keep fighting, my good pious bhagat! In the battle for dharma, Bhole Nath will sooner or later bring us victory!"

Thousands of hands at Mangarh hill appeared to be rising in approval.

Kuriya merged with the adivasi groups that had gathered at various places in the hillocks below Mangarh.